"HAVE YOU GIVEN THOUGHT AS TO HOW YOU MEAN TO EARN THIS MEAL EVEN AS IT WARMS YOUR BELLY?"

"Do not worry, captain. I will pay you somehow."

"Then I get to choose the method of payment."

"It depends on what you would choose," she countered warily.

He continued to lean there so that she was trapped between his arm and the hard contour of his ribs. She absolutely could not look up at him, fearing how she might respond to the dusky passions alight in his eyes.

"I would ask for a kiss in token payment for your debt. A single kiss, your mouth to mine. Nothing unseemly. Just a brief exchange. Have you something else in mind?"

Eliza stood, rising straight up so that she was within the curve of his arm. He was tall, forcing her head back, her throat into a creamy arch. And she met his dark-eyed stare unblinkingly.

Just when the thick fringe of his lashes fluttered and his head began to drift downward, she said, "I will scrub your floor."

Other **AVON ROMANCES**

A WOMAN'S HEART

ROSALYN WEST

AVON BOOKS ◆ NEW YORK

AVON BOOKS
A division of
The Hearst Corporation
1350 Avenue of the Americas
New York, New York 10019

First Avon Books Printing: April 1997

AVON TRADEMARK REG. U.S. PAT. OFF. AND IN OTHER COUNTRIES, MARCA REGISTRADA, HECHO EN U.S.A.

Printed in the U.S.A.

RA   10   9   8   7   6   5   4   3   2   1

To my editor,
Christine Zika,
for having faith,

and

to Linda and Orysia
for keeping me focused

Chapter 1

Was it tempting fate to feel so fortunate? Eliza Parrish wondered as she continued her brisk walk down Derby Street, but there was no room in her heart for dreary superstition.

Tonight her father agreed to hear William Montgomery's request for her hand in marriage, and she was on her way to hurry him home for the interview.

Everything in her young life was perfect.

It hadn't been easy convincing Elias Parrish that William was the one . . . or at least the right one for her. Though he had no true objection to William, who was seen as a prime catch for any Salem miss, Elias held the belief that no man of substance came to the countinghouse except by the quarterdeck. Dear William, unlike her brother Nate, was no sailor.

And Eliza was no fool. Her father's true reluctance was due more to father than son. Justin Montgomery was as abrasive as William was mild. Beyond that, their politics conflicted. The Parrishes were old-line Federalist merchants: old money, old ideals, old blood. The Montgomerys were Republican upstarts, part of the nouveau riche who strove to rise to the top of society with an aggressive style the old guard

1

found to be an affront. "Base plebeians" she'd oft-times heard her father grumble.

But politics hadn't stopped him from accepting Montgomery funds to underwrite his latest East Indian voyage, making the two men uneasy partners, soon to be in-laws.

Eliza chided her father for his snobbery and teased that it was the loss of his housekeeper he resisted more than the forfeiture of a daughter. She'd been the head of his household since her mother's death years ago, and though he depended upon her in that capacity, Elias swore he wouldn't keep her from the joys of running her own.

And now she would become Mrs. Montgomery. Her heart fairly flew as her rapid steps carried her down to the bustling wharves toward her father's warehouse.

At the foot of Parrish Wharf, Eliza paused to draw a deep breath, releasing it in a sigh. She'd grown up on the waterfront to the mélange of sights, sounds, and odors of commerce. She loved the rich sea smell of the mud flats when exposed at low tide, the way it mingled with the pungent tang of spices and underlying fumes of the tanneries. How she would miss this colorful slice of the world once William moved her to the sedate backwater of Chestnut Street, where she would assume her duties as his wife. She hurried on.

Elias Parrish spent the majority of his waking hours at his countinghouse on Parrish Wharf surrounded by the wealth of his trade. Since a spindly child, Eliza's fondest memories were of perching upon a high stool absorbing hair-raising tales of pirates and profits suitable for a kingdom. Even after Oriental silks replaced the simple wool of her short skirts, Eliza loved to loiter within the high-beamed rooms, daydreaming of the far-off lands her brother was lucky enough to see. She'd always been welcomed within regardless of whom her father was entertaining. So she was understandably surprised when one of her father's clerks stepped up to bar her entrance.

" 'Tis sorry I am, Miss Parrish, but the mister cannot be bothered at the moment."

More startled than offended, Eliza tried to sidestep his thin figure, but he was remarkably agile, finally barricading the door with outthrust arms.

"Really, James, this is too much!" she cried in exasperation. "Let me pass. I must speak to my father on a matter of much importance. He would not want me sent away."

Then she noticed the redness encircling the young clerk's eyes and how hard he fought to keep his lips from quivering. Alarm knifed through her.

"James, what's happened? Is it my father?"

The young clerk's chin wobbled. Above his knotted neck cloth, his Adam's apple jiggled like a turkey's with the strength of his emotion. Prompted by panic, she pushed by him roughly and wrenched open the door to her father's countinghouse.

Compared to the sun-drenched street, the darkness from within seemed ominous. A heavy quietude hung upon those shadows. It was never quiet in the Parrish countinghouse. There was always some plan brewing, always some old salt visiting to spout wild tales. But on this morning, it was still, still as the grave, and Eliza feared the worst.

"Father?"

She could just see his stooped figure, there, back by the casks of fine Madeira. He didn't raise his head at the sound of her voice. Fright escalated with each hard beat of her heart. She crossed the piñon flooring, the shush of her skirts over the straw-littered planks the only sound until she grew close enough to hear her father's breathing. It came in low, hoarse hitches.

He was crying.

That fact shot a bolt of terror straight through her, for the last and only time she'd ever heard him weep was when he heard her mother had died.

For a moment, she couldn't move. To reach out to him meant learning of the awful truth that tore those terrible, tortured sobs from him. On this golden day, this perfect day, she didn't want to hear it. Not on this, the day her future happiness was to be sealed.

"It happened off the Cantonese coast."

The sound of his voice startled her. It was oddly matter-of-fact, as if he were relating some news of interest that didn't bear upon them directly. Which made it all seem much more sinister.

"What did?" she asked.

He took a deep breath. It rasped like a crosscut saw through green timber—wet, raw, fraught with resistance. When he spoke again, the steadiness was gone from his voice. The words quavered.

"A squall. Blew up and over them. It was done in a matter of minutes."

Tremors swept to Eliza's toes and back. She wanted to ask him to explain, but somehow, horribly, she knew. She knew without his saying it.

Her brother was dead.

He went on in a flat tone, a tone as lifeless as her brother and his crew.

"All was lost. The *Peregrine* took on water in near fifty-foot seas. The masts were topped. There's no hope of any survivors."

The silence fell again, so deep, so empty, so like the watery depths that now held her brother in a final embrace.

"No!"

The cry burst from Eliza's lips. Anger surged upon hot waves of denial even as hotter tears burned for release. She blinked them away, refusing to accept without proof.

"No, I don't believe it! How do you know it's true?"

Elias Parrish lifted his head then, and the stark, hollow sheen of his stare pitched a dash of cold reality upon Eliza's desperate hopes. "There can be no mistaking it, girl. The *John D* was running alongside. Her captain saw the *Peregrine* capsize."

"And he did nothing to help? The coward!"

"He was lucky to save himself and his own ship."

"But did he see b-bodies in the water? Is he sure no lifeboats were away?" Eliza's stubborn insistence brought a deeper pain to her father's lackluster stare, but she couldn't help it. If she didn't question, if she didn't argue, she would have to accept.

"Stop it, Eliza! He's gone. The cargo's gone. Every hope I ever had is gone, lost on that damned coast. Now go home, girl. Go home and let me grieve alone. Tomorrow's soon enough for the plans that must be made."

She took a step toward him, thinking to embrace him, needing to feel the strength and comfort of his arms as well. But he put up his hands, bracing them against her tender sympathies, preventing her from seeking solace when her own world was crumbling, too. The barring gesture, holding her separate from his pain, broke the last of Eliza's resolve. With a soundless wail of grief, she fled the countinghouse, leaving her father to his solitary sorrow.

Chapter 2

It was late.

Darkness draped her bedchamber. Eliza lacked the strength to rise and light the lamp. She slumped, limp and drained, upon the cushions of her window seat, her tear-stained face turned outward toward the night. She saw nothing but blackness surrounding the dim outline of her reflection.

She waited to hear her father's tread upon the steps, but no sound reached her in her lonely mourning. How deep it was, that grief twisting down through her soul. Nate, dear Nate, so vibrant and alive. She couldn't imagine that bold life snatched away by a cruel whim of nature. How would they go on without him? Parrish Shipping would never be the same, for Nate was an integral part of her father's dreams, just as he owned an integral portion of her own heart. Both were broken on this day that should have known only happiness.

What was she going to do?

There would be a period of mourning. That meant no marriage. No cargo meant no profits. Hard times, to be sure. But her father would rise above them as always. Her father was charmed.

Like Nate had been charmed.

Another sob rose up to slowly strangle in the dry confinement of her throat. She closed her aching eyes and rested her brow against the coolness of the windowpane. Then, from somewhere below, she heard movement, footsteps. And she sighed, glad her isolation was about to end.

There was a timid tap at her opened door. Puzzled, she turned upon the dormer seat. Her father wouldn't have made such a polite entrance when he was always welcome.

Perhaps William . . .

But it was a stranger poised awkwardly against the shadowed light of the hall. A stranger with grim tidings etched upon the long bones of his face.

No.

No more.

She wanted to moan, to shriek for him to be silent, not to voice whatever ill news brought him to pause, twisting his hat brim at her chamber door.

"There's been an unfortunate accident. . . ."

The funeral was an elaborate affair. Faces of the sorrowful bobbed before Eliza, distorted, just as reality was distorted. She nodded by rote at their sympathies: So sad that father should follow son to the grave so quickly. Elias Parrish, impaired by the amount he'd had to drink, staggered into the path of a carriage on his way home. Quick, they said, more painless than the news he'd received hours before.

William's hand formed a chill casing about her own. He smiled at her, a woeful smile, speaking of his sadness as he vowed, "I will see you are taken care of, Eliza. This I promise."

She nodded, grateful to be rid of her worries while all was numbed by shock and grief. William, of course, would see to everything. After all, they'd been only hours away from sealing their betrothal.

It was later, as the mourners milled about her father's black-draped house, partaking liberally of his excellent drink, that she heard the first whispers. They quickly shushed at her approach as the speakers avoided her gaze. But she'd heard them clearly enough.

Penniless. Destitute. Indebted.

Confused, she sought out William, finding him and his father in the study, her father's private room, going through her father's private papers. They both looked up guiltily. Justin Montgomery's shame was the first to fade.

"Come in, Eliza. We must talk."

William gasped in surprise. "Father, can this not wait? The man is hardly cold—"

"Better it be swift and clean and done in private. Close the door, girl."

Eliza did as requested, then approached the two men warily. The fact of their presence, uninvited, smacked of desecration to her father's memory. "What are you doing in here? Those are my father's things."

Her question displeased Justin. His smile was placating, barely covering his impatience with her. "I am—was Elias's partner. I am trying to see what can be salvaged before his creditors descend and strip everything to the bone."

Odd that he should use the reference to a vulture. Reining in her irritation and her growing apprehension, Eliza waited for him to go on.

"You are a bright girl, Eliza. I do not have to explain the workings of our business to you. All your family's assets were attached to the *Peregrine*. When she went down, the loss of her cargo was the loss of your fortune as well."

Eliza swayed, then held herself stiff and straight.

There it was, laid out plain. That's what her father meant when he'd chased her home. There was nothing left to rebuild upon. He'd known creditors would swarm their doors as soon as they heard. In a way, he was saved that final humiliation by his untimely death.

He'd saved it for his daughter to bear.

"I should talk to our solicitor." Flat, calmly spoken words relaying none of her inner panic.

"He'll tell you what I'm going to tell you. You've nothing but debt as an inheritance. The house, the business, your belongings, none of them will come close to what was owed."

Penniless. Destitute. Indebted.

She drew a shaky breath. She was not a child. Of course she knew the risk of her father and brother's chosen endeavor. Fortunes rose and fell like the winds over the Atlantic. And it was a cold, ill wind sweeping over her now.

Then William spoke up, strongly, forcefully. "I've promised Eliza that we'd take care of her. In this instance, I'm sure the period of mourning could be waived and we could be married right away. I won't allow her to be humiliated by her father's lack of wise investment."

Though the words pricked her sense of devotion, Eliza forgave them. William was just trying to protect her. Even as she exhaled in relief, Justin Montgomery drew himself up like a dark thunderhead and cast down a bolt to tear her dreams asunder.

"There will be no wedding."

Both young people stared at him, struck speechless, as he continued with a logic as cold as it was unfeeling.

"No heir of mine will marry a woman without means. We've lost enough to the Parrishes without assuming the load of debt that would come as dowry. Bad business."

William recovered first to argue, "We are speaking of love, not business, Father."

"They are the same, boy. Grow up."

His usually kind features florid with agitation, William took hold of Eliza's arm and guided her back to the door. "Please wait outside, my love. I would have a word with my father."

Dismissed to the hall of her own home, Eliza tried to hold to hope as voices rose from within the room. The knowledge that her future was being decided without her quickened a resentment strong enough to wake her from her grief. Fear went with it, hand in hand, until after a heated confrontation Justin Montgomery exited the room, striding past her without so much as a glance.

One look at William's face told all. He tried to speak, then tried again, finding the words easier to say with his gaze averted.

"I have promised not to abandon you and I will not. The vows we've spoken to one another will see us through this . . . this unfortunate turn."

Eliza wished he would look at her so she could read the strength of that conviction in his expressive eyes. He didn't. "Explain 'unfortunate' to me, William."

He winced at that demand. His hands gripped the edges of her father's desk, going white knuckled. "Our marriage will have to be . . . delayed."

"For how long?" Anxiousness put a quiver in her question.

William's features clenched and worked fiercely. "Four years."

"Four years? But the period of mourning—"

"That's a period of indenture, Eliza," he said in an embarrassed whisper.

"What! What?"

He sighed heavily with regret and frustration. His resignation put a terrible chill in Eliza's heart. "Apparently, my father is not your only creditor. The weight of debt is, shall we say, crushing. I wish there was a way to put this more kindly, but . . . the only way to keep you from debtor's prison is to sell off papers of indenture for a period of four years."

Eliza stood, paralyzed, wordless. The shock was too total for her to express her dismay.

"For his part, my father will assume ownership of Parrish Shipping, this house, and its contents. That will not cover his investment, but he is willing to accept the remaining loss."

"And I . . . I am to be sold to satisfy the rest?"

He looked at her then, his gaze dark and tortured. "I promised I would see to you. I have done my best. I convinced my father to buy your papers."

"I will be your . . . servant?"

" 'Twill be a gentle servitude, my love, in surroundings to which you are accustomed. My sister, Philomena, is in need of a companion. She's to travel to England, and my mother's frail health prevents her from serving as proper chaperone."

Eliza knew his sister well. Philomena was a spiteful, spoiled creature who envied Eliza for her family's social position. To be placed in her hands, at her mercy . . .

Seeing the rebellion building in Eliza's face, William crossed to her, enfolding her in a tight embrace. "Take heart, my love. I will find a way for us to be together. I will work upon my father's will in your absence. His heart may be hard at the moment, but he is not a compassionless man."

But he was. William's failure to understand that made Eliza want to shake him awake to his father's true nature. But then he placed a tender kiss upon her brow and bid her, "Believe in me, Eliza. You, above all others, have always had faith and that is what sustains me. That and the knowledge that you will be safe and cared for by my family. Take heart and have faith."

"I will," she pledged because she wanted so much to believe him.

And now she was trying to keep that pledge as their ship rocked across the Atlantic on Philomena's tide of tears.

"Elizaaaa."

The sound moaned from the bunk behind her, but Eliza was reluctant to leave the glass through which she watched the wake of their vessel churn like her emotions.

"Eliza!" The call quickly altered in tone from pitiful plea to whining demand.

With a sigh, Eliza turned away from the rippling water and faced her petulant cabinmate. Philomena Montgomery proved no better a sailor than her brother, William. The moment the *Majesty* eased away from India Wharf in Salem, the delicate-natured female took to her bunk and pail, soiling both at regular intervals. It was Eliza's duty to comfort and clean up after the queasy Philomena.

"Eliza, my gown is ruined. Fetch me another."

Wordlessly, Eliza opened the cupboard to select a fresh garment from the dwindling store. Soon she would have to find a way to wash and air the sour-smelling clothes piled near the door, but for now, Philomena's excess in packing proved to be a blessing. Ignoring the sight of her own two good gowns crushed between the volume of her mistress's, Eliza closed the cupboard and returned to the ailing woman.

Philomena's bedraggled form draped limply across the tangle of covers. She made no move to cooperate as Eliza dragged her upright and began to divest her of the damaged gown. It was like tending to a puppet with severed strings. No sooner had she peeled down the bodice than a rumble of intention had her grabbing for the bucket, placing it between her and the green-skinned Philomena until the sounds of sickness abated. She made no comment as she wiped the other's sweat-dappled face and continued with the dressing.

What could she say? It wasn't her place to comment or condemn. Not any longer.

Fate had prescribed that Philomena Montgomery, once her peer, now be her superior, at least until the four years of her indenture were paid.

Freshly garbed and weak, Philomena collapsed back upon the ticking, her eyes closing, dismissing Eliza from her care. Grateful for the silence, Eliza returned to the vista, to her brooding thoughts.

What a disservice William's compassion proved to be. Didn't he understand that there was a vast difference between being a Montgomery wife and a Montgomery servant?

Eliza never considered herself a proud woman, but when she walked away from her own luxurious home with only a trunk of belongings, she refused to let her shoulders bend beneath the shame of it. Those who'd only weeks ago courted her favor at afternoon teas averted their eyes when they saw her. She tried not to care. She'd settled into her household position, aware of the other servants' amusement at her diminished circumstances, aware as well, more painfully so, of how suddenly she became invisible to a family who had once adored her.

A kinder woman would have sympathized, but Philomena held only malicious contempt for the rival now reduced to near slave. Contempt manifested itself in spiteful reminders of her fallen status. Eliza ignored them as best she could. All she had to do was endure Philomena's tantrums and try not to be disheartened by what her mistress's banishment said of Justin Montgomery's hard heart.

Philomena was being sent to England because her unsuitable interest in a lesser-born customshouse clerk had been discovered. Philomena shrieked and cried and begged and cajoled, but Montgomery hadn't lessened his firm decree. His daughter would go abroad until she got the romantic nonsense out of her head completely. The sea air and foreign soil were just what she needed to purge that upstart clerk from her heart. She'd been wailing right up until the point where Montgomery had to drag her aboard, locking her into her stateroom until the ship was under sail. And now that Eliza was her only link to Salem, it was upon Eliza that she vented all her frustrated spleen.

Though it was unusual for two unmarried misses of their age to travel alone together, Justin Montgomery felt the circumstances warranted the risk. Sailing under the captain's protection, they would be met at the London docks by Justin's sister and her family. There was no real threat to the ladies as long as they remained in their cabin. Not that Philomena ever attempted to leave her sickbed once the subtle toss of the sea stirred swells of nausea.

"What are you watching for, Eliza? Some rescuing hero to sail up and sweep you away from paying your debt to my family? Or perhaps you expect to see my brother pursuing you out of undying devotion." Her laughter was weak yet uncommonly cruel.

Though Eliza said nothing to debate her, a taut line of defiance strengthened her jaw. Philomena didn't miss it. Again, the harsh laugh.

"William will never go against my father's wishes, you little fool. Never! Why else do you think you were allowed to work in our household right under his very nose? Father doesn't fear that William will suddenly develop a backbone, so why should you expect that miracle?"

"You speak very meanly of your brother's virtues, Mena." It was a quietly offered reproof but a reproof nonetheless.

"It's *Miss* Philomena to you now. Don't be forgetting that."

How could she forget when her very existence spoke of it so relentlessly?

"I will not be as weak as William," Philomena continued from her sickbed. "I *will* have my Jonathon. After all, it's not as though I'd be marrying a *servant*."

Eliza fought not to wince at that vicious attack. She would not let Philomena see how the words hurt her.

"Oh, Father, why must you be so cruel?" moaned Philomena, part of a familiar litany of misuse. "How can you think this wretched journey would change my mind where my Jonathon is concerned?"

Tuned to her own unhappiness, Eliza was moved by the anguish in the other woman's voice. She turned to offer a soft encouragement. "Perhaps he will relent once he sees how seriously your heart is engaged. I'm certain he views this as a fickle affection, elsewise he would not be moved to such means. I'm sure he's only thinking to protect you." As her own father would have done. She touched the ring she wore, feeling a sudden kinship for Philomena's plight.

Philomena squinted red-rimmed eyes in her direction. A nasty curl warped her lips. "Did I give you leave to speculate about my father's motives? So, you see me as fickle, do you?"

"That's not—"

"A fine choice of words for one used to teasing the Salem beaux along in a pretty dance to your tune. Miss Moneybags with her stuffy name and hoity-toity airs. Not so high and mighty now, are you? Not when you're standing in my shadow for a change."

Eliza paled, wanting desperately to defend against the slanderous charges. To voice her argument would only escalate the other's anger. So Eliza stood silent, bearing the malicious barbs to her character, and in doing so, unintentionally provoked Philomena's ire.

"Go play the martyr elsewhere," her mistress snapped. "I tire of your woeful expression. If you were not so good with my hair, I would have asked my father to have them throw you into debtors' prison or, better yet, have you parceled off to some dockside gin mill where your charms would have found suitable merit—for a price."

Unable to stand ground against such intentional viciousness without venting her own temper, Eliza left the cabin. She'd lost everything, true. Not even the right to an honest anger remained hers.

How was she to survive this reduction in circumstance? Her strength faltered. She didn't understand why those external forces made others who knew and claimed to love her see her as someone—something— other than she was. She was no different, not inside. And inside was where she suffered most from the crumbling of her faith in all she'd believed about herself, in finding out she was worth less as a person without wealth.

She had never known, not really, how much Philomena hated and envied her. She'd never put stock in the social and political differences that made her Philomena's better. She'd been so casual in her acceptance of her standing that she'd never understood its significance.

Until now. Until viewing her former place of privilege through the eyes of a have-not.

A scuffle of sound from above made her catch back her plan to climb topside for some bracing air. She paused beneath the open steps, unintentionally privy to the agitated conversation of the sailors above. In no time, her own troubles were forgotten.

" 'Tis a pirate, I tell you," the one was saying in a frantic tone. "I've heard tell of that ship, and it's bound for no good."

"Pirate? Bah! They swim like sharks in southern waters where prizes be rich for the taking. We be carrying nothing of interest to the likes of them."

"I tell you 'tis Coeur Noir. 'Tis his black ship that bears no marks nor sports a country's flag."

"Black Heart," the doubtful one whispered, the name shaking him from his scoffing certainty. "Be you sure? I heard he was yet languishing in irons."

"Nay. His crew effected a bold rescue right under his jailers' noses. Got clean away on that devil ship. I never heard tell of him circling so far north . . . not since his privateering days."

"What could he be after?"

"All we carry is that rich Salem wench, and I'll not be staking me life for the likes of her, if it's ransom he be meaning to turn."

Eliza didn't wait to hear the rest of his disparaging remarks as she raced back to her cabin.

Coeur Noir.

What *would* a pirate want with them?

Philomena struggled up onto her elbows to glare at

her absent maid as Eliza slipped into their cabin. Before she could berate her servant, Eliza hurried to the window. Puzzled by the other woman's actions, a frown settled upon Philomena's wan features.

"Whatever has you in such a dither?"

Eliza didn't answer at once. She was mesmerized by the sleek dark ship bearing down upon their merchant vessel, a hawk diving at a fat rabbit. "Coeur Noir." The name breathed from her as she watched the ship come about with a skill she'd seldom seen matched.

"What? What did you say?"

Startled by Philomena's shrill cry, Eliza looked back to her. The other female was positively white. "I overheard two of the crew saying our ship was being overtaken by another vessel. They said it was Coeur Noir. Does that name mean anything to you?"

Despite her spiritless demeanor of moments ago, Philomena leaped up from the bed and shoved Eliza away from the window. The instant she spotted the trailing ship, she went pale as death, her words stark as her pallor. "We're doomed, Eliza."

"But our ship carries nothing of value. What could a pirate be after?"

Huge eyes lifted to meet hers.

"He's after me."

Chapter 3

Eliza was about to shame the other for her dramatics. But one look at Philomena's ashen features spoke the other's panic clearly. It was no act.

"Why would he want you? Have you ever met the man?"

Philomena shook her head, then began to pace, her fluttering hands twisting together in restless knots. "N-no, I have never seen him." She glanced at Eliza, then quickly away. Her anxiousness grew with every step as a deeper fright moved through her mind. Her eyes were feverish, like those of an animal caught in a trap and desperate for escape.

"Then why would you think he means you harm?"

Philomena turned upon her with a savage disdain. "Don't be a twit, Eliza. My family has money. That's what he's after." She looked ready to say more but quickly whirled away again, keeping the rest silent. Her anxiety rose as she traversed the small space, breathing in short frantic gasps.

Thinking to still her fears, Eliza said reasonably, "You worry for naught, Philomena. If they are pirates after ransom, harming you would serve no gain. In fact, a prisoner of value is treated with much respect, or so I've heard."

Again, that haunted gaze hinted at things her cabinmate wouldn't share. Suddenly, Philomena went completely still. Her contemplative stare shifted to her bond servant, and Eliza felt a shiver of warning creep over her. A narrow smile shaped Philomena's lips as desperation spun crafty plots within her head.

"You may have spoken the answer. He has never seen me. He does not know what I look like. The captain is the only one who knows me by sight, and I could easily press him into secrecy." Philomena's scheming gaze swept over her. "If you changed into one of your finer gowns, it might work."

Eliza's suspicions quivered. "What might work?"

"Why, if we were to say *you* were Philomena Montgomery, who would know the difference?"

Before Eliza could speak the objections springing to her lips, Philomena caught her hands in a damp, despairing clasp.

"Oh, please, Eliza. You are so much braver than I."

Eliza was no fool. Philomena was asking her to take the risks involved, whatever they might be. A swift, sure rebellion rose up inside her. "Are you suggesting that since my life has little value, I sacrifice it for yours? I do not believe that is part of my indenture contract with your family."

The flare of Eliza's temper momentarily threw Philomena off course. Anger fueled by fear tightened her expression, but the deeper cunning of a woman used to getting her own way quickly surfaced. Tears pooled in blue china-doll eyes. A vulnerable quiver shook her pointed chin. Tactics guaranteed to weaken the staunchest male—but useless against another of her own sex.

"I won't do it, Philomena, and no amount of threat or tears can persuade me. This matter does not involve me."

Philomena drew a seething breath and rapidly re-thought her strategy. "If you will not do it because of any allegiance you owe my family, then perhaps a change in your own circumstance would be motive enough."

Eliza felt the ship shudder as the sails were turned against the winds to bring it to a standstill. Philomena's terrified gaze flew to the closed door. There was little time left for discussion. "Explain yourself."

"If you will convince this pirate that you are Philomena Montgomery, I will see your servitude ended as soon as we return to Salem."

Eliza's hopes surged. Freedom. "You will return my papers of indenture?"

"Yes. As you just said, there is no danger to you. Kidnapping is a business to such men. They would not harm the means to their fortune. You only have to pretend to be me. A small sacrifice for a great gain. What would it mean? A small delay of our journey while negotiations are arranged? Why, it would hard-ly be an inconvenience." Her eyes gleamed with in-spired fervor. Again, Eliza felt that trickle of unease. "Only you must agree now. Hurry!"

It was so tempting, so irresistible. Freedom. Dare she trust Philomena to carry through with her vow? She eyed the other female, seeing her genuine terror at the prospect of confronting a possible kidnapper. It was a chance she could not allow to slip away. What was a little risk when compared to the thought of re-gaining her pride and so much more?

"I'll do it."

"Quickly, then, change your clothing, and here." Philomena undid the clasp to the elaborate necklace she wore. It was fashioned of jewel-studded medal-lions linked to make a chain. From it hung the Mont-gomery family crest. She fastened it about Eliza's

neck, where it lay chill and heavy, to seal the charade.
"Now there will be no question. You are Philomena."

They waited in the isolated cabin, straining to hear
clues as to what was happening above. They'd been
boarded, though no shots had been fired. A good
sign. Perhaps violence was not intended. Eliza
crushed the folds of her skirts to hide the shaking of
her hands. Bravery was easy to commit to with
words, but action was harder. She hoped she could
carry off the pretense. There was no danger, she reminded herself. Just a clever ploy. Too much was involved for her will to go weak now. Behind her,
Philomena was mewling and moaning with fright, her
face covered by her hands.

Heavy footfalls sounded in the corridor. Eliza's
shoulders straightened and she drew a deep, starching breath just as the door to the cabin thrust open.
Philomena screamed, a thready wail cut short as she
buried her head in her pillows. But Eliza stood firm—
as firm as she could atop trembling knees.

Two burly men pushed into the cabin, filling it with
their menacing presence and the stink of their sweat.
They didn't touch her. They waited, silent sentinels,
and so Eliza waited as well, waited for Coeur Noir.
Anxiety stiffened her spine. Purpose held her head
high. And then she heard his approach, the brisk cadence of his stride. And her resolve faltered, if only
briefly.

*What if he was interested in more than a bartering for
gold? Could he mean to slay her in her guise as Philomena?
To what madness had she consented? Was death preferable
to servitude?*

It was on her lips to cry off from the disguise when
Black Heart appeared, halting within the frame of the

door, letting her wide eyes take their fill of him just as he was measuring her.

She'd expected something ... different. A grisly, fearsome man capable of sending babes to quake in their mother's skirts. A snarling, filthy form reeking with brute power, seething with the madness of one who could cut a throat without remorse. A monster whose very reputation had Philomena cowering in her covers.

But Coeur Noir, Black Heart, was quite probably the most breathtakingly beautiful man she'd ever seen.

He wasn't dressed to draw attention to himself as captain of his ship, or with the flamboyance one would attribute to a legend. He wore a seaman's jacket of plain black cloth cut short at the waist in front while curving around lean hips to fall midthigh in back. Loose trousers tucked into high boots. A simple white waistcoat covered an unadorned white shirt, a black silk neck cloth casually knotted at its throat. Simple clothes made elegant by the bearing of the man—not military stiffness but a strong, disciplined grace borne out by impressive height and shoulder breadth.

The stark white of his standing collar framed sundarkened skin not yet dried and cracked by the sting of brine. He wore his black hair close shorn, wind bristled, instead of in a fashionable Byronic tousle. His face was smooth, facial bones exquisitely cut, highlighted by a slash of black brows and a full wide mouth boasting generous curves. Beautiful. Captivatingly male. So much so, that Eliza was momentarily lost in the looking, wondering how anyone could fear this man. Until she met his gaze.

His eyes were black, like his hair, like his coat, as deeply lustrous as the gloss on his boots. And they were cold—chips of raw obsidian. Emotionless, reflectionless. Dangerous. And suddenly filled with loathing when his gaze fixed upon the necklace she wore.

She drew an involuntary breath as his stare lifted, connecting with hers for an intense probing. For an instant, she quailed and considered glancing away in intimidation. Then something pricked within her, a sense of pride, a snap of objection at his rude glowering. Her chin tilted up a notch higher and her gaze narrowed in unblinking challenge. The uncompromising line of his lips shifted, she thought, for a smile. But it was a gesture never completed.

"Mademoiselle Montgomery, it is indeed a pleasure." His tone indicated otherwise.

"Perhaps for you, sir. Why have you delayed this ship?"

Instead of answering, he glanced away as if her question held no merit. "Take her."

His words were so curt, so cold, it took a moment for her to comprehend his meaning. When one of his burly crew grasped her arm, it became all too clear.

"Let me go! What are you doing?" She pulled back, trying to twist out of the imprisoning hold, but succeeded only in hurting herself. "I demand to know your intentions!"

"You demand, m'am'selle?"

Those black eyes pierced her right to the soul, a soul that knew a sudden shiver of peril. She went still, struggling not to betray her fright.

He did smile then, a thin, coldly formal smile that made his gaze seem blacker, if possible. "Since you demand to know, my lady, I will tell you." His voice was low and soft and thickly accented. A deadly purr. "Your father owes me, Mademoiselle Montgomery, not just for the years I was imprisoned. There is a debt of honor to be paid as well, a fee for services your father thought not to pay. He will pay now, and he will pay dearly if he wants you returned—alive. Let him learn that Coeur Noir, like his friends the Lafitte brothers, will not be crossed without consequence. *Allons!*"

With that threat chilling her very marrow, he turned away to stride up the stairs, leaving her to the hands of his men.

They were going to take her off the ship.

What hadn't Philomena told her? Was this a random act of abduction or something more personal? Something that could turn deadly?

It was more than a matter of playing a role, defying an angry pirate from the safety of her cabin. She was to be dragged from this ship as prisoner, made to suffer she could only guess what, for pretending to be who she was not. Where she would endure whatever vengeance the black-eyed pirate planned. Alone. But this was not her lot. This fate was not to be hers. She was not a lady of worth. She was a bond servant, a valueless pawn.

"No." That objection escaped her as consequence settled, deep and dire. She began to shake her head as one of the men motioned toward the door. "No," she repeated a bit more frantically. "You don't understand. I'm not—"

Philomena's arms bound suddenly and tightly about her, squeezing the words of confession from her lungs. "Be brave, Mistress Montgomery," she cried in a shaky voice, worried not for Eliza's safety but that her own deception be discovered. "I'm sure you'll soon be free."

Free.

Eliza clung to that tantalizing word. It teased her

fears, taunted her for her reluctance to continue the charade.

"You may take your maid, if you wish," one of the men said.

Eliza felt Philomena's violent start, and that returned her calm. She stood away from the frightened woman to exclaim, "No! I will go alone. I would ask that you allow my maid to return to my father's house to tell him that I have not been harmed." *Yet*.

She swallowed down the metallic taste of her fear.

When her guard nodded, Philomena gave a relieved sob and embraced her once again, murmuring gratefully against Eliza's ear, "We will come after you, and your freedom will be your reward. Bless you for your courage."

With Philomena torn abruptly from her and pushed aside, Eliza was propelled forcefully toward the door.

"My trunks, my belongings—"

"The captain said to bring you," one of them growled. "He didn't say nothing about toting your baggage."

So without as much as a clean shift and just a cloak to cover her, she was hurried toward the stairs. She could hear Philomena sobbing in the background, not with anguish but from relief, as she was marched up the steps out onto the deck, a prisoner.

For a moment, Eliza was so grateful for the fresh air and sea breeze, cold as it was, she almost thanked her captors for rescuing her from below. But then she saw the group of armed men holding the *Majesty*'s crew at bay and the plank linking this ship to the dark vessel bobbing alongside. Her mood dimmed beneath a cresting terror. As she was being led toward the side, the captain of the *Majesty* approached. Though she tried to hide her face within the loose folds of her hood, the wind caught it from her chilled fingers, tearing it back off her head and sending up a swirl of red-gold curls to frame her features. Confusion lit his gaze when he beheld her and not Miss Montgomery. A brief warning shake of her head held him silent as to her identity.

"I am sorry I could not protect you better," he told her somberly, "but we are not a ship of war."

"I understand, Captain, and I do not blame you for not risking the lives of your crew in a foolish endeavor."

The captain bowed slightly. "You are kind to say so."

She reached out a trembling hand to him, and his rough palms engulfed it. "Promise you will see my servant safely back to Salem."

"I will, my lady."

She was helped up onto the slippery boarding plank and eased across the depthless green waters to the pirate vessel. When the last of Coeur Noir's crew crossed over as well, the plank was withdrawn and the boarding lines were cast off.

Eliza stood on the deck between the brace of rough sailors, watching stoically as the *Majesty*'s sails caught wind, snapping the canvas taut to guide the two ships apart. A great swell of isolation overcame her as the distance increased and the sad-eyed captain on the other ship became faceless, then formless.

She was alone.

Anxiousness compelled her gaze up to the forecastle deck, where the sleek ship's captain stood. Icy wind rumpled through his close-cropped hair and molded the fabric of his trousers to spraddled thighs. He made a heart-stopping picture, those gloriously chiseled features turned into the brunt of the ocean breeze.

And then, as if he felt her studying him, he turned

his penetrating gaze upon her, that look relentless in
its fury, intense in its intentions.

Shivering from the unexpected chill, Eliza called
herself fool for entrusting her life into his care and
her future to Philomena's promise.

Coeur Noir still held his isolated stance when approached by his second mate. He didn't turn as the
man addressed him.

"She's stowed safely below, Captain."

A pause, then a flat "Good."

"Wouldn't the hold be a better prison than your
own quarters?"

Black eyes slanted a look at him. A cold dagger-
edged stare. "I want her unharmed. Unless I choose
to harm her."

"Luc—" his second began uneasily.

A clipped gesture cut him off. "You have your orders, Mr. Sterns. Is there some problem in understanding them?"

"No, Captain. You've made yourself very clear."

The young Frenchman turned his hard gaze back
to the sea. "Very well. Signal Mr. Symms so he'll
know to deliver our terms as soon as we are safely
away."

"Aye, Captain." Then less formally, "You should
be pleased that all goes well."

"I am."

"Then smile, Luc."

He was greeted with a somber stare and a grim,
"When it is over, *mon ami*. When it is over."

Pushed inside the captain's quarters in the ship's
broad stern and left there without a word from her
guards, Eliza rubbed her arms, trying to restore her

body heat, trying to rekindle her courage, while taking stock of her surroundings.

It was a man's room, filled with male scents of leather, tobacco, and rum. Those same smells that signified security and welcome within her father's chambers seemed threatening now. She looked about in desperation and caught sight of a pair of crossed sabers adorning one wall. She moved to them, possessed by a grim purpose. Bringing one down, hefting its weight in her hand, her confidence rallied.

"Who's helpless now, Monsieur Black Heart?"

She studied the curve of steel as it gleamed wickedly. Could she use such a fearsome instrument in her own defense? Could she wield it to part head from shoulders if her own life were in the balance? The razor-sharp edge glinted.

She thought of the pirate captain, of his stunning features and soulless stare.

She remembered all too vividly the tales Nate used to tell to scare her, of blood-thirsty pirates who preyed upon innocents on the seas.

And juxtaposing those hair-raising tales with the stark look of malice in the pirate's eyes, she knew herself capable of swinging a fatal blow. Unlike Philomena, she had no one to turn to for an immediate rescue. Only her own cunning would serve until William arrived.

She would keep herself safe until that time.

Carrying the sword with her, she continued her search of the cabin. There was little to discover, just a seafaring man's possessions: maps, charts, navigational tools, clothing, all in the stark hues of black and white more befitting a man of the church than a pirate on the prowl. An ornate sea chest served as one seat before a heavy oak table, and a cushioned armchair, another. A single berth was built out from one wall, but she didn't allow her gaze to linger there, nor her thoughts, either. Cupboards built into the other wall yielded decanters of amber liquor and, more surprisingly, books. Hundreds of volumes, more than she'd seen in some libraries. The spines told of French titles, not just history and navigational diaries but novels and poetry as well. Coeur Noir, whatever else he might be, was a learned man. She found that somewhat unsettling, though she was not sure why. It was as if the proof of his intelligence made him a more deadly adversary.

Restlessly, she paced the floor, cold and frightened, dragging the saber behind her. Shadows lengthened and the rumble of her stomach told the lateness of the hour. Finally she lit one of the lamps hanging on either side of the door, comforted by its warm glow. Her spirit knew no comfort, her mind no rest, even when, in near exhaustion, she lay down upon the bed wrapped up in her cloak and its covers. She brought the sword to rest on the mattress next to her. Just in case. No one had threatened her yet, but that did not mean danger would not come.

She closed her eyes, meaning to rest them for only a moment. Weariness dragged her lids down and weighted them there when she willed them to open again. Her mind drifted. How long, she wondered, until the Montgomerys sent a rescue ship after her?

What lay between Justin Montgomery and the pirate Black Heart?

She must hold the truth of her identity silent, at least as long as it took to see the *Majesty* out of harm's way. Then when it was discovered that she had no value, she would be returned to her New England home, to a grateful family's embrace.

And she fell asleep, smiling, reveling in those happy thoughts, unaware of the dark shadow of a man watching over her as she dreamed.

Chapter 4

She was asleep in his bed.

From where he stood out of the light, he could see the soft slope of her cheek, the sweet part of her lips, the feathery curve of her lashes upon fair skin. Fiery hair splayed out upon white linens like beams of molten sunlight. He'd heard she was a comely eyeful and that she was.

He'd also heard she was every inch her father's daughter.

He'd planned this vengeance long and well. While rotting away in a prison cell, he'd had plenty of time to plot against the man who cheated and betrayed him. This was that man's spawn, the tool of that revenge.

Having heard much about Montgomery's golden prize—a nasty little creature by all accounts, spoiled by wretched excess—he had little trouble building his vengeance around her. He would not view her as a helpless female, nor would he soften to her fears. He'd been helpless and afraid and no one had come to his aid. Why should a Montgomery expect mercy from him?

Except he hadn't expected her to look so young, so vulnerable as she did while huddled in her cloak upon his frigid deck. And now, curled within his covers. Such a sight quickened protective instincts she had no right to command, not from him.

Planting a booted foot against the rounding of her backside, he shoved hard and was rewarded by an indignant squeal as she toppled out of bed in the tangle of her cloak. Her eyes snapped wide open, momentarily confused. Blue-green eyes, as changeable as the turbulent seas.

"No one invited you to make yourself at home, m'am'selle. Those are my sheets, and I'm choosy about who shares them with me."

Far from being intimidated by his frigid tone, she sat up quickly, throwing off the cloak and covers. It was then he saw the saber, its blade as sharp and gleaming as her glare. She brandished it before her with the awkwardness of a novice in close-quarters arms.

"I'm not afraid of you," she challenged with all the brass of a kitten showing its claws in the face of a mastiff.

He took a step forward, causing her to scramble backward. His smile was mocking. "Yes, you are. You are shaking right down to your corset stays with the fear that I mean you unspeakable harm."

To her credit, she never blinked. "Would I be right in thinking that?"

"Yes."

He reached out suddenly, closing his fingers about the blade. She gasped in surprise at that bold, fearless act but didn't move. One swift pull from her would cost him his hand.

"But you're safe for now," he added, "as long as you give this to me. I have no patience with being threatened in my own cabin. Release it. Now."

Her gaze delved into his, searching for the truth of

his words within his steady stare. Ignoring the bite of the blade into his palm, he began to pull the saber away from her. The instant she saw a line of crimson creeping toward his cuff, she gave another soft gasp and quickly released the sword into his possession. He grabbed the hilt and took a second to examine his palm. The cut wasn't deep but stung nonetheless— like the memory of her father's treachery.

He caught her regretful gaze as he sucked at the gash.

"What's wrong, m'am'selle?" he asked when the pressure of his mouth stilled the bleeding. "No taste for spilling blood? Or are you used to others doing it for you?" When she had no comment, he returned the saber to its place on the wall, leaving them in plain sight to remind her of her weakness. Whatever sympathy he'd seen in her sea-green gaze was gone when he turned back to her. The combatant look was back. He preferred the fire to the frailty of moments before to keep himself *en garde*.

"What do you plan to do with me?" Stubbornly said, despite the obvious fear.

His reply intentionally chilled with menace. "Perhaps it is better that you not know."

Her lashes flickered, a quiver betraying her fright, but her stare never faltered. "Better for whom?"

"Me, of course. Why should I care what you think or feel?"

Again she had no answer but sat silently, contemplating him and her situation with an unwavering gaze. Both the silence and the stare angered him. He'd dreamed long of her panic, of her mewling for her father's rescue. Her calm cheated him of that satisfaction.

Finally, she stated, "I will be worth more if untouched by you and your crew."

So, she thought his plans included ravishment. Yet, still she failed to plead for his compassion. His stare slid over her with an insulting detachment. "The rumors of your voluptuous beauty are grossly overdrawn. I have no interest in skinny women. As for my crew, as long as you stay within this room, you needn't find out what they think."

A glimmer of hurt was quickly overcome by fire. "You are very rude and vulgar, sir. What care I for the opinion of a lowly pirate?"

His jaw set in a harsh square. His tone cut sharper than the saber's blade. "I am no pirate, mademoiselle, no lowly thief. It would be better for you if I was, for pirates travel under codes of *honneur* that require them to pay courtesy to a guest. I am under no such obligation to be charming, so be warned."

Her chin thrust out in challenge. "If not a pirate, what are you, then? I saw no supplies taken from the *Majesty*. Surely she was carrying things of value."

"Not to me. I took only what I wanted."

"Me." That was a faint echo bolstering into a stronger demand: "Why? Thief or kidnapper, wherein lies the difference?"

"The difference is I take only what is owed to me." He stopped for a moment to control the anger trembling through his tone. "I am a man of the sea. My profession is one of pride and *honneur* abused by those of greedy purpose, those like your father."

For an instant, it looked as though she meant to argue on her father's behalf; then her jaw clamped shut and she remained silent once more. What argument could she give in defense of the bastard? It was common knowledge even among his own peers that Montgomery's ambitions were not to be trusted.

Again, annoyed by the way she so neatly pricked his temper, he stalked to the lamp and turned the wick down until it sputtered out in the glass base. The sharp scent of oily smoke stung his nostrils, obscuring the sweeter fragrance of woman. He drew a deep cleansing breath and turned.

"Where do I sleep?" she asked at last, a reluctant question that made him smile slightly, knowing well she could not see his expression. She was more afraid of his answer than she would have him guess.

He grasped a blanket and threw it down off the foot of the bed. "There. I suggest you make yourself comfortable. But if you would rather sleep here with me, be warned: I retire *sans* clothing."

And he began to strip down to bare skin to prove his point. He heard her scamper on hands and knees around the far end of the bed. Unmoved by her modest horror, he stretched out on the mattress with a sigh of contentment, vaguely disturbed by her scent lingering upon it. He listened for a moment, hearing the rapid cadence of her breathing. She was afraid, just as he intended, but one more thing needed to be said before he could close his eyes for a decent night's sleep.

"If you consider murdering me in the night, do think again. Remember that my goodwill is all that keeps you from sharing the fo'c'sle hammocks with the rest of my crew. They are even more rude and vulgar than I."

She was wordless for a moment as consequences sank deep. Then her retort came, crisp and cutting. "Rest well, pirate. Your throat is safe for this night. I am quite comfortable where I am."

A lie, for at that moment, Eliza's mind crawled with disturbing images kindled by too many stories told at her father's knee. She pulled the blanket about her trembling shoulders and slid to the floor. Not a pirate. She dared not believe him. What other manner of man prowled the sea wearing no nation's colors?

And what manner of revenge did he have in mind?

Hungry and cold and frightened beyond reason, she curled in the scant covers, alert for every sound. She'd known loneliness and heartache in the past months, but now she experienced the raw edge of fear. Uncertainty over her future was never more keen. Closing her eyes, she sought solace in her memories of her family and of William, who would soon learn of her abduction. He would be anxious, true, and worried, rightly so. But would he fly into a rage and demand his father launch a rescue?

She hoped so.

Vigorously.

Prayerfully.

Eliza hadn't expected to sleep, but suddenly the brightness of the new day played against her eyelids, making them flicker of their own accord.

She woke with a jerk of remembrance to find herself curled upon thin ticking on unyielding floorboards. Her body ached; her muscles were cold and stiff. More immediate matters pressed upon her, needs she couldn't tend to unless she was alone. Was she?

Get up you ninny. Stop cowering before this cur. Bold, prideful thoughts spurred her into the necessary action.

Slowly, she peeked over the footboard and then froze. Her pirate was still in residence—all endless bare inches of him.

He lay on his stomach without benefit of the bedsheet, despite the cabin's chill. A long darkly furred leg bent up at the knee, leading the way to a curve of muscular flank and other shadows she dared not explore too closely. Her unschooled gaze fluttered along his exposed flesh, fascinated by the color separation between pale hip and darkly tanned middle. His arm was stretched upward, curling about his head, pulling skin tautly across his ribs to bunch powerfully at his shoulder. Her stare followed the heavy swell of his upper arm, an impressive display of corded strength, all the way down to the slack spread of his fingers.

She'd never seen an unclothed man before. The sight did strange things to her breathing, the air seeming to thicken within her lungs.

He was glorious. Sleek, powerful, and more dangerous than she'd imagined. One glance revealed a vital energy, a strength to be feared and respected. No soft merchant, used to the easy life, he was shaped by the harsh ocean winds, knotted like the heavy bowlines, taut as sailcloth straining in a gale. Built like his dark ship, for speed, for power and agility. Elusive yet ultimately deadly. A shiver took her, partly from awe, partly from anxiousness. How could she hope to defend herself against such a man?

Abruptly, he muttered in his sleep, shifting his hips, rolling with knees tented, over onto his back.

Gasping with maidenly shock, Eliza ducked out of sight, but not before her wide eyes were filled with the vista of broad brown chest and a mat of crisp dark hair funneling suggestively downward. She crouched on the covers, wondering if exposure to such sights would damn her. Such knowledge of the male form was supposed to be kept sacred for the wedding night, for one's own husband. But, oh, how intriguing it was—all that firm muscle and dark skin, even the threatening mass of masculine body hair. She swallowed hard, trembling with a forbidden sense of excitement and shame that nearly overshadowed the fear.

And she was ashamed of herself for doubting that William would look thus in a state of undress.

She heard the deep male rumble of contentment as he came awake, the creak and crack of his joints as he lengthened in a limbering stretch. His bare feet appeared over the end of the bed, toes spread, then curling like a big cat's. She was mesmerized by the sight of those long, slender arches.

He was awake and aware of her.

What would happen now? Would his coldly formal mood of the day before prevail? Or would he be turned to darker purpose?

What if he decided a greater lesson would be dealt her "father" if she were forced to endure her captor's attentions?

He could rape her. She held little hope that she could stop him, not after viewing the strength of his lethal form. She began to breathe faster, in anxious pulls of dread. Then he spoke, the sensual lilt of his accent doing little to ease the sense of threat from pounding heart.

"I see we both survived the night unscathed, m'am'selle. This bodes well for our future association."

She exhaled noisily, dizzy with relief. At least he wasn't contemplating rape. For the moment. Though tempted to retort that she planned no lasting relationship between them, her own discomfort prevented a confrontation. She'd learned restraint in her dealings with Philomena.

"I—I should like a moment or two of privacy," she ventured, hoping she would not have to explain further or in detail.

Silence, then the silken cadence of his reply. "I fear I am not an early riser. I prefer to linger abed until my cabin boy brings me breakfast."

"I cannot wait that long." Her admission brought

a hot embarrassment and a deeper desperation that he understand her urgency.

She heard him shifting on the bed and then the scrap of something skidding across the floor in her direction. An empty chamber pot. She stared at it in horror. Surely, he didn't expect—

"There is a storeroom on the left that will provide you with privacy. Do not take too long tending to your vanity. I should not like to come looking for you."

Refusing to thank him for such basic civility, Eliza stumbled to her feet, pot in hand, careful not to glance in his direction. She was sure his own modesty hadn't called upon him to cover himself. With a stiff dignity, she headed for the door, knees pressed tight together, then hurried into the small adjacent room.

Relief. With it came the awareness of her situation. She had no change of clothing, not so much as a brush for her unruly hair. Her gown was crushed into a mass of wrinkles, adding to her sense of untidiness, leaving her off balance in her willful battle with the pirate captain. Her appearance was the only thing under her control. For all her blustering front, her courage was too frail to consider other tangibles—such as the threat to her life and virtue. Better she fret over small, inconsequential matters that wouldn't overwhelm her. The silliness of bemoaning a lack of hairpins magnified within her stress-filled mind until tears wobbled in her eyes.

How could she be brave when her hair hung askew?

She was trying to restore some order to her coiffure when the door unexpectedly opened. She found herself face-to-face with an equally startled lad of about fifteen. Shockingly blue eyes appeared huge against his swarthy skin and the black hair poking out in disarray from beneath his seaman's cap. He closed his sagging jaw to stammer, "Begging your pardon, my lady. I—I had no idea." Blushing brightly, he ducked into an awkward but no less respectful bow.

Something in his flustered humility and polite deference was just the bolstering shock she needed. To this boy, at least, she was a lady. Not a servant, but the lady she'd been raised to be. It was no part she was playing; it was who she was. And the pride in her upbringing was there to serve her.

She touched the boy's shoulder and said, "It's all right. You needn't apologize. I'm sure you are not used to ferrying female passengers."

He glanced up, encouraged by her tone. Then, wary as a young wolf pup as he remembered that she was their prisoner, he grew bolder. "No, my lady. Yer not our usual cargo, that's for certain." Then he flushed again at his choice of words, struggling to achieve an as yet to be reached maturity. "I—I didn't mean to say that like you was so much baggage."

"I know what you mean. I know I am not exactly a guest upon your ship."

He cleared his throat, shifting uncomfortably from foot to foot, at a loss for an answer. His averted gaze slipped back to assess her shyly. Had he a few more years behind him, she would have been insulted. But he was young, and easy to forgive.

"Excuse me," she murmured. "I must return before your captain fears I've jumped overboard to cheat him of his gold."

"Be you making sport of my cap'n?" he growled with eyes fiercely narrowed. "Such talk will not be tolerated aboard this ship."

"By his rule?"

"By mine, lady." He drew himself up with that claim and stared her straight on with renewed bold-

ness. Cockiness that would evolve into arrogance with
time.

"Then I beg your pardon."

He eyed her suspiciously. Seeking some sign of
mockery but finding none, he relaxed. "You are ex-
cused, madame. Considering your circumstance, I
guess you can't be expected to show us any respect."

"Only if it is earned."

He nodded, accepting that with an oddly grown-
up grace.

Eliza hesitated, taking advantage of the moment
and the blustering boy to ask, "Answer me something, if you would, to put my mind at ease. What
kind of man is your captain?"

"Captain Black Heart? He be shrewd in battle,
quick as a cat on his feet, afraid of nothing, afraid of
no one. Any of us would sail off the edge of the earth
at his command."

Eliza digested this. "You've told me of the kind of
captain he is. What of the man?" Was he cruel? Was
he unpredictable? Was he the type of man to harm a
woman in the name of revenge?

The lad looked puzzled. "Guess that's not such an
easy question. Can't say that none of us *know* him,
'cept maybe the second mate, Mr. Sterns. Keeps to
himself mostly. Guards his privacy like a monk, he
does, but that don't make him any less a man to my
thinking. He be the captain, not our friend. He ain't
one to sit about with the crew laughing over a jug of
rum and tellin' tales, but there's not a one of us who
wouldn't lay down our lives for him."

"Is that what you did when breaking him out of
prison?"

He fidgeted uncomfortably, then replied, "Yes, my
lady. Best you be getting back where you belong." He
dodged aside. As she passed, he was emboldened to

say, "My name be Remy, if you be needing anything."

She graced him with her most fetching smile, needing an ally upon this foreign vessel. "Thank you, Remy. I may call you on that offer."

He seemed stunned by her attention, then blinked and muttered, "Yes, ma'am," in a more surly tone.

Once she stood outside the cabin door, Eliza hesitated, still in the dark as to what kind of man waited on the other side or what degree of danger she was in.

Black Heart. She'd never heard the name in her brother's boastings. Maybe his was too terrible a tale to tell to a young, impressionable girl. But she'd heard enough stories to be duly afraid. Stories of atrocities, of unthinkable cruelties.

She shivered, her hand staying on the knob, reluctant to turn.

Was her handsome captor the monster Philomena feared? Would she live long enough to enjoy the promised freedom?

She drew a breath, willing herself to open the door. Would she find the virile Frenchman still languishing in a state of undress? Determinedly, she entered the cabin without knocking and realized an immediate relief to see him sprawled across the bed in recently donned canvas trousers. He didn't bother to open his eyes to acknowledge her presence, so she decided to ignore him as well, crossing, albeit cautiously, to the windows to look out over the endless seas. He seemed content with the silence, but it made her nervous. She was all too aware of his indecently clad form lounging an arm's length away, seemingly at ease yet coiled with tension.

"It looks as though a squall is brewing." She glanced at him for his reaction.

His dark eyes blinked open at her comment and his

head tilted back. His features were impassive, a beautiful blank of expression. "What know you of the sea and her temperament?"

"I was raised in a—in a seaport, Captain."

She bit her lower lip, wishing she could bite back the reckless words. She'd almost said she'd been raised in a family of seafarers. She had to be careful to remember who she was, or rather, who she was pretending to be. Philomena knew nothing of the oceans from which their town reaped its income. Would he know that? He seemed well versed on her mistress's shortcomings. She glanced at him again, wondering if he'd caught her near slip, but he was studying her with an inscrutable air, giving away nothing of his thoughts. It was time to shift the subject. "What shall I call you, Captain? Black Heart, or have you another name?"

For a moment, he was completely still, as if unwilling to share the niceties of conversation. Then a small smile curved his lips, making her experience an odd yearning to see that gesture come to full fruition. No matter what else he was, he was very handsome.

"I am sure you have thought of many names with which to credit me." When she didn't deny it, he answered with his oddly formal dignity, "I am Jean-Luc Gautier. You may call me whatever you wish as long as you do so respectfully in front of my crew. I have a reputation for not allowing disrespect in any form. I have already cut you considerable latitude, m'am'selle, with your slur of pirate. Do not press my good nature."

She made a harrumphing sound as if to doubt he had such a thing and returned to her study of the sea. Inwardly, she made a mental note not to push his questionable patience. "I have heard much of your reputation and would guess you are aptly named as

Coeur Noir." She could feel his stare upon her, unsettling in its intensity.

"I am, *chère*. You would be wise to remember that."

Just then a soft knock sounded and one of the captain's men entered bearing a tray of food. Her stomach gave a lusty rumble as the odors teased a responsive hunger. The tray was placed on the heavy oak table, and the sailor withdrew without a word. Eliza looked at the portions in dismay. It was a meal for one.

Jean-Luc dragged himself up off the bed and traveled on bare feet to the table. Without a glance in her direction, even though he must have heard the complaint her stomach made, he applied himself to fork and cup with single-minded purpose. A purpose that didn't include sharing.

"Is it your plan to starve me?" she blurted out in apprehension.

He paused, fork halfway to his mouth. Black eyes touched upon her briefly. He finished the bite and, after swallowing, remarked frigidly, "You are much too thin to please the eye as it is. You are under my protection because it suits me. But be reminded, you are not my guest. Your comfort could not concern me less. On this ship, all are equals, m'am'selle. You will not be treated like a princess. If you wish to eat, you will work for the privilege."

Then he turned in his seat to regard her with unflattering aloofness—a monk, Remy had said. But there was nothing monkish in his meaning as black eyes lingered upon her lips, traced down the curve of her bosom, then slid with deliberate purpose to her hips. His voice was a smoky rumble.

"Perhaps you can tell me exactly what you are good for?"

His insinuation took her like a hard slap to the face. And she wished mightily for the weight of his saber in her hand, for this time, she would not hesitate to swing.

Chapter 5

"**I** assure you, Captain, I would rather starve than play harlot for you and your crew."

"Since we have no call for a society hostess, I cannot see that you have any other skills to offer. Of course, if you fear you are unqualified for the other position, no experience is needed. We have been long at sea. My crew would require little in the way of, how you say . . . encouragement. And by the end of our journey, you would have learned a barterable trade." His bored indifference increased the insult.

Fury drove off all threads of fear. Circumstance had brought her low, but never to the level he suggested.

"I think not, pirate. That is not a profession I've ever aspired to."

"A pity for your future husband's sake."

The very thought of William desiring such tawdry knowledge in his bride outraged and horrified her. She spoke with a virginal hauteur. "My intended would not care to have me learn from such a disreputable school."

He regarded her levelly, the impenetrable mask of his expression never flickering. "I am not boasting when I say I have never had any complaints over the manner of my teachings."

Eliza flushed crimson, shocked by his statement. The sinfully gorgeous man—no, he probably hadn't. Mortified and strangely breathless, Eliza put her back to him, afraid he would see speculation mixed with her disgust.

Unfazed by her indignation, he returned to his meal. Eliza watched him, covetously, as he continued to eat, the pinch of her appetite now a savage gnawing. He was a brute, a savage yet mannerly cad, and she was afraid of him and what lay behind the facade of politeness.

But he had breakfast and she was hungry.

"I am not opposed to putting my hands to honest labor."

He regarded her with brows soaring, his bland expression mocking her. "Indeed? What do you know of honest labor? Have your dainty hands ever raised a callous? Your tiny feet a blister? Have you laundered clothes, scrubbed floors, emptied chamber pots?" When she blushed at that last, he snorted. "I thought not. *Vaurienne*. You offer nothing I need or desire."

Good-for-nothing. That last was said with a steady black stare as if he didn't see her as a female capable of tempting him with the remotest twinge of lust. Even though lust was the last thing she sought to kindle in her captor, a jab of slight pierced her. Had she been Philomena in truth, with all her practiced wiles, she would have had every man on the ship at her beck and call. But she was not Philomena. She fell, as her jailor succinctly put it, far short of Miss Montgomery's notable charms.

And Philomena was probably, at this very minute, nearly safe in her family's embrace.

In angry desperation, she unfastened the heavy

necklace and extended it for his scrutiny. "Is this worth the price of my meals?"

His narrowed gaze fixed upon the Montgomery crest. Something very dark moved behind his stare, outweighing any greed for the value of the gold and gems. "I want nothing with that damnable mark upon it."

Eliza snatched the fork from his hand, and as he watched, unmoving, she used the tines to pry open the links attaching the crested medallion to the others. When the chain was restored, she dropped it beside his nearly empty plate, keeping the single gold disk for herself.

"There. You could buy supplies to feed your entire crew with what it's worth."

Jean-Luc picked up the piece, turning it within his palm so that the jewels strobed with varicolored fire. "Worth is subject to circumstance. Since our larder is fully stocked, this is of no great value. Like you. Just pretty stones." He let them trickle through his fingers to the tabletop. "They will buy you supper, nothing more."

"Supper?" She gaped at him, aghast.

"Tomorrow we shall see if you've anything else to barter."

"But I have nothing else!" she cried.

Again, that thin formal smile, that detached assessment. "I would not say that, m'am'selle." When her expression remained immobile, he sighed and pushed his plate away. "I am finished with this. It will be scraped over the side—unless you wish to clean the plate."

Her gaze dropped slowly to the remains of his meal. He was offering her his table scraps, as if to a dog, waiting to see if her pride would allow her to bend before that humbling insult. On this day, it would. She reached for the fork, and when he stood, she slid into his chair to begin devouring the leftovers with an indelicate urgency.

Surprisingly, he didn't laugh at her. He followed the quick movement of her fork as it chased the last of the morsels about the plate.

"Have you never been hungry before?" he asked in an odd quiet.

She spared him a brief glance and a truth. "No, I have not. I do not find it a pleasant experience."

His mood chilled slightly, like clouds blocking the sun's heat. "No, it is not. You would be amazed at what one will do when pangs are twisting in the belly."

Eliza slowed her eating, studying him in apprehension. Was that a threat? Did he mean to manipulate her will by withholding food? She couldn't allow him that leverage. "There are limits, Captain."

He shook his head at her naïveté, mocking and a bit mournful. "You are wrong there, my *belle ingénue*. Someday, perhaps, I will enlighten you." And he turned away to pull a clean shirt from his sea chest.

"Where are we bound, Captain?" Now that her stomach was appeased, her mind turned toward other matters. Toward the idea of rescue. Or escape.

Jean-Luc glanced over his shoulder, the unreadable chill back in his gaze. "No place for a lady."

She refused to react to the threat. "Do we travel far?"

"Far enough. I wish to be away from the reach of your family as soon as possible."

That suited Eliza, too. They were sailing south, paralleling the coastal waters, toward the islands, perhaps. The warmth there would be welcome after the chilling New England clime. And the farther from Massachusetts, the safer she was in her disguise, freeing Philomena to return to her family with word of her heroics. Rescue would be soon forthcoming. Then freedom.

She imagined William's pride and gratitude.

"Something amuses you, *princesse*?"

Eliza glanced up in alarm, unaware of how her features had softened into a small smile. "No, Captain. Only amused that you are foolish enough to think any distance would be far enough. My family will come and you will be very sorry."

The stark black mood took control of him, as it always did when the Montgomerys were the topic. "They have made me sorry about many things already. It is time I returned the favor."

The food suddenly lost its appeal.

By dusk, the storm she'd predicted was upon them. Alone in the cabin, Eliza fought both fear and boredom. She paced. She tried to sleep. But she didn't test Jean-Luc's advice not to stray out of the stateroom. So far, the captain had proved to be a reluctant gentleman. She felt no need to see if the same was true of his men.

Though she was grateful for the solitude, it also chafed upon her hour after hour until she found herself anticipating the handsome Frenchman's return. Idleness never agreed with her. She understood some French, but the prose in the captain's library was beyond her basic knowledge. She longed for a change of clothing, for an end to the suspenseful waiting. For the supper she'd already paid for with Philomena's jewels.

A brisk tap on the portal announced one of the ship's crewmen bearing a platter of savory dishes. Eliza watched in anticipation as the mate set service for two upon the table, pouring two hefty goblets of wine.

And from the doorway, Jean-Luc watched her, his dark eyes inscrutable.

She puzzled him, this woman of fire and indomitable spirit. From what he'd heard of Montgomery's daughter, he'd expected her to whine and moan about her circumstances instead of launching a prideful battle of wills with him. He enjoyed mental sparring with an equal, though she would not see him as one.

She was a Montgomery.

That knowledge had not lost its sting.

He entered the room with a determined indifference and a wry, "I trust you find the meal adequate, *chérie*, even though you see the company as lacking."

She glanced up from the spread of food, her gaze wary of his mood. "Do you plan to join me, Captain, or to spoil the meal with your glowering?"

"I was not aware I was glowering."

"You would curdle milk in the cow, sir."

The corner of his mouth twitched. "Indeed. A talent of the trade, I assume. M'am'selle, if you will allow me."

Genuinely surprised when he pulled back his chair to seat her, she sidled up to ease down in it, alert for any suspicious movements from him. He nudged the heavy chair in behind her and lingered at its back for a moment. She reached for her wine in her nervousness, refusing to look up at him even though awareness of him had her figure tense and close to trembling.

Though logic bid him not to, Luc remained where he was, his gaze mesmerized by the expectant part of her lips as she raised her glass to them.

Sacre ciel, she was sweet.

Sweet forbidden fruit off the Montgomery tree. Out of reach yet tantalizing by its very unavailability.

It had been so long since he'd chanced upon such unspoiled beauty. The deck of a ship was no place for aesthetic appreciations. He'd forgotten how easily moved he was by the *beaux-arts*. And she was an extraordinary work. Strange sentiments shifted through him, tender memories buried deep in a past he'd thought safely hidden even from his own heart.

Before he could catch himself, he reached out to rub the backs of his fingers along one smooth cheek. Like finest porcelain.

Her reaction was immediate and expressive.

She bolted upright out of the chair, surging away from him and his touch. Their stares locked: hers wide and wild, his carefully masking first surprise, then a flicker of disdain. She released her breath in a shiver of apprehension, holding herself still while waiting for him to do his worst.

"You act as though I put a knife to your pretty throat."

She stiffened at his chill tone, some of the glaze of panic thawing into a preferable irritation.

"Your motives are a mystery to me, sir. I know not what they might yield."

His jaw hardened. "And which is it you fear most, m'am'selle? The threat of my cruelty or the anticipation of my kindness?"

Her gaze said both were equally dangerous in her mind.

Luc drew a deep breath, inbred manners forcing down his animosity. "Sit. It was not my plan to frighten you away from a meal honestly purchased." When she hesitated still, he waved toward the seat and said more tersely, *"S'il vous plaît."*

But she wouldn't relent until he moved back, circling the table to assume a spot on the sea chest. Only then did she ease down into the chair, her movements yet strained.

Luc viewed her with vaguely concealed contempt. "What happened to your bold oath not to fear me?"

"Perhaps it was premature, Captain."

As premature as his belief that he would be impervious to her charms. Even poisonous species could be beautiful. "Eat," he commanded.

It was then she noticed the damage done the front of her gown. Wine sloshed from her glass stained its bodice in a dark pattern. She made a sound of dismay and blotted at it ineffectually.

"It's ruined."

"It is just a robe."

"It's all I have," came her uneven accusation. Brightness glittered in her gaze.

"It will wash out."

She shook her head, the glittering more apparent, as was the traitorous hitch of her shoulders.

"Then take it off and put it to soak before the juices set." Frowning at her dramatics, he got off his seat, opening the lid to withdraw a clean white shirt. "Here. Put this on to preserve your modesty, if you must."

She took the hastily flung shirt, regarding him in mute despair, her chin beginning to quiver. Muscles jumped along his tense jaw.

And as he turned his back to allow her privacy, he cursed himself for letting down his guard for even a moment. She was his enemy—a prettier package but no less treacherous than her father. A vain and silly female flying into hysterics over a bit of damaged cloth. He didn't know how to contend with a weeping woman. That made him feel twice the fool.

He listened to the sound of her shimmying out of

her dress. A salacious image sprang to mind, startling him, of her in her thin underpinnings, wisps of sheer batiste clinging to slender limbs. A tortuous ache built heavily in his loins.

"Are you quite finished, m'am'selle, so that we might return to our meal?" How angry he sounded. He hoped she would credit it to the frivolous interruption and not, rightfully so, to an unbidden rumble of lust.

"You may turn around, Captain."

He did and he regretted it. No image in his mind could create as tempting a picture as her swaddled in his shirt. It revealed nothing yet hinted at everything. His mouth went dry as a good wine.

She paid him no mind as she dipped the gown in their washbasin and scrubbed at the stain.

At the table, Luc put his wine to better use, gulping it rather quickly.

After a moment, she sighed and set the gown aside. "It is useless. The damage is done."

"Then might I say you make a fetching picture in my cambric."

His wry comment put her back up. "You think me foolish."

"You do not want to know what I think."

And his tone was just dark enough for her not to wish to challenge that claim.

"Will you sup with me, *chère*?" A more neutral invitation.

Hanging her ruined gown upon the bedpost, she returned to the table only to pick at its offerings.

"You mentioned an intended. Some respectably stuffy merchant, I presume."

He was rewarded with the expected flash of defensiveness.

"A fine man of sterling qualities with which you would be unacquainted."

"And which of these sterling qualities allowed you to go unescorted on an Atlantic voyage only to fall into the hands of . . . pirates?"

" 'Twas through no fault of his. We were to announce our engagement when . . . when an unforeseen misfortune struck. My father's business partner was killed."

He missed the suspicious moistening of her eyes as fury rose to blacken his thoughts. "And your father was so busy gobbling up his former partner's holdings, he didn't have time to give you away as a bride."

Her gaze canted down to the tabletop, and a certain tightness thinned her lips. Anger with him for his statement or for the truth of it? He doubted that she would tell him. She was too much a lady to criticize her father's choices. Or perhaps too wise to agree with them while in his presence.

"So," he drawled out. "Who is this paragon you mean to wed?"

Her gaze shot up, full of fire and deeper turmoil. "I will not discuss my personal affairs for your amusement, sir."

He shrugged. "I do not find them all that amusing, m'am'selle. Such affairs of the heart fill me with ennui."

"I suppose one would have to have a heart first. Forgive me for boring you with the trivial details of my life. I am sorry I haven't such colorful tales to draw upon as you, sir. Leading a respectable life does lend a certain lack of excitement."

"Yes, it does. And don't you sometimes regret that?"

He grinned suddenly, shocking her into dropping

her guard with the way that gesture transformed his face. Surely, her heart skipped a beat.

For a moment, her lips pressed tight, a smile threatening. But in the end, she lowered her gaze to her plate once more and the moment passed uneventfully. Her dismissal made for moody company, shortening Luc's temper.

Why should he care if she described her fiancé in such glowing terms? Someday a woman of worth would acknowledge him in the same manner—perhaps would have already done so if not for Montgomery. He was a fool to lose sight of that, to let this woman's clever banter dull the edge of his well-honed revenge.

And perhaps she was making him more the fool by manipulating his passions with shrewd intent, seeking to sway him with her amicable charm. He had never heard a charitable word spoken in regard to her but volumes as to her spoiled affectations. Was this a trick, then, this comely front disguising a darker center?

He shoved away from the table, his dark scowl earning an anxious glance from his dinner companion.

"I have things to attend to. Enjoy the wine and the remains of the meal. You've paid for the pleasure."

But troubled thoughts would not leave him even after a tour of the ice-slicked decks. The fierce howl of the wind echoed the lament in his heart, the churn of the waves, his inner turmoil. For a moment in his cabin, just for a moment, he'd been lulled into lowering his reserve. In that undefended second, anguish poured back into his soul. Sensations of loss and loneliness that he could ignore when standing firm behind his wall of detachment were crippling when the barriers slipped down. He would not expose himself to such black misery again.

It was she and what she represented. A life abandoned half the world away. She would not upset the orchestration of his revenge. Not by quickening the pain of a past best forgotten. He was Coeur Noir by choice, in both thought and deed. And she would find no mercy in him.

His humor was black as the scudding clouds by the time he encountered his second mate, Shamus Sterns, on his starboard watch. Sterns, a huge irascible Irishman whose features resembled the craggy surrounds of his homeland, had only two soft spots in his heart: one for the sea and one for Jean-Luc Gautier. And it seemed not to bother him when neither affection was returned.

"Evenin', Cap'n. Only a warm woman could drive a man outside on a night this cold."

Luc regarded the grisled seaman darkly. "Have a care, Shamus. I am in no mood for your wit this evening."

"As bad as that, eh?" The older man chuckled, unafraid of his young protégé's ire. They had sailed from Canton to Calcutta together, into the mouths of British guns and into hell itself. Luc, as his apprentice, learned the ropes and the rules with a quickness that endeared him to the old salt.

Together, they'd crossed the line of the equator, and the young Frenchman had been welcomed into the brotherhood of the sea. He'd endured the hazing of the seamen, from being shaved with an iron barrel hoop to being forced to eat vile concoctions a sow would refuse, to earn his rank of "old salt." But being salty didn't lessen seasickness, fear, and loneliness in some men. Luc was not one of them. He thrived on the sea and its varied moods, sharing a respect for it that won a niche in Shamus's gnarled heart.

But the sea wasn't the bond that held them. It was the darkness of the past.

Luc leaned upon the rail, unable to relax even in his mentor's company. But the old Irishman's tart tongue was just the medicine for his brooding soul. He allowed the man many latitudes, one being an opinion freely voiced.

"What is it, young Luc? Vengeance not the sweet ambrosia you expected?"

Luc shrugged beneath the weight of the other's big hand. "*Non*, it is not that. My mouth yet waters at the thought of Montgomery's pain."

"'Tis the lady, is it not? I warned ye, didn't I, lad? It takes a darker heart than yours to misuse a woman thusly."

He bristled at that suggestion. "I am not misusing her."

Another chuckle, just a lusty rumble against the roar of the waves. "Nay, of course not. You just stole her from her family to terrorize them. That's not misuse, but rather gentlemanly behavior."

Shamus didn't wither beneath the fix of his black glare.

"So, what am I to do? Forget my rights? Forget my pain and what is owed me? Because a vain, silly woman casts big seemingly innocent eyes in my direction? I think not! When Symms bears word of the exchange, I will return her without a bite of conscience."

Shamus smirked at him. "Then what be yer problem, lad? 'Twould seem you have all well decided in your mind."

But not in his heart. And that was a truth Jean-Luc would not speak, even to his oldest friend.

Shamus pushed his palm against the side of his captain's dark head. "Go below, boy. Stand by your choices without a whimper. You've every right to what you do, as well we both know. The Montgomery clan is owed no sympathy for all their lies. Remember that when those soft eyes go asking you for favors. Yer not the one responsible for her situation. This is her father's doing. All is put in motion. By now, Benji will be making his move in Salem to tell them of your terms. Rest easy and without reprisals from that conscience you claim not to have. There is naught you can do tonight."

Luc smiled at him thinly and gave a brief nod to that wisdom. It would be over soon, and the payment of debts would free him to follow his own dream. Until then, he had only to harden his mood toward his unwilling passenger's plight. And he was an expert at self-denial.

He returned to his quarters, cold, weary, and yet restless, only to find the source of his aggravation had retired for the night.

She was curled at the foot of his bed, huddled in search of warmth within her scant blankets.

"*Enfer*," he muttered. Refusing to examine his motives, he tossed an extra measure of covers over her shivering form before throwing himself, fully dressed, atop his own bed to seek an uneasy slumber. There, he had dreams less pleasant than her lush form to taunt him.

Chapter 6

The hard bump of her head against the bed board woke Eliza from her sleep. Beneath her, the ship rolled upon an agitated sea, rocking her in a less than soothing manner within her blankets. It must have been well past dawn, but the room still hung with grayness, unrelieved by the clouded skies. She sat up stiffly and worked the kinks from her back and shoulders as her fingers touched the heavy covers placed over her during the night. An unexpected kindness. She glanced cautiously over the footboard. Jean-Luc was still asleep, thankfully in full attire.

Hurriedly, she snatched her dried, if ruined, gown down from the bedpost and replaced his oversize shirt with its familiar feel. Her fingertips lingered over the rough weave of the pirate's shirt until she caught herself caressing the fabric almost wistfully. Then she discarded it with an ill-tempered toss.

A tap on the door announced breakfast. Eliza was quick to answer it, taking the tray from a suspicious seaman who was obviously wondering if she'd murdered his captain in his bed. She closed the door in his face before his questioning gaze could find an answer.

Setting the tray upon the table, she observed the

single serving, then cast a jaundiced eye toward the sleeping man. Determinedly, she drew up his chair and sat herself down to his meal, addressing herself to the crispy potatoes and harsh coffee with ravenous appreciation while both were yet steaming.

She was skewering the final chunk of potato when a lazy mutter sounded from the bed. She popped the last bite in her mouth with a smug sense of satisfaction as her captor roused himself in gradual degrees, finally sitting up to drop his booted feet to the floor.

He was rumpled and rough-edged, and the combination completely captivated for some reason unknown to Eliza. His black hair was standing at bristling attention, though listing in various directions. Angular cheeks were dark with an aggressive stubble. Clothing collapsed upon his frame in untidy peaks and wrinkles. But his eyes drew Eliza in—dark, dewy, dulled by the dreams yet lingering in his mind. The boyish quality struck a nurturing chord as his hands scrubbed at traces of sleep, washing the vulnerability away with that rearranging gesture. He blinked up at her, slow to take in the empty plate.

"Have you at least saved me some coffee?" His voice was husky, like smoke unfurling about her senses. She shivered, then chastened herself for the reaction.

"There is some in the pot, Captain. I am afraid it's tepid at best."

He sniffed and blinked his eyes into focus. "You didn't wake me." It was a statement, not an accusation, and Eliza felt tempted to tease.

"I did not want to share."

"Ahhh. But you did not save me so much as a scrap. How unkind to take such advantage of me. Now I shall starve." His tone was soft, almost congenial. Almost human.

She smiled slightly, thinking him overly dramatic. After all, who was taking advantage of whom? Wasn't she his prisoner? "Have your crewman bring you more."

"There is no more. Once it is gone, it is gone. This is not the fancy kitchen of your home, m'am'selle. It is a ship's galley. The cook carries a large blade and is not to be trifled with. If I were to send an order for seconds, most likely he would feed me my own— well, I think you understand what I mean."

It was on her lips to say she was sorry, but she bit back the impulse proudly. She was his captive, not his guest, as he had so bluntly stated. She owed him no courtesy.

Still, she felt bad that he would now go hungry. She had, and she hadn't liked it.

"Besides," he continued, standing and stretching his arms overhead to bend to the left then right. It was a strong graceful movement, like a sapling oak swaying in the wind. "With the ship pitching, it is not a wise idea to keep the fires going below."

He came to the table, reaching over her to pour some of the lukewarm brew into the cup she'd been using. She kept her gaze downward, trying not to look or feel guilty as he drank and grimaced slightly.

"Was it good?" He gestured toward the scoured plates.

"Yes."

"I'm glad it did not go to waste. A lesson for me to be an early riser. I cannot force myself to rest lightly when surrounded by the safety of my crew. To make up for all the nights I slept not at all."

He stared into the cold coffee as if seeing his past there in the grounds. Then he glanced at her uncomfortably, as if feeling he'd said too much.

"Have you given thought as to how you mean to

earn this meal even as it warms your belly?"

"Do not worry, Captain. I will pay you somehow."

"Then I get to choose the method of payment?" He was standing close behind her. The heat of his nearness seemed to press upon her even though they did not touch.

"It depends on what you would choose," she countered warily.

He set the cup down upon the tabletop and continued to lean there so that she was trapped between his arm and the hard contour of his ribs. Her heart was beating frantically. She absolutely could not look up at him, fearing how she might respond if there were dusky passions alight in his eyes.

"What sort of favors did you bestow upon your Salem beau?"

Her head snapped back, her stormy stare colliding with his. "That, sir, is none of your concern."

"Ah, do not tell me he never asked you for one." His accented voice became a mildly mocking caress. "Too much of a gentleman? A pity. Were I not his equal, I would ask for a kiss in token payment for your debt. A single kiss, your mouth to mine. Nothing unseemly. Just a brief exchange. We would not even have to enjoy it. *Non*? Have you something else in mind?"

Eliza stared up at him, the combatant edge dissolving into panicked pools of deep sea green. That wide gaze touched upon his lips, lingering there, following the generous upper arcs and firm lower swell, watching as they slowly parted in unbidden anticipation.

And she heard him saying *nothing I desire*.

But wasn't that the most elemental type of desire burning in his stare?

Eliza stood, rising straight up so that she was within the curve of his arm, her bosom brushing his mussed shirtfront as she refused to give even an inch. He was tall, forcing her head back, her throat into a creamy arch. And she met his dark-eyed stare unblinkingly, delving into it until the center blackness increased, engulfing the whole in a blaze of naked want.

And just when the thick fringe of his lashes fluttered and began to drift downward, she said, "I will scrub your floor."

The descent of his lids halted.

"Qu'est-ce que c'est?"

"Your floor. It is stained with last night's wine and countless boot prints."

Plainly astounded, he let his gaze detail her mouth with a sweep of frustration. "But the kiss, it would be much less effort."

"For whom, Captain?" She pushed at his chest and, caught off guard again, he stumbled back a step or two. "If you would be good enough to call for a bucket and brush, I will waste no time."

And so she scrubbed her first floor for the price of a breakfast, and it was by far the most satisfying wage she'd ever earned. Even as her back ached and her knees groaned and her delicate hands burned from the harsh solution, she knew her sullen captor was glowering at her in his disapproval. He would have obviously preferred the kiss.

As would she, came the treacherous truth as she renewed her vigorous motions. Part of the energy behind her actions was spurred by that guilt. Poor William. How worried he must be, and here she was, contemplating a pirate's kisses.

She slopped out more soap and applied a fierce pressure.

William.

Gentle William, with his pale, poetic looks, won her

over completely within the small circle of merchant society. He was quite unlike the men she'd met through her family's associations, weather-stropped titans who walked down Salem's Derby Street as if it were a deck rolling beneath them. While those seafaring men were about business, striking deals over ale at Goodhue's Tavern, William was more and more often her squire at teas, pig roasts, and afternoon outings. From the first time he'd taken her carefully in his arms and guided her to the strains of a piano and fiddle reel, she'd known he was the one. Kind, intelligent, socially sensitive, and adoring. What more could a woman want?

From deep within her came a quiet rumble. A woman wanted a man who would keep her safe. A man who would not bend before his father's edicts to sacrifice the woman he claimed to love.

And once that whisper began, she couldn't still it. Perhaps she was being unfair. Perhaps William really had done all that was possible.

Then why wasn't she his lawful wife instead of here scrubbing decks for a pirate? Resentment ate at her trust.

Finally, after rubbing her hands and knees raw, Eliza straightened and glanced over at Jean-Luc. He was seated on the bed, propped up by a bank of pillows where he'd been reading the same page of verse for the past hour.

"Does all meet with your approval, Captain?"

He scowled with a bruising detachment. "I stand corrected, m'am'selle. You would make a tolerable scullery maid. But I doubt that the floor will need cleaning again before supper time. Be thinking of what other talents you may have hidden."

"That is a long while away, Captain, but I shall be thinking."

And from across the space of his cabin, their gazes met, mingling with a surprising intensity. And somehow, they seemed to have forgotten that they were enemies. For the moment.

A different sort of tension built between them. A restless, itchy kind of expectation.

Madness. Foolish madness.

Nervous now that there was no activity to occupy her, Eliza said, "You must have great faith in your crew to loiter here whilst they are above at their work."

He set the book aside, finally giving up the pretense of reading. "I take nothing from them, *princesse*. I will most likely be on deck throughout the night, when the worst of this storm rears its ugly head. We shall sail right into its teeth." He smiled grimly, the gesture never touching his black eyes. "Then let your lover try to follow."

Eliza turned away, a great hollowness filling her chest.

The room was too small, the dark Frenchman seeming to fill it with his potent virility. She had little experience with this type of male. And her naïveté was going to cost her dearly if she were not careful in her baiting of this unpredictable creature.

"Captain, would it be possible for me to go up on deck, just for a moment? It is so confining down here, and I long to feel the sea air upon my face."

He eyed her cautiously. "It would be dangerous, *chère*."

No more dangerous than remaining below with him.

"I am not afraid. I won't wander near the rails."

He stood to say gruffly, "You will stay close to me. The deck of a ship about to enter hell's fury is no place for a stroll."

"I'll be careful."

"Just for a moment, then." He relented, but he didn't look pleased about it.

The moment Eliza stepped on deck and the frigid Atlantic air slapped against her, she almost regretted her choice. The cold stung to her very marrow. Crystals of ice and snow swirled about her, dancing on the sharp-edged wind. Her cloak billowed out behind her like a sail turned into the breeze, leaving just her gown and undergarments to fend off the pervading chill. She took a quick step back as another gust pummeled her. And just as quickly, a firm wall of solid warmth pressed up behind her, blocking her retreat, bracketing her up close with a sudden tight embrace.

"Easy now, *ma belle*." The accented voice crooned against her ear, raising to be heard above the wail of the wind. "It would not do for you to misstep."

"I'm sure you wouldn't want your bounty to wash overboard, now would you, Captain."

She felt the vibration of his laugh against her. She'd never heard a sound of genuine amusement from him before. It made her wish to see the warmth of its accompanying smile.

"*Oui*, m'am'selle, that would be a tragedy. I would mourn the loss of all my careful planning."

But not her.

Eliza stiffened and would have pulled away from him except his arms banded about her like brass barrel fittings. One curled beneath her bosom, the flat of his hand spreading wide upon the curve of her ribs. The other caught her cloak and wrapped it snugly about her. But what enveloped her was the surrounding sense of the man himself.

For a moment, the violence of the storm seemed calm in comparison to their awareness of one another.

Oh, but he was big and strong, forming a block

against the worst of the wind and a shelter in which she could enjoy the bite of the salt air. Almost as much as she was enjoying the feel of him. The way his palm burned through the silk of her gown. The way his powerful grip made her go all weak with yearning while still vibrantly alert to those quickening sensations. How easy to forget who he was when overcome by what he stirred within her.

As his breath brushed against her temple in warm, intimate strokes, she leaned back, her head upon the lea of his shoulder, her body a submissive bow as she lifted her face to the slated sky. She noticed the way his breath caught and his arms hitched up in an almost restrictive pressure. Her eyes closed, her senses filling with sea and storm and the wild elation of her effect upon this stoic, dangerous man. He wanted her. A thrill of delicious power came with that knowledge. Braced between the spraddle of the captain's sturdy thighs, she felt no danger of being swept away. Except, perhaps, by the captain himself.

Then, abruptly, he stepped back, the chill of separation waking her from her languorous fancies. She straightened within the now loose circle of his embrace, and to cover her own embarrassment, made a point of watching the crew working the ice-encrusted lines as the sea flung them hard to port, then back again.

"She's a beautiful ship, Jean-Luc," she called back over her shoulder, casually using his given name as she admired his vessel. "Sleek and fast. A privateer, yet bigger than our Salem-bred craft. She's French, like you, is she not?"

"*Oui*," he said in some surprise, but warming to the topic was far safer than warming to the woman. "You know your ships. I would trust nothing but a fellow countryman upon these changeable seas."

"What is her name?"

"*Galant Sans Coeur.*"

"Heartless lover," she mused. "How fitting. 'Twould be difficult for another vessel to overtake you."

His cheek pressed to her wind-whipped hair as he murmured, "Impossible, *ma petite.* So you can stop looking behind us for the sight of pursuing sails."

How smug and sure he sounded and, she feared, rightfully so. Rigged for speed as she was, his vessel was a predator, capable of striking without warning and disappearing on the horizon without a trace. Like a vengeful spirit. Nothing the Montgomerys owned could pace let alone catch them. Her head bowed slightly, resigned to that truth.

Feeling her brave spirit ebb, Luc sought a way to bolster her without offering any direct sympathy. He nuzzled his wind-stung cheek into her hair. Beneath her cloak, his palm moved in a leisurely circle upon the snug fit of her silk gown, his thumb tracing the lower swell of her breast. When he felt her gasp in time to the sudden jump of her pulse, he purred silkily, "I had not expected you to admit defeat so easily, *chérie.*"

Her response was as hoped. Her head gave a jerk, catching him in the nose with a stunning force. Her elbow drove back at the same time, smacking him sharply in the ribs and earning her the space to whirl out of his arms.

"Captain, I wish to exercise more than my patience. Surely you'll not deny me a quick turn about the deck."

His moment of jest became a somber frown. "I cannot allow—"

"Who knows how long this storm will last. It might

be days before I've the chance again. I've promised I will not jump overboard."

"I'll take her," came the sudden offer from his second mate.

Luc scowled at Shamus, not appreciating his interference but grateful for it anyway. Yes, some distance was needed between him and his lovely hostage. He would go quite mad if forced to endure the soft press of her for another minute. The storm bandying the ship about was nothing compared to the tempest brewing in his loins. He'd been chaste too long to withstand the upheaval as well as he wished to.

"Take her," he growled at the big Irishman. "Do not lose her."

"Aye, Cap'n." And the old man allowed a smirk of amusement to tease in his smile. "Come, Miss Montgomery. Let me escort you." He took her cold hand, tucking it through the bend of his elbow. Though he was a big, burly man, Eliza felt immediately safe entrusting herself into his care.

"Thank you, Mister . . . ?"

"I be Shamus, miss. At your service." He paid no attention to his captain's snort as he bowed to the lovely young captive. "Promise me that you'll mind your step. These decks be polished as glass."

"Be careful that you do not trip over your silver tongue," Luc grumbled after them. He watched them walk toward the forward deck, knowing the lady was safe with his second and wondering why he wasn't more relieved to be shed of her.

The sudden violent pitch of his vessel woke him to his duties. He cast his gaze heavenward to gauge the angry roil of black clouds. Flakes of snow had turned to tears of ice, freezing in his hair and on his lashes, burning his skin. Another burst of wind sent him stumbling back against the companionway. His attention jumped instantly to the forecastle, but he needn't have worried. Shamus had the lady in a protective grip. The wind tore into the sails, sending shudders through the vessel. The rolling of the ship caused the mast shrouds to slacken, then snap tight with rending force, a danger to be dealt with if they meant to keep afloat.

"Remy, Jeffries, scale the main and cut away the rigging!"

The young seamen were quick to climb upward at his command. Luc watched impassively from below, head cocked, listening for the perilous sounds of creaking hull or straining spars. He didn't relax his pose until his orders were met. He didn't fear for the ship; she was built to take anything the Atlantic could throw at her, but he'd as soon not lose his parade of canvas to the rip of winds.

Relieved, he was making his way forward to where his second and his hostage were braced against the pitching seas when a terrified cry rang out from above. His head jerked back in time to see Remy Leverett snapped off the ratlines like a flea with the flick of a finger. The boy's downward plunge halted when his foot caught in the rigging, dangling him upside down almost thirty feet above the deck and raging waters.

Cursing, Luc flung out of his jacket and was kicking out of his boots even as he raced to the web of ice-coated ropes leading upward. Barefooted and bare-handed, he began to climb, ignoring the claw of the wind threatening to tear him free of his precarious grip. It was like gripping a wild horse determined to throw him, and more than once the sole of his foot slipped through the holes, leaving him hanging by one hand while the whole of the rigging shook and snapped beneath him.

The higher he went, the crueler the winds, buffeting him to and fro while ice shards ripped at his unprotected flesh. He didn't consider his own fate, concentrating instead on each firm hold before releasing the other.

The climb seemed to take forever, but finally he dared glance to the side where Remy swung like a sandbag in the harsh breeze. The boy's wide gaze met his. He was obviously terrified but unharmed.

"Stay still, *mon ami*! I will come out for you."

"No! 'Tis too great a risk. We'll both fall."

"Do as I say!" And Luc began to edge out, the muscles of his arms and legs spasming with tension and strain. One hand. One foot. Inch by cautious inch as the ropes groaned beneath his weight and failed to provide honest purchase. He wove one arm and leg through the network of knots until he was safely anchored, and only then did he reach for the frightened boy.

He caught only shirt fabric with his first attempt. Then the canvas of his trousers. Luc held on, working his way over to the boy's waist.

"Grab on to me. Careful now. Not too fast."

Remy's fingers bit into the muscle of his forearm just as his foot slipped free of the ropes. Luc cried out as the full brunt of the boy's weight yanked on his arm sockets, but he refused to let go. Remy swung like a pendulum below him, causing both men and the rigging to groan with the strain.

"Grab the ropes, Remy."

"I'm slipping, Cap'n! Don't let me go!"

"I won't!"

"Don't let me fall!"

"I won't! Do as I say. I cannot hold you much longer. Grab for the lines. Get your toes on them. Do it now!" And with the last of his strength, he swung the boy flush into the rigging, where he would either catch on or plummet downward. He caught and held, and for a moment, they both hung, tangled in the lines, gasping for breath while tremors of shock and exertion rattled through them.

"Thank you, Cap'n," the boy wheezed at last. "Thought I was a goner."

"Can you make it down on your own?"

"Aye."

"Slow and careful. Get on the windward side so 'twill blow you into the ropes instead of away from them." That was Shamus talking through him, an old lesson learned well.

"Aye, sir."

And Luc watched as the boy crawled down, waiting for his own strength to return so he could do the same. He was aware now of the stiffness in his joints, of the numbness in his hands and feet as he withstood the punishment of the weather. Chills rode through him viciously where the sweat-dampened shirt plastered to his skin. He wouldn't last much longer if he didn't start down, but after a few rungs, he noticed a dangerous weakness in his muscles. They refused to respond or support him.

"*Sacre Mère*," he panted, fear as icy as the ratlines twining through him.

He tried to force his fingers to curl, to clasp the frozen cordage, to hold just a little longer. But they were as responsive as twigs.

He felt his foot slide, his toes grazing the lines but failing to find a point of balance. His numbed hands disobeyed his order to close fast. He saw himself dropping away from the rigging, felt the swoosh of air at his back, saw the roiling mass of clouds above, swirling in merciless fury.

And he fell.

Chapter 7

To Eliza, all ceased to exist beyond the heroic rescue playing out in the rigging far above.

Unaware of Shamus's grip upon her arm, she strained into the stinging wind to follow Jean-Luc's progress up the treacherous netting, caught by the boy's fear, the crew's dread. Breath suspended, she watched as this fearless man who had countless others at his command asked none to do what he would—risk all for one boy's life.

At that dangerous moment, a dramatic shift occurred within her frantically beating heart.

All her years she'd hung upon stories of the sea, of the kind of man it took to tame those wild waters. She'd listened to her brother and his peers speak of the hard work, poor food, Spartan conditions, and long hours, of the tedium punctuated by moments of stark terror when a boy became a man in an instant or took to a cold, wet grave. She heard them boast of their various captains, expert seamen and navigators all, with iron strength and endurance, carrying the trust of their crews because it was well earned, where success required a sharp mind, grace under pressure and—she'd blushed then in her eavesdropping—balls of polished brass.

Here was such a man.

It didn't matter what path he followed to what end. At this moment, in her heart and mind, there was no man braver, no man more noble, no man more deserving than the handsome young Frenchman battling the elements for the sake of one of his own.

She, too, weakened with relief when Remy was guided to safety. She went light-headed with thanksgiving as he began to wend his way down the tangle of ropes to where his fellow crewmen waited to slap his back and fill his cold hands with a mug of gut-warming rum. The smile froze on her face as she glanced up at Shamus. His uplifted features twisted with horror.

"Luc . . ."

The name moaned from him as he released her and began running. Her stricken gaze followed to where his was riveted, to the icy webbing of lines from which Jean-Luc Gautier fell.

He dropped like a hawk shot from the heavens, limp, soundless, and so very, very fast, to the deck below. She was saved the horror of seeing him hit but the cry that wailed from Shamus was just as terrible as the older man struggled over the thick roll of the lowered mainsail. Eliza followed, skidding, slipping perilously on the rocking deck, too stunned to realize she was praying as hard as old Shamus and young Remy.

He lay spread-eagled upon the thick bundle of shrouds, eyes closed, pale as marble, limp, as if every bone in his body had been broken. Shamus hovered over him, afraid to touch him, murmuring his name again and again in a dazed chant. Eliza was pushed in closer by the sheer press of the crew. She struggled, rearing back, wanting to escape. This was not how she wanted to see him, broken in body and soul. She'd lost too many to mourn one more. A soft sob slipped from her.

It was then she saw his lashes flicker. Just a twitch as snow gathered upon his otherwise still face. Perhaps she'd imagined it. She stood, staring, waiting, hoping she'd not been mistaken. Another flutter, a bit stronger than the first.

And a low, awful gasp sounded, as if his chest were fighting to rise from beneath a crushing weight.

Jean-Luc's eyes opened, glazed, for a moment wild with panic as he failed to draw a decent breath.

He was alive!

Eliza followed the men bearing their captain back to his quarters. Shivering with cold and delayed shock, she hung back out of their way as they checked for broken bones and wrapped his frozen feet and hands. Wordlessly, she supplied Shamus with rum from the cabinet so he could force some between the colorless lips. She was dimly aware of a teary-eyed Remy at her side, of the way his bright eyes flooded with remorse and guilt at being the cause of his captain's near death. Without thinking, she banded an arm about his middle, and they leaned into one another for strength.

The storm's rage hadn't quieted, calling the reluctant men back to their positions until just Shamus sat at his friend's bedside. Eliza approached cautiously.

"Will he be all right?

Shamus chafed one still hand between his own rough ones. His voice was thick. "Grace be to God that the furled sails broke his fall. Had he met the deck or the waves . . ." He shook his head, unable to finish.

Eliza came closer, offering the elder man a hefty mug of rum. He took it gratefully and gave a silent toast to his motionless captain.

"You've sailed together for a long time?" she asked, surmising that his distress went deeper than a mate's for his captain.

Shamus smiled. "I taught the lad all he knows about the sea. I care for him as if he were my own son. But don't let on that I told you as much. He doesn't hold with such sentiments."

"Coeur Noir," Eliza muttered.

Shamus harrumphed. "Black Heart, indeed. Soft heart and softer head be more like it. Almost got himself killed because of it again. Foolish boy."

Eliza frowned slightly. Softhearted? This cold, emotionless pirate? She thought not. She'd seen the darkness in his penetrating stare. Too much darkness to believe him capable of tender mercies.

But he'd gone aloft to save the boy, fearlessly, without hesitation, well aware of his own risk.

"I don't understand," she said aloud, then was embarrassed that she had spoken.

Shamus chuckled. "I'm not surprised, lady. 'Tis not a side of himself he'd likely show to you."

Again that hint of bad blood, going beyond a captor's regard for a prisoner. "I've done nothing to harm him. I don't even know him. Why has he this hatred for me, as if I am somehow to blame for his lawless acts?"

Shamus stared at her as if surprised she could ask. "Lawless acts? Perhaps you should question your father more closely when next you see him."

Since that was unlikely, she persisted. "Perhaps you can tell me why I or my family should apologize to him because he was convicted of piracy and given a just sentence."

Instead of answering, he held up one of the slack hands for her to examine. "Just. Call you this just?"

She glanced, then could not look away. There was

an odd thickening around the joints to each finger of Luc's right hand. A strangling horror rose in her throat as she whispered, "What did they do to him?"

"They asked him to give up the location of his ships and the names of his crew. Each time they asked and he would not answer, one of his fingers was broken."

"B-broken . . ." Sickness swelled at the thought. "Who—who called for such barbarity to be done?"

Shamus met her wild, angry stare. "Your father, Miss Montgomery."

Eliza gasped, wanting to deny it but somehow unable to form the words. Justin Montgomery . . . William's father . . . Her gaze riveted to the slightly crooked fingers.

"Aye, and what was worse was having to rebreak each and every one of them so they would mend properly and he could use his hand again."

She didn't need to ask who performed that awful service. The old man's pale eyes were rheumy with remembrance as he gently placed Luc's hand within her own.

"Now, lady, tell me again that justice was done and that he has no right to hold ill will against him who ordered it. But that is not the least of it. Not at all. But 'tis all you'll learn from me. The rest he'll have to tell you himself." He rose up stiffly and took one last look at his still friend. "Aye, a tender heart, for 'twas me, I'd have slain ye and sent yer lifeless body back to the bastard that bore you."

Shocked by those savage words, Eliza watched the second mate leave, her own spirit in turmoil. A confused gaze returned to the man she'd called pirate. To the awful twist of his fingers that told a different tale than Philomena had confided. Brutal acts were done by men like Coeur Noir, not by civilized merchants, not by the father of the man she would marry. She wanted to say no, it was not true, but she'd seen another side of Justin Montgomery, a dark side that could order a pirate thusly abused, that could turn away the daughter of a friend because she had no fortune. Absently, she rubbed those exaggerated joints, tears pricking her eyes when considering his pain, wonder seizing up in her heart when she considered the courage it would take to remain silent.

The impact shattered through him, shocking his being with a force that sent the spirit flying from his body.

I'm dead, he thought for a disoriented moment. In a place of calm distance, he watched his crew and his captive gather around the disjointed figure he'd once claimed. They were weeping, but he felt none of their distress. His emotions were floating—soft, airy sensations—as if carried on a spring breeze. Nice. *I'll lie here awhile*, he thought in a pleasant bliss. Until he saw the lady's face, the way grief sharpened each feature, the way tears glistened in icy trails.

Mon Dieu, she's weeping for me!

The idea so surprised him that in a heartbeat he lost his hold on that peaceful plain and was back within the aching confines of his human form.

He couldn't breathe. He couldn't move to convey his dismay. He choked, suffocating as his ribs refused to expand. Now the thought of death chilled through him, no longer pleasant, no longer peaceful, but rather a frightening unknown to be denied, to be defied.

Air rattled noisily down his windpipe, inflating his lungs, sending a fresh spark of life to every fiber. And it felt so good, for a minute he was able to ignore the pain. Until they lifted him and then, no matter how careful they were, his joints, his muscles, even his thoughts were afire with agony. Things went dark, but it wasn't a restful place that held him, and soon he was fighting his way back to awareness, this time prepared for the waiting pain.

He heard voices, fuzzy and indistinguishable at first, then sharpening into those of Shamus and his captive. Lacking the strength to participate, he listened. It was hard to hear the emotion in Shamus's tone when he spoke of resetting his fingers, hard because it brought back a full host of sensations, from the cold unyielding feel of the rail to which he'd lashed his own arm, to the slogging of rum churning warm in his belly in its failed effort to numb him. To the terrible waiting, the dread, the *knowing.* Then the surprise of discovering it was somehow worse than he'd remembered. The sound, that splintering crackle followed by his own screams echoing in his ears as if they were a stranger's. Screams he'd been somehow able to contain that first time when among enemies but not here, among friends. The praying, over and over, for unconsciousness to take him from the hot spears of suffering. And even through all his misery, the hardest part had been seeing Shamus's face, the terrible pinch of grief inscribed there upon that craggy surface, the regret, the apology.

How his hatred flourished that dark day upon those red-black swells of agony. The hunger for revenge kept him alert to the very last snap and grind of his bones together. In the fevered days that followed, he'd lain the firm foundation for his vengeance, plotting, planning, through those endless sleepless hours when pain beat in each fingertip and darkness hardened about his heart.

He hadn't expected the intensity of those feelings to fail him.

Yet, when Philomena Montgomery, the tool of his retribution, sat at his bedside, gently stroking cool soft fingers over his own, he lost the heat of his fervor. And when she lifted his palm to the dampness of her cheek, he was lost altogether.

"Shamus talks too much."

Eliza was startled by the sudden statement. Guiltily, she started to release his hand, but his fingers curled, enfolding hers in a weak press, so she continued to hold it.

"How do you feel?"

He blinked woozily and wet his lips. "I don't know. I'm not certain. I'm afraid to move lest I find I've done myself harm."

"Don't move, then."

"Remy?"

"The boy is fine. He came down safely."

A sigh escaped him. "Good." He drifted for a moment; then focus returned. "The ship?"

"In good hands and weathering the storm well enough without you."

"And you?"

"Me?" She wasn't sure how to answer, uncertain of what he was asking.

"Are you well?"

"Yes, Captain. Though I confess to have aged several years during your fall."

A small smile touched his lips. "I apologize for any gray hair I might have caused you."

"It was very brave, what you did."

His smile twisted. "And also very foolish. Next time, I shall pause for a moment of reflection before hastening to my doom."

But she knew he wouldn't. He was a man of immediacy, of action, not of pondering and weighing risk. A man who cared deeply despite his outward shunning of demonstrations.

And that knowledge rattled her.

He drifted again, allowing the quiet to settle over him. It was then he felt the curve of her hand against his cheek. He opened his eyes just in time to see her face come down to his, filling his entire field of vision beautifully.

Her kiss was a shock of sweetness, a soft press upon the contours of his mouth, a gentle shift to find an exquisite fit. His lips parted as he breathed it in and exhaled in wondrous yearning. Then she was lifting away, and he was too weak to follow.

"For the supper, Jean-Luc."

What about breakfast? he wanted to ask, but he was already sinking deep under the waves of slumber, hoping to dream of what that fare would offer.

Eliza straightened, the moist tingle of the kiss lingering on her lips. She was thankful for his lapse of consciousness, for how would she explain her impulsive act to him when she didn't understand it herself? She was at a loss as to the attraction, how to defy it, how to resolve it, when her future was properly engaged to William Montgomery. She was playing a lie here on this ship, pretending to be who she was not. Nothing was real, not the role, not the feelings, not the situation. She must remember that.

Eliza brushed her mouth with unsteady fingertips, wondering how to regain her balance. It tumbled out of control in her fascination with this unsuitable man. A man who professed to despise what she was—or rather who he thought she was. Passion was what she felt for him, the same lustful interest he returned. Nothing more. Nothing deeper. This was not love, this warm liquifying of her sensibilities. Love was not the excitement pounding within her breast nor the panic sparked by his nearness. It wasn't love that drew her to kiss him so boldly upon the mouth—or to enjoy it so despite her best intentions.

What, then? Something to be denied until safely removed from the source, until fondly returned to the familiar. Then this adventure would cease in its charm, and the Frenchman would no longer hold her both captive and captivated.

At least, that was her hope.

He dreamed. It wasn't of a lovely young woman serving him kisses for breakfast. He dreamed of pain, throbbing up from his shattered hand, twisting within his empty belly. Of darkness and wet stones, chains that chafed and bound him in helplessness. Of air too dank and awful to breathe because it was thick with death and disease and despair. Of solitude and loneliness so deep it echoed to the soul upon wails of madness. Of hope deserted, of life abandoned, of trust destroyed.

Horrible dreams that were really memories.

He woke with a soft cry, disoriented by the heavy shadows in the room. For a moment, he lay trembling in his own sweat, thinking himself back there, shackled, imprisoned, forgotten. Then the lulling movement of his ship reached him, and the tang of salt air cleansed his nose of the fetid stench of helplessness. His lips moved in a silent prayer that it had been a dream and not a waking nightmare. And he wondered what breathed the whisper of past terror back into his slumber.

Then he saw her slumped over the curl of her arms, head pillowed there upon the tabletop. Philomena Montgomery. The bastard's daughter. The means through which to purge his past and regain his future dreams.

He would not, could not forget that again, not as long as the frightful reminders haunted his mind and tormented his soul. He would look upon her lush lips

and see the unspeakable things he'd had to force between his own in order to survive. He would see his
own suffering reflected back in her fearful gaze. And
when she would offer tenderness and passion with
gesture or word, he would recall the hateful glare of
her father, lying bastard that he was, as he said,
"Break his fingers until you break his silence." Her
misery was naught compared to his own.

They owed him, those pampered Montgomerys,
and they were going to pay.

In making that promise to himself, the blackness
was back surrounding his heart, a blackness no
woman's wiles could penetrate. A darkness no
amount of desire could brighten.

Only in vengeance could he gain freedom.

Only through this woman could he realize his right-
ful dreams.

He would have it and he would have them—no
matter what the cost to his lovely captive.

And the memory of tear-filled blue-green eyes and
the tormenting tenderness of a single kiss were
drowned in the surge of that tidal fury.

Chapter 8

D eep, gusty groans of misery woke Eliza from her sleep. She straightened in surprise to see Jean-Luc not only out of bed but struggling to put on his boots.

"You shouldn't be up!" came her cry of concern as she pushed back the chair. He didn't reward her with so much as a glance.

"I must see to my ship." And he gritted his teeth as boot leather scraped over the nearly frostbitten bottoms of his feet.

"You've others to tend to that chore. See to yourself. You almost died yesterday."

"Almost, unfortunately for you, is not the same as fait accompli."

He looked up then and she could see the anger darkening his eyes, tightening his features into an uncompromising mask. This wasn't the same man who held her against him, shielding her from the winter winds. Nor the dangerous seducer trying to tempt her into a kiss. He was once again Coeur Noir, grimly set upon his purpose.

"I cannot believe you're actually doing this. A sane man would listen to reason."

But he had no reason to heed her, not when he wouldn't listen to his own limitations.

"Breakfast is on its way, with extra coffee this time."

He ignored her attempt at conversation, saying curtly, "Good. I'm hungry."

"How would you have me pay for my meal?"

He swiveled toward her and she knew from the way his gaze flared, then narrowed, that he, like herself, was thinking of the kiss they'd shared. The tip of his tongue swept his lower lip. He wiped the moisture away with a quick backhanded swipe of denial.

"Have you that gold medallion featuring your family's crest?"

Puzzled, she nodded and produced it.

"I will have that."

She placed it in his extended palm, watching as he curled his fingers over it. He clutched it there in his hand until his knuckles whitened, until surely the raised image was cut into his flesh. Perhaps this was as he intended, a reminder of where she came from and how far they stood apart.

Despite his claim, he touched little of what was on his plate, anxious to get up on deck—and away from her. Eliza did nothing to delay him now that the distrustful tension was between them once again.

Eliza took advantage of his absence to beg a washbasin and soap from Remy when he came to take the breakfast tray away. Her own garments were soiled beyond further endurance. Wedging the chair beneath the door handle, she stripped to the skin and bathed as best she could before donning one of Luc's shirts and a pair of his canvas trousers.

Having never worn anything but delicate linens against her bare flesh, the rough feel of his clothing provided a disturbing friction. She wasn't sure if it was the chafing or the fact that the fabric had been next his skin. Better not to explore that too deeply, she decided as she turned to a vigorous scrubbing of her single set of clothes. After dashing damp tendrils of hair off her brow countless times, she finally twisted her hair up away from her face, securing it there with one of the ribbons from her gown. She was wringing the last of the soap from her chemise when a sudden bang against the door startled her into nearly spilling the basin.

Hurrying across the room, she slipped the chair away from the portal, and at once, Jean-Luc was pushing his way inside, his features thunderous.

"What are you doing that the door needs be barred? Did you think to keep me from my own quarters?"

"I was bathing, Captain. I hoped to save us both the embarrassment of an untimely intrusion."

That stopped him in his tracks and his tirade in midbreath. Against his will, his dark gaze scorched the length of her, making her painfully aware of her inappropriate garb and the fact that she was wearing it without his permission.

But those things never occurred to Luc. He was stunned by the unexpected sensuality of her wrapped in his billowing garments. She had surprisingly long legs, well-rounded hips, and a temptingly narrow waist. And though he'd taunted her about being too skinny to draw his notice, he couldn't wrest his attention from the plump curve of her bosom where his damp shirt clung like a second skin. The longer he stared, the sharper the impression her nipples made against the wet fabric.

She was aroused by his attention.

That knowledge nearly broke his hard-pressed resolve.

Suddenly, all he could think about was her, splendidly naked, sponging cool water between those pert breasts.

Cursing direly, he strode to his cabinet and yanked out a bottle of rum. He drank from the bottle, not bothering with a glass. The heat of the harsh liquor pooled in his gut but was cool in comparison to the fires raging lower. He hurt all over. It was agony to move, yet all he could picture was the two of them falling upon his bed in the throes of urgent passion. The fierceness of that urge made it difficult to breathe, to think, to speak. He who had so much control over matters of the flesh. He who had sworn off female companionship that might distract from his cause.

He took another deep draft and closed his eyes, willing the hot swirl of need to go away. He touched the Montgomery medallion, which he now wore about his neck on a thong of leather. His thumb rubbed over the raised impression.

"Captain?" Her tentative tone lapped over his senses in a caress. "Are you in pain?"

Oh, if only she knew the half of it.

"Can I call someone?"

"Call me fool," he muttered, downing another huge swig.

"What?"

"Nothing, *Mademoiselle* Montgomery." He said her name with bitter emphasis to remind himself and her of their positions. "Do not waste your sympathy on me. I would not were the roles reversed." And he hobbled to the bed, knowing that if he went down, he might never get back up, but unable to bear his own weight another minute. He eased onto the mattress, breathing heavily into the pain as he rolled onto his back. Helpless to do more than lie there, he squeezed his eyes shut, teeth locking against any outcry, as the shudders of distress rode through him. Gradually, his abused muscles relaxed into a dull throb of complaint, and he took another drink from the bottle he'd brought with him. And he waited impatiently for the liquor to dull his hurts, those of the body and the soul.

It did no good.

He could still hear her, feel her, smell the fresh scent of her.

His head pounded in time to the lower ache that would not be stilled.

He gave a start as something damp and cool draped over his brow, settling across his sore eyes. He didn't want her ministrations of pity and was about to toss the cloth away, but in truth, it felt so good, so soothing, he couldn't complete the gesture of contempt. Instead, he soaked up the sense of relief and drifted into a restless sleep of minutes or hours. Whichever it was, he woke in no better a mood. He fumbled for the rum bottle and flung the cloth from his forehead. And his first sight was of his captive *princesse* standing in the sear of setting sun, her poignant gaze upon the waters.

Something about her wistfulness disturbed him more than he cared to admit. Especially when those dying embers reflected in the moisture trailing down the curve of her cheek.

"For which of your luxuries do you weep, *enfant gâté*?"

He saw the brief tremble of her chin before it firmed with that unquenchable spirit. Her tone was soft yet underlined with strength.

"For my freedom, Captain. 'Tis a longing you should understand."

"*Oui*, m'am'selle. That I do."

She turned toward him with angry animation. "Then why subject me to this?"

He regarded her long and unblinkingly. "I believe that is exactly the reason, Mademoiselle Montgomery."

"For cruelty's sake?"

"That, and to earn back what should have been mine to keep."

She looked back out the window, snubbing him with the deliberate toss of her head. His already soured mood darkened.

"Think you will see him riding our wake?"

"Who?"

"You lover, of course. Do you believe it is you he pursues or just your promising fortune?"

"Me, of course." But there was a hesitation to her clipped reply.

Spurred on by the loosening effects of the rum, by his hatred for her family, by his own unfortunate desire for her, he wanted to hurt her because he was hurting.

"Ha! Believe what you will, but no man of your pristine circles would accept a woman without wealth. To them, it is money that makes the measure of a man, not deeds, not merit."

She regarded him through eyes ablaze with feeling. "And is that what you believe as well?"

"*Non.*"

His answer surprised her. "Then why you are so hungry for your ransom, if not for the respect you hope it might lend you?"

"I want what is owed me, nothing more." But in this, he protested too much, and recognizing his denial, she gave a superior little smile.

"Really, Captain Pirate. I do not believe you."

He came up off the bed, bounding up without wisdom to meet the full blunt of his body's anguish, reeling within the daze of rum. He was angry enough to ignore the first and relish the second. "Indeed. Think I care for your opinion?"

She fixed him with a level stare and a penetrating, "Yes, I do."

He sucked in a startled breath but could find no ready retort. Damning the liquor for dulling his mind, he turned to another tack.

"And this paragon you mean to wed, he values your opinions?"

"Yes, he does."

"Either you be a lucky woman or he be a henpecked man."

"He is no such thing!"

"A man of virtue and unfailing confidence then, that he would hear a female's voice over the convictions of the day."

"Yes," she threw back to his face.

"And who is this man, this god, this wonder of unnatural equality?"

She blinked, then held her head high. "Why would I give you his name? So you can blackmail another for a tidy fortune?" And how could she, in her guise as Philomena, claim William Montgomery as the man she waited for?

"Afraid he would not deem you worth the price, m'am'selle? Think he would not part with any amount to save you from the likes of me—pirate, rogue, black-hearted defiler of women? Wouldn't a decent, honorable man rush to the rescue of such an innocent, to save her from that fate worse than death?"

As he spoke, his accent thickened with passionate feeling, a storm of fury gathering, ready to tear asunder. She cried out when he flung the bottle of rum at the wall, where it shattered like his control. His hand shot out, clenching the front of her shirt, and with a savage jerk, he tugged her up against him, flush to the hard wall of his chest, where hot, liquor-laced breath scorched her face.

"*Bon*," he hissed. "That's exactly what I want them to do. I want them to writhe with the thought of you in my care. I want them to spend sleepless nights imagining you warming my bed, a helpless vessel for my every depraved wish. I want visions of us together squirming in their minds so that they will hurry to cater to my every demand to get you back." A coldly clever smile twisted his lips. "And therein lies my greatest revenge. For no matter what you tell them, they will believe the worst. Though you will vow you remained untouched, they will be forever tortured by what they think you suffered at the hands of me and my entire crew. Just try convincing them that a man of my reputation would not think of polluting his flesh in joining with a Montgomery."

He thrust her away, glaring at her with a dispassionate pleasure. "As I said, the perfect revenge, one that will grow with every rumor, strengthen with every doubt. No matter how many lovers from your genteel class you are whispered to have taken between those slender thighs already, 'tis the stigma of one so beneath contempt wedging there against your will that will be the undoing of your family's pride."

"And I will be ruined," she echoed in a stricken tone.

"Yes. You will pay the price of your father's treachery though innocent of his schemes, just as I did." And there was no trace of mercy in his obsidian glare, just a hard gleam of justice done through any means.

A timid tap at the door interrupted his angry outburst, and at his harsh call to enter, one of his seamen brought the supper tray to his table, an anxious glance darting between the two of them as he made a hasty retreat.

Jean-Luc stalked to the table, inhaling the fragrance with dramatic delight. "Ah, the chef's lobscouse. You will enjoy this, m'am'selle, providing you have the means to pay for the privilege. What tokens do you yet hold; what favors are you willing to barter?"

She met his dark glance with a stiff silence.

"Nothing? It is a long journey to New Orleans, and you doubtlessly will be ravenous by then and eager to bend to any offer."

"Perhaps by then I will be," she countered with a quiet dignity. "But on this night, I have no appetite."

"*Non?* For the food or for the terms of payment?"

"Neither, Captain."

His gaze raked over her, pausing at the fist of frustration formed by one small hand. "And what of that trinket you wear? Let me see it. Perhaps it is worth a bite of bread and nip of ale."

Her other hand flew to cover the ring on her right hand. Her tone was guarded. "Only to me, sir."

"Let me see. I will be the judge."

"No!"

Her step back in denial was all the provocation needed. He was aching for the opportunity to knock her pride down a peg and prove his own mastery. Yet when he grabbed her arm, he was unprepared for her vigorous rebellion. The sting of her palm set his head ringing, and almost at once, she began twisting, wriggling in his grip. It was no longer about the ring. He had no true interest in the inexpensive circle of gold. It was about subduing her spirit once and for all, breaking that which held him fascinated. Then he would be free of her bewitchery and able to go on with his plan without suffering pangs of remorse.

"Give it to me."

"No! 'Tis mine. A gift from my father and you'll not sully it with your possession."

"From your father? Then it is valuable to me."

He didn't understand, of course. He couldn't know she referred to her own father, Elias Parrish, now dead and buried. He couldn't know the ring was the only thing she retained of a personal nature, the only piece of her own jewelry not taken and sold off to lessen her family's debt. It was the link to her past, to the love of her family, and giving it away would be surrendering up the last of her identity.

But in the end, he was stronger and his might overcame all of her objections. He caught her flailing hand and, despite her clenched fingers and scratching nails, stripped the ring off it. Once he had the ring, she gave up her fight, wheeling away so he wouldn't witness her tears.

"It is nothing special," he commented as he turned the plain gold band within his palm. "One would think a man of your father's wealth would give his child something a little more . . . ostentatious."

"Return it to me," she demanded hoarsely. "As you said, it is worth little, save in memories."

"Then I shall keep them safe with me." And he added the ring to the length of leather already sporting the Montgomery crest. Both lay against his chest, a taunting reminder of her position. "Now sit. Enjoy your meal."

"No."

"You paid for it, m'am'selle, so you might as well eat."

"No." Her back was to him, so he couldn't guess her expression. But her words were fiercely, flatly spoken from a defiant heart. "You said you would only take what was owed you. If I do not eat, what you hold is unfairly stolen."

Jean-Luc was dumbfounded. What a brilliant defense, albeit impractical. He laughed out loud. "A bold gesture, m'am'selle. One you may hold to for this eve, perhaps, tomorrow. But in time, you will relent and accept it as a fair trade."

"Until that time, you are naught but the thief you claimed not to be."

"I will endure that temporary stigma, my lady. Whilst you tempt that lacking appetite with the smell of this excellent fare, I shall be on deck. Stand firm. Do not disappoint me by giving way too soon." With a mocking bow, he left her.

Eliza collapsed atop the sea chest, despairing the loss of her cherished ring. Because he'd made light of her determination, she would hold fast despite the way the aroma of the meal woke complaints from her belly. If he were a man of any honor, he would relent when he realized how serious she was, and restore the heirloom into her care. Until then, she would mourn its loss as she mourned the loss of those it symbolized.

And she would have to consider the truth of his vile words.

Whether the daughter of a wealthy merchant or just a bond servant, the shadow of her days—and nights—upon the sleek pirate vessel would take a toll upon her virtue. Though not the target of his punishment, she would suffer it just the same.

Would William want her for a wife even if she yielded up her maidenhead in proof of her virginity? Or would he bend once more before opinion and cast her off as tainted goods? She hated not knowing that she could trust him to stand strong in her defense. Every hour spent upon the *Galant Sans Coeur* lessened her claim of innocence. Heartless lover . . . exactly what Jean-Luc Gautier was, whether in fact or malicious fiction.

Rescue had to come soon. It had to. Or all her sacrifice, even her freedom, meant nothing.

Chapter 9

Jean-Luc let the crisp salty air clear his head as he turned about the deck. Distracted only by the greetings of his watch crew, he had time to consider what had transpired in his cabin—and to regret it.

He fingered the two items suspended about his neck: the crest representing the goal toward which his hatred steered him, the ring signifying the means to reach it. He tried to make it that simple within his mind, but his rebellious heart had other notions.

Despite his moniker, he had no taste for taunting women. He was raised to believe the smaller, gentler sex was to be handled with respect and deference, catered to with tender court, and coddled with every luxury in return for their devotion. But he had also been raised to believe men would behave honorably if treated thusly. And he knew that to be false. He'd steered clear of the female gender since his youthful days of exploration and indulgent conquest. He didn't need the mysteries of womankind clouding his purpose.

The kind of females he met in the various ports to which he'd traveled weren't the kind to inspire romance. They were creatures of the moment, eager to tempt a man's passions for the gleam of his gold. As his gold was precious to him, he kept his passions under a tight rein. There would be plenty of time for passion when he'd accomplished everything he'd set out to do. Why, then, did those years of frugal discipline fail him now, when he had so much more than a few coins to lose?

Philomena Montgomery embodied everything he despised about the class system in the supposedly classless Americas. She symbolized the wealth, the privilege, the separatism that held her away from those of his society. He'd come to this country seeking the equality won in blood in his own France. He'd come dreamy-eyed with visions of achieving all through hard work rather than pedigree, having been lured by the idea that any heights were obtainable. And to a point, that was true. The Montgomery family was not of old money. They'd bought their way into fashionable circles. But once there, they turned their backs on their roots, closing ranks behind them to prevent others from following to that exclusive plain. A system surviving on snobbery not substance.

All he'd wanted, all he'd asked for was a way into that elite circle without compromising everything. Land, his own fine lady, respect—that was all he required. It was his due, after all, if no longer his birthright.

And Justin Montgomery let him know, bluntly, that such ideals would not be borne. A lesson learned most painfully and not easily forgotten, no matter how many tears shimmered in those lovely blue-green eyes.

He let the twin tokens fall back against his shirtfront. The quixotic Mademoiselle Montgomery confused him, that was all. She made him remember back to a time when his heart was not hard and his future lay golden.

By the time he headed back for his cabin, the effects of the rum were almost gone save a dull reminding ache behind his brow. Now, calmer of mind and emotion, he regretted the words they'd exchanged and his rough actions. Of course, apology was out of the question. A kidnapper did not beg forgiveness of his captive.

He hoped he would enter his quarters to find the meal devoured and his guest in a milder mood.

Such was not the case.

The food lay cold upon the plates. His lady's demeanor was even colder.

Her turbulent gaze touched upon the tokens he wore. Then, without so much as a word to him, she retired to her thin pallet of covers, presenting him with her unyielding back and softly curved backside.

And so passed the next few days in a silent battle of wills. While Luc made no mention of the impasse, he displayed food for two in a tempting array morning and night. She would not be coaxed. Only sips of water passed her firm lips, not sustenance, not syllables. The standoff progressed from an amusing challenge to a genuine threat as the lady grew pale and spiritless with each forfeited meal.

Watching her huddle in her blankets, wasting away, Luc cursed them both for the stubborn game they played.

After the second day, it wasn't so bad. The cramping sensations muted to a continual gnawing grind deep in her belly. Water sometimes soothed, sometimes aggravated it. The smell of food ceased to be a torment when she fixed her attention upon the ring dangling about the handsome Frenchman's neck. That became difficult as light-headedness clouded her vision and made her momentarily forget why she denied herself. After the second day, he left the cabin with the platters heaping, steaming with beckoning aromas. Would he know if she stole just a morsel? Just enough to cut the edge off appetite? Perhaps not, but she would, and she refused to weaken her stand even as her strength waned.

He was weakening. She could tell by the shadowed guilt in his covert studies. He hadn't expected her to be so strong, and that heartened her. It was a knowledge she hugged close, smiling over it as she lay hungry in her blankets. He would surrender first and her victory would be the sweetest, most satisfying fare.

But when she swooned dead away on her way to the washbasin, the impasse was over.

Eliza ebbed back to consciousness in the warm, soft embrace of his bed. She was lifted within the crook of a sturdy forearm, something delightfully heated pressing to her lips.

"Drink," a firm voice commanded. And she did. It was a savory stock, hot, fragrant, filling after only a few swallows. When she turned her head away, she was eased back into the downy haven, and she slept heavily, dreamlessly for the better part of the day.

She awoke rested and ravenous. And all at once surprised by the familiar weight of her father's ring upon her finger.

"Ah, you are finally awake, I see."

He was standing by the vista of windows with the brightness of the southern sun behind him. Though she couldn't make out his expression, he made an impressive silhouette: tall, bold, fit. A quiver stirred within her.

"I have been waiting for you to wake so we might share breakfast together. I am quite bored with my own company at the table. Would you be my guest, m'am'selle?"

No apology. No words of explanation. And she sensed there would be none. To bring up the matter would call for one of them to admit defeat, and neither ever would, not even with the evidence plain upon her finger.

"I would be honored to be your guest, Captain." For that implied no strings attached.

He watched her devour her meal, his gaze one of satisfaction as if he, indeed, had won some point in their match of wills. She felt generous enough to allow it. But not without comment.

"I am quite overwhelmed by your courtesy, Captain. Can it be that you were worried over my health? Afraid I would expire before you could turn me in for profit?"

He almost smiled, that taunting hint she found so intriguing. "I am a most charming man, m'am'selle, when not kept at rapier point by my guests."

"Guest am I now? Does that mean I am free to refuse your hospitality and return home?"

The smile crept a little wider. "I think not."

"I thought not."

He observed her as if she were some curiosity he couldn't quite understand. But the moment he realized what he was doing, the veneer of formality returned, disguising whatever else was on his mind.

"Our clime has warmed considerably now that we're passing into Caribbean waters," he mentioned as he poured her more coffee. The weather wasn't the only thing that had warmed. His dark stare simmered briefly as it held hers. "Perhaps you would like to go up on deck to enjoy the sunshine. It would bring some needed color back to your face."

"I would enjoy that, Captain."

He nodded. *"Bon."*

"You wouldn't want anyone to think you were not an admirable jailer."

His gaze slitted slightly. "Some are far worse, mademoiselle."

She kept her stare from falling to his hand and decided it best to stick with neutral subjects.

"You said we were headed for New Orleans."

His black brows soared. "Did I?"

"Yes, you did."

"Then it is true. It will be only a few more days. Hopefully, news from your father will find us there."

For a moment, the companionable mood faltered. Luc sipped his coffee, his dark eyes canting downward, but not before Eliza saw the hard glitter within them.

"Your days with us thereafter will be numbered, Mademoiselle Montgomery."

"Call me Eliza. There need be no formality between us, Captain. Philomena is such a cumbersome name. I much prefer the use of my middle one." That would ease the strain of responding with spontaneity to a name that was not her own. And it would ease the association with Montgomery.

"Eliza."

A disturbing heat overcame her with the way he caressed her name in speaking it. His accented voice made it a piece of mellifluous poetry. And for the first time, she felt comfortable in responding as herself.

That sense of self grew as she leaned against the rail of the *Galant*, her face lifted to the warm breeze. Having grown up in a seafaring family, she loved everything about the salty air and rock of the waves. In her younger days, she and Nate traversed the coastline in his sailboat, taking turns handling the lines, and later as the boats became ships, she absorbed all she could about onboard life at sea because knowledge lessened the anxiety of letting her beloved brother head out into the unknown for a year at a time, first as mate, then working his way up through the "hawsehole" to captain by his twentieth birthday. Dressed as a boy, she'd crewed for him on short runs while letting her father believe she went as a pampered passenger. She had no fear of climbing the ratlines or turning the sails into the snap of a gale. The sense of freedom was intoxicating, and she could well understand the draw of the sea to men from all walks of life: the adventure, the danger, and the discipline that left one free from care.

How she'd envied Nate when he'd signed on for his first junket, weeping as much out of jealousy as she had from worry when he'd headed for Calcutta under a full parade of sails. Being a daughter, she would never have the chance to explore new worlds at the helm of a proud vessel. Sensitive to her feelings, Nate spent countless hours upon his returns filling her with exhaustive details of each journey, recounting life in the forecastle quarters, cramped dark and damp in winter, stifling in summer when fouled by the breath of sixteen other men; the meals made from vermin-infested hardtack; the stench of pitch and bilge water—all weighed against the exotic wonders of the port cities for an education like none other. He painted pictures so vivid, she was alive with the taste and smell of the Orient, with the dark mystery of the Gold Coast. And how dearly she'd loved him for sharing those precious insights with her.

And how much she missed them now, knowing she would never be privy to those colorful tales again.

"A fine day, Miss Montgomery."

Brushing a quick hand across her damp cheeks, Eliza looked to Remy Leverett with a smile. "Yes, it is."

He came up to settle at the rail beside her, and for a moment, Eliza was overwhelmed by his similarity to her brother at a younger age. The wiry seaman possessed the same swaggering sweetness she'd so adored in Nate. They were both guided by the bowditch. It gleamed in their faraway stares, in the half twist of their smiles as they dreamed of adventure, then went out to boldly pursue it. No woman would ever hold their heart as ferociously as the sea, and Eliza pitied those who would doubtlessly try.

Then it struck her anew that her brother would never be forced to make that choice between love and wanderlust.

To distract herself from the pain crushing in about her heart, Eliza turned her attention toward the bronze-skinned boy.

"How is it you've turned to the pirating life, Remy?"

He looked at her blankly. "What?"

"How did you come to sail under Coeur Noir's notorious flag?"

The boy gathered himself up proudly to spout, " 'Tis honored I am to be included in such noble company."

"Noble? 'Tis noble to skulk about the seas raiding those helpless to hold their treasures?"

"Begging your pardon, lady, but where did you get such a notion as that?" He seemed plainly puzzled. Could it be he did not know of Jean-Luc's sordid past?

"Most likely from the court's conviction of your captain on that very charge."

Remy laughed, unconcerned by the severity of that judgment. "Oh, 'twas pure nonsense, my lady. Cap'n Black Heart never sailed under no skull and bones."

Eliza sighed. His loyalty was admirable but naïve. "Methinks you paint your captain in too perfect a light."

All Remy's good nature fled from him, leaving him an expression that was far too old and weathered for his years. "Be careful, madame. I'll not allow disrespectful address even from a fine lady. Cap'n Luc may not be a saint to your way of thinking, but he saved me. He plucked me outta the gutters of New Orleans, where I was living off garbage and sleeping under piers. He gave me clean clothes, a dry roof, the chance at self-respect. And I worked hard to earn it. He can sometimes be a stern master but never a cruel one. And he never, never is untrue to his own rules of honor."

"Remy."

The lad turned from his stalwart defense to face its topic. "Aye, Cap'n?"

"Be you on this vessel as passenger or crew?"

"I work for a living, Cap'n." He bowed with a quick formality to Eliza and let his cocky stride carry him aft.

"Out to bewitch my crew from their duties, m'am'selle?" Luc asked with a deceptive smile. He was dressed in sailor garb, simple and utilitarian. Even so, his deportment set him apart from those who sailed under him. Eliza looked back out over the waves, unwilling to let him note her appreciation.

"He was extolling his captain's virtues."

Luc laughed. "And I'm sure you set him straight."

"I tried, Captain, but you seem to inspire a rather rabid fealty in those who serve with you. The sign of a good captain, I understand."

"Why, *ma belle fille*, be careful. That sounded almost like a compliment." He relaxed his stiff pose to assume Remy's place at the rail beside her, leaning on crossed forearms and lifting his handsome face to the salty breeze and warming sun.

"He defends you from the charge of piracy quite eloquently," she said, risking the swift change of his mood. Surprisingly, he didn't bristle up in challenge.

"The boy came from the most wretched of circumstances. Hell would have seemed a paradise to him."

"And you, Captain, what circumstances did you come from? I see a certain regal air about you. Could it be that you're of the same noble class you scorn?"

His evasion was noticeable. "It is not the rank that makes the man, lady, but rather the opposite. What I was is of no consequence. What I make of myself says all."

"And what do you mean to become—hunted by the law and the Montgomerys? Neither will give you peace to be anything but a criminal on the run for the rest of your days."

He met her gaze squarely, his own dark and determined. "*Alors, chérie*, that's where you come into the picture. You are the means through which my good name will be restored."

She gaped at him, astonished. "By tearing me from those I love? By extorting a ransom for my return? How can you equate those villainies to the establishment of a good name?"

His stare narrowed in intensity. "By the end of this, m'am'selle, the true villain will surface, or I will be in my grave and it won't matter to me any longer."

Chapter 10

Who was this man?

Eliza sat near the windows watching Jean-Luc work his navigational charts, questions spinning about in her head.

Was he a vile, cold-hearted terror of the seas, rightfully convicted to prison for his crimes? Or was he the honorable captain capable of commanding unshakable respect from all his crew, as Remy steadfastly claimed?

His own words conflicted with his actions since the day he'd stolen her—or rather "Philomena"—from her ship. Kidnapping and ransom were violent and illegal acts reaffirming what the courts decreed about him. But he continually claimed himself the victim, calling his gestures legitimate retribution. Who and what to believe?

Of course, she didn't have to make a choice. It didn't matter if he were pirate or paragon. She was his captive, his pawn, and there was nothing she could do while in his imprisoning care but watch the drama unfold.

Doubts assailed her—about Justin Montgomery, about William, his son. It was more and more difficult to believe them undeserving of Luc's vendetta. And therefore increasingly difficult to know where her loyalties lay.

What would Luc do when he discovered he didn't have Philomena Montgomery in his hands? Would his wrath turn upon her or would she be released, unharmed, as insignificant? Those factors, too, were out of her control, but they played upon her thoughts with increasing frequency. The only thing in her command was when the truth should be revealed. She'd promised Philomena enough of a delay for her to escape the reach of Coeur Noir. Surely that had been accomplished. What if there were no plans to launch a rescue for the sake of a mere bond servant?

Her father and brother, had they yet lived, would have combed the seas for an eternity for her return. Was there anyone else who would care enough to take on a man of Black Heart's reputation?

In her heart, she wanted to answer *William*. But her logical mind gave another response. Dear meek William had not stood firm on her behalf when the risk was nowhere near this great. Would he now demand his father send ships after the very woman Justin Montgomery deemed too low to be considered for his son's bride? A painful truth lanced through her. She feared not, even while wishing it were so. Her father had warned her of Justin's duplicity, and Elias Parrish hadn't been mistaken in many things—except in his belief that he would always be there to protect his daughter.

William, with his poet's heart, lacked the basic strength of character found in men like Nate Parrish ... or Jean-Luc Gautier. That tender trait once endeared her. Now it was a weakness she could not admire. Not when it was her life at stake and she could not muster the trust to believe in the man who claimed to love her. Would he come for her or consider this an easy way out of an awkward situation?

"You are very pensive this evening, *chère*."

Eliza glanced up to find Jean-Luc's probing gaze upon her. Knowing it was no use trying to deny her melancholy, she admitted to it freely. "I have much to ponder over, Captain. My fate rests in uncertain hands."

His handsome features grew solemn. "I have said you would not be harmed whilst in my care." He sounded offended that she should be fretting over the idea of his abuse.

"'Tis not that, Captain." She smiled wryly. "You have been a most gracious host."

He ignored her sarcasm. "What, then? Do you fear your father will not pay for your freedom?"

For Philomena's, there would be no doubt. Montgomery would have paid any price. But for the daughter of his deceased partner who was now worth only the price of her indenture? Justin Montgomery was a man who knew no personal loyalties. Was he also a man whose treachery had falsely imprisoned the Frenchman sitting opposite her?

"You are slow to answer."

Eliza sighed. "No. I am certain he will pay any amount for his daughter's safe return."

That wasn't a lie.

Luc smiled in relief. "*Bien*. Then you have naught to do but enjoy the voyage."

"As I've enjoyed it thus far?"

He shrugged off her mild complaint in good humor. Just then, dinner arrived, its bearer waiting patiently until Luc had safely stored his precious charts, leaving the tabletop clear. Eliza eyed the setting for two with disfavor, but did not speak it until they were alone once more.

"And how might I earn this repast? Would you check my teeth for gold?"

"I've a much better idea. You are a well-bred female. I trust you know your letters and numbers."

"Yes," she responded warily.

"I speak English well enough, but my reading, it is not so good. If you would . . . how you say, tutor me in my reading of English, I would be most grateful. Grateful enough to welcome you at my table until we reach New Orleans."

"Just help you with your reading?" It sounded simple.

"*Oui*. I desire to make my home here, and in order to be a man of respect, I must know these things."

She smiled ruefully. "It takes more than book learning to command respect from a country that has condemned you to a life in prison."

Though his gaze slitted, he retained his narrow smile. "We will not talk of that. Come. Sit. After we eat, we will begin our lesson. If you are agreeable."

She looked at the feast spread out before them, her mouth watering in anticipation. "I am."

After the meal was finished and the dishes were taken away, Jean-Luc provided a volume and angled his chair around the table so that it butted up against the sea chest that made her seat. Then, after pouring them both glasses of a surprisingly good Madeira, he opened the book and began to read.

He wasn't as unskilled as he'd led her to expect. The words came haltingly, some badly mangled by his accent, but he was able to guess at most before looking to her for confirmation. When he had it, he'd beam in self-congratulations and go on to the next line. This was a new facet, one rarely shown. His intelligence was displayed in the library he kept, his thirst for knowledge in the eager way he devoured each word he read. That was a surprise to her. Few men of the sea had the time or patience for scholarly pursuits. What, then, should she make of Jean-Luc Gautier, with his monkish reserve, his blood-soaked reputation, and his hunger for genteel improvement?

Charmed by his crooning accent, distracted by his nearness, she made the corrections casually. Delivered word by laborious word, it was some time before Eliza actually heard the content of what he was reading. Then she had trouble listening to anything else above the roar of blood to her ears.

He was reading erotic prose.

And she was sitting primly next to him correcting him on his elocution oblivious to the wicked content!

" 'The most delightful kiss is that which is planted on moist ardent lips, accompanied with suction of the lips and tongue. So sweet the emission, exquisite'— *exquis*? Yes? 'More agreeable than honey. A shivering greets the whole body of man, and is more intoxtoxicating than strong wine.' "

The phrases, spoken low, caressed by Luc's melodious intonation, began to throb with blatant meaning. Part of her hung upon every sultry word in forbidden titillation. Another cringed in modest horror, having never heard—never *imagined*—such things. But she continued to listen, when every decent fiber in her upbringing demanded she stop him, stop the flowing descriptions, the scorching prose, the images conjured in her virginal mind . . . of she and Luc doing those things the graphic lines depicted.

" 'A son-sonorous kiss upon the outside of the lips, it gives no pleasure, but one which provokes a delicious volup-tu-ous-ness, belongs with divine congress.' Congress? *Congrès*. *Assemblée*? I do not understand this. *Parlement national des États-Unis*? This makes no sense. What does it mean, this 'congress'?"

Heat flamed within her veins, trailing a molten path through the body she commanded to sit still and stiff with proper decorum. "I do not think it refers to the government, Captain."

He lifted dark brows, awaiting further explanation.

"I believe it refers to . . . relations." Her skin was hot and tingling as if she suffered from too much sun.

"Ah! *Relations. Bien.* The English, they never say what they mean. Where was I? Yes. 'Know that all kisses and caresses be rendered useless if unaccompanied by that most virile member. *Passion* which inflames resembles fire, and as only water can extin-tinguish this, so only can the flood of man extinguish the fires of love.' "

Her thoughts spun wildly, feverish with dismay and decadent delight. The cadence of her heartbeats had grown fast and furious, excited, frightened all at the same time, not so much by the words but by the man and the way he spoke them. As if each were directed to her in the most personal and private way possible. She fought to keep from squirming as an embarrassing pressure built low in her abdomen, like an itch begging to find relief. Instead she reached for her wine, hoping it would cool the fires below.

It was like pouring pitch upon a flame.

" 'Woman is like a fruit which will yield its fragrance only when rubbed by the hands, as the basil; unless it be warmed by the fingers it emits no perfume. The same with woman: If you do not animate her with your frolics and kisses; with the nibblings of her thighs and close embraces, you will not obtain what you desire; you will experience no pleasure when she shares your couch; and she will feel no affection for you. Explore her with all possible activity. Do not let pleasure's propit-pitious moment pass by unheeded: It occurs when you see her eyes slightly moist and her mouth partly open. Unite then, but never before.' "

Without looking at her, Luc could feel her response to the text he was reading. Her breath had quickened into feathery little gasps. Her lithe form fairly vibrated with inner tension and the battle to deny it. Either she was a good girl buffeted by shock or she was a bad girl tempted beyond tolerance.

He'd heard she was a bad girl and that what she was hearing was nothing new.

He continued to spin the hot, exotic verse, not looking at her yet aware of her in every fiber. He drew in that heady fragrance: the smell of her freshly washed gown, the warm perfume of a woman's desire, the rich bouquet of wine upon her lightly panted breaths. Intoxicating, each one. Beckoning as the words made tantalizing pictures against a will he'd vowed to honor. He'd promised not to take advantage of her.

But should she ask him . . .

His rendering of the words thickened, his accent oozing sensuality.

" 'Such perfect symmetry: soft, seductive and perfect in all detail. It is warm, narrow, and dry to such a degree that one would think fire would dart from it. Its form is graceful, its odor suave; its whiteness throws the carmine center into relief.' "

He wanted her. The rawness of that need raged beneath a carefully tempered control. He let the verse seduce her when he could not. He let the words incite her in ways he'd said he would not.

She didn't stop him.

Eliza couldn't stop him.

She was mesmerized.

Her anxious glance detailed his profile. How handsome he was, she thought once more, with those sundarkened sculpted features. Her gaze stroked along the slash of one black brow to the bristle of his raven-sleek hair, followed the whorl of his ear to the cut of his strong jaw. She lingered upon his lips, watching them form the scintillating syllables. And suddenly the urge to touch him, to feel the angular bones of his face, to taste, again, the textures of his mouth, created a dangerous friction upon her will. The need to know versus the need to withdraw, now, while she safely could. But it was already too late for her.

" 'Do not rise yet from her breast, but let your lips wander over her cheeks, and let your sword rest in her sheath. Seek ardently to arouse—' "

She reached over to close the book.

"Enough." The single word forced its way up through the constriction of her throat.

His gaze lifted, registering surprise—and something else, something darker, intense, compelling.

"What is it, Eliza?" He spoke her name in a husky, possessive fashion. "Is my diction so unbearable?"

"N-no." She was panting, breathless with agitation. "What kind of book is that?"

He glanced down at the leather-bound cover. "It is a rough translation of the Far Eastern love sonnets of Sheikh Nefzawi."

Air strangled for release from her lungs. " 'Tis not love it speaks of."

"*Non?* I found it very . . . stirring."

She met his stare then, hers wide and stricken. " 'Twas shameless and most wicked."

His smile was faint, suggestively taunting. Intensity gathered, an approaching storm, between them. "You found no romance in the words? Did they not inspire you to passion? I believe that was their intent."

"No!" she declared too vehemently. "To imagine a decent man and woman indulging in such . . . that they would enjoy . . ." She couldn't finish.

"It spoke of nothing indecent," he argued mildly, his penetrating stare never faltering. "Nothing that could not be enjoyed."

She shuddered with disgust and illicit curiosity. "To kiss like that with open mouths and tongues. I—I cannot comprehend . . ." She swallowed hard.

"Perhaps I could translate better."

He felt her ragged inhalation just an instant before he claimed her lips beneath his. At first her mouth was still and slackened with surprise. His tongue lolled along that soft seam, furling, swirling wetly in enticing patterns until a slight part bade him enter. He delved inside for a quick tempting plunge, then pulled back, meaning to draw away.

As if she guessed his intention, her hands flew up to hold his jaw, his cheeks, urging him to remain. To show her more.

Need crashed like violent surf over the rocky shore of his control as her mouth opened in invitation. Rivers of passion pulled him into delicious madness. God above, she was sweet and wild and hot for him.

His arm snaked about her trim middle, jerking her up into his lap so that her bosom flattened against his chest and she encircled his shoulders in a desperate grasp. His kiss grew hard, demanding, hungry. The soft little moaning sounds of compliance she breathed into his mouth only pushed his passions further beyond the brink of no return.

His hands worked her skirts up over her thighs, the gesture hurried and a little rough, freeing those sleek limbs to spread wide as his knees wedged between them. She straddled him, knees hugging to his waist as he took a brief moment to open his trousers. Still swamping her senses with deep, plundering kisses, he scooped his palms beneath her silky bottom, lifting her, poising that damp gateway to paradise above him. Then gripping her hips tightly, he dropped her down upon his engorged shaft, impaling her there.

The breath exploded from his lungs as dark, wondrous sensations whirled about him, endangering his concentration. She was so incredibly hot and narrow, the demand for release was instantaneous. It had been so long—and never like this, sensations so sharp, so edged with taut restraint, so powerful he felt helpless to hold fast against them. He groaned and grappled for a saving sanity.

But what shocked him back into sobriety was the woman wrapped about him. Fingers that kneaded the back of his neck in restless longing now twisted savagely in his hair. The supple body rocking against him suddenly arched and shuddered wildly. Not in the throes of passion, as he'd first assumed, but in frantic denial and distress.

"Eliza?" He banded her with his arms, trying to still her struggles, frowning because he thought she was playing some cruel game with his emotions, and angry that he'd allowed himself to trust her eagerness.

Then he felt the scalding of her tears against his face, against his neck as she burrowed there.

Understanding dawned, a sunrise over gallows.

He had taken an inexperienced maid. One who was no longer willing. If she had been at all.

He lifted her up gently, tortured by the hard tremors plaguing her slender form, and cuddled her close. At least, he tried to. His palm rubbed up and down her back, soothing, seeking to quiet the spasms of her despair. Panic, frustration, remorse slammed into him all at once, making him demand some absolution.

"You wanted me. You wanted this."

Her head jerked from side to side, and the sound of forlorn weeping reached him.

Mon Dieu!

"Why did you let me believe it was so? Why did you not stop me?"

When she made no reply, he caught the sides of her head between his hands, wrestling it up so he could see her face, but that was far worse a punishment. Her eyes were wide and dazed, glittering with unshed tears of pain and consequence. Seared by self-blame, he let her go and leaped up in a frenzied motion, toppling her back onto the tabletop as he scrambled for escape.

He hastily rearranged his clothing, then paced, taut with unrelieved expectations, unable to look at her while his emotions yet seethed in turmoil.

"How could I have so misread the situation?" he asked himself aloud. He didn't need her answer. He knew why.

Because he'd wanted to. He was cautious when it came to women, never one to love or lie with one in a fit of reckless passion. They distracted him from his goals, interfered with his focus upon the future. He'd been saving himself by choice for the woman he'd have for a wife, wanting to be worthy of her in every way before taking that final step toward permanence. Wanting to be able to provide for her and keep her . . . safe.

Somehow Eliza Montgomery had confused his intentions, had gotten him thinking that maybe she . . .

He ceased his agitated travels, his hands flexing powerfully at his sides. He was facing the sea as he spoke, his words low and gruff. "Forgive me, m'am'selle. I took unfair liberties. I thought—"

"You thought what?"

The cut of her demand was so unexpected, he came about in surprise. She was still leaning against the table, mussed and well used, but her clothing was straightened. And her stormy stare sliced to the bone.

"You were a virgin."

"Were" became the operative word.

"I had not expected that."

Because he made it sound like an accusation, she flung one back at him. "Why not?"

"I had heard . . ." He fumbled, searching for an excuse.

"You heard wrong, Captain."

Indeed.

Guilt was one thing, but taking full blame was incomprehensible. "I did not rape you, mademoiselle. You did nothing to suggest my attentions were unwanted."

"Are you saying I—I *seduced* you?"

He wrapped himself in a chill hauteur. "Clumsily, but quite effectively."

"I did no such thing, you conceited bastard!"

"Bastard, am I? You did not call me that when tearing at my hair and sucking my tongue down your throat."

"You—you tricked me—with that book."

"Just words, *ma belle*. Why protest so loudly when I only gave what you asked for?"

"Asked?" Eliza quivered with rage. "You were the one who took advantage. I did not *ask* to be at your mercy."

Her fragile jaw worked silently, and the glimmering returned to her eyes. Then, just as quickly, both chilled. Only her rapid breathing betrayed her tenuous state.

"Congratulations, Captain. Not only will you have your reward and the satisfaction of having ruined my prospects, you've stolen my honor as well. Such a cleverly plotted vengeance befitting Coeur Noir. You must be very pleased now that you've gotten all that you wanted from me."

It was on the tip of his tongue to deny it, to plead he'd had no such intentions. But he said nothing. Better she believe it was true. So instead of begging her pardon, or her forgiveness, he assumed an arrogant posture and said the purposefully unforgivable.

"You are very naive if you believe that is true." His cold smile mocked her. "They say vengeance is sweet, *ma chère*. A pity we could not have continued to discover if it is so."

He caught a blur of movement from her right hand, giving him just enough time to dodge the wineglass flying at him. She was about to slap him next, but he caught her wrist easily.

She cursed him in language a lady wasn't supposed to know, let alone use. He jerked her up against him so that the shock of his hard physique stilled her verbal abuse. Words sputtered, then failed her. She leaned into him, drawn by the power, the heat, helpless against the needs he quickened. The brace of her free hand against his chest became a restless circling over tempting terrain. The confused gaze lifting to meet his spoke of want, of fear, of disdain.

It was the contempt he focused upon, letting it abrade his pride. It was that or kiss her again, which would be the height of folly.

"Forgive me," he drawled. "I should have known you'd find no amusement in your weakness. How much easier to blame your failing on me, crying deception as an excuse for your own desires. I can see your dilemma, *princesse*. You are a Montgomery and therefore above such baseborn delights with someone of such little consequence." His black eyes sparked with sudden fierce fire as he concluded, "No need to fear that this brief interlude will lead to conception. Lucky for any nameless brat we'd breed together, for your father would doubtlessly drown it like a cur pup whelped upon his prize bitch.''

He ignored her gasp of shock at his language, at his suggestion, and without further word, he shoved her away and took his leave.

Leaving her broken of heart if not spirit.

Chapter 11

Her true misery didn't surface until the door closed behind him. Then it came in great painful waves, rolling through her, dashing her emotions against the hard reality of her shame until she was weak and helpless to resist.

What had she done?

She'd lost the only thing of worth that was still hers to claim.

It had happened so fast. Her senses dazed by Madeira and madness, she allowed his kisses, had returned them in a frenzy of inexperience. How had things gone so quickly from innocent—or not-so-innocent—kisses to the rending of her virtue? She wanted to shriek that he'd pressed an unfair advantage, as he'd admitted, but she could not. She'd wanted what he offered, had accepted it, had demanded it, right up until that final, irreversible step. Had she wanted him to stop, she should have cried no at any juncture up until that last one. But she'd had no chance. Her instincts had been drowned in the fires of delight. A woman living with two modest men, she'd never been schooled in matters of the flesh. She hadn't known to react with denial because she hadn't understood his purpose. She thought con-

summation revolved about marriage vows, proper
blushes, and a gentle foray by two tender lovers in
the dark. Not the wanton straddle of a dangerous
stranger's lap aboard a ship of thieves.

"Foolish virgin, playing with fire. Damn you,
scurvy pirate, for your black heart and your scheming
lusts!"

Her wavering gaze touched upon the book of seductive verse where it sat innocuously on the tabletop. She snatched it up, flinging it after the wineglass.
It made a satisfying thud against the far wall. The
anger felt good, restorative. She sat up straight and
wiped her sore eyes. Her mind spun ahead for ways
in which to salvage what had just happened.

"Who needs to know?"

She whispered that aloud to feel its potential. The
panic knifing through her moments ago ceased its
stabbing. Who would know?

She had no experience in lies. However, if she was
to escape this with any degree of dignity, those lies
would have to roll off her tongue like sweetest honey.
It would mean denying that she betrayed William
with another man. It would mean denying she'd betrayed her own moral upbringing to revel in unbri-
dled lust.

It would mean denying the powerful slam of emotions even now battering away at her heart when she
thought of her dark lover, Jean-Luc Gautier.

He wasn't her lover, not really. What they'd done
didn't involve love, not at all. It was a combination of
the tension and the wine and the potent verse prodding them toward passions best left unexplored.

She closed her eyes, assailed by vivid sensations:
the Madeira-laced taste of his tongue in her mouth,
the power of his encircling embrace, the hard thrust
of him through the breach of her virginity, and the

way that mysterious masterful part of him throbbed so hotly within her untried female flesh. She shuddered, her body still aching from that sudden, fierce possession. Deep feelings edged at her awareness: discomfort, dismay . . . disappointment. She hid her face in trembling hands. That was the worst of it, the shameful admission, at least within her traitorous heart, that she'd wanted it to continue beyond that first invasive hurt.

She'd lost momentary control—no, her sanity.

It would not happen again.

She would continue to play the part of Philomena Montgomery until they reached the port of New Orleans. It would be too dangerous for her to reveal her deception while still aboard the *Galant*. Once ashore, she would apprise Jean-Luc of his mistake. Then, with or without the Montgomerys' intervention, she would make her way back to Salem to claim the future she deserved. A future within the familiar circles of New England society as William's bride.

That was the only way it could be.

It was what she wanted.

Her future held no place for a compelling sea captain and his sinister plots of revenge. Or for the disturbing emotions he quickened within her breast.

So how was she to act now that the awkward fact of intimacy wedged between them?

It proved an unfounded worry, for Jean-Luc did not return to the cabin. Not that night as she lay in the tangle of her covers dreading the sound of his step, nor the next when she listened for it anxiously.

He stayed away and his absence worked upon her will more dangerously than his presence could. Her mood sunk lower with each hour spent in her own company until finally she could stand it no longer.

Comfortably garbed in a pair of borrowed trousers

and a baggy shirt, Eliza stepped up on deck, risking reprisals in order to grab for a breath of fresh air—and to steal a glance at the elusive Frenchman who was never far from her thoughts. She moved out farther into the pooling sunlight when she didn't spot him right away.

"Good day, Miss Montgomery."

She turned a smile upon Remy Leverett as the boy strode up to join her. She took no offense at the poorly veiled interest steeping in his gaze, remembering he was in his youthful prime and full of vinegar. Her father had been fond of that excuse for her brother's reckless behavior.

"And a fine one it is, Mr. Leverett."

He blushed at her formal address and drew himself up taller. "May I be of some help to you, my lady? Were you looking for Cap'n Black Heart?"

"No." Her denial came too quickly to be believed, but Remy was oblivious to the nuances of displaced passions.

"He be aft shooting the sun for our latitude. Shall I tell him you be looking for him?"

"No, thank you, Remy. I just came topside to soak up the breeze."

He nodded, pleased that a fine and frail lady like herself was not afflicted with the seasickness that plagued most dainty females and some of the crew.

"Tell me, Remy, how long have you sailed with the captain?"

"Oh, I packed out with Cap'n Luc when I was but ten. Them was grand privateering days, and we carried our letters of marque proudly in raids on British merchantmen. Many tried, but nary a one caught up to us on the *Galant*. The cap'n would say it was all done for the gold, but none that knows him believes that to be the only truth. He bears a Frenchman's scorn for the English, and 'twas an excuse to strike back at them for all their haughty arrogance and for what they did to his family."

"What did they do?" she asked, more interested than she would admit.

"'Twas in one of their squabbles that Brit troops took his family's home. Killed them all from what I heard, rumor, that is, not from the cap'n hisself. He don't speak of it and I don't ask. Shamus, he might know more of the matter. 'Tis said their paths go back a long way."

"So how did Jean-Luc—I mean, your captain, go from French citizen to American privateer?"

"He swears to sail under no man's flag but his own, to call no country his home, but 'tis a lie. For all his bluster, he loves these upstart colonies 'cause they be bold like himself and not afeared to take on those who would be an unfair master."

"Privateering is not exactly the work of a patriot," Eliza chided, not liking the picture Remy was creating of his captain. It was all too noble and grand, bordering too closely on the ideals her own family held. She didn't want to admire him.

"Not a patriot?" Remy said with an indignant sniff. "What do you know of it?"

"My brother was Salem's finest blockade runner. His crews boasted that he could smell his way at night from Heel Gate to Providence with his eyes shut. Many a morning his ship could be found right under the very guns of the British when the fog lifted, ready to pile on sail and streak for Stonington with cannonballs whistling behind them."

Remy gave her an odd look. "Your brother? I was not aware that your brother had ever taken a turn at the helm."

Caught by her own proud words, Eliza was aghast

at her carelessness. The only way out was to brazen a bluff. " 'Tis a little-known fact. Since then he has found his taste more for the books than the bowditch."

"Swallowed the anchor, did he? There's no shame in retiring from the sea once one's mettle is proven." Remy looked impressed but was not to be outdone in boasting. "Cap'n Luc was with Lafitte down in New Orleans when they broke the British, but he never pirated with the brothers no matter what friendship lay between them. 'Tis false, those claims that laid him up in prison, for a more honorable man I've never known. 'Twas why we went to so much trouble to free him."

"And who made those claims?" she asked, a shaky sickness spreading through the pit of her belly.

"Your father."

Shamus Sterns's voice cut in like a cold northern gale. He met Eliza's surprised stare with an unapologetic glower and didn't break from it as he growled, "Remy, get back to yer duties and quit being so free with yer tales."

"Aye, sir." The boy slipped her a regretful glance, then scurried away.

Left alone to face the second mate's scorn, Eliza squared up before it, ready to defend a position that was not hers to hold. "Were they truths he was telling?"

Shamus squinted at her menacingly but relented when she showed no sign of intimidation. "Aye, the truth as seen through the eyes of an impressionable lad."

"And what truths would you tell, Mr. Sterns?"

"The truth that bad apples don't go falling far from rotten trees."

"And that means what, exactly?"

"I don't know what tricks ye be up to, missy, but stop them."

"I've done nothing to deserve your warning, sir. I am not here of my own will, and I refuse to be blamed for any disconcertment my presence causes you."

" 'Tis not me, lady. 'Tis Luc. I don't know what ye've done, but you stay clear of him, ye hear. 'Tis his flaw to want to believe in things that do him harm. He is a fool for causes best left alone. This time I'll not allow him to be regretting them."

"I don't know what you mean."

"So you say, but we both know ye've bewitched him."

"I—I bewitched him?" It was so ridiculous she could scarcely think of a response. "I am his prisoner, not his paramour. I have done my best to stay out of his way. I am a woman betrothed. How dare you suggest that I would be disloyal to my intended with a man who stole me from my family's care! He is well deserved of his name, this Black Heart you accuse me of enticing. I would as soon throw myself overboard as to entertain his contemptible attentions."

Her anger built with every breath until the words spat from her lips. She let her tirade vent the frustrations of not being in control of her own heart any more than she was of her own destiny. But the moment she said them, she wished they'd remained unspoken. For behind Shamus stood Jean-Luc Gautier, still and stunned by the broadside she'd just delivered.

He looked so weary, as if he'd known no rest for days. His eyes were shadowed with a fatigue that circled like bruises. But still they were sharp as newly fractured chunks of coal, brilliant as black glass. And he stared right through her.

"There is the side, m'am'selle. No one will stop you

if you wish to throw yourself into the sea."

Then he went below without waiting to see if she would or would not.

Eliza followed.

He was seated at the table, his charts spread out before him, dark head bent in concentration. He was working the figures for longitude upon a chronometer. Most seafaring men depended upon lunar angle to plot position in tandem with a clip log and reel. Few were lucky enough to own the expensive and fragile navigational tool Jean-Luc possessed.

He began to dial in the coordinates, then cursed beneath his breath and started the process again. After the third failed attempt, he slammed the instrument down on the tabletop with a startling lack of regard. He pressed the heels of his hands to his temples for a slow massage. A suspicious gaze lifted when Eliza picked up the tool.

"May I?"

He shrugged in disinterest and closed his eyes.

It took her scant time to locate their position on the charts. She'd purchased a chronometer for Nate when he'd earned his first captaincy, and they'd learned to use it together. She hadn't forgotten how it was done any more than she'd forgotten Nate.

"Here is your position, Captain."

He slitted his eyes open to focus blearily on the spot her finger pressed to. The lines blurred before him. "Make note of it, if you would, there in my log."

She found the appropriate space and entered the degrees.

"You're not steering us aground are you?" he asked, only mildly wary.

"No, Captain. I've an interest in getting to New Orleans, too."

He nodded disjointedly and staggered up from his

chair. She gave him a closer look, noting his sudden pallor.

"Captain, are you ill?"

"I should like to lie down, unless you've an objection to me claiming my own bed."

Before she could answer, his knees gave way and she found herself supporting his considerable weight. "Captain?" She angled so that her arms circled his middle. She could feel harsh tremors working through him. Had he taken a chill spending his nights on deck while she squandered the protection of his quarters? Guilt assailed her. "Come, Jean-Luc. Walk with me. Just a few steps."

He managed an awkward effort that got them to the bedside. She tried to ease him down but was forced to release him into an ungainly sprawl. He was quick to burrow into his covers, pulling them up over shoulders, which shook with violent shivers as he drew himself up into a tight ball. She could hear his teeth clattering.

Worriedly, she placed a hand upon his brow while asking, "Who can I get for you? You're obviously very sick."

His fingers closed about her wrist, the pressure hurtful, his spasms transmitting through her. "Shamus. Just Shamus. No one else."

"All right, Jean-Luc. I'll bring him."

He released his hold, his hand clutching the covers instead.

The surly second in command eyed her rapid approach with blatant disfavor. Until she told him in a confidential tone what prompted her to seek him out. Then, without a word, he hurried below. He didn't seem surprised at his captain's state, only gravely concerned as he knelt down at the bedside to place a gentle hand upon Luc's shoulder.

"Lad, be ye all right?"

Luc's hand flailed about, then seized upon the old gnarled one for a desperate press. "Let none of the crew see me like this. Take her away."

"As you wish, boy. I'll stay with ye through the worst of it."

"*Non. Impossible.* Your place is above, seeing to my ship. Without Benji aboard, the duty is yours. Do not fail me as I have failed this crew. Change the course. The coordinates—are there in my log." He spoke with difficulty, words forced out through the clench of his teeth.

"Luc—"

"Do not fail me."

"Aye, Cap'n." He looked uneasy with that concession as Luc was taken by another series of hard tremors. He was clearly torn between loyalties to his friend and to his vessel, each needing his attention.

"What is it?" Eliza asked, watching Luc curl up within the covers to battle the fierce chills.

Shamus didn't look up. " 'Tis a touch of malaria."

Malaria. Eliza stiffened in dread. She'd heard of the mysterious disease that spread like wildfire through southern port cities, taking a terrible toll on their inhabitants along with its brother, yellow jack.

" 'Tis not life threatening," Shamus assured her, guessing at her alarm. "Somehow it failed to snatch away his soul the first time, as it did so many others, but it comes back to haunt him now and again with the chills and fever and sweats. 'Twill torment him through the night hours, but he should be fit again by morning light."

"There's nothing that can be done?"

Shamus sighed heavily and shook his head. "No miracles, my lady. But he is strong and will ride it out as he's done before."

"I'll stay with him, Mr. Sterns."

Shamus regarded her narrowly. "Why would ye do that?"

"To free you for your duties. I've no wish to run aground. My freedom lies in New Orleans. I will watch over him and do what I can to make him comfortable."

"'Twould lighten my load considerably, Miss Montgomery." That was as close as she would ever get to gratitude from the surly sailor. He stood with reluctance, saying, "Send for me if you need to . . . if it gets too much for you to handle." That sounded ominous, but Eliza refused to waver. Shamus sighed again, this time with resignation. "I'll look in when I can."

With her brief nod, Eliza accepted responsibility for the fate of his captain, and Shamus didn't look pleased with that prospect.

"Go tend to the ship, Mr. Sterns. We will be fine here."

With a last look at the figure huddled beneath the blankets, Shamus sketched a curt bow to Eliza and carried the log's coordinates above.

Leaving her alone to face Jean-Luc's demons of delirium.

Chapter 12

By nightfall, it was almost more than she could handle.

Once the wracking chills abated, Jean-Luc began to toss off the cocooning covers as fever consumed him in a roaring blast. He tore at his shirt with restless gestures, anxiously seeking cool air against the scorch of his skin.

"Let me," Eliza offered, pushing his ineffectual hands aside to efficiently strip off his shirt, then his boots. He quieted briefly and turned a momentarily lucid gaze upon her.

"I thought I told you to leave me alone."

"So you did, Captain. And I thought you'd have learned by now that I'm not one for taking orders."

"Where's Shamus?"

"Steering us into Gulf waters at your command."

He nodded at that, his overly bright eyes closing. When they opened again, the edge of alertness had dulled considerably.

"Who's at the helm?" he asked again.

"Shamus," she told him patiently a second time.

He rolled his head from side to side, his gaze losing its focus. She wasn't sure he'd heard her.

"Jean-Luc?" She touched her palm to his forehead, alarmed by the searing heat.

"Je ne me sens pas bien. J'ai mal à la tête."

"I'm sorry. I don't understand." She'd taken conversational French as a young woman, and was versed in polite parlor chatter. Unfortunately, the phrases she knew were useless, and he spoke too fast for her to translate more than a few scattered words. "Your head? Your head aches?"

"Oui. J'ai mal ici." To stress his meaning, he slipped his hand over hers where it rested upon his brow, gripping it anxiously, then pushing it away. *"Il fait chaud.* So hot . . . go away. *Allez-vous en!"*

His agitation grew into a forceful thrashing as heat consumed him from within. Hoping to calm him, Eliza bathed his face and bare chest with a cool damp cloth, trying to detach her thoughts from the chiseled perfection of his features and intriguing swells of his muscular torso detailed in passing. When she draped the freshly moistened cloth across his brow, his restlessness eased.

"Merci. Je vais mieu."

She took it to mean he felt better and was relieved. But it was too soon to feel confident. The fever quickly reasserted itself, and she spent the next hours routinely cooling him with the sponging baths and physically stilling his frantic struggles, exhausting work that showed no signs of ending. She was able to take a short break when Shamus stopped to check on him. She used the time to consume several mugs of strong coffee and stretch her sore muscles. The meal she had more than earned went untouched.

Jean-Luc didn't know his friend. Fever-glazed eyes held no recognition as his gaze wandered the room in erratic circles. Frowning slightly, Shamus pressed the back of his hand to one flushed cheek and pronounced, " 'Tis the worst of it he's fighting now. Once the fever breaks, 'twill be better." He glanced up, and for the first time, no hostility shone in his eyes. "You are doing a fine job, lass. My thanks."

Eliza was too overwhelmed to do more than nod.

The minute the brawny seaman left the cabin, Luc's concentration seemed to gather. "Shamus?"

Eliza rose up wearily. "I'll fetch him for you."

But Luc rambled on, apparently unaware of his surroundings and who was or was not with him. "Shamus, see what they've done. See what the bastards have done to me." And he put out his hand, the one with the distorted joints, and said in an oddly sober voice, "I cannot remain on the sea lest I have one hand for the ship and one hand for myself. I won't let them steal that from me as well. Go on. Do it now . . . all at once. I can bear it, I swear to you. Promise you'll set them squarely so one day I can close them around the neck of that son of a bitch, Montgomery. Promise me, Shamus, then do it, quickly. Do it now." His eyes squeezed shut, and his features set as if in preparation for the agony to come.

Gently, Eliza enveloped his unsteady hand between both of her own, bringing it up against her tear-dampened cheek. "No one will harm you, Captain. 'Tis but a memory from the past that troubles you." Her lips brushed along the ridge of his knuckles, her heart breaking at the thought of his bravery and his pain. "Hush now, Jean-Luc. 'Tis the fever that feeds your fears."

His fingers opened to stroke along her jaw. When Eliza gazed down at him, she thought awareness sparked in his eyes, he was staring at her so intently.

Then, with a low, tortured cry, he pulled her down to him, his arms enfolding her in a fierce embrace. She could feel his kisses, hard and frantic against her hairline, and the soft moan of his voice as he wept raggedly against her ear.

"Oh, Evonne. Evie, I am sorry. Forgive me. I could not protect you. I know not how to avenge you. *Je suis de bon coeur. Je suis désolé.* I will never love again."

Caught in his embrace, Eliza drew an anguished breath. Who was this Evonne who had broken his heart? A lover? A wife? Someone he'd cared for so dearly he clung to the memory still. Uncomfortable with his misplaced mourning, Eliza leaned away.

"Jean-Luc, I am not your Evie."

He searched her face in confusion, breath escaping him in rapids gasps. It caught in a hoarse sob of grief. "You are not Evonne."

"No, I am Eliza."

He shook his head in a dazed fashion, her name meaning nothing to him in his fever-fed state. He touched his fingertips to her lips. "You are very beautiful. Are you an angel?"

She smiled. "No."

Comprehension lit his gaze. "Oh. *Excusez-moi, mademoiselle. Vous êtes une prostituée.*"

Before she could protest that startling assumption and what she feared might follow, she was surprised again by his abject apology.

"*Pardon, ma belle.* I have mislead you. I have no coins to spend on you or your sisters. I must go."

When he began to lever himself up on his elbows, Eliza stopped him with a hand upon his bare chest. "Stay, Captain. Rest awhile. There is no charge."

He sagged back down with a grateful sigh. "*Merci.* You are most generous." His eyes closed, flickered, opened again. "But I am taking your bed."

Anxious to keep him quiet, she said, "We shall share it, if that is all right with you."

He nodded that it was, too drained by sickness to

think up an objection. He raised his arm, opening a tempting cove next to his body. Unable to do otherwise, Eliza sank down beside him, gasping slightly when he hugged her in close so that her head was pillowed in the lea of his shoulder and her figure molded along his strapping length. She felt his chest expand in a sigh.

"*Bonsoir*, m'am'selle."

"Sleep well, Jean-Luc," was her husky reply. She could feel the pound of his pulse beneath her palm gradually slowing as he surrendered to a weary slumber. And he slept while she lay agonizingly awake.

So this was what it was like to bed down with a man for the night.

She'd never shared her bed with anyone save a cocker spaniel pup when she was a child. This was completely different. She was aware of the hot male scent of his fevered skin, of the pulse of his heart beneath her hand, of his sleek, hard near-nakedness. He was asleep. She could have slipped away without disturbing him. What kept her at his side were thoughts more disturbing than she wanted to examine.

Eliza closed her eyes, lost to the swirl of confusing sentiments.

And even as she reveled in the comfort of Black Heart's embrace, she sent out a desperate prayer that rescue would soon find her—while she could yet be saved.

Jonathon Prine locked up the customshouse as usual, but instead of beginning his solitary walk to his boardinghouse rooms, he turned covertly into a darkened alley and into the arms of his love. Their kiss was hurried and fueled with the danger of what they were doing. Finally, he broke away breathlessly only to hear the same lament he'd been ignoring for the past few days.

"Jonathon, we must act now. 'Tis too risky to go on as we have. You forget how easily I could be recognized; then all would be for naught." Of late, her melodious tones had taken on a strident quality he did not like. But then she was kissing him again and he forgot his objection.

"Please, Sweet Pea, you know how this intrigue distresses me. Why can we not be honest in our approach of your father?"

Her laugh was harsh, almost insulting. "You do not know my father. He would never consent to this match."

"But think of the worry you've put the poor devil through, believing you in the hands of cutthroat pirates."

Philomena Montgomery smiled, pleased by the notion of her father's despair. Fair recompense for all the trouble he'd put her through to thwart his bullying plans. She sweetened that smile to bedazzle her love. "Oh, Jonathon, don't you think I wish it could be another way? I know you will prove yourself worthy in his eyes, but for now this is the only way we can be together. Would you rather I be in England suffering the court of countless noblemen?"

Jonathon scowled at that, and his impassioned embrace tightened until she squealed in delight.

"Oh, my love, you do understand that there can be no other way for us to be wed. Providence has bought us the time we need to escape my father's yoke. No one suspects that silly merchant captain put me secretly ashore thinking he was helping to save my life." She laughed at the man's gullibility. All men, she'd found, were easily led, all but her father. That was why this deception was so delicious and it was so imperative that she succeed.

She stroked the young clerk's lapels. "Come away, Jonathon. Let us flee to Marblehead, where I've friends that will hide and abet us in our struggle toward happiness. We can be wed there and live secretly as man and wife. By the time my father discovers I've not been kidnapped, I should be hopefully ripe with a Montgomery heir."

Jonathon blushed, disturbed by her blunt speech and a little bit by her aggressive manner. He told himself that it didn't make her less the gentle girl he loved. It just proved how intolerable their situation had become to so harden her tender spirit toward trickery of those who loved her.

Sensing his worry, Philomena smiled and leaned up against him, coaxing his arm about her once more. Her melting gaze befuddled his mind and scrambled his protests.

"Just think, Jonathon. By the time we seek our slumber on the morrow, it will be as man and wife. And when I've conceived our child and present myself upon my family's doorstep, they will be so happy to see me safe, they will not think to deny us our future together. Do you want to go on grubbing for a living under the customshouse rule when you could be counting money for my father, our moneys?"

Jonathon said nothing for a moment, considering the lure of what she presented: a beautiful, wealthy wife; a fat, lucrative business future.

"I'll turn in my notice in the morning, withdraw all my funds, and we can be off before noon. And by nightfall, you will be Mistress Prine." He hugged her enthusiastically, missing her smug smile of victory.

Now her father would know her wishes were not

to be denied. Let him fret about her fate for a time so he would truly appreciate her.

Caught up in her private schemes, Philomena easily forgot the word she'd given to Eliza, for what right did a lowly bond servant have to demand her fate be weighed as more important than her mistress's happiness?

Luc woke to the cool pastels of daybreak and to a sketchy memory of the past dozen hours. His fever had crested in the early hours of dawn, finally allowing him some rest. He held to vague remembrances of someone's gentle care, of cold cloths applied to his aching head soothing away the heat and relentless pain. The lull of soft assurances, the tender regard of a sea-green gaze. All his senses snapped to a sudden attention around that one detail.

Eliza.

Had hers been the touch that quieted his fears? Hers the calming whispers he clung to when all else spun so maddeningly out of his control? Hers the unfamiliar form nestled up against him in the night? Or was it all part of the delirium baking his brain?

He opened his eyes carefully, slitting them against the brightening sky reflected off the Gulf waters that carried them toward his home. He could tell by the movement of the ship, by the lap of the waves against the hull, that they were making good time under a full parade of sails. Shamus had seen to his orders. And Eliza had seen to him.

She was standing at the windows, staring pensively over their wake, over waters she'd travel soon in a return to her life a world away. She was dressed once more in her crumpled gown, her hair a tumble of fiery curls about the fatigued slump of her shoulders. Her features were drawn and wan with worry and some woebegone sentiment that struck a poignant chord within his heart. Was it her fate she feared for or what passed between them that wore so on her spirit? He hoped it was the former.

He shifted slightly upon the bed, and her attention came round immediately, her gaze alight with concern. A fragile smile played about her lips when she saw he was awake.

"Good morning, Captain. I see you have indeed survived."

"With, I suspect, you to thank for it."

She shrugged off his compliment. "You give me too much credit, sir. The battle was yours, fairly won. How do you feel?"

He took a brief assessment and reported, "Like I have escaped from hell slightly worse for wear." But, he had to admit, not as bad as he usually did when rousing from the fever's grasp. Ordinarily, he woke to a sticky unpleasantness reminiscent of a night soaking in bilge water, sweat caked upon his skin as if he were a cask of salted meat in the galley. He placed his palm upon his bare chest, finding his flesh cool and clean, with all the residue rinsed away. He was covered by a fresh sheet, though the one beneath him was still soggy and stiff. She'd bathed him . . .

In some alarm, he lifted the sheet to peer below, seeing nothing but naked skin all the way to his toes.

. . . all of him.

When he glanced back at Eliza in an inexplicable embarrassment, he found her head purposefully averted. Was she blushing? Would she stammer some apology that would make everything so much more awkward?

No, she did not. Instead, she remarked in an admirably level voice, "When you feel up to it, Captain,

I'll fetch you some clean clothes and order you breakfast."

He slumped back against his sodden pillow, his dazed mind trying to take it all in. She'd cared for him during his fevered ramblings, had lain beside him, offering comfort and her own heat, had cooled him and washed him—all over—and now was waiting to call for his breakfast.

A sudden tightening about his chest sent alarm spiking through him. He chose to call that anxiousness suspicion, though it could well have been something else altogether.

The worst part of his malady wasn't the discomfort or even the unexpectedness with which it struck; it was the helplessness, the absolute vulnerability while in its thrall. The idea of being without wits or resources while dependent upon the aid of another put a terrible fear into him, a frustrated dread only Shamus knew and understood. And only Shamus was trusted with his weakness.

Until now.

Until this woman of despised background became privy to his secrets, stripping him bare.

It scared him into a fierce defensiveness.

What would she do with this knowledge? What repayment would she demand? Would she hold her acts of mercy over his head, expecting leniency from him? Perhaps free passage back to her hated family? His dark eyes studied her with an angry speculation. Now would come the shameless bartering, the carving away at his conscience, the blatant manipulation of his momentary failing into leverage for personal gain. His mouth thinned into a bitter line as he waited.

"Who is Evonne?"

The question struck like a lightning bolt flashing

down from a cloudless sky. "Where did you hear that name?" His accusation was soft and stricken, bringing her about in a posture of apology.

"You spoke of her . . . last night." She was quick to take in his dramatic pallor, his anguished gaze that said clearly that she'd wounded him to the marrow. "Forgive me, Captain. I've meddled in something too personal."

Her sincerity shook him back to his senses. He sucked a cleansing breath. "She was my sister. She's dead."

Tears swam in her gaze, making her eyes gentle seas of sympathy. "I'm sorry—"

"It was many years ago," he answered curtly. Then his tone deepened slightly. "What did I say?"

"You mistook me for her." She didn't want to draw that explanation out any further.

He stared at her for a silent moment, then said, "Yes, I can see the resemblance now. Not in the face but—" He broke off before he made a fool of himself by canonizing her brave spirit.

Eliza smiled faintly. "You also mistook me for a harlot."

Black brows soared. "Did I? I did not pay you for any services not rendered, did I?"

"Your purse is safe with me, Monsieur Pirate. My services do not come with a fee attached." Then realizing what she'd just said, a fierce stain of crimson rose in her cheeks. Again, her gaze darted away from his shyly, yet when it returned, she met his stare with a stoic grace. "Would you like your meal now, Captain?"

"I would like my trousers first, if you do not mind."

When he sat up, she followed the drop of the sheet to where it pooled about his hips. A glimpse of pale flank was enough to send her skittering about in search of his clothing. Blood warmed her face, for try as she might, she could not dismiss from her mind the sight of him in all his naked splendor. She'd done nothing wrong in removing his sweat-soaked garb. Her first and only thought had been of his comfort and recovery. She'd tried to bathe him modestly with her eyes averted, but the blind fumbling proved more distressing than the purposeful cleansing with Samaritan intentions.

She passed the trousers back to him without a glance in his direction and stood stiff and still while listening to the shush of the canvas drawn up over his long legs.

"I'll call for breakfast." Her voice was oddly hushed.

"*Non.* I should like to go above first."

He didn't need to elaborate. He needed to put in an appearance so his crew wouldn't speculate about his absence.

However, Jean-Luc overestimated his strength. He was able to stand, but balance was beyond him. Eliza stepped up to hitch an arm about his middle, steadying him.

"Captain?"

"I am fine," he growled.

"You're weak as a kitten and have no business tending to your ship in this condition."

"Do not scold me, mademoiselle. I do what I must."

"Then you will do so with my assistance."

"No!" The idea appalled him.

"You were not so stubborn last night. I must say, I rather prefer you out of your head than out of your mind, which you must be now to insist upon this foolishness. Lean here." She'd brought him to the table, leaving him to the support of his chair back while she found a clean shirt in his sea chest. He allowed her to drape it about his shoulders before he started determinedly toward the door. His steps wobbled, forcing him into a humiliating dependence upon Eliza's slender shoulders for balance. The moment they topped the deck, he stepped free of her, holding to the rail for orientation. She watched in begrudging admiration as he squared up beneath the attention of his crew, and save for his poor color, none would guess what torture he'd endured over the last twelve hours.

"Captain," Shamus called gladly. "The helm be yours and welcome to it."

"Thank you, Mr. Sterns."

And as he went to take control, Eliza got her first glimpse of their destination. Of New Orleans, where the truth would finally catch up to her.

Chapter 13

Though it looked like any other port town, Eliza was quick to notice the differences in New Orleans. The heat was the most apparent: a sticky, thick, moisture-laden air that clung to the skin and soaked up the scents of the dock area like a redolent sponge. The sound was unique, too, laced with foreign cadences: the richly musical French, the earthy patois of the natives, the mysterious East Indian accents from the bearers on the wharf. Whereas New England was crisp and clean, New Orleans was musky and exotic. To Eliza, it felt both magical and malevolent.

As soon as the *Galant* was adequately moored, the crew was quick to scramble ashore, grabbing up armfuls of the dusky beauties who lingered there, laughingly displaying their charms. The blatancy shocked Eliza, who knew well what sailors did in port behind closed doors, but nevertheless was stunned to witness the lusty rituals right out in the open air. She averted her eyes, peeping occasionally as the crewmen hurried their giggling ladies to the nearest establishments where they would soak up rum and more of the bartered delights.

Waiting anxiously for direction, she looked to Jean-Luc, who was busy securing his ship. Once that was done, he strode for the gang plank with an unwavering stride, his weakness overcome. Never once did he glance her way. Apparently, she was to be handled as cargo, not as a companion. His snub made that abundantly clear.

"Come with me, Miss Montgomery," Shamus said from her side. His hand curled firmly about her elbow, steering her toward the shore. A prisoner.

Though dressed no differently from the rest of his men, Luc wasn't swarmed by the port's harlots. Perhaps it was his unsmiling visage that warned them away or the air of intense distraction that told them he was looking for something other than a warm and willing armful. He stood planted on the dock, looking about, his gaze never touching upon any of the lewd females casting luring looks his way.

"Eh, Jean-Luc!"

Just as Shamus and Eliza came up behind him, Luc was approached by the hailer. If a pirate could be recognized at first sight, this man was one, with his gleaming gold tooth and multihooped ears and garish selection of clothing and jewels. He grinned broadly as he pumped the more reserved Frenchman's hand and that expression widened to include Eliza as his speculative gaze swept her from top to bottom. She repressed a shiver beneath that crude undressing stare.

Luc was quick to rid himself of the clutching hand and wasted no time with pleasantries. *"Comment ça va, Etienne. Y a-t-il des messages pour moi?"*

"Messages? Oui. Un moment. First, you come with me. I get you rooms . . . nice rooms. Come." He gestured and grinned some more, and though Luc was obviously impatient, he followed, trailing Shamus and Eliza behind him.

Nice rooms. Eliza held to her dismay as she

scanned the filthy squalor of Etienne's establishment. One glance into the parlor room told her plainly what type of business was conducted under his roof. Ladies in various stages of undress fawned over men, mostly sailors, who were involved at cards and drink. A huge man, the first African Eliza had ever seen close up, stood guard at the bottom of the winding staircase. He was magnificent with his ebony skin and flashing dark eyes. She tried not to stare, but every place she looked startled her sensibilities.

"What you think, Jean-Luc? Nice place, eh? How many rooms you need? One for the *belle fille* and another for you?"

"One room."

Etienne gave a sly chuckle. "*Oui*, one room and a promise no one will disturb you. First, we share a drink, *non*? A toast to your journey and your return home."

The grinning bordello owner wound his way back to a corner table, waving Luc into one of the seats and collapsing into the other. He glared up at Shamus and growled, "You. Fetch us a bottle and glasses."

Shamus stood his ground until Luc nodded up at him. Left alone, Eliza crowded in close behind the French captain's chair, seeking shelter from the hungry gazes of the men around her. She refused to call on Jean-Luc for a sign of his protection. She wasn't at all sure he would extend it.

"What news do you have for me, Etienne?"

"The drinks first, Jean-Luc. It is unlike you to rush things. You would have me believe it is the information and not my company that brings you here as my guest." Etienne pouted, hoping to win an apology, but Luc offered none. The greedy gaze rose once again to Eliza, taking her measure. "A comely wench, Jean-Luc. After all these years, I was beginning to think you did not favor the company of women." His smirk was vile and suggestive.

"Not women I have to pay for," was Luc's bland reply.

"This one then is not . . . uh . . . a working woman?"

"*Non*. She has other value to me."

Etienne sighed dramatically. "A pity. So fresh. She would bring a ransom."

Luc did smile then, a thin close-lipped smile. "That is my hope." He looked about for Shamus but couldn't spot the burly seaman in the cramped quarters.

Eliza smelled the man before she actually saw him. Waves of particularly offensive odor swept over her: sweat, heat, dirt, and other best unnamed scents. He'd angled up behind her so silently, she had no warning until he reached out to touch her sleeve, rubbing the silky material between filthy fingers. She gave a start and shrank against Jean-Luc, repelled by the sight of beady ratlike eyes and a leering gap-toothed smile.

"How much for the night with you?" he asked, lust thickening a nearly undecipherable accent that was not quite French but an earthier, muddied variation.

"You could not afford me," she hissed. "Go away."

"An hour, then. 'Tis long enough to get things done. Several times."

She pulled away from his pawing hands, disgust curdling in her belly. "No." She was aware of Luc's disinterest in her plight as he continued talking with Etienne. Anger and a deeper fright shivered through her.

The swamp rat persisted, edging closer until she was backed into the corner, nearly overpowered by his stench. His hands were surprisingly agile, roaming her breasts, her hips, tangling in her hair.

"Leave me alone." She struggled to make her tone

curt, without a quiver of the distress she felt while batting his hands away. "There are others here who would welcome your coin."

"But none of them I like so well as you."

She felt a sudden chill as a piece of silver was dropped down the front of her gown, catching between her breasts.

"For a touch or two. Right here."

And before she could fish out the presumptuous payment, his dirty hands were rucking up her skirts, running roughly over the bared flesh of her thighs. Horrified, she thrust up her knee to block his fumbling, catching him in the chin and clacking his remaining teeth together. He backed away, but only to reassess the situation. Rubbing his jaw, he glared at her through black eyes bright with fury. Eliza knew right then he wasn't going to leave her alone until he found some satisfaction.

Panicked by the feral meanness in his glare, she petitioned desperately, "Please. I cannot take your money. I—I belong to him." And her hands closed rather frantically upon Jean-Luc's shoulders, calling upon him to intercede. She lifted her chin proudly, defiantly. "Perhaps you have heard of him. Coeur Noir."

She could see the name sinking in through the haze of cheap rum. The ferret blinked, his beady gaze going from the rounded swell of her breasts to the back of Luc's dark head.

"Coeur Noir," he breathed anxiously. Yes, he knew the name. Then he laughed, smirking at her. "But everyone knows—Black Heart, he don't like the ladies."

She took a giant leap of faith, letting her arms curl about Luc's neck, crouching down to hug him close, her breasts flattening against his back. "He likes this one," she said with a confidence she didn't feel.

Her accoster hesitated. He stiffened when Luc turned to stare at him with a darkly dangerous impassivity. He didn't want to get tangled up with the likes of the infamous privateer. "Be that true, Black Heart. Is she your woman?"

Eliza met Luc's unreadable stare. Their faces were only inches apart. She allowed a trace of pleading to appear in her gaze, asking for his support. He looked up at the impatient Cajun.

"I have no woman."

Eliza's gasp was audible as the Cajun grinned wide and reached down for her. Luc intercepted his hand, cuffing his wrist with a steely grip.

"But she is my property," he clarified, the chill of his words as unarguable as the certain death in his challenging stare.

The swamp rat had enough vermin intelligence to know not to press his luck, but he was still out his money. He stabbed a grubby finger at Eliza's cleavage. "She has me coin."

Luc swiveled on his chair. He hooked a forefinger in the neckline of Eliza's gown and pulled the fabric away from her bosom. Then he dipped the other hand down between the warm soft press of her breasts, ignoring her startled stiffening, to come up with the piece of silver, now well warmed from the heat of her flesh. He tossed it to the Cajun.

"Spend it elsewhere," was Luc's advice, readily taken. The threat gone, Luc turned back to his conversation, Eliza dismissed from mind without a glance.

His property. Eliza trembled with shock and indignant rage. Her hand flattened against her chest, where her heart raced and her skin yet tingled from the invasion of his impersonal touch. She was panting heav-

ily, shaken by the encounter, stunned by Luc's
indifferent claim. *Property.* Rebellion crushed her fear
of moments ago, starching her spine. How dare he!

Anxious to put some distance between them, Eliza
started to stand, only to find herself the center of Luc's
attention once more. He reached out to snag a handful
of her hair, drawing downward to force her to her
knees beside his chair.

"Better you not make a spectacle of yourself, *chérie,*
lest I be pushed to bloodshed in your defense."

"In defense of my trade value, you mean," she spat
at him, using her piercing words to show displeasure,
since his grip discouraged struggle.

"*Exactement.* Sit and behave like the chattel you
are."

Still seething, she settled herself on the dirty floor
at his feet, hating the submissive pose but smart
enough to recognize its inherent wisdom. If she stood,
she would only draw the notice of some other lusty
fool, and the next one might be too lost to rum to pay
mind to Luc's intimidation. He was protecting her.
What did it matter why?

He didn't release his grip on her hair. Instead, he
pulled her over so that her head rested against one
taut-muscled thigh. With her cheek squashed against
the rough canvas of his trousers, she trembled with
an anger best restrained.

"Ah! Here's your man with our drinks," Etienne
exclaimed, cheerfully relieving Shamus of the glasses.
The burly seaman spared a curious glance at Eliza,
then took a stand behind Luc's chair, providing a barrier for his back. "What shall we toast, Jean-Luc?"

"To whatever information you're holding from
me?"

Etienne laughed. "Very well, *mon ami.* Word has
come from your first mate, Benji Symms. He says to

tell you that all goes as planned. Your wishes have been relayed, and the other party is anxious to bend to your will. Whatever that means."

Eliza knew what it meant. Shock had her clutching at Luc's long leg. Montgomery was eager to pay a pirate kidnapper for the release of his daughter.

But she wasn't his daughter.

How could Montgomery not know that?

Her thoughts reeled at that knowledge, struggling to find some explanation. Had Philomena failed to return with news of the deception? Was Montgomery setting a trap for the crew of the *Galant* by playing along with the lie?

Whatever truth lay behind the message from Montgomery, one thing was very clear to her. It wouldn't matter if she told the truth about the switch of identities. Luc would never believe her. He would consider it a poor attempt to escape before the ransom was paid.

She was trapped in the role of Philomena.

As she sagged dispiritedly against his thigh, the clutch of Luc's hand in her hair subtly shifted to an absent stroking. Her mood was soothed by the change even before her mind was aware of the way his fingers twined and lightly teased through the red-gold tangle. Too weary and worried to cast up any further rebellion, she leaned against him with her eyes closed, allowing the repetitive gesture to quiet her misgivings. Her palm rubbed innocently up the inside of his leg.

Suddenly, Luc stood, shaking her off his lap. She gazed up at him through dazed and questioning eyes, puzzled by his look of cold annoyance.

"You said you had a room, Etienne. Show us there. Once I am rid of this distraction, we can settle in for some serious conversation."

Etienne grinned. "I shall have a new bottle opened. This way."

Eliza plodded behind the two men, with Shamus bringing up the rear. She was uncomfortably aware of the feral Cajun's glare following her across the room from where he sat with his cronies, sharing a skinny tired girl between them. Probably all they could afford. Eliza felt a pang of pity for the unfortunate creature.

For all the slovenly appearance of the lower rooms, the upstairs quarters were surprisingly pleasant. Dominated by a big, net-draped canopy bed, there was also a mismatched table covered with colorful bottles of oils and scents. Full-length windows served as a doorway to the second-floor balcony, but upon closer examination, Eliza saw that they were nailed shut, either to keep the unsavory inhabitants of the neighborhood out or to lock the ladies of the house in. Scant, heavily perfumed air trickled in through the louvered slats of the closed shutters.

After glancing about and finding the room agreeable, Jean-Luc produced a set of iron shackles, closing a cuff about one of her wrists before she thought to protest. The other he snapped about the sturdy iron frame of the bed. She pulled against the short two-foot length of chain in dismay.

"What is this?"

"The means to guarantee you will not escape me." And he showed her the key, strung on the thong that held the Montgomery medallion.

With a snarl of fury, she lunged at him, wishing to scratch his emotionless eyes out, but the chain jerked her up, spinning her about to drop upon the bed with the whiplash of momentum.

"Do not wait up for me, *chérie*." Sketching her a

mock bow, he strode out, a frowning Shamus closing the door to her prison.

For several minutes, she vented her ire by calling him every vile name she could think of, then several more, arranging those slurs into different combinations. Finally, her fury exhausted, she slumped back on the bed to consider her situation. *His property. His prisoner.* In his bed. She jumped off the counterpane in agitation and paced to the limit of her iron leash.

An hour passed, then two, and a quiet knock sounded on the door before it swung open to reveal Shamus. He stepped back to motion to someone behind him. Eliza watched, bemused, as a large metal tub was brought in and quickly filled with steaming water. After dismissing the bearers, Shamus unlocked her cuff, observing with some disapproval as she rubbed her chafed wrist.

"Compliments of the captain?" she asked, eyeing the tub with both longing and irritation. How dare he think he could buy her compliance so cheaply?

"No, my lady. Mine. I thought you might appreciate the wash and a change from your rather ripe attire."

She blushed as she considered the stained and sweat-soiled gown she'd worn throughout her captivity. "I appreciate it greatly, Mr. Sterns. Only what am I to put on?"

He extended a thin white wrapper, explaining as her color deepened, "It was the most modest I could find"—he glanced about. "Considering."

She took the filmy garment gingerly. "Thank you, again, sir." She looked to the tub, then to the corridor behind him. "I would not care to be disturbed."

Shamus actually smiled. "I will lock the door behind me. You needn't worry about the captain. He is . . . um . . . occupied for at least the next hour."

Eliza flushed, clutching the gown to her. Was he trying as delicately as possible to tell her Jean-Luc was visiting one of the neighboring rooms? That knowledge left a bitter taste instead of relief. "I shall enjoy the bath and the change of clothing, Mr. Sterns, but pray, what did I do to earn such consideration from you? Last I knew, you were ready and willing to slay me and send my carcass back to Salem."

Shamus shifted uneasily at that reminder. "It's to thank you, my lady, for seeing to the captain when the fever laid him low."

"I would have done the same for any creature so obviously suffering."

Her curt reply didn't lessen his gesture of thanks, for he bowed to her and bid her to enjoy her privacy.

After hearing the lock shot home, Eliza wasted no time preparing for her bath. Sniffing at each one of the glass bottles on the table, she found a pleasingly scented oil and sprinkled it atop the heated water. Then, with a deep, gratified sigh, she sank in, knees to her chest, and let the soothing scent and penetrating warmth ply the tension from both body and mind.

Even with Shamus's assurances, she didn't dare linger. After a vigorous scrubbing of skin and hair, she dried off and slipped into the scandalous covering. It was billowy, the folds of fabric not quite making up for the diaphanous quality of the material. In the moonlit room, she was fairly certain it would provide an appropriate covering, but when a knock at the door came again, she was unwilling to test that theory. The spread from the bed made an ample wrap about her as servants trudged in to remove the tub and Shamus lifted the open cuff to the shackles.

"Forgive me, my lady. Captain's orders." He looked genuinely saddened, so she gave in without struggle, providing her small wrist for the cold metal bracelet. It weighed heavily upon her spirits as she sat once more alone in the room.

She could hear someone playing a piano badly in one of the rooms below. Laughter and muffled voices wafted up from the parlor. And through the thin walls, she could hear other sounds, sounds that made her flush with embarrassment even in her solitude. Love sounds: husky whispers, creaking bed frames, escalating moans, and lusty bugles of completion.

And as she listened to the passion plays going on in all rooms but hers, she wondered if Jean-Luc was in one of them, sating his lusts with another.

The image wounded. For suddenly, unwittingly, she was assailed by sensations—the velvety seduction of his kiss; the taut texture of his man's body, hard and powerful; the ache of anticipation flooding to her female places at the thought of his embrace. The unexpected claim of intimacy, whether a planned possession or not, still made her his. First, for always. Nothing would ever change that, no matter how many careful lies she spun to convince everyone—and herself—otherwise.

He was the first to breach her innocence.

And the knowledge that he was elsewhere sharing those lessons with another wrought more misery than she could bear.

Chapter 14

❧

Luc sat in the noisy parlor room, trying to focus upon the glass in front of him when his attention had a maddening wont to stray upstairs.

Unlike the other members of his crew, he avoided Etienne's harlots to concentrate on his fairly good wine. He kept to a back table, where he had a clear view of the room while he remained hidden in shadow. A long bout of moody silence had encouraged the persistently affable Etienne to leaving him alone. Now, left to his own company, he only had to endure an occasional sullen glance from Shamus, who sat across the room, an eager wench in his lap.

He knew the cause of his second mate's displeasure. The same plague as his own.

Eliza Montgomery.

Chained upstairs like a beast, probably still cursing his every ancestor. The thought should have amused him. It did not. Nothing concerning her was as it should be.

He hated the idea of the shackles, but he couldn't risk losing her in a place such as this. And he didn't trust himself to be her guard. He'd gone suddenly insane whenever she was around him, and he was at a loss as to the cure. Distance seemed to help, but still, images of her prowled restlessly through his mind. It was insanity. That was the only explanation for one willful female's raining havoc upon all his careful plans.

He was not a man to step off a path once chosen. Eliza had him wandering in crazy circles, doubting his heart, his mind, and his right to demand what was denied him. She was just a woman, no better, no worse than any crowded in this room. Except she had all her teeth and smelled nicer. If it was an ease to his lusting he sought, why wouldn't any of them serve just as well?

But they wouldn't.

The few wantons brave enough to approach him stirred nothing but annoyance, no matter how much mounded flesh they dangled before his eyes. Contrary to the snide rumors, he'd had a healthy appetite for pleasure in his younger years, bedding many a willing wench from chambermaid to aristocrat with equal aplomb. But his life had taken a drastic turn with the death of his family. New purpose steeled him against distraction, and female company was a distraction not difficult for him to ignore. He'd made a vow in his muddied yard where crimson stained the puddles in which he knelt, a promise never to allow emotion to tear his world asunder.

From that point on, he'd schooled himself mercilessly to feel nothing, to reveal nothing. He'd become Coeur Noir, a dark specter haunting the seas, all the more frightening because he seemed detached from recognizable cause. He wasn't moved by greed or personal loyalty, or enslaved to any master. His agenda was his own, shared with none but Shamus, who'd been witness to his reasons. Those reasons drove him night and day, with memories more punishing than any lash.

He'd been so close to freeing himself from the yoke of his promises when Montgomery's treachery took everything away from him again. The agony he'd suffered in captivity only reinforced those goals, narrowing his dark intentions along one single line of vengeance. Eliza Montgomery was the key to all and also the lock barring him from it.

He refused to believe he cared for her.

That would be too cruel a twist after all the sorrow he'd known.

Yet if it was not an affliction of the heart, why was he so hesitant to claim his reward for her exchange when it was what he'd striven for, plotted for, and now was reluctant to pursue?

He didn't want to give her up. That was the crux of it, and it was driving him to frustration. Of all the women he could court and claim once this all was over, she would be the one he couldn't have. The only one he wanted.

He swallowed down another glass of wine, but the warming in his belly was mild compared to the burning in his heart.

Another glass set down upon the tabletop, startling him out of his morose thoughts. Shamus settled in the opposite seat, the look of reproach making Luc wish him away.

"You looked so wretched, I couldn't leave you alone whilst you flailed yourself with guilt."

Luc blinked, unaware his feelings were so transparent.

Shamus smiled ruefully. "Oh, don't fret over it. None but myself could see behind that mask you wear so well."

"Since you are so prophetic this evening, what guilt am I tortured by?"

"The sins of the world, if you thought you could carry them," the Irishman grumbled.

Luc bristled up behind his impenetrable facade. "You mock me."

Shamus laughed. "Nay. I admire you. You would be worthless as a man if some remorse didn't gnaw upon your vitals at the thought of bartering away a woman you've come to fancy."

Luc went still, his features freezing over in disciplined denial. He needn't have bothered. Shamus saw right through it.

"Lad, you cannot have both the lady and the legacy of revenge Mr. Symms even now sets forth in Salem."

"I know."

"Decide which means more to you—Montgomery's money or his daughter."

It sounded so simple. It should have been simple. "The one is mine to take. The other I must fetter to hold. I cannot see a choice, *mon ami.*"

"There are always choices, Luc. Always. You must live by the ones you make. Perhaps it's time you put away your graveside oaths and thought to see to your own happiness instead."

Emotions flashed like strobes of lightning through the tormented blackness of his gaze. *"Non!* How can I find happiness with her—with anyone—until I'm worthy? I will not make another commitment I cannot keep. I will not allow those I—"

"Love?" Shamus supplied softly.

Luc took a shaky breath, but his conclusion was fiercely steady. "I will not allow those I love to suffer for my vain promises. Never again. I will not take what I cannot keep. I will not desire that which I cannot protect. I have nothing, Shamus. I have no power, no possessions. I do not mind that for myself, but I will not subject another to the uncertainty of my lot.

It would be too . . . hard." And the quaver of that last word betrayed him.

"Luc, you cannot bring them back. You cannot change what happened. If 'twere possible, I would have sacrificed anything to make it so. You know that, don't you? Don't you?"

He dropped his gaze and murmured an unconvincing, *"Oui."*

And Shamus knew that even after all the time they'd spent together, he'd never really been forgiven for the deeds of the past. That was his hell to bear.

"Happiness," the young Frenchman ruminated. "How can there be happiness for me? Now there is only justice. And justice will be served when Montgomery bends to give me what I deserve!" His fist pounded the tabletop, sending the liquid sloshing in their glasses. Luc quickly downed his and poured another. He must have been well in his cups because he allowed Shamus to put a hand on his shoulder. Normally, he would have shaken off such a personal gesture in a public place.

"Luc, think. Perhaps you can have your vengeance and the lady, too. Would you be satisfied taking something of equal worth from the bastard? Say, a daughter instead of a dowry?"

Luc stared at him, afraid to consider what he was suggesting.

"Would seducing or even wedding his child be an adequate revenge? It would hurt him, and his pride, deeply. Is that not something he values as much as his gold?"

The notion tempted. Eliza. *His*. Oh, how the stuffy New Englander would hate the thought of it. Would that not be a satisfying end to his vendetta? That every time he took Eliza to him as a man to his wife,

Montgomery writhed with the knowledge of that union?

But it wasn't just about what remained unsettled between him and Montgomery. Therein lay the difficulty. It was about Eliza, too.

Luc shook his head. "She would not have me, and I will not keep a woman who needs be chained to endure my presence."

"Bind her with stronger chains."

How?

He was still wondering as he wove his way rather precariously up the stairs to where Eliza waited, his prisoner.

The room was dark and stiflingly warm. For a moment, he thought he was alone, and a spear of panic pierced his chest. Then he heard the soft shush of her slumbering breath, and the tension trembled from him. As his vision adjusted to the darkness in the room, he could see her curled upon the floor at the foot of the bed, concealed beneath a heap of bedcovers. And he was as much a prisoner of the situation as she.

Sighing heavily, he stripped out of his clothes, all the way to bare skin. She'd seen him thus before, and modesty wouldn't be borne on such a sultry eve, not when fires burned from within and without. He stretched out on the bed after dropping the mosquito netting down on all sides. His eyes closed, but the vision of Eliza refused to be banished. Her sea-green gaze swimming with tears as she bent over his shipboard bedside. The haughty tip of her chin as she openly defied him when grown men quailed beneath his frigid stare. The bewitching movement of her lips, the teasing smile, the thinning of disdain, the sweet part of passion as the moisture of his kiss lingered upon them.

Groaning, he rolled onto his belly only to become more painfully aware of her effect upon him. It was like trying to rest upon a mizzen mast. He flopped over onto his back and stared blindly at the ceiling.

Bind her with stronger chains.

What did that mean?

A plague upon Shamus for giving him another worry.

The answer whispered through his thoughts like a tantalizing breeze within the sweltering room.

Seduce her.

Could she be made to love him? Would he be capable of wooing her—and to what end? She would never consent to wedding someone so beneath her, and even if she did come to care for him, she wouldn't go against her father's wishes by coupling with his enemy. Would she?

He was tormented by the remembrance of her mouth opening hungrily beneath his, receiving, encouraging him without the slightest hesitation.

And just as quickly he recalled her unmanning horror as she wept that he'd ruined her.

She would never accept him. Never. The memory of her desolation was his answer.

Eliza woke at the sound of boot steps on the floorboards. Without moving, she canted her eyes downward, hoping to discern who intruded upon her slumber. She heard his weighty sigh.

Jean-Luc.

She lay still, pretending to sleep while listening to the sounds of him disrobing, followed by the creak of the bed frame. She sniffed the air suspiciously, not jealously, she told herself, but could detect no trace of another woman's perfume. Only the bitter fruit of wine. Lots of that. He was drunk. And soon he was snoring softly in oblivion.

Now wide awake, she couldn't relax upon the hardwood floor with the whispering sounds of passion still seeping through the walls. Insects buzzed incessantly, feasting on her unprotected skin. And then she caught the movement of something low and dark scurrying along the distant baseboards. On the same floor upon which she was lying.

Rats! The place was probably infested with them. Her skin crawled with distaste, and a night upon the floor could no longer be borne.

As quietly and inconspicuously as possible, she slipped under the edge of netting and onto the bed. Luc's dark, indistinguishable shape was sprawled down the center, leaving her a scant strip along one side. Because she was yet chained to the footboard, she was forced to lie in the opposite direction.

The mattress was yielding, and the sonorous familiarity of Luc's snores oddly soothing. Though she thought it would be quite impossible, she was soon fast asleep.

Something tickled his ear. Luc muttered softly and reached to brush it away, coming into contact with ... toes?

He blinked open his eyes to find the room still draped in late-night shadow, but when he turned his head to the side, there was no mistaking one small pink female foot resting beside his head.

A foot smelling deliciously like lilacs.

The fragrance brought back a rush of wistful remembrances, of the huge bouquets arranged in various rooms from the bushes surrounding their chateau. Pristine whites, succulent purples, palest lavenders bursting with a scent he'd ever equate with home and family.

He leaned his cheek against the arch of that dainty foot and inhaled contentedly. Sweet, delicate, delightful. Like the lady.

Eliza.

He was surprised to discover her nestled in beside him. Perhaps surprised was not the right word, for he was suddenly cold sober and achingly aroused. His palm skimmed up the slender length of one leg until encountering a wrap of enticingly thin fabric.

The scented oil . . . the wispy material over soft skin . . . her presence in his bed . . . all for him?

The possibility played incredible havoc upon his senses.

It was as if heaven had delivered his every desire.

How could he refuse?

He felt her stir when he pressed his lips to the slender arch of her foot, suckling lightly upon the fresh-scrubbed skin. Her toes curled sensuously in encouragement. Or at least he took it to be so. From there, he licked his way up to her foot, laving along her toes, then sucking and chewing gently upon each one in turn. A sudden spasm shook along her leg. She was awake now. He paused but didn't stop the leisurely seduction. He continued to nibble at her toes and up her instep as he held her foot cradled in his palm. He could hear the sharply altered pattern of her breathing. But she said nothing, her expectation interwoven through the silence.

Slowly, he drew his tongue up the curve of her calf, feeling the muscles bunch and twitch along the way. When he swirled wetly beneath the crook of her knee, she gasped, a startled punctuation leading to a more rapid respiration. He felt her fingertips touch upon his hair, tentative, trembling, then twining fitfully. He needed a stronger recommendation.

"I will not go farther without your *oui* or *non*."

From the darkness came a whispered, "Yes."

Chapter 15

She woke to the wonderfully erotic feel of someone kissing her toes. She was so shockingly
aroused by the tickling, tantalizing sensations, she forgot to protest as those taunting kisses traveled up to
her knee.

It might have been a dream except she was so
acutely aware of everything: the heated brush of his
breath upon her skin, the curve of his strong fingers
conforming to the contour of her calf, the rash of overly sensitized flesh quivering from head to thoroughly
ravished toes. But mostly of the threads of longing
coursing to the throb of her womb. She was on fire.

She reached down to rumple the crisp cut of his
hair, her fingers clenching in unabashed desire, and
never, never had she wanted anything so much as this
man's touch. Everywhere. Anywhere. All of her was
alive with a wild yearning.

"Say *oui* or *non*."

She heard him quite clearly, and in the recesses of
her mind, she knew exactly what he was asking. And
still she heard her own voice, hoarse with anticipation.

"Yes."

Since she was yet cuffed to the foot of the bed, Eliza

waited for Luc to shift around so they could be face-to-face. She assumed kissing would come naturally after her breathless acquiescence.

She assumed wrong.

He edged downward on the mattress, his kisses raining over the tops of her thighs, his palms rubbing the tension from them as he went higher, higher, brushing away the diaphanous gown as he went. She caught her breath as he pressed a hot kiss to the red-gold down covering her womanhood, but her confused relief when he lifted away was short-lived. He rolled onto his back, his big hands clasping opposite thighs, pulling her up and over him so that her knees touched his shoulders and she was kneeling upright and perplexed. She gasped as he nipped sharply at her inner thigh, causing her to inch away from the unexpected pinch of his teeth. Her knees spraddled wider apart, which was his intent. A shudder of anxious uncertainty preceded the stroke of his palms up the inner sleekness of her legs, not pausing, as she frantically hoped, until they reached the timid gates of her femininity, parting them boldly with the wedge of his thumbs. Stunned, she tried to lift off him but was held fast as his hands hooked over the tops of her thighs, preventing the movement, then, actually lowering her despite her resistance.

She said his name with a quavering panic just as he lifted his head for that first shocking contact. Heat shot through her, sizzling along her limbs as he tasted her swollen pink flesh. Nothing, not even the wicked foreign love poems, prepared her for such a thing as this intimate invasion of her body.

She was aware of clinging to his tented knees, hugging to them as shattering waves of bliss shook through her like a pitching ship upon hurricane-driven seas. Then all was calm except the frenzied tingling of her nerve endings as she slumped over his bent legs.

What had he done to her?

What marvelously wicked revenge had he exacted upon her will? Her body was weak and unresponsive as he toppled her carefully over onto her back, where she lingered in a sated sprawl, her eyes closed, her breath coming in labored little gasps of wonder.

She felt his kiss upon the curve of one hip. Her abdomen fluttered as he drew a wet path to her navel, where his tongue swirled lazily before continuing upward. Her breasts tightened in readiness, puckering to taut budded tips by the time his hands slid up to test and gently mold their fullness. He traced a moist trail up the oil-scented valley, then stopped, cupping his hands, burying his face in their soft fragrance. Beneath his palm, her heart was beating madly, hurrying as a state of restless yearning was upon her once more.

"*Oui* or *non*," he whispered again, the words a hot caress over her flushed body.

"Yes," she breathed, then moaned, as he took first one then the other nipple between his teeth for a brief tender torment. By then, her legs were thrashing helplessly, her head tossing from side to side. He stilled her with his hands on either cheek, his fingertips soothing over her feverish brow as he lowered slowly to her lips.

He tasted of forbidden paradise. Of wine and lilacs and of her own musky fragrance. She drank as if she'd thirsted for days. She reached to embrace him and was frustrated by the limits of her shackles.

Wordlessly, Luc slipped the thong from about his neck, using its key to unlock her fetters. Immediately, her arms wrapped about him, pulling him tightly to the cushion of her breasts. As his kisses teased across her cheekbones, over her tenderly flickering lids, her hands roved aimlessly over the hot sleekness of his shoulders, kneading, clutching, desperately searching.

When his mouth settled satisfyingly over hers once more, he lifted up, shifting his weight. She spread her knees in anticipation, welcoming him within their fertile valley. And just as she was arching her back, encouraging him to stake a deeper claim, he paused again to ask, "*Oui* or *non*?"

She was about to reply out of urgent need when he halted her response with the touch of his fingers upon her lips. The gesture made her stop, made her consider what she was inviting and with whom.

In the darkness, his eyes were like gleaming chips of onyx, wide and black with desire and something else he was fighting—fear. Of her acceptance or her refusal, she didn't know, only that it was there. The effort of restraint cut into every prominent angle of his face. He was panting lightly, his lips slightly parted, his gaze plundering hers for an answer. It was because he forced her to think beyond the sensual swirl tangled about them, giving her the chance and the choice to say no, that she was able to respond.

Her mouth moved against the press of his fingers. She touched the flare of his cheekbone stroking down to the underside of his jaw. He held his breath suspended.

"Yes," she told him. "I want you, Luc. I want this."

On the force of his ragged exhalation, his mouth dropped down to claim hers, hard, aggressive, fiercely devouring until the gentle sweep of her tongue tamed the violence of his kiss into a fervent quest for mutual delight. She was touching his face, his ears, his hair, his throat with exploring fingertips, wringing a moan from him that was full of wonder. Then he came up on his elbows, looking down into her eyes with such tenderness and concentration, she understood and tensed for the pain.

"Oh, *chérie, non*. Don't be afraid." He swept back her hair with the spread of his fingers and kissed her long, lavishly until the tension melted away. "I will not hurt you, *ma belle*. Trust me. Trust me."

And she did, expelling her anxiousness in a shaky breath as she lifted slightly to kiss him back, working out her worries with darting little thrusts of her tongue into his mouth. He groaned and mumbled something she couldn't understand. Then he was filling her, one smooth penetrating move that joined them perfectly and, as he'd promised, painlessly.

"Do you need me to read to you to light the fires in your soul?" Slowly, his hips circled, letting her feel his power, his passion for her until her hands spread urgently over the hard contour of his flanks, clasping, tugging, demanding more, that he show her what to do about the intensifying need flaming through her.

"I don't want words."

He obliged with a deep plunge that seemed to touch the very depth of her soul. She said his name like a prayer.

"Am I a bastard still?" And he continued, rocking into her.

"No. Yes," she moaned. "If it's vengeance you want, then take it. Take it now."

Kissing her hard and hungrily, he murmured, "No vengeance could ever be this sweet."

The intensity of years of restraint gathered as if he'd been waiting an anguished forever for this moment, for this woman, to unleash it. When it came, the force of his release was shattering. His body bowed in a taut arch, his eyes closing tightly, his muscles clenching, spasming, then dissolving into endless shudders of relief. Becoming boneless as he buried his face against her neck and let the last of the tension shiver from him.

There was a mystifying degree of contentment in holding him afterward, stroking through the damp bristle of his hair, following the slick ridge of his shoulder with her caress. She listened as his breathing slowed, as his heartbeat quieted. Even as he sighed and bussed her throat with lazy kisses, reality was returning with unwanted clarity.

She'd made love with him. Of her own will. And she'd reveled in it, in what he was doing, in how he made her feel. She, a woman, unmarried, caught in a lie; he, her captor, the man who kept her in chains.

What sort of insanity had overset them both? What did that make her now?

His lover in fact by her own admission.

She'd said she wanted him, and she had, wildly, passionately, without the excuse of ignorance or innocence. And she had no regrets; what he'd shown her was beyond words. It was the settling of consequence that chilled through her.

She pushed at Luc's shoulder, causing him to stir with a mutter.

"Luc, you're heavy." She made it sound like a mild complaint when her every instinct was to hold him tighter, anchoring him where he was.

Mumbling a soft apology, he shifted off her, turning onto his side with his back to her, sinking deeper into exhausted slumber. Yet when she began to sit up, he said her name. She leaned over him, stroking his hair, his bare arm, kissing the cap of his shoulder because she couldn't help herself.

"What is it, Luc?"

It sounded like "Belong to me." Then he was fast asleep.

She lay her cheek atop his shoulder, tears welling

beneath closed eyelids. Such sweet, soul-possessing words. Said to the woman he thought she was. To Philomena Montgomery.

But she wasn't Philomena, daughter of his enemy, capable of providing him with all he desired. She was Eliza Parrish, once a noble woman, now no one of consequence. Worth the papers of her indenture alone. And when he discovered that, he would hate her for her deception, for luring him away from the reward he sought with such single-minded passion. That reward was not her. Would never be her.

And she was only making it worse by prolonging the illusion.

She loved him. Had been in love with him since he'd climbed those icy ropes to save another. Knowing who he was, what he was, didn't stop her from adoring him for his bravery, his honor, didn't keep her from yearning for his touch and, now, for his possession.

If ever there was a more terrible trap, she did not know it.

Except she was no longer trapped. He'd forgotten to secure her in her shackles.

She waited until his breathing relaxed into a soft pattern of snores. Ever so slowly, she slipped off the bed and gathered the flimsy gown and her courage about her. What she planned was unquestionably dangerous, but the greater danger lay there on the bed where she'd given herself to a man who was not her husband, a man who was hunted by the very maritime law her family always exalted. Remaining would only bring them both unpardonable pain. Better she slip away in her role as Philomena than be recognized a coward for who she really was.

Brushing the dampness from her cheeks, she bent to retrieve Luc's cast-off shirt, wearing it to provide some modesty. Without looking back, she eased into the hall, pausing for a moment of panicked remorse before heading for the stairs.

As the door closed behind her, Luc rolled onto his back to stare up sightlessly at the canopy over head.

Bind her with stronger chains.

He sighed bitterly. What did he know of a woman's heart? Certainly not how to reach it. Obviously not how to hold it. He'd given her a choice of freedoms— his love or her escape. He hadn't wanted to, but he'd needed to know before risking any more of himself. He'd hoped. . . . He'd almost believed . . . almost.

Then she gave him his answer.

What a fool he was.

Eliza crept down the dark stairs, her mind already flying ahead in an attempt to push away thoughts of what she was leaving behind. She would find a way to purchase passage back to Salem. Perhaps sneak aboard one of the packets tied at the New Orleans wharves. She would worry about how once she escaped from the immediate problem.

A problem that escalated as she neared the bottom of the steps.

The soft clearing of a throat jerked her up in a quivering fright.

Remy Leverett separated himself from the shadows of the now empty parlor.

She put a hand to her racing heart and tried to smile. "Remy, you scared me nearly witless."

He looked miserable. " 'Tis sorry I am about that. Cap'n asked me to watch out for . . . things. I'll be takin' you back upstairs now."

Understanding struck a cruel blow. Of course Luc wasn't worried about her escaping. It had nothing to do with trust. He'd already posted guards to prevent the possibility. And now she would be marched back up and delivered to him in all humility, like a valuable pet who'd broken the leash and was returned in shame for failing to heed its master's order to stay. She couldn't bear to be brought back like that after stealing away from the man who'd brought her selfless bliss. Anything was better.

She startled the boy by clutching at his arm in desperation. "Remy, please let me go. I don't deserve this treatment. I am not my father, responsible for whatever crimes he may have committed. Please."

Remy twisted uncomfortably, trying to wriggle out of her grasp. "Now, my lady, that's not up to me. The cap'n gave orders—"

At that answer, a flood of tears cascaded down her face, enhancing her pleas, increasing Remy's distress.

"Remy, please. You said I could come to you if I needed anything. I need to get away from here. Far away. Your captain has taken unfair advantage of me whilst I was helpless and shackled to his bed." Shock registered on the boy's face, but she rushed on with her exaggerated story, anxiety fueling the lies she couldn't believe she was telling. "He's *hurt* me after he promised he wouldn't. I'm afraid. Surely you can't want that weighing on your conscience. Don't force me to go back to him. My reputation, my life, my very soul will be stained beyond redemption."

The stricken Remy was clearly torn, but before she could press for the advantage, a polite spatter of applause sounded from the top of the stairs. Her gaze snapped up to see Luc clad in just his trousers.

"Bravo, m'am'selle. An excellent performance. Just the right amount of tears and recriminations."

Eliza's knees went weak, her senses spinning. Only

Remy's hold on her arm kept her from sinking to the floor.

"Come back up, Mademoiselle Montgomery." Luc extended his hand, his gaze alarmingly impassive. "You have taxed poor Remy's loyalties enough for one night. Any more of your sad story and I would be tempted to slit my own throat to help you escape from such a monster." He crooked his fingers patiently. "Come. It is too late for more games."

For one wildly desperate moment, Eliza considered casting herself upon the thoroughly confused Remy for protection, but in the end, she resigned herself quietly, climbing the stairs with as much dignity as she could muster. She brushed by the stoic Frenchman, who made no attempt to touch her, and regally returned to her bedchamber prison. She stiffened at the sound of the door closing softly behind them.

"That is a fetching look, m'am'selle. How far did you think to get in a place such as this before someone was tempted to truly take advantage of what you offer?"

She didn't reply, unsure of his mood, made anxious by the flat tone of his voice. She continued her proud stance as if she'd done nothing to be ashamed of in trying to flee her kidnapper. And she hadn't. But he was more than that now. He was also her lover. Had she hurt him? Was he furious? She was afraid to find out.

He circled around with a slow, predatory step so she could see him. There wasn't much to see. His smoothly set features gave nothing away, and whatever moved behind the blackness of his eyes remained a secret.

"Don't pretend you were surprised," she goaded to hide her fear.

"I wasn't."

Silence hung between them, thick with tension. She expected his contempt, perhaps a smug rejoinder. Nothing. It was intolerable. She struck the first blow.

"Then why this act of injury, as if I'd done you a personal wrong? It's business, Captain. It's just for the money, isn't it?" She couldn't keep her jaw from quivering as sparks flew from her eyes. "Damn you, you cold-hearted—"

"Me? I am cold hearted? And what was that—that little performance below? I expected to be used. I confess, I enjoyed it. But Remy, he is an innocent. He doesn't understand creatures like you. Is there any lie you would not tell? Any depth to which you would not sink? To twist the affections of that boy—to tell him I *hurt* you. By God, woman, that is too low for contempt."

Gritting her teeth against her shame, Eliza extended her wrist for the return of her shackles, resigned yet resistant to the idea of such slavery.

His expression never altered. Not a flicker prepared her for the sudden violence with which he grasped her wrist, his hand becoming that steel band, the other lifting high.

"I could hurt you. Is that what you want? For me to hurt you?"

She gasped, shaken from her courageous pose to cringe back and cry, "Don't strike me!"

Those stoic features tightened, his struggle for control beginning to crack. As Eliza pulled fearfully against his grip, raw emotions sharpened in his black stare. Because he had wanted to be surprised and she had failed him. Because his need for her had never been more frenzied, more explosive. And futile.

His left hand lowered, extending to her palm downward. "Here. If you must break something, I have five of these left. But I've only one heart, and that, mademoiselle, will not be at your mercy."

"Then let me go, Luc. Please!"

"I can't."

One harsh tug brought her up flush to his chest, stunning the breath from her, just as the slanting descent of his mouth stilled her anxious rebellion. He kissed her fiercely, hotly, demanding she prove by her capitulation that at least in this, she'd been honest. It took one second of rough persuasion, then two before she opened to him like an exotic blossom—sweet, soft, incredibly delicate. The pressure of his lips gentled instantly. His moan said he didn't care which of them surrendered as long as they could come to this exquisite point together.

His palms pushed the shirt from her shoulders. The fluttery gown followed. Her own hands weren't still, reaching for the band of his trousers, sliding them down the hard angle of his hips. Tongues mated as their bodies fit together for a long, uncontrolled moment.

Then Jean-Luc scooped one arm beneath her knees, sweeping her into his embrace, carrying her behind the mosquito netting and following her down to the bed without ever leaving her lips. Lost to the magic, Eliza welcomed him in a reunion that took her senses up and away. To a place she couldn't imagine being without him. Or with anyone else.

And afterward, this time, she was the one to sleep within the wrap of his arms, her head tucked beneath his chin while he stroked the tumble of her hair. While he remained awake, staring somberly up into the darkness.

Chapter 16

~~~~~

Eliza stretched languorously within the warm pool of hazy sunlight. A sense of heavy satiation made movement—even the thought of movement—difficult. It was late morning, and the knowledge that she'd slept in was a surprise.

The fact that she was alone in bed was an even greater one.

"Luc?"

She scrambled up onto her knees, clutching the edge of the mosquito netting to her as an ineffectual covering.

"Jean-Luc?"

He was across the room, fully dressed, his back to her as he bent to tug on his boots. She watched the play of muscles beneath his shirt with a hungry appreciation as details of their night together rekindled a throb of longing. As she was considering a way to lure him back into her arms, he said, "I will be back in a few days."

She was too stunned for speech as she followed his movements to where he'd left his jacket. He hadn't looked at her.

"Back? You're leaving?"

He finally turned at that tremulous question. His

face was schooled into impenetrable lines, and his voice, cool as an Atlantic breeze, said, "I need to see to provisions for the *Galant*. We must be ready to sail—to pick up the ransom."

She flinched at the way that was said, flatly, devoid of feeling. But she wasn't put off.

"I'll go with you."

"*Non*." No explanation, just no. Letting her think what she would.

And she was thinking, rapidly, frantically. The idea of separation from him was unbearable. "Send Shamus or the others. Why must you go?"

"Because it is my ship. My responsibility. *Comprenez-vous?*" He was upset and fighting to cover it. She could tell by the thickening of his accent, by his subconscious slip into French. But he was still so terribly remote, as if nothing had happened between them. Or, perhaps, because it had. "I take my vows seriously, m'am'selle. More seriously than those you made to your fiancé."

His toneless words were delivered with the force of a slap. She gasped, rocking back on her heels at the unfairness and unexpectedness of his attack. Because he was right; there was nothing she could say in her defense.

Why wasn't there more guilt, more shame at the mention of William, her intended? But William and those commitments seemed so far away and Jean-Luc was here. What smoldered between them was new and powerful, if yet unnamed. Would he chide her now after enjoying those pleasures fully?

And while she recovered herself, his dark gaze helplessly assessed the way the filmy netting outlined her lush figure, clinging to the supple limbs that had twined so enticingly about him, to the ripe breasts he'd savored like sweet fruits. Her hair cascaded in a riot of color about her pale face and shoulders, making him long to comb the tangles from it with his fingers. He took an involuntary step forward, then stopped himself, too late. She'd seen the smoky heat flare in his eyes and rightfully guessed the reason.

Worries over William were forgotten.

"Do you have to go now? You should have awakened me."

His reply was stiff. "I did not want to share." Not his thoughts, not his wounded heart. And not the splendors of her loving. It was hard enough to walk away from her as it was. He turned toward the door so she wouldn't notice the magnitude of his lie outlining the front of his trousers.

"Don't leave me here."

He hesitated, snagged by the tremor of genuine fright in her tone. His softened slightly. "You will be well guarded." A double-edged comfort.

"Am I to return to my shackles, then?"

He glanced back over his shoulder. "Have you given me reason to trust you, mademoiselle?"

Her smile was rueful. "No."

He nodded and was about to go when her fragile voice reached out to him once more.

"Jean-Luc? Don't be gone too long. I'm afraid of this place."

He might have mentioned that she wasn't afraid to run about it in the dead of night dressed in next to nothing. But he didn't. Instead, he gave her a curt reassurance: "You will be safe here."

"I don't feel safe. How am I to protect myself?"

"Remy will be outside." Then, because she still looked so vulnerable and despairing, he reached into the pocket of his coat to produce a small palm-size pistol. "Keep this with you. It should discourage anyone from bothering you in my absence."

She took the piece from him, weighing it in her hand with an air of speculation. He almost smiled.

"In case you are considering turning it upon me, be warned, it has but one shot. I am not easily discouraged, nor easy to kill, but should you manage to slay me, my men would put an unpleasant end to you."

Her features became almost as stony as his own. "I understand, Captain."

"I will see some clothing is provided for you." Again, his gaze scorched briefly, hotly over her body. There was danger in further delay. *"Au revoir, m'am'selle."*

Again, just as he reached the door, she caught him with a plaintive cry.

"Luc?"

This time he didn't turn. He was afraid to.

"Last night—"

He froze inside. His voice was ice. "Was last night. It is over, *fini*," he concluded, stepping out and locking the door behind him.

Eliza collapsed into the rumpled bedcovers with a soft cry of despair. Gathering them about her as a shield for her nakedness, for the impersonal comfort of their closeness, she held her tears of confusion at bay. She had to think. She had to find a way out of this turmoiled dilemma before she lost herself completely to this man who thought of her as a means to an end.

Belong to me.

What had he meant by that? Too late to ask now, after her failed desertion.

Could she return to William now with those same lies, claiming her innocence while yet longing for Jean-Luc's touch? Had she so lost herself to deception that the truth was an enemy to be hidden from either man? A truth equally hidden within her heart?

A gentle tap on the door distracted her from the threat of weak tears. She sat up, binding the sheets about herself for modesty's sake, as Remy entered bearing her breakfast tray. He kept his eyes carefully averted.

"Good morning, my lady," came his subdued greeting. "I've brought you some decent clothing. I'll allow you time to dress before I replace your . . ." He glanced miserably at the shackles dangling from the bed frame. "I'm sorry, Miss Montgomery. Cap'n's orders."

"Is he gone, then?"

"Yes, my lady. He's left me in charge of your safety. If you need me for anything . . ." Then he broke off, head hanging in misery because she'd come to him in need and he'd turned her away. His anxious gaze rose at last, touching upon her shyly, worriedly, and she realized he was searching for signs of abuse. "How be you this morning, my lady?" His voice choked over that question, and the power Eliza might have held over him for the purpose of manipulation failed before her tender sympathies.

"I am fine, Remy. Your captain did not harm me. Those things I said were just to gain your help in getting away."

"Truth?"

She allowed a small smile. "Truth."

The boy's shoulders drooped with the evidence of his relief. What a wretched anguish he'd been suffering, fearing he'd aided his idolized captain in the unforgivable mistreatment of a woman he admired.

Eliza watched the ancient-looking clouds of guilt clear from the lad's youthful features, and she was glad to have relieved his pain. Again, she was reminded of Nate, and the poignant twist about her heart bound her to the boy. "Forgive me, Remy, for misusing your noble intentions. I will not do so again."

In making him that promise, Eliza forged a link of trust between them. And more than that, a tentative friendship on equal terms.

Remy smiled, a hopeful gesture she quickly returned.

"I shall be back after a bit. Enjoy your meal, Miss—"

"Eliza. Please."

"All right. Eliza."

After he'd gone, she eagerly donned the clean clothes. The undergarments were of cheap fabric and unadorned, nothing like the thin batistes elaborate in their laces and embroideries she used to wear, but they felt good against her skin. The gown itself was a simple high-waisted cotton print, something a maid might wear. The sleeves were short, the neckline a low vee edged with a prim white collar, both a relief from the promised heat of the day. Her present situation had no place for vanity, but she longed for a mirror as she worked the snarls from the loose waves of her hair. Perhaps it was better she didn't see how she looked after being long away from pampering comforts. Did she look like the type of woman who would wear this dress? Is that how Luc would see her? As a lowly chambermaid?

A grim slice of reality stopped her vain thoughts. Wasn't that what she was? A lady no more. High birth was no replacement for low means. How cruelly she'd learned that lesson. This was what Eliza Parrish was. A woman destined for coarse cloth and slovenly rooms. A woman who would never again know the sumptuous feel of silks, touch costly French perfumes behind her ears, walk upon the arm of a gentleman to see to the comfort of her guests.

Then a somber Remy returned to clasp the proof of

her circumstances about her wrist. After that, she had no appetite for what was on the tray.

A wave of bittersweet regret swept over her, shaking the practical foundations of her will. For a moment, she allowed herself to weaken, to curl upon the bed she shared with a renegade, to weep lonely tears for what she could never reclaim. Had she been dreaming, then, that William would ever come for her, that he would ever accept her back with open arms? Had her hopes of fitting back into Salem society been childish and impossible? Was it time, then, to release the past and to look toward the future she might make for herself? With Jean-Luc?

Belong to me.

Was it her he wanted or the triumph of owning a Montgomery?

When Luc returned, she would ask him. She would tell him the unvarnished truth and take a huge chance upon his generosity. Upon his capacity for forgiveness. The first she'd witnessed. The second she could only pray he possessed. And then she would make her plans dependent upon his answers.

Belong to me.

Was that what she wanted? Or was it all that was left her?

She'd resigned herself to the wait and to her ultimate fate when the door to her room opened an hour later. Expecting Remy, she stood, readying to hand him her emptied tray. Then the smile on her face froze into an expression of dread, for it wasn't Remy standing on the threshold.

It was the snaggletoothed Cajun from the night before, leering boldly as he stepped in and closed the door behind him.

*   *   *

It took the entire day to refit the *Galant* and lay in supplies. A hot, restless day for Jean-Luc. A day of tiptoeing to avoid their captain's temper for his crew. Because he never displayed fits of anger—or any great demonstrations of any kind—the men worried and whispered among themselves. And in the end, they turned to Shamus Sterns for answers.

Shamus found the moody Frenchman alone in his cabin, seated on his sea chest before the open expanse of windows. A sultry breeze filtered in, ruffling through Jean-Luc's hair. No expression revealed itself as the captain brought a nearly empty glass of rum to his lips as he stared at the ripening moon.

"Captain."

There was a long pause, and Shamus began to think he hadn't been heard. Then came a soft reply.

"I am not fit company, Mr. Sterns."

"'Tis not your company I seek, Luc. I've come to give you counsel."

"I fear I'm in no mood for that, either. Go away, Shamus. Leave me alone." A toneless command, easily ignored.

"Luc, the crew be worried about you."

No flicker of response. "Tell the crew to mind their own damned business."

"Beggin' your pardon, Captain, but you be their business."

Dark, flatly opaque eyes shifted toward him. "There you are wrong. They have their orders from their captain, do they not?"

"Fed to them at sword point. You are not yourself, Jean-Luc, and they grow . . . concerned."

Passions flashed through his stare, lightning through black heavens before the void returned. "Not myself? What do they know of me? Have I ever given them leave to an opinion on how I feel?"

"You've never given them anything except commands to be obeyed. They see you as cut in cold stone; you're Coeur Noir to them. But now you've given them glimpses of the man behind the mask, and they be curious and a little afraid, I'm thinking. They do not know what to make of the change."

"Am I to confess all the inner workings of my heart to them and beg for their sympathies?" His tone sharpened with scorn, and a touch of discomfort.

"At least they would know you had a heart, Luc. 'Tis no great shame to admit to that, lad."

"Maybe not for you. But for me, there is." He tossed back the rest of his rum and closed his eyes tight, waiting for the burn to subside. Waiting for the pain to dull. He took a shallow breath, his control returning. "And what does the crew suspect is the cause of my malady?"

Shamus held nothing back. "They believe you are in love with Miss Montgomery and that you no longer wish to collect the ransom."

Not a twitch betrayed him. "Is that what they think? You may tell them they are wrong."

"I will not lie to our crew, Luc."

Luc fixed a fierce stare upon him, the muscles of his face going taut and lean. "Love her? How can I love her? She is everything I find reprehensible: spoiled, too wealthy to notice there's a cruel world outside her door, addicted to privilege whilst others suffer for it. Love her? That is ridiculous." He grasped the Montgomery medallion, unconsciously rubbing it between his fingertips. "She is a tool, Shamus, to use and discard when no longer of use. I will trade her to her father for the money he owes. Do you think she's any different than her sire? Do you think she would not betray me and my foolish crew at her first opportunity, then wash her hands of our fate?"

Shamus said nothing for a long moment. Then he replied, "No, I do not think so. You don't either."

"You're wrong!" He surged to his feet and prowled the room, stride abrupt in agitation. "You're wrong, *mon ami*. She is no different. She has no *honneur*. We will take her back to them and good riddance. Once we collect our debt, she can go off to marry her paragon and raise a brood of equally treacherous brats."

"Then you've made your choice where the lady is concerned." He didn't sound happy about it.

Luc paused in his pacing, his back to his old friend. "It was made for me." That was revealed so grimly, Shamus felt compelled to insert his own opinion on the matter.

"You are afraid to act."

"Afraid? Of what?"

"Afraid to love, to care for another. Luc, if you love her, don't discard this opportunity by hiding behind that indifference you wear so well. Solitude can become its own prison, and you're about to lock yourself away forever."

Jean-Luc spun toward him. His features were sharply chiseled by the stress of restraint. When he spoke, his words were thickly accented and coated in ice.

"Who are you to be so free with your suggestions? You are not my father. I have no family, as well you know."

Shamus replied with equal frigidity. "Forgive me, Captain. You are right, of course. I am nothing to you." With a stiff bow, he withdrew from the room, leaving Luc alone with the shame of what was said.

"Shamus!" But the door remained closed to him. Luc squeezed his eyes shut, cursing himself a thousand times as a fool. He let his shoulders sag and his head hang low for a moment of oppressive defeat, then stirred once more. "Forgive me, old friend," he spoke aloud, a little too late.

He was a pot too long aboil, things bubbling, roiling, pressing for the means to escape while he desperately clamped the lid down. Eventually, the pressure would be too much for him to contain, and Shamus was right; thought of the inevitable explosion terrified him.

Eliza was the flame, firing his passions, igniting a spark that now raged out of bounds. If he was not careful, he'd be left with nothing but hot ash for a heart.

The sooner she was on her way to Salem, the safer he would be. Just knowing she was nearby, waiting in that room where they'd made such wild sweet love, was a temptation he couldn't ignore much longer. The need for her was a fast-spreading ache, not beginning at his loins but rather massing within his chest. Not even the fact that she was Justin Montgomery's daughter seemed to matter anymore. It was her refusal of him that would make it possible to surrender her up and go on without her, no longer the thought of revenge. It wasn't as sweet when the cost was his heart. Shamus was right about that, too.

Accomplishing nothing by sulking alone, Luc climbed up on deck and observed firsthand the odd way his men were regarding him. Had he become so detached from emotion that the slightest display of it was received with shock and suspicion? Was that the kind of man he wanted to be, Coeur Noir? That had never been his intention.

Seeing him, Shamus approached, his weather-worn features still stiff with affront. "She be ready anytime you are, Captain. We should be getting word on a place of exchange from Benji any day now. Montgomery wants his daughter back without delay. Could be the fiancé has a hand in the hurry. I would be anxious to have such a prize returned to me, were I him."

The sentiment tasted bitter, but Luc didn't comment. His gaze lifted to the masts and rigging. "Tell the men they've done fine work for the *Galant*."

"They did the work for you, Luc. Tell them yourself." When Luc recoiled in surprise and reluctance, Shamus sighed. "Afraid a personal word of thanks will invite them to think of you as friend? Don't worry. They don't think of you as flesh and blood. Never mind. I'll tell them. They should hear it from someone." With a shake of his head, the older man started to walk away. Then, thinking better of leaving with words that needed to be said, he turned to confront the stoic young Frenchman.

"As a captain, you command the respect of every man here because you've earned it with your skill and cunning. They would jump to your every order without question. But if you let them know you as a man, they would follow you into hell, Jean-Luc. Do you think they risked all to free you from that prison just because you're a fine navigator? Have you ever taken the time to thank them for your freedom? My guess is not. I've gone these ten years without the slightest gratitude for saving your wretched life. Or did I? I sometimes wonder if what I saved was alive at all or merely a dead man walking. By your leave, Captain, I'll convey your heartfelt sentiments to the crew." His bow mocked; then he strode away from the unbending figure.

With the moon gleaming down on black water and the stifling heat below, the crew gathered on deck to share laughter and outrageous tales over melodies from the squeeze box and pennywhistle. Such events were ribald and relaxed and attended by all but their self-contained captain. So when Jean-Luc made an appearance in their midst, in his shirtsleeves and bared feet, it was enough of a surprise to bring an instantaneous hush.

Luc hesitated on the fringe of their gaiety, knowing himself the reason for their silence, until one of the men asked properly, "Ye be needing something, Cap'n?"

"*Non.*" The answer croaked from him, and he was tempted to turn and leave it at that. But then he caught Shamus's perplexed gaze, and his courage was refortified. He signaled over his shoulder, and several casks of good rum were brought up on deck and deposited before him. "I would ask that you share a drink with me." The request felt odd on his tongue, as did the invitation. Silence greeted it. He searched their bewildered faces and began to regret the overture.

Then Shamus called, "To what do we raise our glasses, Captain?"

Luc topped the first cask and dipped in a cup, lifting it in his second's direction. "To the finest crew a man could ask for. And a belated thanks for restoring me to your helm."

"We will drink to that . . . Jean-Luc."

Luc managed a grim smile as the big seaman came to take the cup from his hand. Shamus hoisted it somberly and took a long swallow, then returned it. Luc drained the rest of it. Shamus's laugh boomed good naturedly.

"It's a fine vintage, laddies. Help yerselves."

The barrels were swarmed, and standing in their midst, Luc was anchored in place by the weight of Shamus's heavy hand upon his shoulder, pushing him like a reluctant child into a crowd of noisy strangers. Having never been a part of this camaraderie, Luc would have shied away from the attention if not for Shamus's imprisoning grasp. After the first cup of rum, the crew were more willing to relax around their remote, formal captain. The cook, O'Malley, came to press his beefy palm to Luc's for a rough shake and a hearty claim of, " 'Tis glad we are to have you back, Cap'n Luc. Ye had me worried that yer standoffishness was due to me lack of talent at the tables."

Luc looked askance at Shamus, desperately uncertain of how to proceed.

"Tell me, Luc," his second said, draping an arm about his rigid shoulders. "Ye've dined in our colonial prison. How does the food compare to what O'Malley serves us?"

Luc offered a tentative smile. "Mostly what they provided had hard shells and was yet wiggling, so I can see little difference."

That brought a round of guffaws even from the blushing O'Malley.

And gradually Luc relaxed. The sense of belonging embraced him with an unhurried fondness, and he found himself seated cross-legged on the deck in the casual circle of others laughing over the boatswain's bold stories. Inch by cautious inch, his guard lowered. It was like waking from a long sleep, his emotions tingling uncomfortably from disuse. But there was such a never experienced pleasure in being included in the almost tribal closeness.

Raised by servants, a gently bred mother, and oft absent father, surrounded by younger sisters and taught singly by tutors, he'd never learned to interact with his peers. Shamus was his closest claim to friendship, and he'd never allowed himself to enjoy even that small luxury. He hadn't wanted to care for those who served him, needing to keep them at a distance—just names and duties and nothing more personal.

Now he felt that loss keenly. Perhaps it was not too late to make amends.

Warming a cup of rum between his palms, Luc's thoughts shifted from the companionable company to another ache none of their jovial camaraderie could soothe.

His longing for Eliza.

Chapter 17

The hour was late, the rum nearly gone. Luc staggered up to his feet, drawing Shamus's curious glance. Something must have shown in his expression, for the older man frowned slightly.

"Are you all right, lad?"

"A little too much rum and conversation for a monk like me." Then he let go with a wide grin that was startling in its affability. "I am overwhelmed, is all." Then a poignant hunger softened his gaze as he looked toward the city's center. "I think I will go ashore. Will you stay with the *Galant* and see that no one sinks her or falls overboard?"

"Aye, Cap'n." He had the nerve to smirk. "Give the lady my regards."

"I will, *mon ami.*"

By that admission, Shamus knew his captain was monkish no more. He was hopelessly enslaved. Chuckling to himself, he reached for more rum.

Etienne's business was going full bore when Luc pushed his way inside. He didn't see the amiable host in the throng of pleasure seekers, so he headed straight for the stairs. The huge ebony-skinned guard barred his way for just a moment too long, then word-

194

lessly stepped aside. As Luc climbed the stairs, a feeling of unease pricked at his nape, and he was alert for signs of danger. Remy wasn't in sight, either, but perhaps he was inside the room keeping Eliza company.

He tapped on the door, embarrassed by a rush of eagerness just to see her face, hear her voice. He dared not hope for more than that lest he succumb to the fever she quickened in his blood. He refused to thoroughly disgrace himself by courting the favor of a woman who did not want him.

It was taking her a long time to answer. He knocked again.

"Eliza?"

The knob turned easily in his hand. A cold shiver of alarm streaked along his spine. Standing slightly off center, he pushed the door open, too cautious to rush in without assessing the situation.

The room was dark, no smell of lamp oil or sound of slumbering breaths to tell him the room was or recently had been occupied. It felt empty.

Holding tight rein on his emotions, Luc eased in and lit the lamp. The filmy gown that had fluttered about Eliza's supple limbs lay discarded on the unmade bed. The remnants of a breakfast tray sat undisturbed on the floor.

And secured to the footboard hung one half of the broken shackles.

Eliza was gone.

A fierce oath ripped from him. What a fool he'd been to trust her. Somehow she'd managed to convince someone to aid in her escape, and the absent Remy was the most likely candidate. How that stung, the lack of loyalty a bitter blow. With a woman like Eliza, what chance did Remy have of resisting when Luc could scarce manage that feat?

The sense of loss and betrayal slapped him completely sober. He would find them. They couldn't have gone far undetected. Etienne would know something. Someone would have seen a boy and a beautiful woman slipping down the stairs.

Like a territorial wolf on a scent, he turned, eager to begin the trail. And he pulled up short, his attention snagged by an irregularity in the door jamb. He looked closer, where the wood was freshly splintered away, and found a small ball embedded there. The right size for the pistol Eliza carried.

Whoever had Eliza hadn't taken her willingly.

"Cap'n?"

Remy Leverett sagged against the other side of the door frame. His gaze twirled with an odd lack of focus, and his bones seemed strangely flexible. At first, Jean-Luc thought he was drunk. Fury caught him in a strangle hold as he snatched the lad up by his shirt front.

"Remy, where is Mademoiselle Montgomery?"

The boy's features loosened like melting butter. "I— I don't know—"

Luc shook him, a terrier with a rat. "Where is she? What has happened here whilst you drank yourself into a stupor? I left you with orders to guard her!"

"I don't know, Cap'n. One drink and it weren't rum. I swear to you. I wouldn't have let anything happen to her."

His face hard and unreadable, Luc's thoughts spun with a cold reasoning. "One drink. With whom?"

"I'd taken Miss Eliza her breakfast and was waiting for her to finish. Your friend who owns this place invited me to share a cup of coffee with him. I remarked on its strange taste, and the next I knew, I was waking up with the garbage out back." The boy's chin quivered. "What's happened to Miss Eliza?"

Luc's hand unknotted from the lad's lapels, leaving the sailor to totter on his own. His voice was low and heavy with its native accent.

"That is what I mean to find out."

Etienne Moreau was immersed in his favorite activity. Greedy fingers stacked towers of gold, coins from the evening's entertainments. A good take, especially with the huge sum he'd managed quite unexpectedly and with so little investment on his part.

Suddenly, his grin became grimace, as a strong hand closed about his throat. His eyes bugged in terror as they met Jean-Luc Gautier's stony face.

"Where is she?"

He couldn't have forced a sound if he wanted to.

A wickedly curved dagger whipped up to fit above the crushing grip. Blood welled warmly where it nicked his skin, and, never a brave soul, Etienne all but wept the truth.

"What could I do, Jean-Luc? They threatened my life. They said they'd burn the roof over my head! For a woman? You could not expect me to make such a sacrifice. Could you?"

Luc's gaze assessed the amount of coin on the table and came to his own conclusions on the cost of Etienne's courage. But now was not the time to exact his revenge on the sniveling coward.

"Who?" he demanded, death chilling his words. "Who took her?"

"Those Cajuns who took a fancy to her last eve, led by T-mon Beauclaire. They would not take no for an answer. They left this morning bound upriver. They won't be traveling fast. I told them you would be gone for several days." And he smiled slyly as if he'd done Jean-Luc a great favor.

Luc leaned in close until they were cheek to cheek

over the unwavering dagger. "Tell me, Etienne," he asked softly. "How much was she worth? Your life? Because if I do not return with her, I will exact that payment from you and toast you with your own blood."

He stood, jerking the blade aside. The tip caught the brothel owner beneath the jaw, slicing upward to his ear. Etienne hissed but was wise enough not to wail. He put all his energies toward begging.

"Please, Jean-Luc . . . I did not know she meant anything to you. How was I to guess? I will gladly share in the profit I made off her—"

The rest was cut short by the force of Luc's fist.

By the first gray of dawn, he was on the river, paddling along the still backwashes and into the deep bayous. The delay frustrated him but since he wasn't bayou bred like the men he pursued, he had to get all the information he could before setting out after them. They had the advantage of numbers and swamp savvy. He had surprise in his favor. He wasn't afraid, not for himself.

But for Eliza, he went half mad with worry.

The physical exertion was all that kept him sane. The steady stroke of the paddle drove him as relentlessly as his fear. He didn't know the men he followed, but he knew those like them. Animals, more dangerous when running in a pack, ruled by nothing but brute strength and basic lusts. His panic deepened into a nightmare of grief and fury. They had Eliza. Confident of not being chased, they would have taken the time to camp, taken the time to . . . to . . . He paddled faster, not wanting to think about what they would do with a woman like Eliza among the six of them. Insidious suggestions crept in, noxious as the still waters. Tormenting visions.

He would kill them.

He paddled faster.

By noon, with the sun blazing mercilessly overhead, he was dizzy with the heat and shaken by fatigue. Touches of weakness left by the malaria added to it. Insects buzzed about his head, feeding upon his sweat-soaked flesh. He didn't notice. His heartbeats became the rhythm for his dipping oar: hard, strong, tireless. His mood primal, his senses focused, he only looked ahead, toward his goal of finding Eliza. Of killing those who'd taken her.

He wasn't by nature a brutal man. More scholar than brawler, he preferred to think his way out of bad situation. He'd never taken a life, at least by his own hand or with planned intent.

But as the day wore on, he began to think about torture.

His only consolation was that they would keep her alive. They'd paid a tremendous price to enjoy her, and they'd savor every coin spent.

He sank deeper into the darkness. Images of them beneath his knife blade, screaming for relief, writhed through his mind.

Darkness finally stopped him. He was afraid to go on, afraid of missing them in the night. He knew he was close. His whole body tingled with awareness of them. And his thoughts ached with the knowledge of what they would be doing.

He slept in the bottom of the shallow boat, drifting in and out in short, restless snatches. And with the first slivers of daylight he was on the trail again.

He found their camp toward noon, empty now but still a wealth of information. They were drinking heavily, careless about their safety. With minds dulled and pounding, they would be traveling slowly. He would be on them by nightfall.

He found Eliza's chemise, ripped by impatient hands and bloodied. He crushed it in his hands, a black swirl of violence engulfing him, shaking him like waves of sickness, spiraling to his soul until he became somehow different in his despair. Dangerously capable of anything.

He was beyond physical pain, beyond mental torment. All focused into a pin dot of purpose.

Voices wafted out on the heavy bayou air, jerking him out of the semistupor he'd fallen into as darkness settled. Luc stilled his paddle and sat, listening. Again, he heard the coarse echo of laughter. Then a raw female scream. Tension gripped him, rippling up his spine, exploding within his head. And it took every scrap of his control not to plunge head-on to his death.

What good would it do her if he were to die recklessly?

He clung to that, repeating it in his mind until it fettered his fierce mood. Rushing them in a wild impulse would solve nothing and certainly would not change Eliza's situation. He had to think, to plan, to chart his course carefully.

And he had to do so while ignoring her thready cries of helplessness and fear.

While the Cajuns laughed and drank and pleasured themselves upon their captive, Luc skimmed the edges of darkness like a deadly shadow. He settled deep into that blackness to wait for his opportunity, crouching in the muck, tormented by insects, tortured by Eliza's hoarse pleas. His head hung low, his arms crossed over it, his knees squeezed in tight to shut out the sounds, sounds that altered subtly from one woman to several, the scene from a Louisiana bayou to the French countryside and back. He rocked upon his heels, biting his lips until they bled to keep back the moans of anguish as time and place confused themselves in one hellish nightmare. Weakness trembled through him with that remembered horror, threatening to cost his rigidly set control.

He hadn't been able to protect his family, and they'd been slaughtered like innocent sheep. And he hadn't protected Eliza any better.

He raised his head slowly, eyes glittering, cold and dark. Eliza wasn't going to die. She was strong of heart and will. And he was here to rescue her. Suddenly, the need for retribution paled beside that purpose. Vengeance could wait until Eliza was safe. Then he would come back and descend upon them like the wrath of God.

Deciding that, his mood quieted; his soul grew calm and still. And he waited, unaffected by his surroundings or by his own discomfort, for the right time to strike.

By daybreak, the Cajuns lay sprawled about where they'd fallen in their drunkenness, all but the one guarding Eliza. He was tamping the makings of a smoke into a crudely carved pipe, totally oblivious to his own impending death.

Eliza slumped bonelessly where she'd been tethered like an animal to a fallen tree. Her dress was filthy and torn. Matted hair hung about her face like a dull curtain. She was silent and unmoving.

Luc eased up out of the murky swamp like one of the avenging demons whispered to inhabit it. The first rays of morning glinted off the blade in his hand as he sliced through the Cajun's vocal cords and arteries in one swift, soundless pull. He caught the guard as he fell and settled him noiselessly to the ground in a spreading pool of crimson. Luc stepped over him without another thought.

He knelt beside Eliza, uncertain of her state. Was she awake, alert? Would she cry out and give him away? Carefully, he slipped his hand through the spill of her tangled hair, clamping it firmly over her mouth. She reacted with a startled jump, her mewling cry effectively smothered by his palm. Quickly, fearing her struggles, Luc brushed the hair from her face so she could see him, then was dismayed by the blankness in her hollowed eyes. And then was outraged by his first glimpse of her.

Her lovely features were badly bruised. She'd been beaten either to subdue her or just for the sport of it. Hot rage surged within him, along with the desire to calmly stalk amongst the slumbering beasts, coldly slitting their throats. But one outcry, one sound and all could go to ruin. It was a risk he couldn't take for the sheer satisfaction of knowing them dead for their cruel deeds.

Later, he promised himself. Later.

For now, it was imperative he get Eliza away.

He touched his forefinger to his lips, warning her to be silent. There was no awareness in her dull stare, no signal that she understood or even knew him. He mouthed a soundless curse and reached to cut her bonds. The instant she realized her freedom, she became a surprising adversary. Her knotted hands swung at his head like a club, catching him unawares and knocking him back upon his rump. Then she was on her feet, running—in the wrong direction. She was heading right toward the center of the camp.

Acting quickly, Luc swept her legs out from under her. She fell hard, and before she could recover from the stunning force, he was atop her, clamping his hand across her mouth once more. She writhed beneath him, all hellcat fury and desperate ferocity. Trying not to hurt her, Luc pinned her with his greater mass, containing her flailing arms within the grip of one hand. He flipped her over, terrified that any second her thrashing would stir the camp.

She lay on her back, glaring up at him through wide, terrorized eyes. Her bosom heaved mightily beneath the crush of his chest. He tightened his fingers to keep her from biting him. Then he risked all by speaking, whispering the words as softly as possible against her ear while trying to avoid the butt of her head.

"Eliza, it's Jean-Luc. It's Luc. I've come to take you away from here. Look at me."

She stilled, her bright eyes fixing upon his intense features.

"Do you know me? I need you to be silent and come with me. If you understand, nod your head."

For the longest second, she didn't move, panting, trembling, staring up at him in confusion and alarm. Then a touch of sanity returned to her gaze, and her head jerked a slight affirmative. Cautiously, Luc removed his hand, ready to slap it back in an instant as her lips parted for the draw of a deep breath. But she didn't scream. She mouthed his name in silent recognition. He smiled grimly in return.

He stood, pulling her up against him. For all her struggling, she was frightfully weak, clinging to him for balance and looking askance. He gestured to where he'd left the pirogue and again signaled for silence. She nodded again, with greater comprehension. But as he led her out of the camp, past several of those who'd brutalized her, he could feel the shock shuddering through her. Her face turned into his shirtfront as they stepped over the corpse of her guard. He could hear the softest of whimpers working its way out of her. But that was all. She went with him docilely, silently, as quickly as she could, then huddled in the bottom of the boat, clutching her knees, her battered face buried against them.

It was too soon to feel relief. Luc poled out into the faster-moving waters, then began to paddle stealthily upstream. No cry of discovery sounded behind them. Still, he didn't relax. When out of hearing range, he prodded Eliza with an extra oar. She cringed away from the contact.

"*Princesse*, if you wish to save your skin, I suggest you help me paddle."

She looked up then through those dazed eyes, blinking as she focused on the oar. Then she took it from him and began applying it with urgency, because each stroke carried her farther away from the source of her fears.

Chapter 18

They stayed on the water for the better part of the day, Eliza matching him stroke for stroke. She said nothing, nor did she look back at him. He knew her demons were driving her but knew of no way to ease them until they reached their destination.

As the landmarks grew more and more familiar, Luc began searching for a spot to go ashore, finally finding one in a barely visible niche hidden by dense grasses. There, he nudged the pirogue up onto dry ground and helped Eliza out. She watched, clasping her arms about herself, as he waded into the water and punched several holes through the bottom of their boat, leaning on it until it was completely submerged. Then he rearranged the tall grasses to conceal their passing.

"Come on," he told her as her gaze lifted in mild question. "It is not far."

She didn't ask for details, falling in behind him as he pushed his way through the thick undergrowth. Nor did she slow him down even though her slender body was shaking with fatigue. The fear of being caught was greater than the weariness.

It rose out of the tangled surroundings like an ancient ruin. Vines overran the front pillars, myrtles

choked the delicate balustrades. But to him it was
Mon Coeur Desir, his heart's desire, and nothing had
ever looked so close to heaven.

Not realizing he'd stopped, Eliza staggered into
him. His arm whipped about her waist to keep her
from falling, but she slumped over it limply, courage
finally giving way to a faint. He swung her up into
his arms easily and bore her across what would someday be the gracious green of his front lawns, up to
the house he'd carved out of a wilderness.

He'd been away for over a year. The sense of homecoming was bittersweet when he thought of all that
had gone undone in his absence. Time, unfortunately,
had not stood still. Evidence of its unkind passage
was redolent in the air, the dank stench of mildew
everywhere. He'd built Coeur Desir to resist the en-
croaching clime, so the damage wasn't as serious as
it might have been, but still, it pained him to see so
much in varying states of decay.

He carried Eliza into one of the double parlor
rooms because it held some of the home's scanty fur-
nishings. When he pulled the covering off one of the
chaises, dust momentarily blinded him. The sumptuous brocade he'd paid dearly for had been eaten away
by some sort of vermin, exposing much of the seat
padding and bare wood. The destruction wounded
like a personal attack, plunging him into angry despair directed at the cause: Justin Montgomery. While
he'd rotted away in prison, so had his home in his
forced absence.

The soft mutter of Eliza's breath against his throat
pulled Luc back to the immediacy of their condition.
He eased her down to the dirty floor, then carried the
cover outside to shake it as dust-free as possible. It
wasn't a fine brocade, but it made a respectable surface to cradle his lady love.

And how very desperately he loved her.

Now that safety surrounded them, emotions he'd suppressed as unwise came lapping back in a steady tide. The crippling fear of losing her. The agony of believing her treachery behind it. The panic propelling him after her, willing to face any odds for her return. The possessive fury twisting into primitive knots when he thought of others misusing her. The sacrifice of revenge just to keep her safe. All those things massing to an overwhelming whole. It was too much to contemplate all at once.

She was here with him, worse for wear but his at last.

How was he going to keep her?

First, by keeping her alive.

He shook off his pensiveness and shifted into a more familiar pattern of action. They would need water, food, light. It felt good working toward a goal, much more comfortable than abstract emotions. He was pleased to find his well still good, yielding up buckets of fresh cold water. There was little in the way of sustenance. A barrel of salted meat managed to resist tampering. He chewed a piece thoughtfully as he returned to kneel at Eliza's side. Dipping a wadding of cloth into a pan of clean water, he began to bathe her face, gently blotting away the dirt to expose the true nature of her injuries. By the time he was finished, his jaw ached from the grinding of his teeth. He took the evidence of her pain very personally.

Bruises mottled her face and neck, disappearing down into the ripped bodice of her gown. His guess was that they continued all the way down, but he didn't check. Her situation was too fragile, his control too perilous. Instead, he lifted her hands, grimacing at the sight of her wrists. They were raw from rope burns. The broken shackle still dangled from one hand. With the key from around his neck, he opened it and tossed the ruined metal aside. Then he began to carefully bathe her wrists and hands, too.

And that's when he noticed her father's ring was gone. Somehow, that sparked even hotter rage. They'd stolen the ring she'd nearly bartered everything to keep.

He was going to kill them slowly.

He was so involved in his thoughts of punishment, he didn't notice she was awake.

He heard her inhale, slow and sibilant, and glanced up to find her gaze upon him. Her eyes were green as a New England forest and just as wild. Only when he felt her pulling did he realize he was gripping her wrists tighter than he intended. He gentled his hold but didn't release her. His thumbs stroked softly within the well of her palms.

"Eliza, it's Jean-Luc. You're safe now. I'm not going to hurt you."

Gradually, he let go of her, then waited for her to strike out at him or scramble for escape. She did neither. Her arms dropped slackly, as if too heavy for her to hold, and her head turned to the side, her gaze fixing blindly upon the ceiling. She was still in shock from all that had happened. His initial impulse was to gather her up close, but he feared he would only frighten her more with any physical demonstration. Instead, he kept his voice pitched low, in a crooning cadence.

"Would you like something to eat? I bet you are hungry? Some cool water, perhaps? I'm afraid there is not much else I can offer in the way of . . ." He trailed off because her eyes had closed and her face turned against the back of the chaise. He sighed, wanting to touch her but not quite daring. "Rest, then. Call me if there is anything you need."

He waited for some response and got none. Reluctantly, he stood and as a tender afterthought, stripped out of his jacket to lay it over her. Her fingers curled over the lapels, hugging it tightly about her.

It had been so long since he'd cared for anyone, the feelings were awkward, bursting. Frustrated and restless, he left her to the healing solitude, stepping out onto the broad front veranda to breathe deeply of the settling night.

His home. It was, yet it wasn't. He'd built it with that plan in mind, yet somehow had never been able to instill a sense of belonging to its large empty rooms. Now, with Eliza inside, a bewildering sensation of peace secured itself around his heart. And he knew, as odd as it seemed, that Coeur Desir had been waiting for Eliza. He'd built it for her. For them to share together.

She woke with a cry wedged up in her throat, the sound strangling there in a pathetic whimper. She lay still, afraid to move, uncertain of where she was. Terrifying memory, never too far from the surface, assailed her, and it was like enduring the attacks all over again. Her body shuddered with revulsion, tears beaded on her lashes, but she struggled to hold in the sobs, not sure who would hear them.

It was dark. She wasn't lying on the ground. Where, then? The smells of musty disuse and mold were thick about her, but threaded in with those potent odors was a milder, richer scent. A scent that was musky, male, and compellingly familiar.

Eliza stroked the jacket that blanketed her, fingering the buttons hidden by the turned back lapel. A seaman's coat.

"Luc."

His name came out as a whisper, as frail as her

hopes. Somewhere in the blackness and panic of the past few days, she remembered his voice, spoken low and filled with sweet promise.

I've come to take you away from here.

Her breathing quickened. Had he been real? Had he come for her? Was she now safe with him? She was afraid to believe it, afraid to wish it were true. The only reality she'd clung to was the hope of his rescue, darkened by the fear that he had somehow orchestrated her sale to the Cajuns.

Which was true?

She got up off the chaise, clutching Luc's coat about her. She wobbled for a moment, her balance tenuous. But the need to know before she could close her eyes again drove her onward, even as terror trembled through her, warning her to run, to hide while she could. She took one step, then another, shuffling toward the central hall of a house she didn't recognize.

She saw the figure of a man on the porch, staring out at the darkness. Panic seized her at the sight. She muffled a cry with the press of her fist against torn lips. Instinct screamed for her to flee even as she recognized the powerful silhouette.

"Luc?" She forced his name from the constriction of her vocal chords.

He turned at once, his quick stride toward her halting when she shrank back in alarm. He paused there in the heavy shadow, tense, anxious. His voice was unusually soothing.

"Eliza? Are you all right?"

A waking blackness came up and over her so fast, she was caught unawares. Chills rattled up through her. Panic swelled and crested with enormous force. She couldn't seem to breathe right, air coming in small, insufficient gasps. She felt hands upon her, cupping her elbows in support, but they became different in her anxious mind—pawing, hurting—and her fragile control snapped.

With a moaning cry, she flung her arms wide, trying to fend off the invading hands. At the same time, instinct responded to the memories of horror, prompting her to protect herself. To run . . .

Luc saw the change. One minute, she was weak but lucid. In the next, sanity drained away like the color from her face. Her eyes grew huge and haunted by what he could not imagine. Horrible sounds clawed their way out of her throat, prickling the hair at the nape of his neck. Wild and wounded, she stumbled back, fighting him off with frantic hands, those terrible cries prompting a twist of alarm. She didn't know him.

What was he going to do? He couldn't let her run out into the night in her frail state. Yet he couldn't bear the thought of restraining her, even for her own good.

"Eliza, *ma belle*, you are safe with me."

The sound of his voice provoked her to action. With surprising agility, she dodged to one side, meaning to circle him and disappear into the darkness. Luc caught her arm, halting the attempt, pinning her in close to his chest when she began to shriek and struggle.

With his arms banded tightly about her, he effectively stilled her notion of escape. She writhed against him, her mewling cries muffled by his shirtfront. His eyes squeezed shut, Luc rested his cheek against the top of her head. He continued to hold her, keeping her pressed close, hoping to overwhelm her fears with his familiar presence.

But he wasn't familiar to her, not anymore, not while the darker demons prowled through the confusion of her mind.

Finally, she surrendered, her body going slack, shivering loosely in his arms. He did nothing for a long moment, cradling her in his embrace, absorbing the cherished feel of her. Her heart thrummed a frenzied beat. Her breath puffed in short bursts. But she was quiet, at least on the outside. He had no idea what raced through her thoughts. His lips brushed over the tangle of her hair.

"Oh, *chère*, I feared I would never find you. Don't let me lose you now to this madness."

And even as he whispered that hope, a cold dread seeped in, murmuring that it might already be too late.

Because it was too dark to wander about the rest of the house, they slept in the parlor, Eliza on the ruined chaise, Jean-Luc on the floor alongside it—where she'd fall over him if she tried to slip away before dawn. Despite his best intentions, he slept hard. Knowing they were safe, at least temporarily, he could no longer hold to the exhausting pace. His mind and body shut down for the remaining hours of the night only to come awake with a jerk to a room flooded with sunlight—alone.

Wide awake with his first blink, he took in the significance of the empty chaise and cursed passionately. How would he find her if she'd headed out afoot? He was no tracker, with no special knowledge of the land. His only hope was she hadn't gotten far. He was rushing to the hall when he heard the sound of water. His knees went weak.

She hadn't left him.

Eliza was washing from the basin on the veranda. She'd stripped off the torn gown to stand gloriously naked against the verdant setting. Sunlight gleamed against fair skin, highlighting the supple curve of her back and gentle flare of her hips as she bent down to run the wet cloth over her arms and shoulders. Water droplets shimmered like diamonds along that sleek expanse, teasing him with the remembered feel of her, all satiny smooth beneath his palms. Never had anything stirred him quite so deeply as the sight of her nude innocence in such pagan surroundings. A healthy surge of lust would not have surprised him, but this warm spreading sense of possessive pleasure took him completely unaware. As if he could have stood there forever lost to the looking, content with that chaste adoration.

Was that love, then? The willingness to sacrifice the physical for the emotional satisfaction? Odd, he wouldn't have thought it could be that way between a man and woman. Or was it just this woman?

He noticed, too, the marks upon her body, testaments to the cruelty she'd borne. Bruises mottled her arms, ribs, and backside. Dark smudges that could only be the imprint of a man's hand marked her upper thighs. Fury growled through him.

She must have sensed him standing there, for abruptly she swiveled around to regard him in stark dismay. She clutched the cloth to her breasts as an inadequate covering. Their coral tips quivered with the force of her erratic breathing. She'd already washed her hair. It hung past her shoulders in a heavy curtain of wet silk. She looked wild, beautiful. And absolutely terrified.

Very slowly, Luc unbuttoned his shirt. Her wide eyes riveted to the movement of his hands, her fear growing. He shrugged it off and extended it to her.

"Here. It is not clean, but it will cover you until you can wash your own things."

She stared at the shirt, her gaze darting between his offering and him as if searching for some sign of a trap. She reached out a trembling hand, cautious, oh, so cautious it made him grit his teeth against the desire to cry "I won't hurt you!"

Her fingertips nudged a sleeve. Then, fast as a snake, she snatched it from him, wiggling into its concealing folds. She stood by tense degrees, taut as a doe ready to take flight. Luc made no move toward her.

"Do you know who I am?" he asked.

After a moment, she nodded.

"Who am I?"

She moistened her cracked lips nervously. "Jean-Luc." Her voice was a hoarse whisper.

"And you know I would not hurt you. You know that, don't you?"

Again, the jerky nod.

He focused on her stare, trying to win her confidence. He smiled encouragingly. She didn't return it.

"Where are we?" Again, that fragile whisper.

"I own this land, this house. I thought we would be safer here than trying to venture alone back to New Orleans. I left word with Shamus so he would know where to find us."

She considered this somberly, then accepted it with another nod. Fear gave her eyes a depthless quality, like the warm seas of the Mediterranean. Luc found himself diving in without wisdom. He took a step toward her and she a quick one back.

"Eliza, I won't hurt you."

She didn't answer. She didn't look convinced, either. Shadows darkened the tranquil waters of her stare with an undertow of uncertainty and pain. He was drowning in those pools of sorrow yet helpless to save them both. The only thing he could do was pull back.

"I will leave you to finish here. I need to open the

house up to the sun and air before it falls down of rot around our ears.''

One of the hardest things he'd ever done was turn away and leave her unguarded upon his porch. There was nothing to stop her from running away, and he hoped that would convince her that it was safe to stay. She had to start trusting him, and the only way he could foster it was by trusting her in return. He, who had little faith himself, was beyond anxious as he climbed the curved cypress stairs to the second story, struggling to resist the need to look behind him to see if Eliza was still on the porch.

The master bedroom lay heavy with dust, but it was nothing a good stiff broom and sunny breeze wouldn't cure. He threw open the windows to stir the stagnant air and stripped protective cloths from the giant tester bed he'd had shipped from France. He lingered a moment, caressing the silky wood of the frame, eyes closing to recapture the happy squeal of children bouncing on the counterpane with gleeful abandon to awaken slugabed parents. He expressed a heavy sigh and turned from the poignant images only to come face-to-face with Eliza.

She clutched the door frame timidly, her great green eyes fixed upon him both worriedly and warily. If she was afraid of him, it seemed she feared being left to her own company more. He smiled faintly. She shivered in apprehension.

Deciding the best thing would be to go about his business as if she weren't there, Luc strode out into the hall, chagrined that she shrunk back against the wall as he passed her. He went from room to room, inviting in the fresh air, shaking the musty coverings out over the gallery and leaving them draped there to absorb the sun. She followed, a frail shadow, keeping him within sight but at a distance. Which was fine with him.

Traversing his home, he fell in love with it all over again, aching for the loneliness of its empty rooms. Such a house should know laughter and life. He glanced at Eliza. Perhaps it would again.

"These acres were granted to my family by the French crown before I was born." He spoke of the history to put Eliza at ease as he swept unoccupied webs down from the elaborate ceiling medallions. The details of his story seemed far distant to him, as if retelling someone else's life.

"In my grandfather's day, the big river came right up to the door, but now it's taken a turn the other way, leaving behind some of the finest, most fertile soil imaginable. It will yield spectacular crops."

He glanced to where Eliza sat curled in a pool of sunlight at the gallery rail. Her head rested against one of the whitewashed spools, her gaze fixed vaguely upon some distant spot. He guessed she was listening.

"I suppose you think it is odd that a man of the sea could know something of the land." He paused, hoping she'd show some interest in the answer. When she remained unmoved, he continued. "My family comes from a long line of those who till and reap what the soil rewards. My earliest remembrance was my grandfather pressing a lump of warm earth into my palm, telling me, 'Respect the land and it will always provide for you.' He was so proud of the legacy he thought to leave me. It is all gone now, just as they are gone—all but this land and this bed." He paused. He'd never spoken of the past to anyone but Shamus, and not even to him for many years.

But the sight of Eliza sitting straighter, her head

cocked slightly in a pose of attention, encouraged him to go on.

"I never loved the sea, not the way my father wished I would. It's the land that holds me. My dream has always been to hold my own great house, to look out over acres rich with prosperity. This is my *coeur desir*. The foundation was built of brick laid by workers provided by the Lafittes in exchange for services done them. The upper floors are cypress, plaster, and mud. I oversaw their construction and design. I saw myself living in these rooms, entertaining below, beginning a family above. A wonderful dream that was not to be due to the greed of—" He broke off abruptly, remembering to whom he spoke. He swallowed down his bitterness and cast a look her way. She was staring at him intently.

"Because of the Montgomerys," she supplied.

His features worked into harsh angles. It was impossible to disguise his ire, so he turned away with a curt, "Yes."

"How very much you must hate them." She spoke softly, almost as if she wasn't included in their number.

In control of his expression, he looked to her again. "*Non.* Not you. I do not hate you." A rich timbre crept into his tone, a resonant rumble of all he suppressed inside. Eliza either didn't hear it or chose not to react to it, for her gaze was unblinking.

Needing to change the subject, he set the broom aside and smoothed the aged counterpane with his palms. "I must go for supplies. We've next to nothing in the larder—"

"No!"

He turned to see her gazing up at him through anxious eyes.

"It is not quite a mile to the neighboring homestead. I should be back by nightfall. You rest—"

"Jean-Luc, don't leave me." Terror trembled in her voice, striking an answering chord of tenderness within him.

"I will not be gone long. You are safe—"

"No! You said that before, didn't you? I won't be left behind." She stood on unsteady legs, clinging to one of the cypress colonettes for support. She looked ready to faint.

"Eliza, it is not an easy journey. The terrain is rough—"

"I don't care."

"*Non*. You will remain here. You will be fine as long as you stay inside. I will only be away a few hours at most and you can—"

His reasonings died in his throat as she approached him with a hesitant stride. Her fingers plied the buttons of his shirt, shaking fitfully as they opened it. Then, before he could register in his mind what she was doing, she'd shrugged out of the garment, leaving her naked beneath his startled gaze.

"Don't leave me, Jean-Luc. I will do . . . anything."

Chapter 19

❧ ⌒ ◯◯ ⌒ ❧

Even though Jean-Luc had been in a perpetual
state of arousal almost since the moment he laid
eyes on her, carnal pleasures were the furthest thing
from his mind at this time.

"Non, chérie," he murmured thickly as he bent to
retrieve the shirt.

Her hands trapped his face in the wedge between
them, directing his wide, startled gaze to the intensity
of her own.

"Don't leave me, Luc. Don't let them take me
back."

Before it could register that she was bartering herself for his protection, her mouth was on his, hard,
relentlessly seeking his response. He tried to turn his
head away, but her fingers twisted in his hair, becoming fists at his temples. As he straightened, her nude
body swayed against his, molding along his lean,
strong length like a second skin. As her tongue jutted
aggressively into his mouth, his body rose of its own
accord, pushing hot and full between them. She
sighed as if relieved by the evidence of his desire.

"Love me, Luc."

Was this what she needed? Luc was confused. After
what she'd endured at the hands of those animals,

219

lying with a man was the last thing he would think her interested in. Perhaps, then, it was something she had to prove to herself, that she was capable of responding as a woman.

If that was what she wanted . . .

His hands came up slowly, fitting against the curve of her spine, at the hollow between her shoulder blades, pressing her to him, alert for signs of resistance. There were none. Her painful hold on his hair relaxed, her fingers combing through it restlessly, urgently as his mouth opened over hers. He held her, kissed her, lingered over the tempting interplay as a host of wild, sweet emotions broke loose inside him. He'd been so afraid, so afraid of losing her. His kiss deepened, his arm lowered to hook behind her knees, lifting her, turning them both toward the bed where he'd always dreamed of making love to the woman fate delivered for an eternity. He could imagine being in it with no other. He laid her down. Her grasp refused to lessen, drawing him over her.

He wanted to be sensitive to her mood, willing to withdraw the moment she betrayed signs of discomfort. It was hard to hold to those noble ideals with her hands tugging at his trousers, shoving them down over his hard flanks. He meant to go slow, to court her gently, but her voracious little mouth scrambled his ability to think clearly as it sucked on his lips, on his tongue, sending spears of flame all the way to his toes.

She wriggled under him, fitting his hips between the tenting of her knees, inviting him in with the press of her palms to his buttocks, arching to encourage him. He needed little encouragement. He was overwhelmed with sensations of relief, of gratitude, of love and desperate desire. He'd never wanted anything so much as this passionate reunion. He'd never had a woman make love to him with such insistence. His mind was dazzled, his hunger for her raged beyond caution, out of control. He thrust into her.

Eliza gasped against his mouth, tension bowing her body. She was tight, hot and dry, not nearly as ready as she'd led him to believe. With supreme effort, he remained unmoving within her, denying the hard impatient throbbing of his sex as it demanded satisfaction.

This was wrong. It felt wrong to him. Confused, he began to withdraw. Her long legs wrapped about him, keeping him from pulling away.

And in a voice harsh with feeling, she said, "What's wrong, Luc? Don't you want me now?"

Not want her?

Nothing could have been further from the truth.

He surged within her, faster, deeper than he'd planned, but there was no tempering the frenzied nature of his need. He drove toward his release, gasping when it came, stunned by its intensity.

He collapsed, drained and dazed, his labored breaths feathering Eliza's hair.

It was then in those slow, recovering moments that Luc realized all that had happened. At some point in their lovemaking, Eliza had ceased to participate. Her arms stopped their clutching to lie limp at her sides. She'd averted her face to avoid his kisses. His passions were spent within a form so lax, she might well have been sleeping. With awful, ugly suspicions curling through him, Luc lifted up onto his elbows. Eliza's eyes were open, staring sightlessly at the far wall. She flinched when he touched her jaw to guide her attention to him.

That blank, inanimate stare said it all. It had been a sacrifice. Whatever she'd felt, it wasn't an answering passion. Her emotions were suppressed beneath a impenetrable sea of green. And all the beauty of the moment died.

"Take me with you, Jean-Luc." It was a flatly delivered request, stating plainly that he had received what he wanted; now she expected the same.

Feeling used and disturbed, Luc got off her, jerking up his trousers with a gruff, "All right."

She didn't smile. It was no smug victory. Eliza slid out of the bed and into his shirt as if they'd just exchanged handshakes instead of passion.

They made an odd-looking pair tromping through the tough saw grass beneath the graceful sway of Spanish moss. With just his jacket over the bare expanse of his chest, Jean-Luc strode along the vaguely remembered trail with Eliza stumbling behind him. He tried to offer his assistance, but she pulled away from his overture. So he left her to her own devices, keeping a covert eye on her progress.

Finally, Luc drew up beside a great live oak. Just ahead was a simple raised cottage where he hoped to barter for supplies. He turned to Eliza, bidding, "You must stay here, out of sight." Then he forgot the rest of his cautionings.

She sank down at his feet, trembling and breathless. Her bared legs were scored with scratches, and her unbound hair was tangled with wisps of moss and leaves. Yet when she looked up at him, there was no sign of distress, just a quiet desperation.

"Don't leave me behind."

He knelt down, heart seizing up when she cringed away. He managed a smile. "You are not exactly dressed for a social call. They would think you my *petite amie*, and that is not how I would wish you known."

Eliza's thoughts stirred dully. *Petite amie?* Did that

mean sweetheart? Was he ashamed to claim an association with her? After all that had happened, she
shouldn't be surprised. She looked away, suppressing
her pain beneath the swell of ready numbness. It blanketed her emotions and allowed her to hide from
many truths.

Luc saw her awareness dim and sighed regretfully.
He placed one of his hands over her cold ones and
pressed lightly. He tried not to let it matter when she
snatched them away. He withdrew the gesture, standing.

"Eliza, I must go speak with these people. You stay
here."

Immediately, she was wound around his leg.

"Don't leave me."

He tried to untangle her twining grasp, gently,
firmly, but she wouldn't be discouraged. He grew impatient because he was dangerously close to yielding
anything she desired.

"Eliza, stop." He thrust her away a little more
roughly than he'd intended. She crouched there, hugging her knees, plaintive gaze ripping into his heart.
He spoke harshly to chasten her and his own weakening sensibilities. "You will remain here, out of sight.
I will stay in plain view. You can watch me from here.
I will not go in the house. You have my promise. All
right?"

Finally, he had her sketchy nod. But the moment
he turned away, he heard her soft fearful cry.

"Luc."

He crumpled. Bending down, he scooped her chin
into one palm, holding her steady as he touched a
brief kiss to her brow.

"My promise, *ma belle.*"

* * *

Eliza huddled at the base of the massive oak, lost in the fog of ceaseless fear. Her anxious gaze followed Jean-Luc with a despairing reluctance to let him go. Instinct told her she was safe with him, even though a deeper fright had her shivering at his touch. She seemed to remember him through the jumble of her mind. Sometimes, she recalled him clearly as Jean-Luc Gautier, her brave privateer, and sought his protection. Yet at other times, he blended in with the anonymous blur of threatening male, to be avoided and feared. Her memory was filled with blissful blanks. The missing details were vague and sinister, whispering of pain. There were moments when she wished the barrier away, sure she could face whatever it hid for her own good. But when it began to lower, and she glimpsed the darkness, the horror it held at bay, she gratefully succumbed to blessed oblivion once more. Coward, she called herself, while thankful for the ignorance.

Luc meant safety. Of that she was sure. As long as he was with her, nothing bad could reach her. His absence wrought such horrific anxiety, she couldn't bear to be apart from him, even when his presence was almost as disturbing. As long as he allowed her to be near him, the waiting darkness stayed away. To be near him, she would do anything for the fragile peace of mind it gave her.

She had a hazy recollection of him declaring nothing was given for free. If she wished his protection, she had to pay for the privilege. And all she had left to barter with was her body. On the detached plane her mind had found comfort in, it didn't matter that he took her. Sensations were far removed from her physical self. She didn't remember why, only that it was for self-preservation. Let him use her empty shell of a self. He couldn't reach her heart or soul to spoil them.

She watched him speak with a wary couple. Luc. She swayed toward him. He was handsome. The sight of him warmed her with a faint tingling she should have recognized but didn't. Intense yearning rose within her, the need to touch him, to be close. He'd promised he wouldn't leave her. Why didn't she trust his words? Had he broken them before?

She quit wondering, afraid such probings would bring back a rush of memory, and there was too much she still wished to avoid.

He came back toward her at last, a bulky burlap sack hoisted over his shoulder. Gladness rushed in a tide, carrying her to him at a run. He had time to drop the sack and catch her up in his arms.

Eliza hugged herself to him, enveloped by a sense of security, a balm to her tattered spirit. She breathed in the scent of him, absorbed the strength of him with the stroke of her palms along muscle-sculpted arms. He said nothing, simply accepting her within the circle of his embrace, holding her close until she squirmed to gain her freedom. When she stepped back from him, attuned to wariness once more, she worried over the lambent heat in his gaze. It wasn't lust. It was something deeper, more possessing. Nervously, she glanced away, toward the parcel he carried.

Shaking off the tender pleasure of her greeting, Luc knelt down to open the sack.

"I was able to trade for quite a number of necessities. Here. This is for you."

She stared at the leather breeches.

Luc smiled. "Not very fashionable, I know. But they will protect you on your walk back. Hurry now. We must go. I do not know the way well enough to manage in the dark.''

She tugged on the trousers without further protest and waited docilely for him to lead on. Again, she made the lengthy walk without slowing him down or begging for a chance to rest. His admiration for her soared, along with his concern.

She skirted behind him, a shadow, a vague sliver of her former self. She didn't speak. Her expressive range narrowed down to two emotions: fright and desperation. Traumatized by her captivity, he guessed her mind and body were too shocked by abuse to return to normal functioning. Did that mean they never would? Would she be forever shrinking from his slightest gesture, accepting his commands with meekness instead of the combatant spark he missed so dearly? He remembered his father speaking of such things happening to men in wartime, where the horror of death sent their souls into hiding, leaving an empty husk behind. Would he ever have her back again, or had those animals stolen away her lively spirit?

The big house was draped in latticework shadows from the majestic live oaks spreading near. A chorus of frogs and night birds began down in the swampland, making a special song only heard here in the bayou. Music that reached to Jean-Luc's soul. He entered the house, engulfed by the feeling of coming home, gratified by the sound of Eliza scurrying after him. And as he prepared them a meal off the provisions he'd gotten, he talked because Eliza's silence was painful to listen to.

"That man I met with, Didier Tournadier, he is a genius at working wood. He carved the wooden chandeliers hanging in the hall and dining room and many of the medallions, door frames, and moldings. Such a waste, talent like his, hidden out here in the back-waters. Apparently, he is on the run from a noose. I did not ask the particulars. It would not have been polite. He and his wife and their three sons work the neighboring plot of land. They are good neighbors, keeping to themselves. He was happy to trade these goods for a little sweat from me. I will be lending my back for the next few days to help him clear one of his fields."

Eliza's stare darkened, but her anxieties went unspoken as Jean-Luc brought her a plate of fried okra and red beans. She stared at the food unblinkingly.

"Eat."

What Luc wouldn't have given to hear her snap "What will it cost me, pirate?" But she said nothing, picking up her spoon obediently. Disheartened, Luc concentrated on his own meal.

By the time they'd finished and Luc had put away all their bartered goods, darkness had settled completely. Knowing he had an early start over to Tournadier's in the morning, Luc lit the way upstairs with a lamp. He'd gone halfway when he noticed Eliza wasn't following. She stood at the bottom of the steps, hugging the newel post. Light from the lamp was faint, not doing justice to whatever played upon her upturned features.

"Eliza, come up," he called coaxingly. "It is late. We are both tired and in need of a good night's rest. Come up. I won't hurt you." He added that last, hating the need to say it.

Still she hesitated, and unable to think of any other way to persuade her short of force, Luc continued up the curve of the stairs and went into the big master bedroom. Setting the lamp on the side table, he threw back the ancient counterpane and stripped out of his clothing. He'd just slipped beneath the thin top sheet when a gliding whisper of movement caught his eye.

Eliza approached gingerly and lingered at the foot of the bed. Her arms were hugged across her chest, and great, luminous eyes studied the empty space on the bed as if it held both lure and threat. Luc patted his palm upon the mattress; then he turned down the light.

He waited in the darkness, feeling her reluctance to join him, wondering if she could overcome it. Finally the slightest dip announced her presence beside him. Determined not to betray her trust, Luc rolled away. He closed his eyes, trying to summon sleep, but his every sense was alive, focused upon her.

After a time, the sultry heat and lulling music of the bayou night soothed him into relaxation. He'd begun to drift pleasantly toward slumber when a gentle bounce of the bed was followed by the alarmingly soft fit of Eliza's form along his backside. Her arm curled over the slight concave of his waist, her balled fist coming to rest over his heart. He lay motionless, startled. He felt her weary sigh brush the nape of his neck. Smiling to himself, he closed his eyes again and, this time, slipped easily off to sleep.

Luc woke with a start, fully alert for danger. He reached for the pistol he'd tucked beneath the bedding when he heard again the sound that broke his slumber. Leaving the pistol where it was, he rolled toward Eliza.

She was knotted up in a tight ball, limbs tense and trembling. Small whimpering sounds escaped her as she dreamed, no doubt, of her past nightmare. Tenderness overcame him.

Whispering her name, Luc turned her onto her back, rubbing the rigidity from her shoulders and arms in the same way he would warm her from the onslaught of cruel elements. Wasn't it the same—weather tormenting the body, her dreams tormenting the soul? Both needed careful attention to coax them back to normal.

"Eliza? Wake up, *ma petite*. You are safe now."

He knew the moment she crossed the line to awareness. Her palms flew up to brace against his shoulders. Her knees drew up to protect her from violation.

"It's Jean-Luc, *chère*. You've nothing to fear."

"Luc?"

He felt her hesitation, her uncertainty, the great and possibly insurmountable barrier of her terror. Then, with a soft cry, she cast her arms about him, hugging hard, shuddering violently.

When he would hold her and comfort her gently, Eliza drew back, panting lightly. He waited for words, but she answered with actions. Her sudden kiss sent a shock of sensation scalding through him. He tried to pull away, but she clung fast, forcing a response.

Her tongue touched to the seam of his mouth, sliding wetly, probing at his resistance until, with a ragged groan, he opened for her. She swirled inside, conquering his reluctance with an unpracticed ease. How had she discovered so quickly how to mold his desires to her will? His hands fit to her face, and she didn't recoil from his touch. It incited her to greater demonstrations of need. She tugged him over her, feeding his urgency with provocative stabs of her tongue to mimic what she would ask of him. What was honor and good intention when tempted with his every dream?

"Make me belong to you, Luc."

That whisper against his lips struck down the last of his resistance. With a groan of compliance, he lifted her hips within his palms and slid inside her. She took him with a fierce trembling. It might have been passion. He wanted to believe that. She kissed him as if it was true.

Mine.

That word teased him, taunting up visions of her being used by other men. Brutally, violently, they'd stolen the treasure this woman had become to him. They'd taken her spirit, her fire, her passion, and he wanted it back. He wanted to reclaim her soul even as he claimed her body. He would wake in her the heart-shaking pinnacle they'd reached that first night in New Orleans. He would stir in her the need that even now overwhelmed him. She was his, and he would have her back, erasing the memory of those before him.

Driven by that purpose, he plunged into her heated core, working toward a surcease of passion, finding it, alone.

Frustrated by his inability to satisfy her, Luc tucked her up against his side, determination easing to tender sympathies as her arms banded tightly about him. He kissed her hair and sighed.

"It will take time, *ma belle*. I'm here for you. I will not leave you. You're safe with me, Eliza. You do believe that, don't you?"

Silence.

Very softly, he vowed, "You will."

As he sank into an exhausted sleep, Eliza lay wide awake, hearing whispers of danger in the placid night sounds. And she clutched at the man beside her to keep them at bay.

Chapter 20

A wake but unwilling to stir, Jean-Luc let the strange sense of contentment embrace him. His home. His ancestral bed. His lady love. Afraid to move lest the mood be broken, he absorbed it all, filling his long-sorrowing soul with what it had hungered for. Permanence, family—still an illusion yet tangible enough to tempt such thoughts.

Eliza slept beside him, her gloriously bright hair strewn like tangled sunbeams across the pillow covers. Her bruises were fading, blotches of ugly color against otherwise flawless skin. How he wished her emotional injuries could heal so effortlessly with time.

Time called him from where he longed to linger. He had a debt to pay and would not ask his neighbor to wait. The instant he moved from the bed, he felt Eliza's anxious stare upon him. Purposefully, he didn't look her way. His will wasn't dependable, and the sight of her, all morning soft and available, could easily be his undoing. He dressed hurriedly.

There was no way to steel his heart against her panicked expression. It struck him the moment he turned around. She didn't speak; she didn't plead. Her great luminous eyes did it for her.

His tone was gentle in its prompting. "If you are

coming with me, you had best make haste.''

Relief flitted across her face. It was thanks enough. She grabbed up the leather breeches, giving him a tantalizing view of sleek back and rounded bottom. He stalked from the room, groin tight with torment.

Again, Eliza kept silent pace with him on the walk to Tournadier's. In her breeches and borrowed shirt, with her coppery tresses bound back in a heavy braid, she looked more the rugged frontier woman than a sheltered Salem miss. The look suited her. And it suited him as well. The glow of good health was back in her cheeks, dimming the evidence of her misuse, but shadows remained in her ever alert and anxious gaze.

She was wise in her worry. Jean-Luc hadn't said as much, but he was far from at ease with their situation. He hadn't invited Eliza along just for her company or to soothe her fears. He didn't want her to go unguarded for any length of time. He'd no doubts that the Cajuns were looking for them, and these were their swamps. No one could hunt him and Eliza better.

They knew who he was. Their first act would be returning to New Orleans, where his ship was still at anchor and Etienne still held their money. It might have been as easy as a return of the price paid for Eliza—not that Etienne would be forthcoming with a refund. But money wouldn't make up for the loss of one of their own or the loss of their property, not to men like these hardened bayou rats. They'd be out for revenge. Luc would be safe only as long as they couldn't find him. He was a landowner but had never been free with that fact. They only knew him as a man of the sea. It wouldn't be a simple matter to track him down, nor an impossible one, either.

And if they came after him before Shamus arrived

to provide escort back to the city, Eliza's fate was in his hands. He knew he could never allow them to take her back. At least, not while he was alive.

She belonged to him now, and he would protect her. And he no longer pretended, even with himself, that he wasn't in love with Eliza Montgomery. It was that simple. That complex.

At Tournadier's, they were met by the slim, homely Creole who, with a curious glance at Eliza, invited them in to share breakfast. Eager for a cup of the rich brew that had his nose twitching in the morning air, Luc was quick to accept. With a guiding hand on Eliza's back, he urged her forward, hoping she wouldn't balk and force him to any awkward explanations. Though Tournadier was too polite to demand any, it would place an uncomfortable breach between them.

His wife was another matter.

One look at Eliza's discolored face and Claire-Marie Tournadier was ready to fillet the meat from his bones. She didn't say anything. She didn't have to. She made the connecting glare from Eliza's bruises to his hands, her black-eyed stare lifting to Luc's to convey her contempt. Though Luc shared her disgust for anyone who would so abuse a woman, he did not feel the need to exonerate himself from her blame. His chin took a defiant notch higher.

"Woman, coffee for our guests," Tournadier called. "Have your forgotten your manners?"

Claire-Marie muttered a meek apology and went to fetch them the savory brew while her husband spoke of the work ahead and his stripling sons ogled Eliza shyly. Luc watched uneasily as the woman tried to make eye contact with Eliza, but to the dispirited younger woman, none existed aside from him. She followed his every move with her needy gaze, oblivious to the other female's attempts at kindness. He took some satisfaction in that, shallow though it was.

And when the coffee was gone and the men shouldered their tools for the fields, Eliza rose anxiously, looking to Luc for direction.

"Your young lady is welcome to stay here with me," Claire-Marie suggested, careful to convey none of the censure snapping in her dark stare.

Luc didn't have to answer. Eliza leaped to do it for him with the quick winding of her arms about one of his.

"She will come with me," Jean-Luc said, knowing that clutching gesture could not be misinterpreted. "I thank you for your offer though, madame."

Her glare slashed right through him before she turned coaxingly to Eliza. "Are you sure? 'Twill be ever so much more comfortable for you here."

Eliza drew a panicked breath. "Luc." Her gaze cast up in beseechment.

Curse the woman for her meddling, Luc thought as he quieted Eliza's fright with a small smile. When he reached up to pat her arm reassuringly, Eliza doubly damned him by shrinking away. His mood hardened.

"She will be fine, Madame Tournadier." His tone brooked no argument, nor did the lady's husband's chastening stare. Claire-Marie said nothing more, holding her tongue with obvious difficulty. Luc could see he'd made an enemy.

The heat increased with the hour. By noontime, Luc ran with sweat. Following Tournadier's example, he stripped to the waist, using his shirt to fashion a head covering. The work was brutal, exhausting, but Eliza created a constant bright spot whenever he glanced over to where she sat in the shade of a huge live oak looking drowsy and delectable. It was easy to fantasize about a shared future with her as his lady, as easy as it was to forget what brought them together: that she was a tool of vengeance against her father, a society creature already bound to wed another. She was his captive, not his willing concubine, but in the sweltering afternoon hours, he could imagine her as more. Much more. Such pleasant fancies made the time fly faster.

Until he glanced over and saw Claire-Marie in urgent conversation with Eliza within the deepening twilight shadows.

As he approached, he realized it was more Claire-Marie talking *at* Eliza, who was looking up at her with a bewildered frown. Her gaze leaped to Luc with apparent relief.

"Madame Tournadier, how good of you to stop out to keep my lady company."

Claire-Marie leaped back guiltily, fear flickering briefly in her gaze before it congealed with wrath. "We were just getting to know one another. It's lonely out here for me without another woman to talk to."

Luc made no comment. The statement was innocent. Her manner was not. He didn't need another problem to add to his mountain of worries, and he wondered just how much trouble the Creole's wife could be. Plenty, if she discovered who Eliza was and what had brought her into his care. Claire-Marie Tournadier seemed the sort to forget that one minded one's own affairs. His severe glare of warning was interrupted by a call from Tournadier.

"Bright and earlier tomorrow, eh, Jean-Luc?"

He raised a hand in affirmation and put the other one down to Eliza.

"Shall we go home, *ma petite?*"

When Eliza hesitated, her confused gaze fixed upon his palm, Claire-Marie spoke up.

"It would be no trouble if you would care to join us for our evening meal."

"Thank you, madame, but we must decline." His tone was frigidly polite as he willed Eliza to accept his hand. Finally, she did so, possessing it anxiously between both of her own. Luc's chill smile turned upon Claire-Marie in triumph as he lifted Eliza to her feet and tucked her into the shelter of his arm.

And on the walk back to Coeur Desir, Luc weighed two evils. Was Eliza safer alone at the house or in the sly Madame Tournadier's company?

"What did Madame Tournadier talk to you about, Eliza?" He posed the question later, casually, as they climbed the stairs for bed. When she had no answer, he looked to her, impatient in his concern. "Eliza, did you hear me?"

She was staring anxiously at the darkened floor below as if expecting it to yield up her faceless terror. The sharpness of Luc's tone caught her attention but not her focus. She stared up at him in panic.

"Are we safe here?"

"Yes, of course. What did Madame Tournadier say to you?"

She stared up blankly, as if the name meant nothing.

Luc sighed and his temper softened. He couldn't be angry in the face of her confusion. "You are safe here, *chérie*. I will not let anything harm you." Then he suffered the childlike innocence of her grateful embrace. There was nothing childlike in his response to it, to the sweet press of her along his hard and hungry planes. To take advantage of her in her bewildered state would make him no better than the animals who pursued them.

Yet that night, when she turned to him all soft and invitingly naked within the big bed they shared, noble sentiments gave way before a deeper yearning. He hadn't the strength to turn down her offer, that offer of momentary bliss. Lost within her yielding heat, surrounded by her silken limbs, a swirl of desperate longing overwhelmed him, every bit as sharp and intense as his physical release.

It wasn't until afterward, when he tried coaxing an answering warmth from her with his searching kisses, that he was again frustrated. It was like trying to encourage a response from one of the porch posts. She didn't reject his overtures, but neither did she react to them. Her mouth was cool and malleable beneath his, as indifferent as a tired whore's. That correlation slashed through his ardor.

And as she curled up close beside him, confident that her protection had been paid for, Luc held her, chafing in a hell of his own making.

They fell into a pattern, a rhythm complementing the tempo of long, steamy days and sultry nights. Each morning they drank Tournadier's strong chicory coffee before heading out to his fields. Each day, Eliza waited uncomplainingly within plain sight, content with the tedium. Each night, she offered up the pleasures of her body in exchange for a sense of safety and each night, though he vowed not to, Luc surrendered to his passion for her. Always, he hoped to inspire answering emotion; each time, he was doomed to disappointment.

She got no better, and Luc fretted over it. The glaze of remoteness blanketing her feelings was a constant reminder of how he'd failed her. He couldn't break through it, not with talk, not with touch. It was as if she'd removed herself from the potential of further pain, and in doing so, also denied any possible pleasure.

Hadn't he done much the same thing all those many years ago?

And on the eve of his last day working off his debt to Tournadier, he stood in the silent cavern of his rooms, pondering what to do.

It was so empty, his dream. A home he couldn't afford to finish, a woman whose heart he couldn't claim. He glanced to where Eliza sat on the uncarpeted stairs. She regarded him unblinkingly, looking, as always, on the ragged edge of hysteria between a senseless scream and mindless placidity. He was so tired of seeing it, of not knowing how to relieve it. Was he a fool, thinking to keep her with him? Would she ever recover her wits in surroundings that reminded her of her trauma? Could she ever be made to respond to him as a man instead of as her captor, guardian of her safety?

"What am I to do, *chérie*?"

His words echoed back to him as hollowly as Eliza's stare. He sighed.

"In my mind's eye, I have seen these rooms awash with lamplight, alive with laughter. I have placed every picture on the walls, arranged every table, every chair. I planned to the most minute detail how I would open the doors to the cream of New Orleans in one of the grandest events in their memory, and how they would embrace me as one of their own. I know what I will be wearing, what wines to serve, what music will be playing. All these details kept me from madness while I lay in chains. It was the dream that kept me alive."

He crossed to the stairs, painfully aware of Eliza shrinking back to the opposite side of the steps as he leaned upon the meticulously carved newel post. He caressed the smooth wood of the rail wistfully, his mood one of melancholy.

"How sad to lose one's dreams. This one was so close, within the touch of my hand. I could have had it all if not for your father's treachery." He stared upward at the darkened hall above, leading to rooms that would never house glittering company. The silence mocked him, as did Eliza's failure to show any emotion. He kept talking aloud, to provoke both things with his increasing upset.

"Did he tell you of how he tricked me, *ma petite*? Did he boast of his cleverness while you laughed together at my expense? Was it, perhaps, the moneys he owed me that would have paid for your grand wedding whilst I rotted in prison? Moneys I would have used to complete this dream of a fine home and family? What care you for my dreams, eh? What difference be I pirate or privateer? Neither would be acceptable to one such as you, would they, *mon amie*? What price is *honneur* to one who can afford deceit?"

Eliza no longer looked at him, but he could tell by the angle of her head that she was listening. And somehow, atop all else, that indifferent attention was the last straw. Resentment at his tangled situation burst like a noxious fruit. He wanted—needed—to place the blame somewhere because none of it was his fault. He hadn't lied. He hadn't hidden behind false honesty. But he was the one paying the price for another's foul deeds. And now he was impotent to collect upon them—unless he turned in Eliza for the ransom.

He stalked the hall, angry and agitated, trapped in his own scheme of revenge. To have everything, he had to forfeit the only woman who meant anything to him. Again, Montgomery won. There was no justice, after all.

There was just Eliza.

He couldn't hate her. He couldn't blame her. And he couldn't lose her.

Where did that leave him? With the shell of a dream and a spiritless lover. He was still in prison, and Montgomery held the keys.

Too weary in body and mind to continue the pointless agonizing, Luc opted for bed. No decisions would come on this night. As he started for the stairs, Eliza flattened against the rails, alarmed by his dark mood and brooding countenance. For once, he had no patience with her fears. He strode past her without pause. Halfway up the steps, he heard her creeping after him. He took no pleasure in her reluctant shadowing nor, on this evening of restless passions, in her presence. He stripped out of his clothes and dropped onto the bed, tensing when she joined him.

He stared up at the tester overhead. This was the bed on which he and his siblings had been conceived. Where he'd planned to begin his own dynasty an ocean away from his past. It was never his intention to have other than a cherished bride upon this ancestral bower.

Eliza's hand brushed his bare shoulder. He shrugged it off. Sheets shifted. Suddenly, she was flush against him, soft breasts conforming to his forearm, palm pressing to his taut middle, knees notching in next to his in a posture of false intimacy.

"Arrêtez!" With that growl, he flung himself over onto his side, away from temptation.

But she followed, fitting to the denying curve of his body in mute supplication. His resolve trembled. But on this night, he wouldn't allow it to give way.

He pushed her back, angling for a saving distance between them.

"Stop, Eliza. I do not want you. Not like this."

Bold words considering how graphically his own body betrayed him.

She stared at him through wide, bewildered eyes. Panic skirted her expression, desperation prompting her to reach out again. He flinched from beneath the stroke of her fingertips as if the contact seared him. He caught her wrists and again pushed her away.

"No! Not like this. Not when it means nothing."

Her eyes welled up in confusion and fright. She understood his rejection but not his reason.

"Luc . . . I belong to you."

"*Non*, you do not! I do not wish to own you. I do not wish to take you like bartered goods in exchange for your safety. I will not allow you to hold yourself so cheaply. Not for me. Do you understand? I will protect you, Eliza. You do not need to . . . pay me. It is not your gratitude I want. It is your—" He broke off abruptly, seeing no point in going on. He sighed heavily, struggling to explain what he could scarcely understand himself. "I only want what you wish to give. *N'est-ce pas?*"

She stared at him, features impassive. Whatever thoughts moved behind her impenetrable gaze remained her secret.

He extended his arm, opening a close haven beside him. "Come, *chérie*. Rest. You are safe. Sleep without fear."

Cautiously, she edged in next to him, pillowing her head on his shoulder. Her supple form was tense, disbelieving. But as minutes ticked by and he made no move toward any liberties, she gradually melted with relief into a languid relaxation.

Such was not the case with him.

As she slept deeply, soundly, he remained awake, tormented by his nobility, tantalized by her nearness.

* * *

She was in his dining room pouring coffee at his table.

Jean-Luc relaxed in a quiver of delayed panic. When he'd awakened to find her gone, he'd assumed the worst. The contrast of discovering her here, in this domestic scene, undid him.

Something was different. It was more than the performance of this voluntary chore. It went beyond the fact that she'd washed and dressed with care. She wore the simple working-class costume he'd bartered from Claire-Marie, a three-quarter length jacket with pushed-up sleeves and a crossover front and a plain dark skirt. On her, the lowly garment looked regal, as if she were a rich planter's wife attending to genteel morning rituals. To him, she was the most beautiful sight he could imagine.

"Bonjour, mademoiselle."

She gave a start at the sound of his voice, coffee spilling from cup to saucer. For a moment, she greeted him with the blank-eyed terror he'd come to equate with the scars of her ordeal. Then a faint smile of recognition. Indeed, that was something.

He beamed in response.

"I—I made coffee."

"Merci. It smells very good. May I join you?"

He waited for her agreement. It took a long minute; then she nodded slightly. He approached slowly, not wanting to frighten away this first gleam of renewed spirit.

"You rested well, I trust." He hadn't been disturbed by her nightmares. Again, encouraging progress.

"Yes." She pushed a second cup toward him as he settled in an adjacent chair. When he reached for it, her gaze focused on his hand. He stilled it as her fingertips brushed lightly over the thickened knuckles. He didn't move. Gently, her touch explored the length of each of his fingers, her expression unsettled and then poignantly tender.

"How horribly they must have hurt you. Oh, Jean-Luc, I am so very sorry." It was the most she'd said since her rescue. He was almost afraid to reply.

"I survived it."

Her gaze lifted to his, hers bright as dew-drenched grasses. "How?"

Carefully, he enclosed her hand in his, carrying it up to place a light kiss upon it before lowering and releasing it. She hadn't resisted. Another positive sign.

"By clinging to this dream. By wanting it too badly to let them take it away."

She considered his words for a silent second, then said, "I have nothing left." Curious words, morosely spoken. He didn't argue because she obviously believed them.

"Then find a new dream, *chérie*, one that gives you hope."

Her sigh was soft and heart-wrenching. "Not so easy, Captain."

Captain. She hadn't called him that for a long time, since before. Was her memory coming back? Dare he clutch at that optimism?

Too soon, she fell silent, the waxen doll-like quality returning to mask true feelings. He was disappointed, wanting to call back the spark of self she'd shown him, if only briefly. He drank the coffee, ate the hotcakes she'd made from Tournadier's flour and eggs. And he watched her, wishing to see more in her immobile face.

"I should be finished at Tournadier's by dusk."

Eliza glanced up and surprised him soundly. "I should like to remain here. I have some washing to do."

Fear embittered the taste of Luc's coffee. His first

reaction was to deny her. She couldn't stay here, not alone. The danger was too great. Then suspicion tinted his thinking. Why did she wish to remain when she'd sought his constant company so desperately to this point? Had she some scheme in mind, some thought to escape him? Her features betrayed no clue.

"It would be better for you to stay with me." His reply was carefully neutral.

Her gaze dropped in fragile defeat, the flicker of independence gone. And suddenly, he couldn't bear to see it extinguished.

"You must be very careful," he began. Her gaze darted up, catching his with a grateful animation. "Stay close to the house and be alert."

"I will."

She looked down at the pistol he placed on the table. Was she remembering the other time he'd made this futile gesture?

"If you need me, fire a shot and I will come."

Her hand closed firmly over the stock, and she drew the gun down into her lap. Relief etched itself in her smile.

He hated to leave her. His heart and mind were in a quandary of misgivings, part fearing for her, part doubting her motives. But he went because he had to show her this small trust. His last image was of her upon his front steps, his heavy pistol hanging down against her skirts. Anxiety chewed at him throughout the long humid hours of morning as he worked beside Tournadier and tried to come up with an excuse to return to Coeur Desir that wouldn't compromise him or Eliza.

And then he heard the shot.

Chapter 21

E liza stood in the front hall of the quiet house. Luc's house. It should have felt empty, but somehow the sense of him lingered, giving comfort, calming her anxieties. A thin veil of confusion peeled away, allowing in more light of reason, more cognizance of her situation. She was a toddler taking wobbly steps toward sanity, and the journey seemed impossibly long.

She stood in the foyer, soaking up all that she saw with a new clarity, fully aware of her surroundings for the first time. The house was really quite beautiful, with high cypress ceilings and sleek exposed wood, but a sense of sadness hovered within the largely unfurnished rooms, a feeling of time suspended. A feeling echoed within her own heart and mind. She, too, was hollow, waiting to be filled with new hopes and dreams, and a kindred bond formed between her and the big silent house.

Perhaps all they both needed was care.

Luc's seaman's jacket hung on a peg by the door. Eliza lifted it down and slipped into its generous folds, not because she sought warmth but because it enfolded her with his presence. His scent clung to the fabric. She breathed it in. A stronger purpose steadied her easily frayed nerves. Time to venture out from her protective cocoon to test the limits of her control. Time to move forward, not back, where the darkness of those dreaded days could find her. Slowly, wobbly, a cautious step at a time. Until she found a new dream to sustain her.

She found a large tin tub on the back porch and filled it with water heated over the kitchen fire. Adding harsh soap, she stirred the dirty clothes in with a long paddle, taking pleasure in the simple task. After they'd soaked, she rinsed and wrung them, spreading them to dry over the porch railing. Satisfied by the result of her labor, she was about to return inside when a furtive movement in the bushes sent a bolt of terror up her spine.

Someone was out there, watching.

She'd left the gun inside.

Then Claire-Marie Tournadier emerged from the underbrush and crept swiftly toward the house, an expression of grim determination on her face.

"Quickly, child, before he returns. Come with me."

Weak with relief, Eliza crumpled dizzily to her knees. Through her partial swoon, she felt the other woman's hands cupping her elbow, urging her to stand.

"Hurry. We've not much time to get you to safety."

The word "safety" cut through the fog of her thinking. Her head shot up, her gaze fixing upon Claire-Marie. "Luc. Where's Luc?" Panic began a second surge.

"With my husband and sons in the fields. I can have you away before he returns."

Eliza shook her head. "Away?" Why would she want to leave?

"Quickly. A riverboat passes by every other week.

If you are there on the shore, it will stop for you and take you to New Orleans."

"New Orleans," she repeated dumbly. It made no sense to her. "What about Luc?"

"What about the bastard?" she spat. "You can have yourself well hidden before he comes to find you. Then he'll never have the chance to lay a mean hand on you again. Hurry now. I'll show you the way." Her pulling grew stronger, lifting Eliza against her will.

"I can't leave Luc."

Claire-Marie dragged her toward the steps. "You can. You must before he kills you. Don't you think I know what goes on between you? I know. I suffered the heavy hand of a beastly man before my Didi stole me away to save me. Like you, I was too afraid to do anything to save myself. I don't know how many more of his beatings I could have endured if Didi hadn't forced me to run. The monster was my husband, you see, and no one else would act against him. They said it was his right." She panted in her fury, remembrance quickening the sense of helplessness once more. "No man has that right, Eliza. If you don't have the strength to escape him on your own, let me help you."

Eliza shook her head, comprehension slowly dawning. "No." She set her heels against Claire-Marie's tugging. "No, you have it wrong. Luc has never harmed me."

"You lie to yourself, girl," the other woman argued. "I can feel the marks he's made upon your soul as clearly as I can see the ones he's left upon your skin!"

"No," she moaned as Claire-Marie dragged her to the edge of the porch. "It wasn't Luc." Harsh, leering faces swam before her, horribly distorted by her fear. "It wasn't Luc!"

"I'm taking you from here for your own good."

Warned by the sudden fierceness of her tone, Eliza caught sight of the chunk of wood in Claire-Marie's hand and knew instinctively that the other woman meant to club her with it. Then she would drag her, unconscious, away from this place, away from Luc, the only security she knew.

"No!"

She struck out first, the heel of her hand slamming into Claire-Marie, the unexpected blow above her bosom, knocking the other back, winded and shocked.

Eliza scrambled up to hands and knees, lurching toward the house. Claire-Marie gripped her ankle, pulling hard. Eliza sprawled out, her chin hitting the porch boards with mind-blackening force.

"It's for your own good," she heard Claire-Marie wheezing. And Eliza knew that log would be descending at any moment to rob her of her failing senses.

"Luc!"

Driven by sheer desperation, Eliza kicked out, twisting free to claw her way across the threshold. There, she saw the pistol.

Claire-Marie's step sounded behind her.

Eliza lunged forward, her hands closing on the smooth wooden handle. She rolled frantically, bringing the big bore of the gun up to bear. Stopping a startled Claire-Marie in her tracks. There was a thump as the length of wood dropped from her fingers.

"Get out! Get out and leave me alone!"

Angry, frustrated, Claire-Marie tried one last time.

"Eliza—"

The boom of the gun was deafening. The sound reverberated like thunder, scaring them both into slack-jawed amazement. Part of the door frame disintegrated. Then Claire-Marie fled. Eliza kicked the door shut behind her, sobs breaking free at last.

She didn't know how much time passed as she sat braced against the door, weeping over her tented knees. The anguish was insurmountable. She wept with relief, with fright, out of pain for all she'd endured. The well of her grief was endless. Then the sounds stopped, her throat aching, too swollen to emit further cries. Her ribs hurt as if she'd been beaten all over again. The distancing haze of confusion was lifting from her mind. Unprotected from the horror of her memories, she tried to burrow back into herself, but she could find no safe place to hide. Wave upon wave of fear and recollection crashed over her as she whimpered for relief.

"Eliza?"

She raised her head weakly. "Luc." It was a hoarse whisper.

"Eliza!"

She could hear him racing from room to room, calling her name in escalating panic. She pushed up from the floor and staggered across the room.

"Luc!"

He crossed the threshold so suddenly, they nearly collided. They stared at one another. His expression was stark, stripped naked of all but fear. He gasped for breath, and she knew he'd run the entire distance to answer her call for help.

She was in his arms. Whether he made the first move or she did, it didn't matter. His grip was crushing. Tremors raced along the circle of his embrace as his heart banged a frantic tempo.

"*Mon Dieu*, when I heard that shot . . ." His words fractured, failing him. Winded and faint with relief, he sank down to the pantry floor until she was cradled upon his lap. His hold on her hadn't lessened. "Are you all right, *mon amour*? What has happened?"

"Claire-Marie . . . she thought you were the one . . . the one who . . . hurt me."

"I know, *ma belle*. I should have confided the truth to her." Claire-Marie. He processed that fact, using it to stem the rapid pulse of alarm, pushing away his unrealized terrors.

"She came to take me away from you. I was so afraid. I wanted to make her go away."

He pressed a hard kiss to the crown of her head, vowing, "No one will take you from me again, *ma petite*. This I swear to you."

She gave one small, heartbreaking sob.

"They hurt me, Luc."

With that one admission, all the barriers gave way within her. He held her, rocked her, saying nothing because there was nothing he could say to change what had happened. As hard as her words were to hear, he knew they must be hell to speak.

"I prayed at first that it wouldn't be so bad. I kept thinking of how it was . . . between us, but it wasn't like that at all. It wasn't." She panted softly against his throat, her fingers working in anxious spasms in his hair as the awful moments replayed themselves in her mind. "They didn't care that they hurt me. They—they weren't nice."

A harsh sound rumbled through Luc, but his words to her were infinitely gentle. "Men like that are animals, *chère*. I only wish I could have done something. . . ."

Eliza lifted up to look at him. Her damp eyes glistened, green as emeralds, soft with a surprising tenderness. "But you did, Luc. Don't you see? Because I'd been with you, I knew the difference."

He tried to speak but no words formed.

She touched his face lightly, fanning her fingertips across lean cheeks, feeling the muscles flex at his jaw.

She searched his dark gaze intently, needing to convince him of the importance he'd made in her life.

"You were so good to me, Jean-Luc. If they had taken me first, before you—" Her courage failed. With her head nestled upon his shoulder, she was able to finish. "If I hadn't held the memory of you so close to my heart, I would have found a way to end my life to escape my shame."

"*Non, chérie*. The shame, it is not yours. It is mine, for not protecting you better, for valuing my vengeance more than your safety. If there is a villain to blame, I am that man. If there is guilt to bear, I will—"

Her kiss halted his self-flagellating words. He was instantly lost to its forgiving message.

"You already bear more guilt than you'll willingly share," she whispered against the moist part of his lips. "I'll not add to that load, Jean-Luc. You saved my life. You saved my sanity. There is nothing to forgive."

She would have kissed him again, except he turned his face away, guiding her head back to his shoulder with the weight of his hand.

"You are too generous, *mon coeur*."

As he'd been generous, she realized, with his time, with his tenderness, with his patience. It couldn't have been easy caring for her in her state of perpetual panic. Most of the time, she hadn't known who exactly he was, any more than she'd had a true understanding of who she was herself. He'd given her exactly what she'd needed: security, comfort, allowing her to cling in an effort to push the past away. She'd lived only for the moment, afraid of what had happened, terrified of what was to come. There was only now. And there was Luc. Her constant, her consoler.

Her lover.

Through it all, he had sustained her. And his were the words coaxing her back from the sanctuary she made within her mind. *Find a new dream. . . .*

She felt his hand move over her hair, the gesture gentle, and suddenly, unbearably sensuous.

Perhaps she already had.

His magnificent shoulders went rigid with the first shirt button she opened. His breath escaped in a long hiss with the second. By the release of the third, his full erection prodded her through the fabric of his trousers even as he began to frown.

Her palms pushed inside his shirt. His skin was hot, sleek, stretched taut over muscle.

"Eliza . . ."

Wary and weakening, he tried to pull her hands away. She kissed him. His lips were warm, deliciously pliant, then thin with self-denial.

"Eliza, you do not have to do this."

"I want to."

His mouth slackened with surprise, and she took full advantage, slipping her tongue inside for a slow search that left him trembling. His hands were on her shoulders, tightening to pry her away but pressing her forward at the same time in a confusion of desire. She came to him easily, languishing upon his chest, her arms circling his shoulders, her hands holding the back of his head. He felt good. Kissing him felt good. No trace of memory rose to haunt her as she feasted lightly off his lips. He responded with an obvious reluctance. When she leaned back, he kept his eyes closed, breath chugging heavily.

"Jean-Luc? Luc, look at me."

His eyes blinked open. The black of his pupils swelled.

"Luc, I want you to give me back the pleasures of our first night in New Orleans. I want you too badly

to let them take that from me. I don't want to be afraid
any more. Not of you or of what I'm feeling. Will you
make love with me, Luc?''

"Yes."

He kissed her back, a long, luxurious exchange
meant to encourage.

She thought she was ready, for him, for this. Until
his hands skimmed the edges of her wrapped jacket
away from her breasts, and the ugly bruises were
there to see, standing out plainly against pale flesh in
the sun-washed pantry. He looked at the marks, his
expression tightening, and Eliza wanted to turn away,
to cover herself and the evidence of her shame. It was
shame, no matter what he said. It curled in her belly,
hot, bitter, blaming. She should have been able to stop
them. If she'd only fought harder. If she'd been more
clever, she could have gotten away before . . . before
they stopped that first night and put their dirty hands
on her, leaving the discolored testimony of where
they'd been and what they'd done.

How could Luc help but despise her for her weakness, for submitting? How could he stand touching
the same flesh they'd violated? Her eyes squeezed
shut so she wouldn't have to witness his disgust. She
deserved it. She'd let them take whatever they
wanted. They'd done terrible things, some so vile,
she'd go to her grave before speaking them aloud.
Especially to Luc, who had yet to ask. Remembering
was bad enough.

What if she was with child?

A soft sound of anguish escaped her and was
caught up short by the sudden warmth of his hands
bracketing the sides of her breasts. He buried his face
between them. His breath blew hot upon moist skin.
His stubbled cheeks abraded pleasantly. And a tremor
raced to her soul.

He kissed the bruises, every one of them he could see, tenderly, purposefully, as if his mouth held the power to heal them. Maybe it did, because little by little, the pain went away. Not the physical pain. That had dulled days ago. But the deeper, searing hurt, the bruises left on her spirit.

She held his dark head, her fingers restlessly combing through his hair. She arched her back, coaxing a shift in his attention. He turned it to her right nipple, sucking until it hardened with pleasure, flattening it beneath the press of his tongue, then flicking it into a taut pebble of arousal.

Sensation poured through her like a river.

Luc came up onto his knees, tipping her torso toward him as he lavished equal seduction upon her other breast. Eliza knelt as well, rising up in supple invitation. The floorboards were hard beneath her knees, as hard as the swell of Luc's manhood against her belly. Garnering her courage, she put her hand down to his lap, feeling the power of him through the canvas trousers. He groaned and rocked into her, kissing his way up to her collarbone.

With a few tugs and a bit of fumbling, she freed him for her cautious touch. Silk over steel. She curled her hand around him, remembering the fit of him inside her, the exquisite peaks to which he'd lifted her. Heat pooled low, flooding to that throbbing point of urgency.

Without thinking, she hoisted her skirt. She wore nothing beneath it. Her underthings were drying on the porch rail. With her hands on his shoulders, her mouth covering his, she settled over him, swallowing his gasp, riding out his jolt of surprise.

His hands cupped her bottom, lifting her, easing her down by increments of intensity until he was deeply, completely embedded. Then he held her there, unmoving.

His eyes opened, dark and passion-drugged. He licked his lips, tasting her upon them, shuddering from the way she gloved him. The difficulty of restraint ripped through him.

"Not like this, Eliza," he murmured hoarsely. "Not on the floor. I want to make love with you on the bed of my ancestors."

"We already have, Jean-Luc." She was impatient, anxious to feel him move within her now.

"*Non*," he told her gravely, his stare mesmerizing. "No, we haven't. Not the way we are going to."

She moaned in anticipation.

They made a precarious trip up the stairs, Eliza wrapped about his shoulders and waist, his trousers hanging off his hips, their bodies joined, their mouths mating with tender fervor. They survived a few stumbles without separating for balance or breath, parting only as Luc laid her down on the big bed.

She sat up long enough to remove her clothing. Then she lay down on her back and waited nervously for Luc to join her. She wasn't afraid of him. She was afraid of disappointing him.

Their first encounter was deified by her memory. Perhaps she'd just imagined its splendor as a defense against the horror that followed. With her brutal captors, she'd been stunned by the pain and mental agonies, forced to withdraw from her physical being in order to endure. Later, with Luc, she'd felt nothing beyond a numbing sense of safety. He'd stirred nothing with his kiss or his caresses. She'd been a willing vessel for his desire, filled only briefly, then empty once more. He hadn't hurt her, nor had he brought her any pleasure.

What if she never got those special sensations back again?

What if those filthy creatures had killed that potential within her?

But no. She'd felt it spark moments ago in Luc's embrace. She'd tingled at his kiss, a slow awakening. She'd enjoyed an expectant burning when he'd suckled at her breasts. And there was no denying the sweet shock of satisfaction when she'd taken him inside her.

But what if that was all? What if she remained barren of the remaining delights he'd shown her?

What if she'd lost her ability to love?

Some of that panic must have shown in her face because Luc paused in his undressing, concern creasing his brow.

"Second thoughts, *ma belle*?" How carefully he put that, his neutrality as deceptive as his flat stare.

Eliza managed a slight smile. "Not about you, Captain." She lifted her arms.

He came down to her, still wearing his open shirt and trousers. How perfectly he fit the circle of her embrace. His mouth was silky, persuasive. Her hands trembled as they pushed the fabric from his hard shoulders. She let her fingertips linger along the firm swells of his upper arms. How strong he was, powerful, capable of breaking her in two. A shiver shot through her before she reminded herself that this was Luc, and there was no need to feel afraid.

"Tell me what you want of me, *ma petite*. I will move heaven and earth to see you have it."

"I want you, Jean-Luc. Inside me, now."

Her bluntness startled him, but he was quick to comply. She gasped at his filling stroke and held to his massive shoulders. As he moved, she closed her eyes, willing, *Now, let me feel paradise, now.*

Nothing.

She felt herself drifting away from where the two of them were joined, as if she were watching a pair of strangers through uninvolved eyes. As if Luc were making love to someone else, not her.

Not like this. Not like this! She wanted to feel, to soar, to sizzle with bursting pleasures. What was wrong with her? She loved him! Why couldn't she enjoy his loving?

It took her a moment to realize that Luc was no longer moving. Her eyes flickered open, glittering with unshed tears, swimming with misery.

"I'm sorry, Luc. It's not you." She hid her eyes behind the brace of her forearm, blocking out the sight of his handsome face, etched so darkly with leashed emotion. "It's not your fault. I'm so dead inside. I'm never going to be whole again."

Gently, firmly, he pushed her arm aside so she couldn't evade his intense gaze. "Perhaps we go too fast, *mon coeur*. Perhaps you are not ready—"

"I am," she argued with a sudden fierceness. "And I want you." She kissed him hard to prove it, perhaps more to herself than to him. "I do want you, Luc."

He studied her, looking unconvinced. Eliza feared he would pull away. She tightened her knees, trapping his sturdy thighs between them.

And then he did the unexpected. He rolled onto his back, bringing her up and over him.

"Perhaps if you lead, you will pay more attention to where we are going. This time, you come with me or we go not at all."

Chapter 22

Eliza hesitated, unsure of what to do with the sudden power he'd given her.

"Don't be afraid."

She was about to deny his quiet words, telling him she had no fear of him. But it would have been a lie. Because she was afraid, terrified, not of him but of what they were about to do. Primitive terrors burrowed deep, well beneath the wants of heart or mind, down to where the most basic instincts dwelt. She was afraid to let down the guard holding them inside, afraid that if she let the feelings go, they would be ones of ungovernable horror, of remembered helplessness and pain.

"They hurt me," came her raw whisper, her answer for everything.

"I won't. I won't hurt you."

She drew a fragile breath, tears clinging to her lashes, falling hotly upon his smooth chest to scald through to his soul. "I know you won't."

His palms rested atop her thighs, pushing up and down in leisurely strokes, feeling her tense and tremble. "Do you trust me, Eliza?"

He was asking her to set aside her doubts, to surrender her fears, to place herself totally in his hands, emotions stripped bare. She wasn't sure she could do that yet . . . or ever.

"I want you."

A small smile quirked his lips. "That is not what I asked, *ma petite*."

She let herself look deeper, beyond the soothing sentiments, past the handsome visage and the relentless black eyes. He was waiting for her response, allowing it to be her choice. Just as he had the night before when he refused to take less than her whole self. That was what she wanted to give him now. Everything: scars, fears, desires, all.

"I trust you." Frail but firmly said.

"Then trust yourself with me."

His hands revolved to the underside of her legs, lifting slightly, moving her atop his turgid shaft, letting the movement become coaxing instead of invasive. Her hands clasped over his, gripping tightly as her breathing hurried in small gasps. She was so frightened.

"Say my name."

She focused on him instead of upon the building anxiety. She found him beautiful, a dark angel.

"Jean-Luc. Coeur Noir. Coeur Desir." Her tone grew husky as long-cold fires glowed and stirred back to flame. And slowly, she began to take the initiative, controlling the pace and depth of penetrating pleasure.

It was pleasure. Slow, stroking, sliding pleasure. She came alive with it.

He could see it in her eyes as they darkened to stormy seas and fluttered shut. Her body arched and her head fell back in acceptance of those feelings. Though his need was all-consuming, his body aching, rigid with the effort of control, Luc saw to his promise to see her fulfilled. He palmed her gently, using his deft touch to guide her, to heighten her sensitivity until her breasts rose and fell with the rapid jerk of her breathing. Her soft, throaty moans dragged him up to the tenuous edge that was a balance between heaven and hell. His mind went blank; his body gripped with tension.

Now! Mon Dieu, now!

He thrust into her hard, fierce in his demand.

He felt the first shudder rip through her. Her body clenched about him like a hot fist, contracting, spasming, pulling at him. A harsh cry exploded from him as his restraint burst at last in an answering flood.

She wilted across him, quivering, weak as water. He couldn't muster the strength to hold her. He felt her kiss nibbling at his jaw and managed to turn his head far enough to seek out her lips. Their kiss was languid, lazy with sated satisfaction. Finally, Eliza lifted up to smile down at him.

"You are wonderful."

He made a rumbly noise in his throat, a sound of agreement. *"Éclatant,"* he murmured contentedly, eyes closing. "Magnificent. *Et vous—très belle."*

Eliza felt beautiful, desirable, and whole as she snuggled against Luc's side. She sighed happily and rubbed her palm over his yet laboring chest. "Black Heart." She chuckled. "You need a new name, pirate. That one no longer suits you."

How right she was. The heart he claimed not to have was hammering frantically, crowded with enough pure emotion to burst through the restraint of his ribs. He carried her provoking hand to his lips, pressing a kiss upon it. "Pick a name, if you know one better."

She thought a moment. "Coeur Solitaire."

He held her knuckles against his rueful smile. "Yes, that is most fitting." Lonely heart. For far too long.

Eliza's hand opened, fitting to the side of his face, turning him toward her. Her kiss was soft, sweet, filled with tempting promises. Promises he wanted her to keep.

He returned the kiss and the caresses that followed into a slow, satisfying intimacy. And afterward, they basked in the sunlight and contented silence.

When sunbeams began to angle across the bed, Luc woke to his responsibilities. With another brief kiss upon Eliza's sleepy lips, he sat up. "I must go back to Tournadier's, to explain things."

"Like why I tried to shoot his wife off the back steps?" Her crooked smile said best of luck.

"They are our neighbors. We must maintain their goodwill." He reached for his trousers, shimmying into them, stepping into his boots. Eliza remained sprawled upon the sheets, watching him with a languorous appreciation, making no attempt to hold or follow him. He slipped on his shirt, leaving it loose and open to appease the heat of his body. A different sort of heat arose when he let his gaze linger over his love. "I must go."

She nodded.

He came down to her with a groan, kissing her soundly, lifting up only to fall back upon those sweetly parted lips once more. Lonely Heart? Not when she touched him, held him, swallowed him in a sea of sensations, each more powerful and frightening than the last. He stood away with difficulty.

"I must go," he repeated rather hoarsely. Unable to resist one last taste of heaven, he drank from her lips again, savoring her slowly, like a fine wine. He moaned his reluctance and pulled himself off her mouth, striding to the door lest he weaken.

"Luc?"

He paused, looking back.

"Tell Claire-Marie I do understand and that I thank her for her concerns."

He sketched a brief bow and was gone.

Eliza continued to luxuriate on the big bed, feeling, instead of its emptiness, the incredible sense of fullness within herself. Luc had given her back her inner beauty. Through him, she'd found her center, her strength.

What was she going to do now?

She was in love with her lawless captor, the man who planned to ransom her back to a family she didn't belong to. She thought of William then, for the first time in many days, and realized that though he'd touched her heart, he'd never sent it racing. And he never would. What she felt for her Salem beau was a poignant wistfulness for what would never be. There was no going back to assume her place at his side. Not after where she'd been and whom she'd been with. William would never understand. He was a gentle soul, unused to violence and basic survival. He would never accept her violation at the hands of other men any more than he could forgive her desire for Luc. Her charade could go no further.

It was time to find a new dream.

The dream she wanted was here, with Jean-Luc Gautier. Tending to his lonely heart. Caring for his neglected home.

Loving him. Bearing his children.

She touched her palms to her flat middle, feeling a flutter of alarm. No. If she conceived a child, it would be his. She'd think of no other possible alternative.

Luc's child. A contented warmth stole over her.

All she needed was his name . . . and his love.

Would he give either thing to her if he knew who she really was?

Restless now that doubts shadowed her blissful

mood, Eliza rose and dressed, taking a minute to straighten the bedcovers with a wistful care. Would that it could be her marriage bed. She returned to the pantry, retrieving the recently fired gun and placing it in her jacket pocket. Then she saw to the drying clothes, and she allowed herself to dream.

Belong to me, he'd once said. But would he want Eliza Parrish as much as Philomena Montgomery? Was it the woman he loved, a poor indentured servant instead of the wealthy socialite? She had nothing to give him, nothing but her devotion.

Trust me, he'd bidden her. But would he trust her again once he knew of her elaborate deception?

He'd been careful with his promises. He hadn't offered her his heart or his home. Oh, how she wanted both things. He'd been lover, protector, comforter, but never had he surrendered the role of captor. He hadn't spoken of permanence, only of passion. Was that because he saw her still as the daughter of his enemy?

If that barrier was removed, would he take her for his bride?

She would find out as soon as he returned by telling him the complete truth. After facing the horror of her bayou abduction, she couldn't allow herself to fear Luc's reaction. After so many lies, the trust would have to begin somewhere.

She busied herself within the house to make the time go faster till his return. Instead of fear, a sense of pending relief sustained her. After pretending for so long to be who and what she was not, she could act herself, speak for herself again. Eliza Parrish. Somehow that person had got lost within her, first with a stripping of her social standing, then with a confusion of her identity. But she was the woman who loved Jean-Luc Gautier, the one who was willing to remain here with him forever.

She had nothing left in Salem. It was a world away, a lifetime past. No family waited. No friends who would claim her after her fall from financial grace. Only misery and drudgery remained for a servant where she'd once been pampered guest. Here, with Luc, she could be an equal, she could know freedom.

If he would allow her to stay.

He did care for her. He must to have gone through so much on her behalf. If he felt love—if he even knew what love was—she didn't know. She could show him. She could use each sultry southern night to teach him about gratitude and affection. He already knew about passion. She smiled to herself as she began their evening meal. Her anticipation simmered just like the sausage in her pan. And she practiced what she would say.

It wasn't so easy when she tried to put it in words.

Luc, even though I've lied to you since our first meeting, you must believe that I love you.

Not very convincing.

What I did, I did out of duty, for a chance at freedom. What I choose to do now, I do out of love.

Much better. Duty. Freedom. He understood those things.

The meal was ready. Her speech was prepared. But Luc didn't return.

She waited, beginning to pace the front hall. What could be keeping him? Her imagination supplied sundry explanations, none of them good. Had the Tournadiers refused to hear his apology? Had they done something to harm him? Had the vengeful Cajuns waylaid him on the trail back?

Were they even now lingering out in the seeping shadows?

She hugged her arms about herself, clinging to a ragged calm.

Luc, where are you?

It grew dark and Eliza's panic thickened with the massing blackness. She clutched the pistol before her, refusing to succumb to raving madness.

What would she do if he didn't come back for her?

How helplessly isolated she was out here in this foreign surround, cut off from all but the Tournadiers. She hadn't realized how dependent she was upon Luc for provisions as well as protection. She had nothing of her own, not a single possession. Her thumb rubbed over the base of her ring finger where she'd worn her father's gift since she was a child. Nothing, not even her own clothing. No past, a lean present, and a very uncertain future.

What could have happened to Luc?

Fright trickled in cold rivulets, the sweat of fear icy against her body. It was completely dark now. Hours, hours had passed. She knew something bad was keeping Luc away. She paced, gnawing her lower lip, hand damp upon the pistol stock. Should she go out into the night and try to find him? Try to retrace his steps to the Tournadiers'?

What if he needed her?

Galvanized by that thought, she changed from her gown into shirt and trousers. And when her fear for him prompted her to take action, a thump of sound upon the front steps refocused her terror inwardly.

Someone was outside.

And if it wasn't Luc, the alternatives were terrifying.

Gun in hand, she crept toward the door. If it was Luc, why hadn't he come in? Chills ravaged her, but she forced her mind to remain clear. She couldn't lose control now. If she did, she'd be lost forever.

The porch was darker than her worst nightmare. The air hung thick with the scent of azaleas, camellias, and dogwood. Humidity clung to her skin like a cloying fog. She could hear her own heartbeat, thundering in her ears.

"I have a gun," she announced to the night with a cold bravado. "I'm not afraid to use it. Show yourself."

A low murmur of sound came from the bottom of the front steps. She edged forward, cautious, on razor points of dread, until she could look down and see who or what was there. She made out a huddled shape, indistinguishable at first as man or animal. Than a head rose slowly.

"Luc!"

She came down the steps in a reckless sprawl, tumbling to her knees before him. Her first thought was that he'd been shot or somehow injured, but a touch of her hand to his brow told her all. He flamed with fever.

He mumbled something she couldn't discern and fought off her attempts to aid him.

"Luc, it's Eliza," she soothed, catching his flailing hands and compressing them between her own. She could feel him quake with chills, could hear the clatter of his teeth. She didn't have to see his face to know malaria consumed him. "You're sick, Jean-Luc. I must get you inside. Do you think you can stand?"

Again, he muttered something unintelligible, but he gathered his feet under him, struggling, tottering, swaying up to lean heavily against her support.

"Come on, Luc. It's only a few steps."

They climbed them together. Eliza steered him toward the parlor sofa, knowing she'd never get him up the stairs.

Luc collapsed upon the chaise, fighting against the

ravaging tremors, hating the weakness, the helplessness of the incessant disease.

He'd made it to Tournadier's without any trouble, blaming his hurried heartbeat and overwarm state upon the cherished moments spent with Eliza. But when he sat down in his neighbor's house, a sense of unease spread through him, and by the time he'd finished his coffee, he knew he'd be lucky to make it back to Coeur Desir on his own power.

Claire-Marie wouldn't hear his explanations, demanding her Didier shoot him where he stood. Thankfully, her husband was of a more reasoning mind. Once Luc laid out a frank account of how he'd followed Eliza and her captors into the bayou—deleting, of course, that she was his captive to begin with—Claire-Marie wept openly and kissed his hands, begging him to forgive her. Uncomfortable with her praise, he turned instead to Tournadier, who had grown grim with his telling. What the man told him had Luc racing back to Eliza, desperate to beat the debilitating chills. He'd crawled the last few yards to the porch but lacked the strength the climb it. His chattering teeth prevented any outcry. It was there that his brave and beautiful Eliza found him, in a vulnerable heap, unable to help himself, let alone her.

"Must go to Tournadier's," he managed as Eliza brought blankets from the bedroom to cover him. He clutched at the covers, trying to catch her hand as well. The gesture was ineffectual. "Eliza—"

"Shhhh." Her hand stroked his wet brow. But instead of soothing him, he grew more agitated.

"Not-t-t s-s-safe," he rattled.

"It's all right, Luc. I won't leave you. You must rest now until all runs its course."

He shook off her reassurances with a toss of his head. "*Non* . . . Eliza, listen . . . to me."

"Don't try to talk." Her fingertips touched to his lips. He jerked his head to the side in frustration.

"Not safe . . ."

"Shamus told me of the malaria, Jean-Luc. I know what to do. Please trust me to see to you."

"No . . . must go to Tournadier's."

"Hush, now, Captain. You're in no shape to travel." He could see her vague form seated on the cushions beside him. The fever already distorted his vision. He shoved her hand away from his cheek.

"Leave me." He tried to sound firm, but a petulant moan was the best he could do. "You must . . . Eliza, please."

She wouldn't listen to what he was trying to tell her. That she was in terrible danger if she remained at his side.

For earlier that afternoon, Tournadier had seen strange men on the river, rough-looking, deadly-intentioned men, who could only be after one thing.

Their property.

Eliza.

Luc's fever lasted throughout the hours of the night, and through it all, Eliza tended him. Once his savage chills abated, she coaxed him upstairs, where he could rest more comfortably upon the bed. It was terrible to watch him suffer, but the attack was milder than the first she'd witnessed, so she took heart.

In his delirium, Luc's agitation didn't lessen. It spiked whenever Eliza bent near. He rambled frantically that she should leave him, that she should go to the Tournadiers'. Alternately, he begged her forgiveness for some unnamed crime. He took no comfort from her absolutions, and she was at a loss as to what else to do other than stay close and try to calm his ragged cries. When she tried to wrap blankets around him, he flung them off, shouting hoarsely about rats feasting upon him while he was bound and helpless. Delirium, she hoped, not memory. She didn't want to think such things had truly happened while he was imprisoned.

The fever broke near dawn. Eliza returned to the bed chamber with a cool basin and fresh toweling to find Luc sitting up on the edge of the bed. His head hung low between spraddled knees, and he shook it from side to side as if to clear it.

"Luc, it's too soon. Lie back down."

He gazed up at her, his dark eyes bright but focused. Sweat slicked his skin, making it gleam in the lamp light.

"Eliza, you must go. Now."

She smiled to humor him. "You know I can't leave you." She brushed the dry cloth across his brow, then gasped as his fingers clamped tight about her wrist. His stare blazed.

"You must! Leave me. I am dead already."

She frowned at his upsetting words. Thinking they were fever-bred, she pitched her voice low and gently crooned, "I know it must feel that way now, but you will be fine—"

He jerked her down to him. She cried out as his grasp abraded her tender flesh. "Listen to me! Forget about me. Do you still have my gun?"

"It-it's downstairs."

He panted harshly, struggling to hold to his strength. "Go get it. Lock the doors. Douse the lights and stay clear of the windows." He swayed against her, resting his wet brow against her breast. His eyes closed to deny the swirling weakness. She tried to stroke his sweat-drenched hair, but he lunged back, his expression fierce. "Do it, Eliza. Now!"

"If you will lie down and rest until my return."

He groaned in frustration but bent before her bargain, allowing her to lift his booted feet. He dropped onto his back, chest heaving in anxiety, wondering wildly what he'd forgotten to tell her. By the time his head unclouded enough to permit keen thought, she was on her way down the stairs and never heard him warn, "They're coming."

Most of the floor-to-ceiling windows had no draperies, so Eliza stayed deep in the shadows. It didn't matter that she didn't believe Luc's urgent pleas. The starkness of his tone invited caution. She latched the front door securely, pocketing the pistol she'd left by the couch before hurrying toward the rear pantry. A sense of threat spurred her on. She would feel better once she was with Luc again. Now that the worst of his ordeal was over, she would curl beside him on his big bed and snatch a scant hour of sleep before morning.

Then, when he was stronger, they would discuss their future.

She shot the bolt on the rear door, her thoughts consumed with her lover and the rest of the life they would share. Her soul knew a moment of perfect peace just as she turned, anxious to rejoin him.

And her gaze swung fleetingly across one high window.

She froze, a scream wedging up in her throat.

The unmistakable silhouette of a man moved along the gallery. It wasn't Tournadier.

It was the Cajun, T-mon.

Chapter 23

❧～⟋⟍～❧

Terror sent her scurrying up the back stairs on all fours like an animal. Simple, raw panic pounded through her. Run. Escape. She could not let them take her back. Those survival basics beat against her brain. Tempering them was one thought. Luc.

No matter how great her fear for herself, she could not leave him at their mercy.

This was what he'd tried to warn her about. She saw that now with crystal clear hindsight. Too late for self-recrimination. She needed her energy elsewhere, in getting herself and Luc to safety. They would kill him. She'd no doubt. And they would take her. And take her.

She ran faster, crouching low. The mindlessness of moments ago evolved into a grim determination.

Luc lay on the bed where she'd left him. His eyes were closed, his breathing shallow. Pale flesh hugged the bones of his face. Eliza paused, shaken. How desperately ill he appeared.

She knelt beside the bed, slipping her hand over his mouth before saying his name in a penetrating whisper.

His eyes flew open, alert, aware.

"They're here," was all she needed to say.

He nodded and she took her hand away. "How many?"

"I don't know. I saw only one."

He used his heels to push himself into a half-seated position against the headboard. His breathing was labored. Sweat streamed into his eyes. He wiped it away, then reached out for the gun. She surrendered it without protest. His hand closed about the grip. It shook wildly. Features grim, he brought it up to lie against his chest. His gaze was surprisingly calm.

"Go. I'll hold them for as long as I can."

For as long as he was alive.

"No." That sob of objection tore from her heart. "You come with me or I won't go!"

He shook his head, his eyes somber, gaze riveted to hers.

"Luc, we can make it together."

"You can make it alone."

"They'll kill you," she sobbed, knowing he was right, knowing he hadn't the strength to sustain an escape. How many rounds did he have with his gun? Not enough. "Luc, please . . ."

"Save yourself," he commanded.

Craven terror demanded she accept his order. She could run and hide and be safe. They would never have the chance to put cruel hands on her again. She panted anxiously, considering it, then considering the man who was offering his life for her. Something solidified within her chest, an emotion too big to name.

"No, Luc. I won't leave you. I will not let you die for me."

Her answer frustrated him. His expression tightened with it. Dark eyes stared through her, to some haunting memory that made his gaze grow frantic. He was angry and impatient, his words a fierce hiss. "I cannot protect you, and I will not leave this world with your fate hanging on my soul. I carry too many already." A sudden calm fell over him, a sense of things resolved. "I will not let you become a sacrifice for my sake."

And as she watched, incomprehensibly, he turned the barrel of the gun around, angling it beneath his own chin, muzzle pointing toward the top of his head. His unblinking stare never left hers.

Her shock snapped.

"No!"

Realizing what he meant to do, she grasped the barrel with both hands, jerking it to one side so it would discharge harmlessly. He didn't fire. Nor had he the strength to fight her as she tore the gun from his hand. She was weeping uncontrollably as she hugged him, her damp cheek mashed to his.

The sound of glass breaking below brought her up, away from him. Her eyes glazed. Then she sucked a quick breath and the daze was gone. She looked at him ferociously.

"Together. We go together."

His hand clamped behind her head, holding her fast. His smile was small, awed, as was his whisper.

"*Mon Dieu,* you amaze me."

His arm slid about her shoulders so she could lever him up. The malaria drained him of resources. He could scarcely stand, but for Eliza, he tried, wobbling as she tucked the pistol into the band of her leather britches and snatched his work machete off the night-stand before circling his middle with her free arm. He staggered beside her as she pulled him toward the windows. They opened onto the wide gallery. She dragged Luc outside and shut the windows behind them.

The house was big. It would take them awhile to search it. Long enough, she hoped, to get them secreted away in the shrubbery. Time was not their friend. Darkness gave way to deep lavender shades of dawn and soon would betray them to the searching eye. She scanned the length of the balcony, finding a heavy twist of vine that looked promising. She guided Luc toward it.

"Can you climb down?"

He nodded. It didn't matter if he could or not. He had no choice.

She leaned over the rail, searching the darkness below for any sign of threat. Seeing none, she turned to Luc.

"Be careful. Hang on."

He looked so weak and unsteady. Anxious tears pricked her eyes, but she blinked them away. He gripped the rail, leaning heavily upon it, but try as he would, he couldn't swing his leg over.

"Help me."

She swung one leg over for him. As he lay prone upon the rail, she snatched a precious second to kiss him, hard, deep, and perhaps for the last time. Then she bent, grasping his other ankle, and lifted it over as well. Luc balanced on his belly, breathing deep to collect his waning strength. From within the house came the sounds of rampant destruction. His features tightened. Determined, he pushed off the rail, disappearing into the shadows.

Eliza hung over the rail, watching his descent, her breath suspended. He made it halfway before his reserves gave out. She heard him grunt as he hit the ground hard. She swung over the rail and grasped a sturdy vine, easing downward through the tangle of foliage until her feet found solid purchase.

Luc lay where he'd fallen. Eliza shook him. When he didn't rouse, her hands fisted in his shirt. She hauled him toward the bushes, backpedaling as fast

as she could, expecting at any moment to hear a shout
of discovery. None came as she burrowed into the
concealing brush. Branches tore at her face and hair,
but she pushed in farther, until she was sure they
were completely hidden. Only then did she sit back
with Luc's limp form cradled in her arms. Only then
did she surrender to the fear terrorizing her. She
shook fiercely, clutching Luc's dark head to her
bosom. She clenched her jaws so her teeth wouldn't
clatter as loudly as Luc's in the throes of his fever.

They were safe . . . for the moment.

Slowly, Luc stirred in her embrace, finally pushing
free to sit up. Still he sagged against her, dependent
upon her for support. His breathing sawed harshly
through the silence.

"Will they look for us?" she asked.

"When it's light. They will know we were here."

Eliza thought of the uneaten meal on the stove and
cursed herself for her carelessness. Too late to remedy
it now. She thought ahead, seeking an avenue for
safety.

"Can you make it as far as the river?"

"*Non.*"

"To the Tournadiers'?" Desperation snagged at her
voice.

Again the soft, inevitable, "*Non.*"

"Luc—"

He touched her damp cheek, his fingertips gentle.
"Eliza, *mon coeur*, I cannot run and you cannot carry
me."

Her breath shivered, but she didn't look away from
his intense gaze. "Then we'll wait here until they
leave. Maybe they won't find us." Her eyes begged
him to agree.

"And maybe they will. Eliza—"

"I won't leave you."

He sighed and leaned his forehead against hers. "You are a foolish, stubborn woman."

"And I love you, Luc."

She felt his slight recoil. Her timing was far from perfect, but she wanted him to know the way of her heart while she could yet speak of it. He didn't answer her claim directly, but his hand caressed her face tenderly.

"Then we wait."

She'd never been so scared or been faced with such tremendous loss, not at the same time. She wanted to weep. She wanted to run away. She did neither. Her arms slipped about Luc's neck, and she rested her head upon his shoulder. Their hearts beat together in a frantic unison. As they held one another in the slowly lifting darkness, Eliza reached several sobering conclusions.

Without Luc, she had no reason to go on. Life as the Cajuns' captive held no appeal.

"Promise you won't let them take me from you."

Luc was a realist. He understood immediately, as she knew he would. His body stiffened, his arms tightened, but his reply was firm. "I promise."

Satisfied with his word and oddly content now that her fate was settled, she closed her eyes, relaxing against him.

It was eerily silent. Dare she hope the Cajuns had got bored and simply gone away?

Then it reached her, a pungent, unmistakable smell. Fire.

They'd set fire to Coeur Desir.

Luc bolted upright. A sound escaped him, a low moan of injury and pain. He squeezed his eyes shut in helplessness, features taut with despair. They were destroying his dream.

Eliza gasped, her own heart constricting. It was her dream, too.

And they were burning it down.

Damn them!

After all they'd taken from her, her body, her confidence, her free will, and nearly her mind, Eliza rebelled. How dare they strike at the dream she and Luc would share!

She crept through the underbrush until she could see the house. Smoke curled up from the back, thick, menacing tendrils against the grays of daybreak. There was no sign of any movement in the house or around it. Could they have left, satisfied with a petty revenge?

She jumped as Luc's fingers closed about her arm. She looked to him hopefully.

"I don't see anyone. I think they're gone."

His pain-filled gaze turned toward the house, and he shook his head. "You do not know that for sure."

"Luc, the house is on fire!"

Tension etched his cheekbones into sharp relief. "I know."

"It might not be too late to save it." She started easing out of his grasp. She drew the machete and placed it next to him.

"Eliza, *non.*"

"I'll be careful."

And she slipped through the thicket like a fox, red-gold hair a flash, then gone.

Cursing, Luc tried to follow. He levered up onto hands and knees, but his weakened limbs buckled, unable to support him. He lay facedown, sucking in the scent of earth, tasting his terror, writhing inside at his helplessness. Praying wildly, fervently that she was right, that they were gone.

Then, for the second time that day, a single pistol shot predicted the end of everything.

Eliza raced to the house, slipping up next to its protective shadow, skimming along it in an alert and anxious pose. Her hands were damp on the pistol grip, yet determination stilled their trembling.

The smell of smoke was stronger as she rounded the corner, crouching low to stay below the line of the raised porch. She moved quietly, senses taut and straining for any sign of danger. She could hear the pop and snap of the flames but no hint of the fire starters.

She eased up slowly to peer between the porch rails. Unnatural brightness shone through the windows of the pantry in wavering flashes. Urgency warred with caution. Finally, after making a careful scan of the surroundings, she lunged from hiding to snatch up one of the bedcovers still draped over the rail to dry. She ran into the house without hesitation, using the damp bedspread to beat at the hungry flames licking up the woodwork.

The heat struck back at her, blistering, intense, but she refused to retreat. Jarring coughs wracked her as she swung the smothering covers in tireless arcs, flattening the closest flames even as others spread beyond her. Logic told her it was an impossible feat, but she couldn't stop; she couldn't let the destruction go unchecked. Tears streamed down her face from eyes burned by smoke, aching with loss.

A creaking sounded behind her. She turned, thinking it might be a cracking timber. Instead, she confronted another source of danger. Scraggly features twisted in a tobacco-stained grin. She didn't recognize his face, but she knew what he was. One of her violators. Terror congealed, freezing through her.

"Knew we could smoke you out," he said with a smug chuckle. "Where be the Frenchie? Tell me quick, girl, or it'll go all the worse for you."

And a hard punishing mask settled over his features. She remembered the look well. Panic was no match for the fury surging inside her. She would not be his victim.

"Go to hell."

Enraged by her defiance, he took a fierce stride forward. The sight of the gun in her hand didn't stop him. But its bullet did.

Shock registered dumbly as he staggered back, crimson flowering upon his breast. He stumbled into the flames, fire engulfing him as he fell. His shrieks were short-lived and horrible. Eliza stood helplessly, unable to wish such a death even upon her defilers. It was over quickly, more quickly than her own torment at his hands. She turned back to fight the flames and found herself face-to-face with another of her attackers.

He pulled the gun from her with a vicious wrench of her wrist. His other hand curled in her hair, twisting into a hurtful fist that tore her scalp. Eliza cried out.

"*Chienne!* You will pay for what you done to Jacques, and pay dear."

His hold on her hair made struggling futile. He dragged her toward the door, using those entangled locks as a lead, and Eliza was forced to follow. He paused on the porch, listening to the sound of shots as Eliza gulped lungfuls of sweet air.

The Cajun laughed. "So much for your pretty lover."

Eliza went to her knees in shock. Truth struck her a dizzying blow. What else could the shots signify? Luc had a machete. The only ones armed were his enemies. Loss swirled in a dark mist through her mind.

Luc . . .

Then came the sobering significance. In dying, Luc failed to keep his word. She was once again a prisoner of these men and their animal desires.

Her captor never expected it. Eliza exploded upward with a shriek of maddened rage. Her fingers clawed for his eyes. Her knee drove unerringly into his groin. The agonizing hold on her hair lessened, and free, she stumbled down the steps. She ran toward the trees, desperation numbing her to the fact of Luc's death. She would grieve for him later in her freedom. Or she would join him before surrendering herself again.

The Cajun gripped her by the elbows, halting her flight. She screamed and writhed wildly but was firmly caught. Before her doubting eyes, she saw the figure of Didier Tournadier emerge from the underbrush, an old long rifle in his hands. He showed no alarm nor did he make any attempt to lift the rifle to ward off her attacker. She sagged in her captor's grasp, confused and weeping forlornly.

"Where's Luc?"

That familiar voice came from behind her. Eliza twisted to cast a disbelieving look. Relief gave before an awful confession.

"Oh, Shamus, they've killed him." She could barely speak through the ravaging sorrow. The seaman's face froze with anguish as she blurted out, "I—I heard the shots."

The seamed features relaxed. "Lass, those were our guns you heard, not theirs."

"Then, Luc—" It seemed too much to hope for. Elation swamped her senses. She pulled free and raced toward where she'd left him.

Only to find him gone.

The threat to Eliza gave Luc the strength to act. Weak and disoriented, he managed to haul himself to his feet nonetheless. With the machete weighing heavily in his hand, he swayed toward the house, his steps uneven and misdirected. Sweat poured down his face, burning his eyes, obscuring his vision as he reeled onward. Finally, he reached the front steps. He clung to the bottom post, legs like water, eyesight wavering as images danced on a choppy sea.

Into that rippling view came sturdy boots, muddied trousers, and burly hands. Luc's attention focused upon a flash of gold on one of the beefy fingers. On the smallest finger, pushed to the middle joint, was Eliza's ring.

And Luc saw red.

His gaze lifted slowly by cold, calculated increments until he beheld the face of the brute who had stolen her last and most prized possession. It was T-mon Beauclaire, the beast from Etienne's. He saw recognition light the other's features, followed by a sneering grin.

"You don't look so fierce now, Coeur Noir." A deadly blade appeared in his hand. "Shall I carve that black heart from your chest and make it a parting gift to your lady? Or would you rather we keep you alive for a while so you can watch us enjoy her charms? I don't need to tell you how considerable they are."

Luc struck soundlessly, brutally, without warning. The machete slashed low, burying deep in T-mon's thigh. With a bloodcurdling yell, the Cajun spilled down the steps, and Luc was upon him.

One look at the Frenchman's face told T-mon of his

mistake. Coeur Noir was not a name given without cause. Black eyes devoid of all but delivering death bored into his, chilling his very marrow with their absence of emotion. He saw his own end reflected there as the stained blade swung high and descended with a sweeping song of retribution.

Eliza was the first to see him as he tottered around the side of the house. He was moving slowly, the dripping machete hanging loosely at his side. His features were ashen, his eyes flat black chips of stone. With a glad cry, she ran to him. He stumbled back from the force of her embrace, making no attempt to return it.

"Oh, Luc, thank God you're all right. Shamus and your men are here. Tournadier led them to our rescue. They put an end to T-mon's men and are putting out the fire." The words gushed from her in a mindless relief. She didn't notice his lack of animation, only that he was solid and alive within the circle of her arms.

Shamus saw more. He took note of the dull glazed eyes and the bloody blade. He approached and carefully took the machete from Luc's unresisting hand.

"Be you all right then, lad?"

Luc stared up at him blankly. Then he blinked and his gaze focused. "As right as can be expected." He levered out of Eliza's squeezing embrace. While she questioned him with her teary gaze, he lifted one small hand in his, the left one, not the right, and slipped her ring onto her finger. He carried that hand to his lips to touch a kiss upon the simple gold band. Eliza's breath quivered, her eyes welling up with fresh emotion.

"Your memories, *mon coeur*. Keep only the good ones, and let the others fall away."

Her fingers curled about his, holding tight. She wished she could suspend the moment, to wipe all else from her mind except this one magnificent gesture.

Then Luc was torn away from her by the goodwill and camaraderie of his men, leaving her to study that symbolic band with heart fluttering.

Damage to the house proved superficial. The flames had been confined to the rear pantry and hall, scorching the walls of the back stairs but doing little other harm. The scent of smoke lingered, a harsh reminder of how much worse it could have been.

The dead were buried. T-mon Beauclaire went to his grave in two pieces, bringing no comment but much respect for the captain of the *Galant.* Luc said nothing of the gruesome deed, but the splattering on his boots said plenty. He thanked each of his crew with a handshake and a reserved embrace. He avoided Shamus's gaze altogether.

As Eliza and Claire-Marie dipped out wine from a cask Tournadier donated to their celebration, the boisterous crew lined the veranda rails, calling for unending toasts. Luc answered each one with a lift of his glass and a sip from its contents, but his thoughts were far away. His gaze covertly followed Eliza, who had changed into the simple wrap-front gown. Her hair was twisted up on top of her head to form a crown of lustrous gold, and her gracious manner befit the most elite hostess. The bruising was all but gone from her face, and only a trace of her ordeal lingered when a too sudden movement or too loud laugh startled her. Then her gaze would fly to where he sat, seeking a sense of security from his presence, and comforted, she would smile and continue serving.

"She is quite the surprise, our Miss Montgomery."

Luc glanced up at Shamus, too weary to affect a decent lie. "Yes, yes, she is."

Shamus's features grew somber. "Is she all right? The boy told us what happened."

He asked for no particulars and Luc offered none, other to say a quiet, "Yes."

"You love her."

His gaze on Eliza, Luc didn't answer. His look said it plain.

"A man could do worse, lad."

Luc was slow to reply, and when he did his words were weighted. "But she could do so much better."

Shamus studied him for a moment, then placed a hand upon his shoulder. "Not if she loves you in return. Does she, Luc?"

And I love you, Luc.

He closed his eyes, shutting out the sight of her as that claim twisted about his heart. It was hell to disavow it. But he did.

"It doesn't matter, Shamus. What could I give her? I've nothing but this shell of a house and a price upon my head. I cannot ask her to surrender all she has known, all she deserves, to settle for grubbing poverty at my side. I had such grand dreams. Foolish dreams ... If I took her, do you think her father would ever let us alone? Do you think he would welcome me into the bosom of his family?" A ragged laugh. "I would be back in irons, back in that cell to rot away the rest of my life. And where would that leave Eliza? I could not ask her to take those chances, to suffer those consequences."

Shamus hesitated; then the sight of Luc's misery prompted him to speak. "And if there was a way to possess enough money to buy your freedom and complete your dreams?"

Luc was all sharp attention. "Do not speak riddles to me now. What is this way?"

"You won't like it, Luc."

"How could I like it any less than the wretched options I already have?"

"You will, Luc. You will hate it."

"Tell me."

As the hours dragged on into late afternoon and the cask emptied, the congenial Tournadier spitted one of his own boars, basting it over a pit of coals. The succulent scent wafted with that of scorched wood.

Eliza had no chance to speak with Jean-Luc, and he was shy with her hopeful glances, his darting quickly away. She could see the weariness etched into his lean face and the shadows of some grave worry steeping within his dark eyes. Shamus watched him, too, she noticed. When she was finally able to corner him for a private word, he looked uncomfortable and anxious for escape. His actions puzzled her, hurting her with their indifference, but the haunted blackness in his eyes drew her to his side.

"How are you feeling, Captain? I'm sure your crew would understand if you wished to retire early."

His fixed stare was bland, as was his reply. "I feel fine. My place is here." And he looked away from her with a studied dismissal.

She refused to be discouraged. Her hand touched the back of his head, stroking lightly. He flinched away, still not looking at her.

"Luc, what's wrong?"

"I suppose the fact that I am yet fatigued from fever, that I've had my home nearly burned down, and that we both were nearly killed is not a good enough answer for you."

She would have smiled had there been any humor

in his tone. But it was flat and emotionless. And her anxiety increased. "Of course it is, if it is the correct one. Is it, Luc? Or is it something else?"

Was he uncomfortable with their past intimacy now that his crew had come to wedge between them?

For a moment, she thought he might answer. He caught her hand in the curl of his and brushed her knuckles against his rough cheek. The gesture was as tender as his mood was remote. The contrast frightened her. He stood.

"I should like to be alone."

She was about to protest that things were unsettled between them, that he wasn't strong enough to wander off to brood. But she didn't challenge him because his brief glance was swimming with unnamed sorrow.

"Don't go far," was all she said.

She watched him walk across the tangle of low bushes that would someday be his front lawn, and she ached for the loneliness of his mood. His shoulders rose and fell beneath the weight of his melancholy. Eliza's heart broke. She started to follow.

"Let him go, lass."

She glanced up at Shamus, both annoyed by his intervention and curious over his expression. "Why?" she asked at last. Her head tipped up proudly. "He needs me."

Shamus only smiled. "But he doesn't want to, and therein lie his troubles."

After the time she'd spent one-on-one with Luc, she felt secure enough to demand, "Why would you say that?"

"Because, lady, we've brought word."

Coldness settled about her heart. "What word?"

"That your father is ready to exchange you for a tidy fortune."

Chapter 24

He stood at the edge, on the outside looking in. From behind him, he could hear the sound of merrymaking, but it didn't include him. His thoughts were too restless for him to join in frivolous pursuits. Darker troubles plagued him.

He walked along the fringe of heavy foliage. One step would carry him within its fold and out of sight of the others. There, he could lose himself, letting down the mask that had become such a burden to bear. But the sound of laughter held him poised upon that brink. There was no gaiety in his heart, no laughter in his life, yet the lightheartedness of his crew pulled a strange yearning through him.

As always, the soberness of his nature and the strain of his circumstances separated them. He couldn't let his men see how alone and afraid he was. He was their figurehead of unerring strength, yet he shivered to the soul with a weakness both physical and spiritual. He wasn't strong or particularly brave. He never had been. It was a role he'd learned to play well. They would follow him as long as he continued to fool them. If they knew behind the bold face of Coeur Noir breathed the anxious spirit of Coeur Solitaire, they wouldn't be so free with their praise.

If they knew how close he was to turning his back on everything, they wouldn't toast him as a hero. If they knew he was considering leading them into hell, they would despise him.

"You've strayed a long way from the fire, Luc. Come back with me."

He glanced up at Shamus, the complexity of his mood coloring his view of his second in command. He saw both friend and foe. He looked back into the stillness of the lush surroundings.

"In a little while."

"Will you? I wonder. You've the look of a man who has gone beyond the point of no return."

His comment startled Luc, but he was a master at concealing his thoughts. Instead of reacting, he merely stared down at his feet. And for the first time, he noticed the blotching of T-mon's blood all over the dusty leather. He studied the grisly pattern, mesmerized until a whole sea of red swam up to drown his vision. Ripples of it, so close to his face he could smell its rich fragrance of life and death. He closed his eyes, but memories swelled upon that crimson tide. His ears rang with the peal of screams and the roar of musket fire.

He reeled on suddenly boneless legs, aware of Shamus's supporting grip on his forearms. Even so, he went down upon all fours to retch up the warm wine. There he stayed, weak and trembling, dizziness sucking him toward a past he struggled to escape.

"Easy, lad." He heard Shamus's voice from an impossible distance. "Drawing first blood is hard on a man. 'Tis my guess that he was a man who needed killing."

Luc nodded, fighting to cling to that fact to keep the others at bay. He settled back on his heels to wipe his damp face upon his sleeve. Though his eyes were yet closed, the spray of crimson still splashed across his memory.

"I was possessed by the most amazing madness," he said at last. "I saw myself doing these horrible things and I could not stop them." He drew a deep breath, tasting again the metallic bite of fear and violence. And the primal exaltation. "I have sent men to their deaths before in battle, but never like this, never man to man. Never with such lust for murder in my heart. I did not recognize myself."

"No one wants to recognize those things within their own soul, lad. 'Tis an ugly fact of life, but 'tis life."

The quivering began to still in Luc's belly, and he dared open his eyes again. He glanced sheepishly up at Shamus. "Forgive me. I fear the returning fevers have softened my mind."

"And I fear your mind is warring with a decision already made within your heart."

Luc frowned as he put up his hand. Shamus gripped it firmly and helped hoist him to his feet. "I have not made up my mind, and my heart speaks without reason."

"It's the lass. She's awakened things in you that scare you to death. You're not the first to suffer from that terror. You've slain a man who dared abuse her. She has changed you, lad, and change is not a bad thing."

Luc stared at him stonily, answering with his silence.

"I do not envy you this choice."

At the Irishman's soft words, Luc sighed. "What would you do, Shamus? Tell me."

"I am not you, Luc. I cannot advise you."

"And the crew? What have they said? How can I ask this of them?"

"Most will follow you wherever you lead. There are a few, though, who would not cross the line." He shrugged.

"And you?" His gaze was dark with unshared emotions.

Shamus clasped his forearm. "We have been to hell before. What's another trip? I would go with you, lad. You need but to set the course."

No longer satisfied with the shadows, Luc rejoined his men, marveling at their easy acceptance of him within their ranks. The sense of inclusion was foreign to him, and he held to it with a fragile care. These men, good men. His responsibility.

And then there was Eliza.

He couldn't keep his gaze off her. With her regal grace and enduring beauty, she adorned his home, lending an air of richness to its barren rooms. As if she belonged there.

He watched her hungrily, wondering what kind of man her betrothed was that she could forget him in her captor's embrace. Would he himself be as quickly discarded if she was returned to her home and her plans?

His gaze followed her as she wound her way among his men, acting as his hostess. His heart beat faster with a new and anguished fullness.

Would she be willing to leave her old life and family behind to stay with him? She'd been ready to sacrifice her life for his sake. Was that the passion of the moment, or did her feelings run deeper? He wished he knew more about matters of the heart. He wished he understood the workings of his own better.

He only knew that the possibility of losing her tore it asunder and that when faced with her defilers, it had hardened to enact a deadly vengeance.

Was that love? Then, yes, he loved her. The daughter of his enemy, the fulfillment of his every dream.

But could he become hers?

"You are very quiet this evening, Mr. Leverett."

Remy took the plate of pork Eliza offered, nodding his thanks, but his mood remained glum. Thinking she knew the cause, Eliza touched a hand to his shoulder.

"I don't blame you for what happened in New Orleans."

"Thank you, miss." His clipped tone said that wasn't the burden on his mind.

"Are you angry with me about something? Come, we are friends. Please speak freely."

He stared at her for a moment, debating that. Then, because his own anguish was too great to contain, he spilled his troubles. "I cannot like the direction you're leading our captain in. I have always been proud to serve on his ship, under his command, but now I fear I must decline further service. Things done under the name of flag and country are one thing. The same things done in the name of profit are another."

"Remy, what are you talking about?"

The boy glowered at her. "Before we left New Orleans to come here, Mr. Sterns was approached by the Lafitte brothers. They again have asked if Cap'n Luc would join them at their pirate camp of Campeche, to aid in their plunder of Spanish ships. They have a long-standing friendship, and the *Galant* is known to be the best ship in the water with Black Heart at its helm."

"But Jean-Luc would never consider such a thing."

"He's considering it now, Miss Eliza. We've been asked to cast our yeas or nays on following him down the path of piracy. I must say nay, though it pains me to quit him after all he's done for me."

Eliza's mind reeled with this unlikely information. "Why? Why would he turn to such means?"

Remy's reply cut to the quick. "Because of you, lady. To keep you."

Jean-Luc felt tension snap through Eliza when she realized someone was behind her, and he admired her control as she turned slowly to face him. Alarm heightened the color of her eyes to brilliant emerald. Recognition mellowed it to a smoky jade, though her features remained tight with some worry. She was about to speak when his fingertips brushed over her cheek. She went still. Her skin was silken, the softest he'd ever experienced. Like the emotions whispering through him. His thumb rode over the fullness of her lips. Lost to the intensity of his gaze, she placed a kiss upon it. Their stares mingled, searching, speaking of things never said aloud.

Unbearably tempted to make a greater display, he fanned his fingers wide, combing them back to loosen tendrils of her hair, twirling them about until his hand was webbed in fiery gold. He heard her rapid intake of breath and its slow, sultry exhalation. And with it, she rose up against him, her arm making a lax loop about his neck. Her breasts mashed deliciously upon his chest as her lips parted, coaxing him down to meet them.

He couldn't resist.

Mindless of the fact that they stood in full view of his neighbors and entire crew, he took her sweet mouth with an urgent slant, curving his free arm about her trim waist to lift her nearer. The desperate way she received and returned his kiss was nearly his undoing. He forced some space between them while he yet clung to a scrap of will.

She gazed up through desire-slitted eyes, her mouth swollen wetly from his. He couldn't look upon her and bring coherent thoughts together. He dropped his stare to the hand she'd placed above his heart. The gold of her ring shone richly in the torchlight.

"We must talk." That was all he could manage.

She nodded.

With an uncomfortable glance at their all too interested audience, Luc gestured toward the house.

Eliza led the way inside, nervously aware of Luc close behind her. It wasn't a fearful knowledge, just an anxious one. His kiss surprised her. So did this sudden wish for a private interview. He wasn't a man to make idle talk, so she knew the conversation was critical to their future. The suspense was about to end. And as much as she needed to know the outcome, she dreaded it with equal intensity.

Was he sending her away? After that sweetly searing kiss? After offering up his life? Or was there something else he meant to ask? Her hopes fluttered on tremulous wings, then abruptly stilled.

Was he planning to tell her of his switch in careers from honorable revenge to unlawful plunder?

The parlor was dim. Hints of smoke hung in the air, making wispy ribbons against the glow of firelight from outside seeping around the closed draperies. Luc didn't open them, nor did he light any of the lamps. What tidings were best suited to darkness? Eliza wondered, her heart beating frantically.

He paused at the room's center, his back to her, his stiffly formal stance inviting no sense of confidence in what he was about to say. He was silent, framing his words carefully while Eliza fretted.

"We did not get off to a good start, you and I."

Her laugh was fragile. "No, we did not."

"I would like to think that has changed, that we no longer are enemies of one another."

"I would like to think that, too," she began, but couldn't let him escape that easily. "Does that mean you're giving me my freedom?"

A long silence, then an evasive, "Perhaps."

He began to pace and her gaze followed. He stopped at the fireplace, where his fingertips traced lightly over the elaborate carvings made by Tournadier. She was seeing both sides of him, the unwieldy juxtaposition of vulnerable center and hardened shell. The desire to reach out to him was quelled with difficulty. Her hesitation supplied the time necessary for him to confess his thoughts.

"My father was a professional seaman. He was the most unyielding man I have ever known, both in principle and in practice. He taught me the value of honor, that to be a man meant upholding that honor and demanding it from others. He said a man needs nothing but his honor and requires only justice as his cause. Before he died, we had no common ground between us. I was a meek scholar, content with my books, scornful of his life of bold adventure. He made no secret of his disappointment. He entrusted me but once in his life. He never knew how badly I failed him. I have lived my life since determined not to fail a second time. And I haven't. Until you."

He felt the warm grain of the wood, a contrast to the harsh nap of his conscience. Thank God his father was not alive to see this final failing.

A chill crept over Eliza as she listened to his starkly expressed words. Though he spoke flatly, she caught the undercurrents covered by his toneless phrases. "In what way have I caused you to compromise what you believe?"

"I had it all planned, you see. Neatly organized,

regimented just as he taught me. A man decides upon his plan and he sticks to it. That's how he rose from swab to admiral. And that is what I did when I stood over his grave. I made my plans. First justice, then honor would be restored, and with them, my family's pride.

"I remembered these lands, untamed and unused, and I knew I had found something to which I could devote myself. My father never understood that love of the land. Oh, he would cheerfully fight and kill for the right to claim it, but he never knew the joy of belonging to it. I knew I could build something of value here, that I could plant the seed of my family deep and let it grow here in these rich soils. And that I could have what he always swore he valued most but never truly understood."

He rested his head against the mantlepiece while stroking the sleek wood. His expression softened with yearning. Eliza had never seen a sight so stirring or beautiful.

"And what was that, Jean-Luc?"

He blinked, shaken from his reverie by her quiet question. And she could tell his answer wasn't completely truthful.

"Permanence. Home. He never appreciated the one he had even as he gave his life to protect it. I swore to myself that I would not be the same way. This house, these lands, this is where I belong. My heart is here. It is my dream. And only you can make it come true for me."

She waited but he didn't look at her. She learned nothing from his handsome profile, so she asked, "How?"

"I stole you from your family, from the future you'd planned for yourself. It was an unforgivable thing done out of a need for justice. I do not apologize. I only ask the chance to explain."

"Luc—"

"Please."

And because she knew he was not a man to utter that word carelessly, Eliza stayed silent.

"Your father contracted with the *Galant* to raid fat British prizes under his guaranteed letters of marque. For my part, I took half the prize for me and my crew. While your father was motivated by greed rather than patriotism, I saw it as a chance to exact revenge upon the British by . . . how you say, counting coupe. The moneys I earned, I put into this land and into the building of Coeur Desir."

He went on to describe the satisfactory arrangement, which proved beneficial to both sides, taking close to one hundred British merchantmen and nearly a quarter of a million in cargo. Though he didn't boast of it, the success was due to the sleek lines of the *Galant* and the skill of her captain. Then, with the confrontation coming to a close, there came an unfriendly parting of the ways.

"I had word from my friends the Lafittes that they were joining in the battle to recapture New Orleans. I felt, as my father before me, that I was honor bound to protect my lands. Montgomery didn't see it that way. He was not willing to surrender the use of the *Galant* for patriotic purposes when many a prize was left to be taken. To appease him, I ran one last enterprise, a very lucrative catch, then headed for the Gulf, leaving my first mate, Benji Symms, to negotiate my share."

He didn't tell her of his part in the Battle of New Orleans. Unlike his father, he wasn't one to tote his personal victories but rather the satisfaction of the whole. He'd sailed back toward Salem with a sense of accomplishment, of belonging—to a country and to a cause. However, heroism proved a fleeting illusion. His tone toughened with a long-chewed bitterness.

"When I returned to claim what was due me, I found your father had betrayed Symms and had a trap waiting for me. I was arrested and jailed. Montgomery swore I sailed under no legitimate letters of marque, that my acts were ones of piracy not privateering. It was not enough to imprison me; he wanted ownership of the *Galant* as well as the capture of my crew. I refused to tell him where she had anchored. My silence . . . annoyed him."

He flexed his hand slowly, as if still troubled by the pain. A pain Eliza felt piercing to her soul. Pirate, she'd called him. How she wished back every word. He was no villain. He was every bit as noble as her own brother.

And he thought she was a Montgomery.

"Luc—"

He held up his hand, still not making eye contact. "Let me finish, *ma petite*. Without the payment from that last prize, I had no way to complete the work here at Coeur Desir. I thought justice could be best served by taking you to force Montgomery to honor his debt. I never—ever—meant for any harm to come to you. I cannot expect you to believe that after all that has happened."

But she did. Knowing him as she did now, she knew it was the truth. And she couldn't stay away from him any longer. She crossed to where he was standing, angled toward the cold grate. She eased up behind him, garnering a moment of courage before twining her arms about his flat middle. He inhaled sharply. She feared he would push away. Instead, he cinched her arms a little tighter about him so that they fit close, back to front, and her cheek rested against the taut line of his shoulder.

"I don't blame you for anything that's happened."

He snorted softly, not believing that generous offer. "How could you not when I damn myself daily? If not for me, you would be in the arms of your intended, still a cherished virgin, instead of—"

He didn't need to finish. She knew well what she was. Still, her tone was absolving. "And that is your fault?"

"They took you through my carelessness. And even if they had not, I would still be guilty of the same offenses myself." He made it sound so awful, as if he'd committed a terrible crime upon her instead of sharing an unforgettable bliss.

"And for that I should hate you."

"*Oui.*"

"And you regret those things?"

A beat of silence, then, much softer, "Yes."

She withdrew her arms. He couldn't make it plainer than that. He was restless in the trap of intimacy they'd been caught in. Terrible anguish flooded up, but a remarkable calm remained in her voice. "I see."

He didn't stop her retreat with action. He did it with words. "*Non*, Eliza. You don't see. You don't have any idea what you have done to me. I was not ready for this, for you. It was my plan to finish Coeur Desir, to make it a showplace along the Mississippi, a place of pride. Then I meant to find a woman worthy of its grace and charm. A bride to restore respect for my family's name. A woman to bear my children and bury my shame. Don't you see, the only way I knew to finish what I have started is by claiming what your father owes me. But to do that, I have to surrender up the only woman I have ever envisioned at my side."

He turned to face her fully then. The mask was gone from his expression. In its place was a fragile urgency, exposing the heart of him to her anxious stare.

"Oh, Luc," was all she could whisper before he seized her face between his hands in an earnest press.

"I know I have not been forthcoming. It is hard for me. It does not help that you terrify me. You make me feel—I am saying this badly."

His head ducked down, and she was quick to redirect his eyes to hers with the guiding stroke of her hand beneath his jaw.

"No." He was saying it beautifully. Tears burned behind her tender gaze.

"I would have you for my wife."

She stared up at him, speechless for a long moment. His wife. Nothing—*nothing* had ever sounded better to her.

Fearing her silence, he rushed on recklessly. "I know you would be giving up much for me. Your family, this man you meant to marry. I know I ask much. Is it too much?" She must have appeared stricken, for he grabbed a shallow breath and hurriedly added, "I know you deserve much better."

"How could you say that?" Her words were thin with distress. "How can you presume to know what I want when you don't know me at all?"

"You are right. I did not know you. I thought you were the spoiled, shallow brat borne of my greatest enemy. I was wrong. You are the most admirable of women, so brave and righteous and loyal. You humble me, m'am'selle. I am in awe of your strength and goodness. I would forfeit my claim of retribution for the honor of having you as my bride."

Her eyes were great, glittering pools of frantic emotion.

"But Luc, what of your right to claim what he owes you?"

He misunderstood her worries, thinking she complained over his ability to provide for her as she was accustomed. He took a staunch breath and swallowed down the bitter pill of his pride. His reply was painfully formal.

"You need not fear that I will deny you the pleasures of your birthright. I know I can never make things right with your father. I will be taking his greatest treasure. I would not ask you to live with me on moneys wrested from your family."

"Then how will you finish Coeur Desir?" She could hear again so clearly the longing, the anguish in his voice when he spoke of his unfulfilled dream.

He faced her then, his features immobile, saying nothing of what worked in heart or mind. "Coeur Desir will be the envy of all New Orleans. And you will be her hostess. I will give you anything, everything."

"How, Luc? How will you do it without the ransom money?"

He was a genius at hiding his true feelings. With a bland nonchalance, he told her, "I have contacts in New Orleans who have offered me a shipping run. I would have to be gone for a time—not long, but when I return, I will have the funds required to finish this house, to make it my—our home."

"And restore your family's honor?"

He went very still as she reminded him of that other great hope he'd held for so long. He was amazing in his inscrutability. He never once faltered as he said, "Yes."

What a lie. Her heart broke at its telling. If he sailed on the road of piracy with the Lafittes, there would be no regaining the pride that was so much a part of him.

"And that's what you want, Luc? To restore your family's good name? To claim the respect you've so rightfully earned?"

His mouth thinned into a tight line as conflict worked his stoic features. He blinked, struggling to hold to his impassive front. "Yes, of course. That's what I want." Then he turned away from her, unable to maintain that untruth beneath her soulful study.

And Eliza knew it had been much easier for him to offer up his life for her than it was now to surrender his sense of honor.

But he would. For her.

How could she demand that sacrifice? She would be asking for his very soul. For what was he without his nobility, without the pride that had seen him through the loss of his family, the loss of his liberty? In letting him go against all the principles he held dear, she would be stripping him of his freedom, of his worth, and oh, how well she knew the agony of that forfeiture.

If she loved him, how could she demand he ruin his life just to have her? How long until that sacrifice became resentment? Could he live under the stigma of villain without crumpling beneath the shame?

What could she do? She was not Philomena Montgomery, with her fat purse and proud family. She was a valueless bond servant who could bring him neither moneys nor prestigious name. If she accepted his proposal, she would be forcing him to make a choice that went against the very grain of what made him the man she loved. She loved him for his honor, his pride, his sense of duty and loyalty to the crew who served him. He would be betraying their trust, betraying his own beliefs. For her.

If she said yes.

She watched him move to the window, where he

lifted the heavy swag of fabric to peer out into the night. His mood was impenetrable as that darkness, but knowing him and what he stood for, she could see his turmoil as clear as day.

If she said no, turning away from all that she desired, he would exchange her for the ransom moneys, never learning the truth of her identity. Then he could carry out his dream of Coeur Desir, keeping the memory of his family untainted by deeds of piracy. He would retain his integrity, and she would not go through the rest of her days measuring her happiness upon scales of guilt and shame.

She'd only heard him use the word "love" in one context: when referring to this house, these lands. She was not his dream, they were. And there was only one way she could give them to him to prove the depth of her love.

Sensing her anxiety if not its proper cause, Luc faced her, awaiting her decision. He withdrew behind a glaze of detachment to ask, "So, *chérie*, I leave it up to you. Will you stay with me or be returned to your family for the ransom?"

There was only one way she could respond.

"I want to go home."

His expression never flickered. It never revealed how her simple phrase slashed through the feelings he'd dared bare before her. "Very well," he said at last. "We leave in the morning."

She tried for a dignified retreat, but halfway to the door, her resolve crumpled. She ran the rest of the way to the stairs, flying up them before he could hear her sobs.

And alone in the parlor, Luc gripped the draperies, his knees buckling briefly as a raw sound tore up from his soul.

Chapter 25

❧❧❧

They left Coeur Desir at daybreak, and Eliza knew she was leaving behind her every hope of happiness. Luc was a stiff stranger. The single time their gazes chanced to meet, his was flat obsidian without a trace of life or longing. It betrayed nothing of what had passed between them the night before, nor did it reflect that she'd broken his heart with her refusal. Only Claire-Marie showed any remorse at her departure, hugging her fiercely and bidding her a good journey and quick return. Eliza didn't tell her neither were possible.

Wearing the leather britches, Eliza marched through the swampland surrounded by the *Galant*'s crew. Luc led the way and never looked back. At the river, two long, shallow draft boats were waiting. She rode with Shamus in one; Luc took the other.

The day was hot, sunlight scalding down through the thick humidity to drench the skin and dampen the spirits. Because she hadn't been able to enjoy the surroundings before, Eliza languished in the bottom of the boat taking in the wildly foreign sights, so different from the rock and sand of the eastern coast. The river was lush and pagan, with its brooding cypress swampland and steaming grass marshes. Wildlife was explosive and deadly. Several times, she was alarmed by the sight of alligators drifting lazily alongside them, some measuring a foot between snout and slitted eyes. Shamus told her each inch equated to a foot in body length. She shivered and stayed low.

This was Luc's home—dangerous, unpredictable, exotic, beautiful. Much like him.

And she loathed leaving it behind.

A sudden nasty shift of weather forced them off the water to spend a soggy, shivering night ashore. Their best attempts could coax only a sputtering fire, so supper was eaten cold, an added misery. Eliza curled upon the spongy ground in the minimal protection of Shamus's canvas slicker. She kept her eyes tightly closed against the distorted images lightning cast between the trees. In her exhausted mind, those flashing silhouettes took on a menacing form, shadows that stalked with remembered terror despite the surrounding safety of Luc and his men. She clutched the coat over her head and whimpered softly, wanting Luc, needing him desperately, but unable to seek his comfort. She would have to get used to being alone.

From the other side of their soggy camp, Luc kept a careful watch over her.

For a second night, sleep eluded him in his troubled state. Though pride would not allow him to go to her, concern for Eliza's well-being consumed him. Would the wilderness surroundings and camp of men throw her back to a time of helpless horror? He could still hear the echoes of her frantic cries, stirring a savage wish that all weren't dead so that he might slay them again. Did she feel vulnerable and alone on this dismal night? He knew he did. Seeing her sit bolt upright as a particularly loud crack of thunder rent the air, muting her cry of disoriented fright, was all the excuse he needed to fling off his noble intentions.

She cringed back as his dark shape loomed over her. He could see the starkness of her fear against the pallor of her skin as he knelt before her.

"It's Luc," he told her gently to ease that mindless anguish. Then he tried to explain his purpose by saying, "I was wondering if you needed—"

She cut off the need for excuses. Her arms curled about his neck in a frantic wrap, her heart hammering against him through the dampness of their clothing. He held her tight, absorbing her shivers of shock, absolving his weakness of will. He felt her tears against his throat, hotter than the drizzling rain.

"Don't leave me, Luc!"

He kissed the wet tousle of her hair, his eyes squeezing shut as he vowed, "I will be with you for as long as you want me." And he ached with the truth of that passionate claim. "I will keep you safe from harm."

She quieted then, burrowing against him for sheltering warmth and security. He wished it could be for more. He drew up Shamus's coat so it tented over both of them, and he continued to hold her, knowing this was the last time he could allow himself that luxury.

She'd wounded his pride with her refusal. And she'd broken his heart. But nothing she could do would change how much he still loved her—and always would.

Gradually, she became aware of him. Her palm moved in a familiar caress against the dampness of his shirt. The fingers of her other hand twined through his hair. Her face lifted and he knew the wise thing would be to pull away then, that to kiss her was to open himself up to the most humble vulnerability. But lost in her sea-green gaze, it didn't matter that she might later scorn him for his weakness. He would have her know how much he cared.

His kiss was bittersweet bliss. A torment of all Eliza wanted but could not claim. She clung to him, her heart crying it was too much, too much to ask of it to let him go. But she knew she must. And she knew she would, without betraying her reasonings because that was the only way she could save him from making the greatest mistake of his life.

He felt her response and wondered wildly how she could so desire him yet not want him. But pride wouldn't allow him to ask for her reasons. He had his answer. Knowing why wouldn't change it to one he'd rather hear.

So he held her tight, giving her his strength this last time. Giving her his heart for all times. And sometime close to morning, when the heavens stilled and the bayous steamed, he slept with her enfolded to the curve of his body.

When she awoke, she was alone with only the memory of his nearness to cling to.

They made good time, entering New Orleans before nightfall. Hot, hungry, and ready to quench a thirst, they commandeered tables at Etienne's, where Benji Symms awaited them in a private parlor.

Symms stepped up to embrace his captain in effusive welcome. He was as small and pale as Luc was lean and dark. His nearly colorless gaze touched on Eliza with curiosity before turning back to his captain.

"What news have you, Benji?" Luc asked as he assumed a seat across from Eliza. He waved off the offer of ale in favor of an answer.

"All be set, Jean-Luc. Montgomery has picked neutral ground for the exchange; an estate on Saint Kitts." He paused as Etienne scuttled up to lay out a new round of drinks. The brothel owner cast an anxious glance at the stony-faced privateer and rubbed absently at the crude bandage where his ear had once been. T-mon hadn't been as polite in his questioning as the aristocratic Frenchman, and he wanted no further trouble. Luc paid him no mind, his attention on his first mate.

"Then he is in agreement to the terms?"

"Aye. His daughter for the money. Do you have her, then?"

"Who?"

"Miss Montgomery?"

Luc gestured toward Eliza without favoring her with his glance.

Symms stared at Eliza's wan features and smiled in uncertainty. "I had not taken you for a man of much humor, but this is a joke, is it not?"

Eliza went very still.

Luc frowned, not at all amused. "Is what a joke?"

"Who is this woman?"

"Philomena Montgomery."

Symms laughed in confusion. "I don't know what name she's told you, but she is not Philomena Montgomery."

Luc's dark stare skewered Eliza's. Nothing registered on his motionless features. "How do you know?"

"I have seen her myself, Jean-Luc, upon her father's arm. She be blond and buxom and a royal shrew. I don't understand. Who have you here?"

His entire body tense, his face chiseled of fine marble, Luc said, "Leave us."

When the men hesitated, the soft order became a roar.

"Leave us!"

Stunned by the violence of the command, his crew

scrambled to obey, even Remy, who cast a reluctant glance at Eliza before following the others out of the private parlor room. Eliza cringed back in her chair, struggling for courage.

When the doors were closed and they sat facing one another alone, Luc asked, "Who are you?"

"Eliza—"

His palms slapped the tabletop, making her leap within her seat. "No more lies." He didn't raise his voice, but it penetrated like a lethal plunge of steel.

"My name is Eliza. I am Philomena Montgomery's bond servant."

His breath hissed out. His face was so tight and strained it looked ready to crack. "The other woman on the ship—"

"Was Philomena," she supplied wearily.

He didn't betray much, just a flicker of dark passions behind his unblinking stare. A thinning of his mouth into a taut line. She could imagine what turmoil whipped inside him: the anger, the hurt, the humiliation. His hands fisted upon the tabletop, balling up to conceal their trembling. His expression was unreadable.

"Brilliant."

She wasn't sure she heard him right.

"A brilliant strategy. Her idea or yours?"

Confused by his almost conversational tone, Eliza said, "Hers. She was afraid you meant to harm her."

"And you rushed to sacrifice yourself, *non*? No? What, then, was the price of your treachery?" His voice shook, just a little, but he was quickly in control. His stare blazed, black ice and fire.

She notched her chin higher. "My freedom, Captain."

"You must have valued it greatly to have thrown yourself so enthusiastically into the deception."

His cool derision stung, but she refused to relent. "I have nothing to apologize for."

"Indeed, you should be applauded. You had me fooled completely. I had no idea you were such an accomplished liar."

He took a breath, unable to say more for the moment. His eyes closed as spasms pulled the muscles of his lean face. Finally, he gave a harsh laugh directed at himself. "Like father, like daughter, our Mademoiselle Montgomery. And me, twice the fool."

He was thinking of all the things he'd said to her—to this deceiver. How he'd laid open his heart, inviting her to share his future, his . . . love. *Mon Dieu!* What a blind idiot he was! And all the while he was being sucked in by her beauty and bravery, his true prey was escaping him, leaving him with nothing. No recourse. No ripe revenge. No focus for his affections. He stared at her, this lovely fraud who'd earned his heart on a platter as her reward.

He hated her. He hated the Montgomerys. He hated how he was feeling.

"When did you plan to reveal the deception?" he wanted to know, his voice an icy purr. "I would think you'd have broken it off sooner to avoid recent unpleasantries."

She paled and glanced down at her hands, where her fingers twisted anxiously. "I meant to do so when we first reached New Orleans. I was afraid—"

"Of what? Me?"

She didn't look up nor did she answer. "I tried to tell you several times but . . ."

"What? You were enjoying yourself too much at my expense?"

Her gaze lifted then, meeting his with a melting earnestness. "No. You know that's not true."

"Do I?" For an instant, his features buckled with

anguish. He shuddered as if in pain. "I know nothing of the kind." He could hear her damnable voice: *I love you, Luc.* Disillusionment writhed inside him. He could endure no more. Catapulting from his seat, he stalked to the door, leaning there, palms pressed to poorly painted wood. A wrenching moan tore from him as he pounded his forehead against the unyielding panel.

Eliza flinched, tears in her eyes. Wishing there was something she could do to ease his torment.

There was a hurried knock, and Luc composed himself as Shamus and Benji entered.

"Lad," Shamus ventured carefully. "The men be waiting your instructions."

Luc looked at him blankly.

"Do we sail?"

A sudden focus lit Luc's features. He turned to Eliza as if he hadn't heard the question. "If you are not Montgomery's daughter, why has he agreed to the ransom demand?"

"I do not know," she replied truthfully. "Philomena was to have gone to her father to exact my rescue. But none has been forthcoming."

Luc frowned. He turned to Symms. "You say he is ready to pay?"

"Aye, Jean-Luc. There is no sign of his daughter in Salem. He truly believes her to be in your hands."

"It could be a trap, Luc," Shamus cautioned quietly.

"Or a delicious vengeance."

Eliza sat silently, refusing to quail under the Frenchman's assessing stare as she grew in value once more.

"Benji, take the *Delight* on ahead to Saint Kitts to see if what Montgomery has in mind is trade or trap. We will follow on the morning tide."

"Aye, Captain. Watch for my signal be it safe to come in."

Luc placed his hand upon the smaller man's shoulder in a uncharacteristic gesture. "You do me proud, Mr. Symms."

A second passed before Symms took the compliment with a smile. "Thank you, Jean-Luc. It's been my privilege to serve you."

"This will be my last venture on the seas."

His announcement was greeted with murmurs of surprise.

"There's no more profit to be made in our line of work, and I have decided not to cross its boundaries into piracy even though the Lafittes have made me a tempting offer. A shipboard life was never my choice. It served a purpose, and now I wish to put those things behind me."

"But Jean-Luc, what of your ships, the *Galant* and the *Delight*?" Symms demanded in dismay. "Surely you don't mean to retire them as well."

"Unlike me, they have many good years left upon the seas. I will continue as owner and let them sail under the care and commission of my two finest captains. Those two, whom I trust above all others, are with me here in this room."

Shamus didn't react to the news, but Symms's pale features flushed with anticipation.

"The *Galant*," he breathed in reverence.

"Will sail under the captaincy of Mr. Sterns. Benji, you will pilot the *Delight*."

This, clearly, was not the arrangement Symms had hoped for. His expression fell briefly before assuming a grateful mien. "I am honored by your confidence, Jean-Luc."

"It is well deserved. Be quick if you mean to catch the evening tide."

"Aye, Captain. I will not forget this."

But as Luc turned away, Eliza watched Symms's expression harden into something less than pleasant before he spun out the door to carry out his orders.

"Luc, I am overwhelmed by your gesture," Shamus said.

"Why? You've more than earned this reward."

Shamus's features darkened as he growled, "I have never been after a reward."

Luc bestowed a rare smile upon him. "I know, which is why I've given you the *Galant*."

"Symms expected to have her helm. He is your first mate, Luc."

"Symms is a good seaman, an ambitious one, but he will not treat the *Galant* with the respect she is due. I know you will. I've not been generous with my friendship, though you've deserved it. Perhaps in this way, I can make amends." Then, looking uncomfortable with the disclosure, he reached for two mugs of ale. "Drink with me, Captain Sterns."

"I will drink to you, Captain Gautier."

And they toasted one another with an awkward familiarity. Then Luc's expression grew impenetrable once more. "Take our lovely impostor aboard the *Galant* and make ready to sail at first light. She can continue her role for our benefit now."

And he stood stiffly, unable to look at her as Shamus led her from the room. Only when he was alone did waves of anguish overtake him. He reeled, blindly searching for a chair. He collapsed into it, dropping his head into his hands.

A lie. It had all been a lie. His thoughts swirled dully, trying to separate Eliza from her pretense as Philomena Montgomery. How had she so easily duped him? A bond servant pretending to be a lady. He drew a tortured breath, hoping to free the tightness in his chest to no avail. How much had she pretended? How much was real?

Where did Philomena end and the real Eliza begin?

She'd tricked him. He could place no real blame for the original plot. It was a clever ploy, meant to fool a dangerous stranger. But later, once she'd learned she had nothing to fear from him . . . why hadn't she told him the truth? If the words had come from her own lips, the lie wouldn't have tasted so bitter. If she'd told him as they lay in each other's arms at Coeur Desir, he would have forgiven her anything. If she'd spoken up when he'd made his ill-fated proposal, the devastation wouldn't be so crushing.

But she'd kept silent, and he had to wonder why.

And until he knew, he didn't trust himself to be with her. His mood was too dark, his heart too raw.

Sometime, somewhere between morning and their rendezvous in Saint Kitts, she was going to tell him everything he wished to know.

Then he would decide if he was willing to let her go.

Eliza saw nothing of the elusive captain as the *Galant* glided across smooth Gulf waters. Her emotional journey didn't fare as well. Though she schooled her mind to accept his absence, her silly heart continued to pine for him. Meals were tendered by a grimly silent Remy, his censure yet another sign of her fall from the captain's good grace.

On the second night, she could stand the isolation no longer. When Remy entered with her evening tray, mournful strains of some sad sea chantey drifted in to match his melancholy mood.

"Good evening, Remy," she called with false gaiety.

He glanced up at her. Then his gaze darted away.

" 'Evening, my la—miss," he amended hastily before turning to leave.

"Remy!"

He canted a look over his shoulder. "Miss?"

"Can you spare a moment to talk with me, or have I suddenly developed the plague with you as well?" She'd meant to say it with humor, but tears pricked traitorously behind her eyes. "Please, Remy. I'm so anxious to hear a friendly voice."

He cast an uneasy glance toward the stairs, then sighed and closed the door. "Aye, Miss Eliza, you be right about a plague. This voyage be like a dirge."

"Any why is that?"

"It be Cap'n Luc. He—" Remy broke off, embarrassed by the notion of breaking his captain's confidence.

"Is Luc all right?"

Her anxiousness won the lad over. He smiled reassuringly. "Oh, don't fret, Miss Eliza. 'Tis not an ailing of the body, I'm thinking, but rather a sorrow of the soul."

Eliza said nothing, wondering how much the boy knew of her relationship with Luc.

Then Remy sighed again. "This is his last turn out as captain of the *Galant*, you know. And as much as we all like Mr. Sterns, we'll be missing him sorely at the helm. Instead of celebration, it feels as if we be burying him at sea by his own request. He speaks to no one save Mr. Sterns and hasn't stood down from the watch since we left port."

She was at fault, Eliza knew. She'd hurt him grievously, and he wasn't recovering well. "If only there was something I could do." She hadn't meant to voice that aloud, but Remy brightened immediately.

"Perhaps there is, miss, if you be willing. What say we liven up this ghost ship?"

He cocked his elbow, offering her his arm. Puzzled, she lay her hand upon it and let him lead her up on deck. The crisp salt air was a slap to her senses, shaking her from her dreary daze. The evening sky made an endless jeweled canopy overhead, stretching from yesterday to tomorrow, and the waters were as dark and slick as a soothsayer's glass. Could she see her own future there? she wondered.

Her presence on deck created a stir of unease through the crew, who weren't sure how to respond to the cause of their captain's malaise. Cautious glances shifted to the forecastle, where Jean-Luc's silhouette stood unmoving against the melting reflection of the moon. If the Frenchman was aware of her appearance, he gave no sign.

"Play something lively, Jacob," Remy called to the concertina player. Then when the box squeezed out an infectious tune, the boy bowed to Eliza, inviting her to join him in a reel.

Though she had never felt less like dancing and gaiety was far from her heart, Eliza forced a smile and allowed the lad to turn her boisterously about the confines of the deck. As her skirts belled out from trim calves and her hair swirled into a cloak of fiery gold, the crew gathered in closer to clap in time to the tin whistle, grateful for the distraction.

The deep-starred night, cool caress of the breeze, catchy tempo, and Remy's grin conspired to lift Eliza's mood, as well. Soon she was smiling with a true enjoyment that sparked her eyes as Remy twirled her beneath the arch of his arm and she returned to find herself facing Jean-Luc.

She froze.

Against the darkness, his features were cut with somber beauty. He held her hand aloft, her fingers lightly clasped in his. For a moment, time suspended as her heart took flight with a song of its own.

He bowed with a fluid grace, black eyes never leaving hers. Then, as the mood of the music altered to a stately pace, he guided her through the complex steps of the quadrille with the practiced ease of a courtier to the awe and delight of his men. Entranced by his dark grace and compelling stare, Eliza transformed the deck into a glittering ballroom floor within her dazzled mind. And she was lost to the illusion.

Until the music stopped and, with a formal bow, Jean-Luc abandoned her without a word to go below.

She was shaken from her dazed reverie when Shamus Sterns came to claim her arm. Instead of leading her into a dance to the next lilting melody, he coaxed, "Walk with me."

They fell into step upon the moon-drenched deck, and Eliza could no longer restrain her curiosity.

"Who is he, Shamus? Will you tell me what put such sadness in his soul?"

"Why are you asking, miss?"

She stopped and met his gaze so he could read of her sincerity. "I would help heal his hurts if I could."

"Because he saved you in the swamps?"

"Because I love him."

Shamus expressed no surprise. Instead, he sighed and led her to the rail. He leaned there to stare out over the dark waters.

"I was a young man when I was called to go to war. It seemed a noble undertaking at the time. Though I was promised a shipboard tour by those who inducted me, I found myself mucking about in the infantry on the foreign shores of France. And I hated every minute of it."

He described the hell of war as one who saw the process as senseless and barbaric. His one longing was to complete his military term and return to his first love, the sea.

"There was one particular French admiral who eluded us at every pass. Like a fox, he was, or a ghost in the night. My commander had a personal loathing for this cunning officer and he believed that to capture him would lead to his elevation in the ranks.

"Since we could not engage the Frenchmen on a battlefield, my commander, Fitzroy was his name, decided to flank the military genius on a private front. We marched upon the admiral's home, tipped off to his recent visit there by one of the man's own domestic staff. We were greeted there by his gracious wife, his three daughters, and his somber son. Fitzroy told them they would come to no harm if they cooperated. He demanded to know where Admiral Gautier's ships were headed, and he grew furious when they claimed they did not know. When Fitzroy's plan failed him, my commander calmly ordered that Gautier's family be slain."

Eliza gasped. "Luc's family." Horror twisted to match the anguish upon Shamus's face.

"War is war, but I did not take up the colors to slaughter innocents to serve a man's vanity. The admiral's wife and son fell with the first volley, but the little girls ran screaming with fright, and we were ordered to shoot them down. And we did. Then we marched away from that proud deed unaware of its futility." Shamus turned his eyes toward the heavens, his features taut with the brutal irony.

"Admiral Gautier went down on his flagship two days before we needlessly murdered his family. And after all this time, after all I've done to make amends, Luc has yet to forgive me. And I have yet to forgive myself."

Chapter 26

Luc's stateroom was steeped in shadows. He stood at the far windows, his mood as enigmatic as the black waters beyond. Drawn by his lonely stance and tragic story, Eliza approached fearlessly, wishing to give both ease.

He heard her step. A stiffening spread up his spine. When he turned, twilight obscured his features. His inflectionless voice gave nothing away.

"Forgive the intrusion, m'am'selle. I but came for a change of clothing."

"Luc, I did not mean to hurt you."

A moment's silence. "I will survive the injury." There was no change in his painfully formal tone. "Now, if you will excuse me—"

"No. Not unless you excuse me for so misusing your trust."

She could imagine his thoughts etched clearly in his unwelcoming stance. *Liar. Deceiver.* His reply confirmed it.

"You ask too much."

He tried to brush by her to end the encounter without further unpleasantness. She'd already said too much, and not enough. The wise thing would be letting him go. But she couldn't, not knowing how greatly she'd added to the burden of pain he bore.

She reached out, her hand snagging his sleeve.

"Luc." A quiet petition.

He paused, not because her grip was strong upon his arm but rather because it was a band of steel about his soul. "Release me, madame. I have ship's business to attend to."

The frigid cut of his words could not best the hurried beats of her heart, quickening at his nearness.

"You have business to attend to here also."

He scowled, his dark glare slashing to the core of her outrageous command. "The only business we have is when I trade you to Montgomery for the moneys you will bring me. Let him play the fool this time, but I will play yours no longer."

How cold he was. How he must hate her. Despite her best intentions, she found she couldn't bear up beneath this latest lie, the one that would have him believe she didn't care for him. It was cruel. Perhaps if she could explain without compromising her reasonings. Her hands clutched at his forearm. She could feel his resistance to whatever she might say in the tension beneath her grip and in the way he pulled against it.

"Do not do this," he commanded with an icy disdain. "Do not cheapen yourself with further dramatics."

She hugged to his arm, crying softly, "Luc, please, I beg you. Do not dismiss all as lies."

To free himself from the press of emotions, he raised his arm and flung her away from him with a violence that surprised them both. She fell back across his bed, banging her head against the curve of the ship's side. A starburst of pain shot through her mind, momentarily disorienting her.

Against that dizzying backdrop, the approach of an

intimidating shadow spiraled her into her worst
nightmares. She scrambled back, retreating until the
wall wouldn't allow it. An outstretched hand carried
horrific overtones. She cried out and rolled away, balling up against what little protection the wall offered.
She tensed at the weight of a heavy hand upon her
shoulder, bracing for what would follow. A whimper
of sound escaped the tight press of her lips.

Gentle fingertips brushed the hair away from her
ear. A soft kiss touched upon it.

"Eliza, *mon coeur. Je regrette*—I am sorry. I did not
mean to frighten you."

Tender words whispered against her cheek.

"Eliza, do not fear me, *chère.*"

He pushed against her shoulder. She quivered but
responded to his light pressure there, easing her over
onto her back. Her arms crossed over her heaving
chest, her fists balling protectively. The mattress
shook with the force of her restrained weeping.

It was the most natural thing in the world to accept
comfort from him, first with the ragged whisper of
his name, then from the answering persuasion of his
mouth. She quieted and opened. And with her capitulation, they were both lost.

He kissed her deeply, hungrily, with an alarming
lack of control. If not forgiven, all was at least momentarily forgotten. She arched against him, proving
how perfectly they fit, one to the other, her soft curves
conforming to his hard swells. Their tongues touched
to invite a hot, plunging intimacy. Her hands were at
the collar of his shirt, impatient with the material.
Clothing was shed in careless haste.

His mouth continued its reckless plundering—frantic, demanding as he drove himself within her with
that same savage desperation. He felt her shuddering
wildly and tasted her freeing cry. His response was

instantaneous. Explosive. Endless. Finally over. He lay atop her, panting, senses spinning. And after a while, he felt her fingertips brushing through his hair, the gesture achingly tender.

He moved, leaving her.

"Don't go, Jean-Luc."

"I do not think I could just yet." He rolled onto his back, body relaxing into a series of deliciously weak shivers. His eyes closed as he savored the sensation. Complete contentment.

Then her head burrowed beneath his chin, her full breasts flattening upon his chest. Reality returned with all its doubts, souring his serenity.

What was he doing, inviting her back into his heart? How easily she undercut his defenses with each sweet surrender. Angrily, he sought a way to lessen the impact of their unplanned passion.

"Are you going to tell me again that you love me?"

She winced at the caustic quality of his question, her own tone softly defensive. "I would if you believed me. But you wouldn't, would you?"

"*Non.*"

"Then I will keep that truth to myself."

She lifted up so they could look at one another. Her beauty knocked the power of rational thought from him. Her fingers played along the whorl of his ear, inciting a fierce tremble of renewed desire. He fought it down.

She rode the rock of his breathing, her study of his face so intense he grew uncomfortable.

"I cannot help how I feel, Jean-Luc."

With a twinge of private pain, he pushed her off so he could sit up. "Didn't I promise that you would enjoy the lessons? You'll find someone to replace me soon enough. Someone more worthy of your affection." How that knowledge scalded. He reached down for his trousers, but her arms circled his middle, restricting his movements. Her cheek rubbed the sleek skin of his shoulder.

"No. I don't know that I'll ever trust another man enough to allow him these same liberties. The thought of any other's touch turns me cold inside."

That sad confession woke a certain degree of satisfaction. He had no retort that might cause more pain than it inflicted back upon him. A confusion of hurt and jealousy clouded his cooler logic, the logic that warned him to escape her quickly. But how could he leave when he desired her company so much, when he would gladly endure the pain she caused him just to bask in a moment's pleasure? And why did she hold to him so tightly after casting him away? He didn't understand.

"If you planned to miss me so much, you would have agreed to stay with me when I asked you."

Incredibly, she replied, "You never asked me."

He twisted around, anger and humiliation surfacing all over again as he cried, "I asked you to be my wife!"

With her gaze fixed somberly upon his, Eliza shook her head. "No, Jean-Luc. You never asked *me*. You offered to share your future with Philomena Montgomery, the gracious, wealthy lady who would decorate your home and win over your pretentious guests. You didn't propose marriage to a simple bond slave."

He frowned, his gaze narrowing fiercely as he sought some defense. "You are no bond servant. You are a lady, born and bred. That is no pretense."

"A lady can fall on hard times, too, Captain, but that makes her no less the lady. My fiancé's family did not believe that and so, here I am, cast down, stripped of all but my pride, and little enough of that is left me."

He studied her, recalculations humming within his head. "I did not know. You were not truthful with your circumstance."

"And you were with yours, Captain? Or should I call you *vicomte*?"

He went still as stone. "That title was never earned and never claimed."

"It could have been."

"Non." Again, he shook his head.

"It should have been."

"Non! I do not deserve the honor. I disgraced the title."

Eliza hesitated, aware how he would receive her next words. But she couldn't leave him without giving him back some of himself, just as he had for her at Coeur Desir. She owed him that freedom.

"Why?" she asked him softly. "Because you lived and they did not?"

He sucked a tortured breath, his mouth moving in a speechless denial. For a moment, he just stared at her in that mute dismay as if she'd struck him between the eyes with a pistol ball. Then he grabbed up his trousers and pulled them on. He refused to look at her.

She could not let him escape without facing the truth. "Luc, you have nothing to prove to them anymore. The only forgiveness you need is your own."

He rounded on her with a sudden self-directed fury. "What do you know of it?"

"Shamus told me."

The fight drained from him as quickly as the color from his face. "Damn him. He had no right."

"But it's right that you continue to punish yourself by keeping those who'd care for you at bay? I think

you take a perverse delight in being Coeur Solitaire.
Why is that? Because you don't think you deserve any
happiness?''

"I do not deserve to live!" His voice broke horribly.
"Not at the cost of their lives. They were my family."

"You did not kill them, Luc." Tears glistened in her
eyes and hung heavy in her throat as she felt his pain.
He gave a ragged cry and spun away from her, reeling to the wall of glass, where he slumped in battering
remorse.

"Yes, I did." His palms pressed to the cool panes
as his breathing sawed hoarsely. "They were my responsibility. My father told me to be brave and to
protect them, and I could do neither. Did Shamus tell
you that? Did he tell you that I watched them being
shot down, that I did nothing to save them?"

"He told me your mother died instantly, before any
of you knew what was happening. That you were
shot in the chest in that same volley and were thought
to be dead. He told me that he was so sickened by
what they were ordered to do that when he saw you
yet lived, he was determined to save you. But you
didn't make it easy for him, did you?"

His voice softened with bittersweet remembrance.
"They were a flock of little angels, my sisters. All sunlight, not darkness like me. Always teasing me for my
somber ways, making me laugh when I was trying to
scold them. *Mon Dieu*, I adored them. I could see the
terror on their faces when Mama fell. Such horror in
their eyes. I could hear them screaming as they ran. I
didn't want them to die alone and afraid. I—I tried
to get up, to call them to me, thinking I could shield
them from harm. I tried to grab a rifle from the nearest soldier, but he put his foot on the back of my head
and forced my face into a puddle that was full of my
own blood. Later, I learned that he'd done that to save

me because he knew he could not save us all. How I hated him for sparing me so that I could see them all slain and buried."

Wearing just his shirt, Eliza slipped up behind him, desperate to console him. The flesh of his back spasmed as her hand touched to his shoulder. "There was nothing you could have done, Luc."

"Yes, there was. I knew, you see. I knew the answer to the question they asked. I knew where my father was sailing. I would not tell them. I did not recognize the monsters that they were—until it was too late."

"It was your father's pride and that man's greed for glory, not a failing on your part."

He went on in that leadened tone, as if he hadn't heard her.

"They left Shamus behind at his request. He was to burn our home but to leave our bodies where they fell as a warning to my father. He set the fires as he was told to keep his troops from becoming suspicious, but only to the outbuildings. And then he bound my wound and buried my mother and sisters. I was so ashamed that I'd let them die, I wouldn't allow myself to cry over their graves."

And he'd never released himself from that emotionless prison since then, Shamus told her, except when he'd wept in the forgiving throes of fever.

He fought those long-suppressed feelings now, his body rocking rapidly, breath hitching in raw snatches. As he twitched away from her comforting embrace, the floodgates of blame continued to pour open.

Between his words of deprecation and Shamus's of praise, Eliza pieced together their awkward circumstances: a gravely wounded young French aristocrat with no family or means, depending upon the care of one of the lowly soldiers who'd slaughtered his family. Knowing no other trade, Shamus headed for the sea once Jean-Luc was able. There the timid scholar toughened beneath the bite of brine and grueling labor, growing, under Shamus's tutelage, into a man of lean whipcord strength who earned his superiors' respect with his keen intelligence and cold daring. By the time he was twenty, he had his own ship and the legend of Coeur Noir was fast spreading. But none of that mattered to Jean-Luc, who retreated further into himself under the relentless torment of his demons.

"I did it all for them," he said, more to himself than to her. "It was the only way I could try to make amends. My father wanted a son who was a fearless fighting man. I was afraid to follow in his footsteps, wanting only to keep to my learned pursuits, to the serenity of the land. How he despised me for my choices. How better to avenge him than to take on the guise of a bold privateer upon the seas that my father loved, striking back at the British for what they'd done. But it was his fight, not mine. I hadn't his thirst for glory. My dreams were too full of the blood of innocents. Coward, I could hear him saying with such disappointment in his voice. There was nothing I could do to please him, nothing I could do to appease my guilt." He leaned back against the glass, eyes squeezed tight against the brutal memories.

"Evonne, the youngest of my sisters, was still alive when the butchers left. I held her in my arms and made her promises I knew I could not keep so that she would not be so afraid. Sh-she was s-seven years old. A baby. Just a baby."

His knees gave way, buckling until he slid to the floor. He hugged his bent legs, his averted face buried within the wrap of his arms. A low mournful sound escaped him. Eliza knelt before him, securing him within the circle of her love. Surprisingly, he didn't reject her care. He leaned against her for long minutes as his breathing rasped noisily and tremors of re-morse shook through his broad shoulders. Even then, she could feel him struggle to contain the ravaging emotions, but his success was far from total. He turned his head slightly, his damp cheek lying atop her shoulder so he could speak more plainly.

"Such irony that I chastise you for pretending to be who you are not when I hide my cowardice behind the guise of Black Heart."

"Cowardice?" Eliza lifted his abused hand, carrying it to her lips. She kissed the misshapen knuckles tenderly. "Would a coward endure such agony to protect his ship and crew? Would a coward go aloft in the midst of a storm to save a lad caught in the rigging? Would he readily sacrifice himself for a woman who's been more trouble than she's worth? I see no coward here, Jean-Luc. Only a man with brav-ery to spare and a heart too full of past pain to rec-ognize his own value."

He straightened, his features once again smooth and unreadable as he said, "Perhaps we only see what we want to see."

"Because we're afraid to see the truth?"

He crooked a small smile at that wisdom, then stood, bringing her up with him. "I did not mean to burden you with my troubles, but I thank you for hearing them. I must go." Yet his hand lingered over the brilliance of her cascading tresses. "Perhaps we can speak later."

"I am not going anywhere, Captain."

And with that, they parted in a poignant truce.

It was near dawn when he returned to find Eliza deep in slumber. Once he was on the moon-soaked deck with only the calm black waters as his witness, his thoughts had opened to things long forgotten.

Like the beauty of little girls' laughter, recalled for the first time for its purity instead of with pain. Like the sweetness of his mother's voice as she read to him in the fragrant arbor behind their chateau and smiled her praise when she listened to his orations. Those things had been lost to him, hidden beneath layers of guilt and shame. Bringing them out into the open at Eliza's prodding had freed them from his soul. He felt lighter of spirit for the first time in all his adult years.

He stared down at her as she slept, at the wonderfully resilient yet relentlessly tender woman he'd known for such a short time and not at all. He hadn't fallen in love with her because of her name but rather, in spite of it. The fact that she wasn't a Montgomery was more blessing than curse. For her to call herself valueless was incomprehensible. How could her fiancé have turned her away when any man would be lucky to claim her as his wife? Including him.

Especially him.

She stirred when his weight leveled along the mattress beside her. Blue-green eyes flickered open, sharp with alarm, then warming in welcome. She rolled toward him, snuggling close, resting her head in the valley between his chin and shoulder while her hand stroked lazily over his now bared chest. Her fingertips paused over the small puckered scar below his right shoulder where an assassin's bullet had come close to stealing his life before it had a chance to flourish.

"Is it morning already?" she murmured sleepily.

"Not quite. I did not mean to wake you." He touched her hair and was lost to the luxury of its texture.

"I don't mind." A purr of contentment that set his heart afire.

"Eliza?"

"Ummm?"

"What will happen if you go back to the Montgomerys?"

He could feel her coming completely awake. It was a time before she answered. "I have three more years of servitude left. I have little hope that Philomena meant to release me from my bond. Like father like daughter, as you said."

"This fiancé who turned his back upon you . . . ?"

"I have little hope there, either." Her tone sounded sad and final. He gave the former fiancé no further thought, privately thanking him for being a fool.

Eliza leaned up on her elbow. "Why the questions, Jean-Luc?"

"As you said, I know very little about you."

His answer pleased her enormously. She retained her smile and said, "What you don't know, no longer matters. I'm not that person. Who I am is the woman who has spent these last weeks in your company and—" She broke off, beginning to study his features with a perplexed frown.

"What is it?"

"You're—different somehow." She stroked his brow. "The lines are gone. Since the first time I saw you, you've had this tension about you, as if you were concentrating with all your strength to give nothing away. That mask is gone. This is the real Jean-Luc I'm seeing, isn't it?"

"A man who's been pardoned from a life sentence."

"Is that a smile?" she teased, running her thumb across the slight bow of his lips.

"It might be." Then he was somber again. "Eliza."

She went still, waiting to hear what returned the intensity to his face.

"If I asked again, if I asked *you* this time, would your answer be the same?"

She stared down at him, not knowing what to say.

Emotion clouded her gaze, regret clogged her heart.
"Luc . . . please don't ask. Things are better as they
stand."

"Better for whom?"

She'd asked that of him once and had not liked the
answer. He wouldn't like hers now, so she said nothing.

He scowled and turned his face away. She coaxed
it back with the gentle touch of her hand upon his
rough cheek. Still he frowned up at her.

"I do not like the idea of you as anyone's slave."

"You had no problem envisioning me as your own.
I seem to remember wearing your shackles." Then she
was the one who frowned. "Nor do you have much
of a problem in selling me back for a profit."

"Yes," he argued. "I do. Eliza—"

She laid her hand over his mouth, stilling the
words. "Take the money I'll bring you and see to your
dream. You deserve it, Luc. You've more than earned
it."

He moved her hand, clutching it over his heart.
"And what if I were to find a new dream? One that
we both could share?"

"That will be rather difficult with me in Salem and
you in New Orleans." Even the thought of that separation woke a crushing despair.

"And if I decide not to turn you over to Montgomery?"

"But Luc, the ransom—"

He smiled. "Monsieur Montgomery is not the only
one who knows how to break a deal with deception."

The *Galant* rode the gentle Caribbean tide off the
coast of Saint Kitts. From a distance, the small island
seemed nothing more than three volcanic peaks rising
from the jewel-toned waters, a paradise of golden

beaches and abrupt green hills. And no convenient harbors or coves to dock in. Only the surrounding sea.

Though there was no sign of the *Delight* on the crystal blue waters, Benji Symms's signal rose from one of the deserted shorelines, a thin furl of dark smoke proclaiming it was safe to land.

Shamus eyed the isolated distance between the *Galant* and the parish of Saint Peter Basseterre. In a long boat, a man would be at the mercy of a fast-moving vessel.

"I don't like it, Luc."

"Benji says it's safe to come in. He wouldn't have signaled if Montgomery had a welcome planned."

The Irishman glanced worriedly at his captain. "I'd feel a lot better if you would let me go in with you."

Luc shook his head. "It is my risk alone. I will not allow another to take it with me."

Shamus scowled, unimpressed with his bravado. "Lad, you must know there's a considerable price on your head for the one who gets you back to Salem—breathing or no."

"If I am not breathing when this is done, turn me in for the reward and give it to her."

Shamus followed the tip of his dark head to where Eliza was waiting near the long boat. "Aye. I'll see she's well cared for."

Luc nodded as if that were his only concern. "Keep alert lest it be treachery Montgomery has in mind. I have no great reason to trust in his honor, either."

"Yet you're still doing this."

Luc gave him a thin smile, his only explanation. Shamus shook his huge head.

"I'll never understand you, lad."

"Perhaps not, but you've been a good friend to me. In many ways, a better father than my own could have been. I thank you for that." He put out his hand.

Shamus stared at the outstretched hand and up at its offerer. His features tightened. Then in a big, engulfing move, he pulled Jean-Luc into a firm embrace. Startled, Luc held himself rigid, then slowly unbent to reciprocate. Knowing his dislike of displays, Shamus quickly stepped away but his eyes were suspiciously damp.

"You take care, lad."

"No matter what happens to me, don't let him take the *Galant*. If I do not return, it and all I own belongs to her as well."

"Luc—"

The Frenchman noted his hesitation. "Do you think I make myself a fool over her, Shamus?"

"No. I just think it took you long enough, is all."

With a rare flash of his wide smile, Luc strode to where Eliza stood with Remy. Both seemed ill at ease.

And Luc stunned Eliza and all his onlooking crew by cupping her anxious features between his palms as he leaned down to kiss her. It was a slow, sliding possession leaving no doubt as to his intentions. He was more a prisoner of this woman than she of him.

She was breathless by the time he stepped back. Only their circumstances kept her from casting herself into his arms. She settled for stroking the front of his unadorned seaman's jacket with her fingertips.

"Please be careful." Her voice trembled with emotion.

"We have much to discuss upon my return."

"I look forward to it, Captain. That, and all that follows," she added in a husky whisper for his ears alone. Her grip on his jacket tightened. "Don't trust him, Luc."

"Have no fear of that. I know what he is and what he is capable of doing." His hands covered hers, pressing briefly, warmly, then releasing her. "Shamus will see you are cared for."

She didn't smile or nod. She wasn't pleased with that suggestion. She didn't want Shamus. She wanted him, returned safely into her arms. And he said nothing more, understanding that.

The long boat went over the side with Luc as its only occupant. He never looked back at the *Galant* as the strong pull of the paddles carried him toward his rendezvous with Montgomery.

After Luc's small craft landed safely and he was out of sight, Eliza continued to pace the deck, anxious and unsettled. Something about the exchange stirred a restless feeling of dread. Perhaps it was a lingering insecurity at being parted from Luc.

Perhaps it was being faced with the scene of so many of her childhood memories from her vastly different standpoint: not as privileged plantation owner's granddaughter but as a runaway bond servant. The sight of the blinding white beaches and rich blue of the sea brought back tender memories of her brother's bold grin as he turned the sail of their tiny boat into the wind and of the happy summers they'd played about the lush tangle of inland green while growing brown as the natives beneath the caressing Caribbean sun.

No, it was more than poignant memories teasing at her heart, more than anxieties for Luc.

She knew Justin Montgomery, and that was why she paced. Luc had told her little of what he'd planned, which added to her misgivings.

"Mr. Sterns, where is Luc to meet with Montgomery?"

"At a neutral property belonging to a long absent owner. The West Winds, I believe he called it."

Eliza went cold. "West Winds. But Montgomery

owns that property now. He took it in lieu of moneys owed him."

Shamus cast an uncertain eye toward the shore. "Are you sure, lass?"

"Of course I'm sure." West Winds had been in her family for generations. Its sugar crops funded the foundation of Parrish Shipping.

And now Montgomery owned the properties. A small lie, perhaps signifying nothing. Perhaps a harbinger of deeper deceptions.

"Mr. Sterns, ship coming up fast off the port."

With glass to his eye, Shamus studied the familiar parade of canvas. "It be the *Delight*." And he let the glass fall, his expression was stunned. "And she be armed to the teeth and piloted by Montgomery's crew."

Coming for the *Galant*.

Chapter 27

"What's happened, Mr. Sterns?" Remy cried in alarm. "Have they taken Mr. Symms?"

Shamus scowled at the far ship. "I wonder." Quickly he called for the hoisting of sails, causing Eliza to round on him in fury.

"You can't leave Luc!"

"Lass, I've no other choice. They be his own orders. We've no way to get word to him."

Eliza's panicked gaze dashed between the second mate and the fast-approaching schooner. "And if I knew a way?"

He stared at her. "I'm listening."

"The West Winds belonged to my family. I used to play here as a child when my father was off on his yearlong voyages. I know every tree, every foothill, every door and window of the house."

"How does that help us when we've no way to get ashore unnoticed?"

"And I also know of a narrow cove hidden from view where a ship as sleek and shallow of draft as the *Galant* could put in, and of a path that leads straight to the house. What say we give Montgomery a taste of his own treachery?"

Shamus smiled. "Show me this cove."

* * *

Luc crossed the gleaming mahogany floors of the country house. His sober attire seemed out of place within the elegantly furnished rooms made to mimic those of the rural English gentry. He had no curiosity about its owner. He was focused on the lean, hard-faced man awaiting him by one of the large glazed windows.

"Greetings to you, Black Heart. You seem no worse for your incarceration."

"I've come for what you owe me."

Montgomery laughed. "Never one for small talk, were you? All right, to business, then." His smile disappeared. "You claim to have my daughter, Philomena. In good health, I trust."

"She has not been harmed."

"What do you want for her return?"

"What you owe me, plus the papers of indenture on her bond servant. And a signed statement that I was under your letters of marque. You may claim it was all a misunderstanding if it soothes your pride."

Montgomery glared through him. "Is that all?"

He didn't seemed surprised by the mention of Eliza. The hair at Luc's nape prickled. He clenched his hand until the painful ache pounding through the joints reminded him to be careful. This man was no genteel merchant. He was ruthless.

"I might well ask for the fingers of your right hand," he growled with sudden passion. Then the calm returned. "Just what I've earned. I ask for no more."

"Damned honorable of you, for a thief."

"We both know who the thief is, monsieur. I have not come to state the obvious."

Montgomery smirked and sat down at a spindle desk. He arranged a blank page before him and scrawled across it in his arrogant hand. When finished, he blew on the ink and extended it. Luc advanced cautiously to take the paper. He read the document with a brief sweep of his gaze. It gave Eliza her freedom. He paused upon her name. Eliza Parrish. That surname was familiar somehow.

"Now date and sign it." He passed it back, and Montgomery did so with a flourish. His acquiescent attitude put Luc on edge. He was being entirely too gracious. "Now, the money and my pardon."

"I should like to see my daughter first." He held up the paper, ransoming it for Luc's answer. Luc snatched it from his hand, quickly rolling it before the ink had completely dried and storing it within his jacket, close to his heart.

"You will pay me and I will leave here unharmed. Your daughter will be delivered to your home in Salem."

Montgomery's laugh boomed. "Do you think me a fool? I just give you the money and trust you to send Philomena safely home?"

Luc stiffened. "I have no reason to harm your daughter."

"You are a liar, sir. You do not have my daughter. Did your whore earn her freedom by slaying Philomena for your amusement?"

Luc blinked. How could the man know so much? He took a step back, assuming an *en garde* stance when he heard the door shut behind him, trapping him within the room. He glanced behind him and was momentarily shocked into inaction.

Benji Symms, his first mate, stood braced against the doors, a harsh sneer marring his pale face.

"You should have just given me the ship, Jean-Luc, and avoided all this unpleasantness."

* * *

Eliza disappeared from the deck for only as long as it took her to slip into the leather trousers and one of Luc's shirts. The small primed pistol was tucked into a sash knotted about her slender waist, and the sword she'd foolishly used in an attempt to threaten her captor on that first night was in her hand. Shamus beheld her with a moment of speechless surprise; then a thundercloud of objection darkened his face.

"No."

"But Mr. Sterns—"

"Luc would have my head if I allowed anything to happen to you."

Eliza assumed a cocky pose. "And just how long do you expect Montgomery to forestall his betrayal while you fumble about, lost in the trees?"

Shamus frowned and before he could arrive at some argument, she pressed her own with a fierce sincerity.

"I owe Jean-Luc this rescue. He saved me from much worse than jail. I will not have his fate hanging in jeopardy whilst I hide aboard his ship in safety. You will never find the cove on your own. Do I go? Decide. We haven't much time."

Muttering a curse, Shamus scowled at her. "You have a bit of the pirate in you, my lady. Show us this cove; then lead us to Luc."

She spared no time for self-congratulation. "There. See that jut of coral. Take her in just on the other side."

"'Tis nothing there but reef. We'll be torn to pieces!" Remy cried.

But Shamus was studying the lay of the current as carefully as the demeanor of the woman at his side. And he called back, "Jordie, take her hard a port."

"But, sir—"

"Do it, lad, and be quick about it."

As the crew held its collective breath, the sleek ship tucked neatly behind the ridge of coral, where only upon making that commitment could the secret cove be seen. The relief etched upon Shamus's craggy face said plainly that he hadn't believed until this moment, yet, on Eliza's say-so, he had been willing to risk his ship and his men. He may not have trusted what his eyes told him, but he didn't underestimate the love growing between his captain and this lady. He'd no doubt that she would move heaven and earth to save Jean-Luc.

But he'd settle for this miracle of nature that sheltered them from the view of the *Delight*.

"You look surprised, Jean-Luc. You shouldn't be. It isn't as if you've ever showed any great loyalty after all I've done." Benji circled his captain, keeping at a cautious distance despite the pistol he held in his hand.

Luc stood unmoving, his expression unreadable. Within, he was reeling with the shock of it. "I do not understand."

"No, of course you wouldn't, closeted away with your books and charts, never a good word for any of us. Never a thought for how we'd get by once your honorable sentiments cost us our livelihood."

"And so you turn traitor because I was not *nice* to you?"

"For the money, Jean-Luc. Some of us are just interested in the money. It was good for a time, the pickings rich on the Atlantic, but you, with your cold nobility where your heart should have been, could not lower yourself to join in with the Lafittes in continued profit."

"I would not have stopped you from joining them if that was your wish."

"But I didn't want to be a member of their crew. I wanted to be one of their captains. All I needed was a ship, a fast ship."

"The *Galant*."

Benji smiled. "Now you're catching on. You always was a quick thinker. So I traded you to Montgomery here for the price of your ship. Only, damn you, you wouldn't give it up. So, I took this opportunity to try again. Montgomery was most eager to learn of your trickery. Even now, the *Delight* under his men is overtaking your precious *Galant*."

"I don't think so, Symms."

Benji frowned. "Sterns is a soft-headed fool. He would not sail off and leave you."

Luc's black stare never faltered, nor did his expression.

"Damn!" Symms raced to the window and pulled his glass. He could see the *Delight* circling in the clear waters, but there was no sign of her prey.

Montgomery showed none of the other's agitation. "Calm down, Mr. Symms. You'll still have the one ship and portion of the reward for his head."

"But I want the *Galant*!" He stormed back to where Luc was standing, thrusting the muzzle of his gun between the unblinking dark eyes. "Where is she?"

"Out of your reach, *traître*."

"Save yourself the bullet, Symms. He'll tell you nothing."

With a roar of frustration, Symms whipped the pistol barrel against the side of his captain's head, causing him to stagger from the fierceness of the blow. He began to pace, plotting angrily while Luc slowly straightened and stared fixedly ahead.

Then Symms began to smile. "Sterns doesn't suspect me. I'll find him and tell him that Montgomery will trade you for the *Galant*."

"No," the merchant growled. "This man killed my daughter. He'll not go free!"

Symms turned the pistol on him. "I don't think you will have much say in it."

Montgomery met his about-face of loyalty with a narrow scowl.

"Shamus has his orders," Luc said stoically. "He will not remain in these waters long. And he will not give up the *Galant*."

"Yes, he will. For you he will. Because unlike Coeur Noir, who cares for no one, he cares for you."

"Which is why I disobeyed his orders. Forgive me, Luc."

All turned as Shamus, Remy, and Eliza entered through one of the full-length windows opening onto the veranda. The Irishman was quick to jerk the pistol from Symms's slack hand and cover him with it. Eliza raced into Luc's arms.

"Let's be quick about concluding our business, lad," Shamus urged as Luc hugged her up tight, then set her aside to confront Montgomery.

"My money."

"You'll get nothing from me, you murdering bastard. She was my only daughter. I'll see that you and your whore are hunted to the ground and hanged for that evil deed."

"We didn't slay Philomena."

He glared at Eliza, lips curling with contempt. "And to think my son held a fondness for you. News of your hanging will do well as a wedding gift to Julianna Wiggins. Their banns were posted last week."

Eliza said nothing, her features paling as she clung to Luc's arm.

"Luc, we must go. Now."

Nodding, he cast a hard glare at Symms. "This is

not over between us. You will regret your choice of greed over loyalty."

"Not today, Jean-Luc."

"Soon," was Luc's promise as he strode out of the room the same way his rescuers had come, Eliza tucked against his side, Shamus and Remy covering his retreat.

Montgomery sat silently at his desk, listening to Symms curse and carry on until several of his own men entered from the main hall. He glared at them with disfavor. "Where have you been?"

"There was a disturbance on the beach. We went to investigate."

"And what did you find?"

"Nothing."

"That was because you were in the wrong place. I am surrounded by fools."

Symms approached cautiously. "What be yer orders? The *Galant* is bound to break for open waters as soon as Black Heart is aboard."

"Can you catch him with your ship?"

"No—"

"Then what good are you?" Montgomery gestured impatiently to his men. "Take him out and hang him."

"W-what? On what charge?" Symms sputtered as his arms were imprisoned.

"For being a greedy fool." And he turned his back as the man was dragged away. His thoughts filled with revenge.

Those thoughts continued to hold the grief over his daughter at bay as he returned on his ship to Salem with the *Delight* following. Coeur Noir had surprised him by becoming a ruthless enemy. Even he, for all his ambitions, would never have thought to harm a female to get what he wanted—at least, not seriously.

What he'd done to Eliza Parrish, turning his back upon her plight, had been a matter of social delicacy. And now she was a plague upon him as well.

He would get them, both the pirate and his scheming harlot. By the time he returned home, it had become his obsession. Philomena's loss was almost a forgotten misfortune.

He strode into the big Parrish house. He'd made it his family's home, preferring its location and prestige. There, a flustered William waylaid him on his way to the study. The last thing he wanted was to entertain his pasty-faced son's whining entreaties over his upcoming nuptials. Left to his own devices, the boy would have wed the treacherous Parrish wench, proof enough that he was incapable of making his own decisions.

"Father, a moment please," William insisted.

"Not now, William."

"But, Father, much has happened in your absence. Astounding things."

"What are you babbling about, boy?"

"Hello, Justin."

Montgomery turned toward the open doorway to the study, his jaw hanging.

"Where is my sister?"

"It's Nate," William gushed unnecessarily. "Isn't that amazing?"

Amazing was not the word Montgomery would have chosen. Finally, he pulled himself together to extend his hand and the most genuine smile he could manage. "Nathaniel! What a surprise."

"A shock, I'm sure, since you are living in my home, in charge of all my father's enterprises." Nate Parrish, looking tan and fit and not at all drowned in foreign waters, took his hand for a dry shake.

"How—"

"How is it that I'm alive? A bit of a miracle to be sure. An even greater one that I managed to rescue most of the cargo with the help of some villagers along the Canton coast. I'm sorry it took me so long to return to tell you of our fortune."

Fortune. Montgomery's head spun. "Your father—"

Nate grew solemn. "Yes, William told me about his accident." He was silent for a moment. "But what I haven't heard is where I might find Eliza. I'm anxious to assure her of my return and that all is well again."

Montgomery understood everything in that instant. Nate Parrish was back, wealthy beyond belief. He no longer had claim to any properties or ventures. Nate would take that all away from him, unless . . .

"Excuse us for a moment, would you, William? Nathaniel and I need to talk."

By the time he shut the doors, he had his plan set in his mind. He turned to Nate with a grim sigh. "I'm sorry, lad, but I'm afraid I have more bad news for you. After all the tragedy—first assuming you dead, then burying your father, we took Eliza in, of course. It was the least we could do for the poor child."

Nate expressed a sound of relief. "Where is she?"

"She and my daughter, Philomena, were bound for England to visit family there, to get their minds off all these terrible circumstances." He paused, taking in the young captain's reaction. Nate revealed nothing but gratitude and the beginnings of worry.

"I appreciate that, Justin, but—"

He held up his hand. It was no great effort to summon a catch of emotion to his voice. "Their ship was set upon by the pirate Coeur Noir. I helped send him to prison, and upon his escape, he sought his vengeance upon my innocent child. Both girls were taken aboard his ship, and I was trying to negotiate a ransom for their release. I have only just learned that my daughter, my dear Philomena, was murdered by the blackguard."

"And Eliza?" His tone trembled.

"He has her yet upon his ship. To what end, I do not know."

Nate Parrish had gone very still, the stillness of a dangerous man. "I need a ship."

"I've one you can take. The *Delight*. She's one of the villain's own, snagged in a trap I'd hoped to make for him. She's yours."

He nodded and strode toward the door.

"Take William with you."

Nate paused to give him a puzzled look.

"They were to be married," Montgomery said. "He should be with you when Eliza is rescued."

"See that he's ready, then."

Alone in the study, Montgomery smiled to himself at the perfect web he'd spun. If Nate Parrish sank the *Galant* with Eliza aboard, nothing of his own treachery would ever be known and he'd be back to a comfortable partnership. If Eliza was rescued, William would be there to woo her into compliance and a profitable wedding could be arranged. If Black Heart sent the *Delight* to the bottom, he would have control of the newfound Parrish fortune.

There was no way he could lose.

Eliza stood alone at the bow of the *Galant* watching her sleek silhouette cut through the jeweled waters. Luc watched her with some consternation, uncertain of her mood. Instead of seeking him out, she'd assumed this lonely vigil. He could console her in her fears, could match her for her passions, but he felt at a loss with this quiet melancholy. He wasn't good at interpreting another's pain. He'd no experience in it, being consumed by his own for so long. But he knew she suffered from some unspoken sorrow, and he wished to reach out to her to let her know that he cared.

She didn't react to his presence, so he simply stood at her side, braced against the sting of the salt breezes while he garnered his courage. Canting a glance at her profile, he saw the evidence of tears upon her wind-flushed cheeks. For what woe had she been weeping?

She didn't move as his fingertips brushed through her hair, as his thumb stroked away the streaks of dampness. An uncomfortable knowledge came to him.

"Your fiancé was Montgomery's son."

He stated it as fact, and she did not disagree. Instead, she vowed, "It doesn't matter now."

Contrarily, it mattered a great deal to him. "Did you love him?"

"I thought I did."

"And do you still?"

She didn't answer. Heart twisting, he assumed her silence meant she cared too much to discuss it with him.

"I am sorry." For many things.

She glanced at him then, and he was struck by her resigned expression. "You had nothing to do with what did or did not happen between William and me. His choices were made under his father's influence. I should have accepted them then instead of holding to foolish hopes. It wasn't William as much as it was what he represented, the life I used to lead. Now it is all gone, and I don't know where I shall go or what I shall do."

His palm curved about her jaw. His thumb rubbed lightly over the last of the bruises to mar her cheek.

She was suddenly very still, her sea-green gaze lifted to his without hope, without resistance.

"Come with me. I will care for you."

"But Montgomery still owes you."

"I don't care about that blood money anymore. I can take care of you, Eliza. I can give you all the things you deserve, all the things denied you. We don't need the Montgomerys' wealth."

She had to look away lest he see the depth of longing in her eyes. "I can't."

He slid his hand around to cup the back of her head, drawing her gently against him. She merely leaned there, taking strength and support from his sturdy lines without demanding more. Without telling him more.

"You said you loved me."

Her eyes squeezed shut. "More than life itself."

"Than why can't you accept what I want to give you? Is it who I am? Who I am not? Tell me! The truth could not hurt more than the not knowing."

"It's the price you're willing to pay to keep me."

Nothing could have confused him more. He slipped his hand beneath her chin, lifting it so he could see her tear-streaked face. "Explain what you mean."

"I can't allow you to throw away your honor, your family pride. Not for me, Jean-Luc. I know the value of those things and I could not bear for you to make that sacrifice."

A frown crowded his brow as he shook his head in puzzlement.

"When were you going to tell me the cargo you planned to ship for the Lafittes was stolen? After you showered me with the profits? Did you think my love so shallow it had to be purchased with the humbling of all you hold dear?"

He hid behind a blank expression, all the light going out of his eyes. "I would pay any price required."

"I cannot accept the gifts you would buy."

He thought of the papers guaranteeing her freedom and of the love he longed to bestow upon her. But those things weren't enough if he hadn't the means to support and protect her. His pride wouldn't allow her to settle for less than she'd once known. She deserved more than a man who had only himself and hardship to give. "Then I have nothing to offer."

She palmed his handsome face, feeling such a turmoil of love and helplessness, she wanted to weep with frustration. Here was everything she desired, right in the palm of her hand but for a trick of fate that denied them the price of that happiness.

Unless . . .

"Luc, what if there was a way to still collect from Montgomery?"

His hand slipped over hers, holding it to the contour of his cheek. "We have no bargaining tool, *mon coeur*."

She smiled. "What if we had his daughter?"

"But we don't."

"What if I knew where to find her?"

Chapter 28

$\sim \diagup \diagdown \diagup \sim$

Philomena Prine wiped the dampness from her brow with her sleeve and hoisted another in an endless series of trays up to her shoulder. She stood for a moment, balancing its precarious weight, having learned that haste made for waste, and spillage was taken from her already near to nonexistent pay. In that instant of hesitation, with the noise and stench of the taproom awaiting, along with hours of backbreaking work, she fought back the tears that so often plagued her.

She'd never known such misery. Clever schemes were forgotten amid the drudgery of her days and nights. She'd been spoiled and naive the scant month before when convincing her penniless lover to agree to a romantic elopement. The fantasy had fast faded. They'd been married, true enough, and had taken brief shelter with family friends. But then reality came to bear, and a life Philomena had never known superseded her own of pampered luxury. She was no longer the daughter of Justin Montgomery but the wife of Jonathon Prine. She'd never understood the difference that would make. She learned fast.

Pressing one hand to the aching small of her back, she started toward the taproom, where thirsty sailors would hopefully be generous with their coin if she bent over their tabletop with a smile to deliver their mugs of ale. A smile that once had dazzled wealthy beaux and earned her whatever whim of the moment was reduced to cajoling bread money from drunken customers.

Pasting on a look of false gaiety, she nudged open the door with her hip and wove a practiced trail between crude tables, deftly avoiding pinches and swats that might lead to spills. Plopping down the tankards and snatching up the sailors' coin, she turned to the next table.

"What can I fetch you this fine eve—"

Words failed her. A surge of icy terror froze her vocal chords. For seated at that table, as coldly handsome as the first time she'd laid eyes upon him, was the dreaded pirate Coeur Noir. And at his side sat . . . Eliza? The heavy tray clattered to the piñon floorboards, and the room began to whirl. Firm hands caught her at the elbows, guiding her into an empty chair.

Finally, her senses returned, but again she saw the same unbelievable sight.

"It is you!" she cried weakly as Eliza applied a cool towel to her brow. With a soft wail of welcome, Philomena banded her arms about the other startled female. "Oh, Eliza, it is so good to see a familiar face."

Stunned, Eliza held her, shifting an uncertain gaze to Jean-Luc. This was not the greeting she'd expected from her old nemesis and mistress. "Mena, are you all right?"

Philomena slumped back into her chair, her wan features lit by a weary smile. "As well as one can be when with child and forced to tend tables." At Eliza's shocked stare, she added with a defensive pride, "I married my Jonathon. I am Mistress Prine now."

Eliza didn't know what to say.

The barkeeper strode over and gave Philomena a rough shove. "On yer feet, ya lazy slut. Conversation don't get drinks on the tables or money in me pocket." Then he gasped as his wrist was cuffed in a crushing grip. His gruff manner abandoned him when he found himself skewered by a frigid black glare.

"Do not mistreat the lady lest the next coins you be concerned with go toward the purchase of your casket."

The barkeeper had no idea who the man was, but he knew who he was not. He was not someone who gave threats lightly. He pulled his arm free and told Philomena, "Take ten minutes, then, but you'll make them up later."

Philomena nodded meekly, then turned teary eyes on Eliza. Her face burned with humiliation. "I need the work. Please don't make any more trouble for me."

Was this the proud peacock of Salem?

"Mena, what are you doing in this place?"

Her smile was rueful. "It was the best position I could find. Fancy manners don't pay for meals. Jonathon works at the customs office. 'Tis a good job, but with the babe coming . . ." She broke off, anguish clogging her throat. "Oh, Eliza, look how far we've strayed from our youthful dreams. You were to have William, and I, all New England at my feet." Her laugh was ragged. "Have you come, then, to gloat over my prideful fall? I deserve it, I know."

Never had Eliza felt less like mocking another's misfortune. She understood Philomena's struggle all too well.

"No, Mena. I've come for another reason. Why

didn't you return to Salem; why did you let your father believe it was you in Black Heart's hands?"

"I wanted to make him pay for spoiling my plans to wed Jonathon. And I got my way, as you can see."

"Your father thinks you are dead."

She sighed heavily. "To his thinking, I am."

"But Mena, he believes I had a hand in your murder."

At Philomena's confused frown, Eliza quickly explained how the deception had gone wrong. Though aware of Jean-Luc beside her, she made no mention of her attachment to her captor.

"A foolish plan made by the vain and silly girl I was," Philomena said when she'd heard it all. "I had not counted upon truly falling in love with the man I married or with this babe I will bear him. Our life may not be grand, but it is our life, built upon our love and not my father's coin. As you can see, I've no further use for your services, Eliza. Few tavern maids have dressers of their own."

"Mena, I need you to come to Salem with us, to prove to your father that you yet live."

"I cannot!"

"But you must! You cannot go on letting everyone believe you were killed."

"Philomena Montgomery is dead," she stated firmly. "May she rest in peace."

"But she cannot! Not when that peace means none for those who are blameless."

Philomena gnawed her lower lip in indecision. "I cannot go home. My father would not want to know what has become of me. I see that now quite clearly. He would be so ashamed. I will not give up what I've found only to be placed under his thumb again."

"That is between you and your father." Eliza gripped her shoulders. "You owe me this, Philomena.

You owe me my freedom, and it cannot be won until the truth is told. You must go with us. You must."

The Philomena Eliza had once known wouldn't have cared about past debts or obligations. But the woman before her was obviously not that same shallow girl.

"I must tell Jonathon first. I would not have him thinking that I was going to beg my father's favor. Never that." A bold courage firmed up her tired countenance.

And for the first time, Eliza found herself liking the other woman very much.

With two women sharing his cabin, Jean-Luc piloted his last trip to Salem at the helm of the *Galant*.

It was an awkward arrangement between two who had never been friends, had often been bitter rivals, and now were forced into embarrassing proximity with the choices they'd made. Philomena, ever the poor sailor, lay abed moaning but as yet had not used the bucket Eliza provided. Guilt tormented her more than the mal de mer as she eyed the almost healed abrasions on Eliza's wrists and the yellowish marks that remained from the punishment she'd endured. She was afraid to ask but knew she must.

"Has he been horribly cruel to you?"

"Who?" Eliza asked in genuine bewilderment.

"Black Heart."

"Luc?" Her use of his given name gave volumes away. "No. In fact, he rescued me from those who were." She touched the scabbing bracelets and was surprised by how distanced she was from the pain. "He is a good man, a decent man. The troubles with your father were not of his doing. He was grievously wronged, Philomena. I hope you can believe that."

This newly matured Philomena could and she nod-

ded. "I have few illusions left regarding my father."
Her gaze grew speculative. "So, this pirate, what is
he to you?"

"He is no pirate, and he is many things. Mostly, I
trust him with my life, and it angers me when others
misuse him."

Philomena had the good grace to blush beneath her
grayish pallor. "What of William, then?"

The pang of it stung anew, but it was a faint jab,
nothing fatal. "William announced his betrothal to another. He did not mourn for me long."

"He would have done better waiting for you," Philomena said sadly, following that admission with a
confession of remorse. "And that's my fault. I should
have kept my promise to you. It seems all have failed
you, Eliza. I wish there was some way to make
amends."

Eliza was silent. There was no way she could reclaim the life she'd led. It was lost as surely as her
fortune.

"Will you remain in Salem?"

"There is nothing for me there, Mena. I have new
dreams to follow now."

As Eliza walked the sun-drenched deck alone, she
realized only Luc had not failed to keep his promises
to her.

She stopped, her heart caught by the sight of him
working the lines off the main yard as if one of the
crew and not its captain, blending in from the view
below with his like clothing and barefooted stance.
She marveled at his capable strength, bringing the
sails about to fill with the chillier coastal wind. She
could never tire of watching him at any endeavor, be
it high above against a parade of canvas or close to
the earth, communing with the soil.

He spotted her on the deck below. Forgoing the rat

ladders, he slid in a dancelike spiral via one of the
mooring lines, touching down easily at her side.

While her only thought was to step into his arms,
he stayed it with a cool question and a cautious look.

"Have you come up in hopes of getting a look at
your home port?"

She looked beyond him, recognizing the rocky
coastline with some surprise. "I hadn't realized we
were so close." So close to having all or losing it. Panic tightened about her chest, and instinctively she
leaned closer to her only source of comfort. Luc's arm
skimmed effortlessly about her middle. She didn't
quite dare look up at him, fearing he'd see too much
with the intensity of his gaze.

The need to speak assurances was momentarily
eased by Shamus's arrival.

"Tell him he be crazy, lass. He means to row in
pretty as you please right next to the India wharf. Tell
him 'tis madness. They'll be on him in a minute."

"It will not matter as long as Mademoiselle Montgomery sticks to her story. I cannot risk bringing the
Galant closer. She would be recognized and taken or
sent to the bottom without first asking questions. This
involves Montgomery and me. He'll not expect me to
come for him in his own camp. I intend to deliver his
daughter and collect my pay."

"And if he won't just give over?"

"It's a matter of pride, Shamus." Luc's gaze turned
to Eliza, the dark depths warming with emotion. "To
rid us of the stain of murder—and of the specter of
M'am'selle Montgomery."

Eliza glanced uncomfortably away. What if she was
sending him to his death? "I should like to go ashore
with you, Captain."

The request took him by complete surprise.
"Why?" Suspicions curled with shadowy whispers

through his heart and mind. "There is no need. Unless
you wish to gather your belongings."

She didn't answer and he knew no relief.

"All right, Luc. Be you determined for this folly, I'll
see a long boat readied."

"I thank you, Shamus." When his friend was gone,
Luc's attention focused upon his fears. "Why do you
wish to go ashore, *ma petite*?"

Next to all her genuine concerns for his safety, his
worries seemed silly and unfounded, goading her into
a curt reply. "Am I to assume your objection means
that I am yet your prisoner?"

"*Non. Non,* it is not that . . . only—"

She tipped her head back to regard him directly.
"Only what, Luc? Either I am your prisoner or I am
free to come and go." She held out her wrists. "Are
shackles needed to earn your trust?"

With an ugly feeling coiling within his breast, he
said, "You may do whatever you like."

She touched her fingertips to his taut cheek. "I think
I should like to kiss you."

He blinked, boyishly confused and soon delighted
to comply. He bent his head down, leaning in for the
perfect fit of his mouth to hers. It was all too brief,
that precious union, but she didn't try to hold to him
as he straightened.

"I shall never forget all that you've done for me."

He heard those words with a cold sinking sensation. It sounded too much like a good-bye. Was he
about to lose her to her memories of the past?

Eliza's palms pushed up and down his shirtfront,
absorbing the feel of him. Suddenly, their moments
together seemed too few, certainly not enough to last
a lifetime. After seeing the happiness Philomena had
found in her lowly station, she wanted to pull Luc off
this dangerous course, to beg him to forget the

money, to forget his pride. As long as they lived, they could live on their love. But if something went wrong in his dealings with Montgomery, perhaps he would not live at all. And she couldn't go on without him. Nothing would matter without him.

Luc was watching her expression closely. She appeared so sad. A terrible truth began to build, one he was afraid to face. Trapped by that fear and his own sense of pride, he couldn't demand what was behind her desire to go ashore with him.

Because he feared it was now her wish to remain.

Unless he could persuade her otherwise.

Pushed by a deep desperation, he took her firmly in his arms, eliciting an anxious gasp at his sudden possessive move. Her huge sea-green eyes flew upward to meet his.

The only way he could hold her now was by admitting the truth burgeoning within his own heart. A truth he'd foolishly left silent. He'd promised to care for her. He'd vowed to see her safe. But he'd never told her, in three simple words, how much she meant to him.

How could an intelligent man be so singularly stupid as to overlook the obvious?

"Eliza—"

"Cap'n, a ship! 'Tis the *Delight*."

Abandoned by his embrace, Eliza staggered dizzily, watching him run toward the bow of his ship. She grasped the rail, trembling weakly, wanting more than anything to hear what he'd been about to say.

Luc snatched the glass from Shamus's hand.

"Do you see that villain Symms?" the Irishman demanded.

Luc shook his head. "I do not recognize her captain."

"She's coming for us, lad. Do we engage or flee?"

The *Galant* was the bigger vessel, with eighteen guns compared to the *Delight's* twelve.

"Luc?" Shamus prodded gently, knowing his young friend's aversion to violent confrontation. "Lad, decide now while we still can maneuver."

Still Luc refused to commit them to either bolting or battle. The crew watched the avenging silhouette approach, growing nervous as they cast their glances at their captain.

"Mr. Sterns?" Remy petitioned anxiously.

Drawn by the tense silence, Eliza slipped up next to the Frenchman. She touched his arm, the gesture both questioning and cautioning. He glanced down at her briefly, then back at the *Delight*.

"We will not run."

Shamus was stunned into a moment of immobility. Then he called, "Ready the guns."

Luc belayed his order. "*Non!* No guns. We will not fire unless fired upon."

Impatient now, with the other schooner's bowsprit nearly down their throats, Shamus asked, "And what would you have us do? Ask them to move over so we can pass?"

"*Exactement.* Remy, bring Mademoiselle Montgomery up so they can see her. They will think twice before loosing their cannon with her on deck."

Shamus beamed at his wisdom, then cast a worried look toward their aggressive challenger.

Eliza shook Luc's arm. "Watch for the ledge. It's torn the bottom from many a ship."

His eyes were on the *Delight*. The ship showed no signs of giving quarter.

"Who is that madman at her helm?" Shamus wondered aloud as the approaching ship slipped dangerously close to the submerged ridge of rock known as

Bowditch Ledge, then gracefully skirted around it. "I've never seen anyone your equal, lad, until this day. Where did Montgomery find such a daring pilot to ram our own ship down our gullets?"

Remy ran up to them, panting heavily. He was alone. "She won't come, Cap'n. She's heaving something awful."

The *Delight* was baring her gun ports, rolling its cannons into play.

"Drag her, man," Shamus shouted at the anxious boy. "Else we all be fish food!"

Luc stared at the other ship, awed and respectful of the opposing captain's courage. This was no enemy to take lightly. The offensive posture of the *Delight* bode ill for them. He curled his arm around Eliza, meaning to push her behind him, but suddenly she was gripping his arm, her fingers sharp as talons.

"Oh my God! It cannot be!"

He looked to her, alerted by her dramatic pallor and shallow breaths. She seemed ready to swoon. Alarmed, he scooped his other arm about her, too, but abruptly the weakness was gone. She tore the viewing glass from his hand, training it on the approaching vessel. The instrument trembled wildly as she lowered it from her eye. Her gaze lifted again to Luc's, dazed beyond belief.

"It's my brother. It's Nate."

"Natty Parrish be your brother?" Shamus gasped.

Parrish. Of course. Of the Salem Parrishes. Jean-Luc was too stunned to react to the news. He stared down at Eliza, his perception of her altering yet again, with dizzying consequences.

"Eliza, lass, you'd best be encouraging a family reunion quick before those cannons blow."

Nate! Eliza's relief was overwhelming, but Shamus's words jerked her back to the grim reality of their plight. She seized Luc's forearms.

"Surrender the *Galant*!"

"What?" He looked at her as if she'd gone mad.

"Luc, please! You must! Surrender to my brother. He'll see you're fairly heard."

Luc's head spun viciously. Surrender the *Galant*. Years of chained misery ahead. Eliza . . . a Parrish! He took a denying step back, rejecting all. Rejecting her.

Eliza would not allow it. She reached up, grasping his face between the press of her palms so he could not look away from her urgent sincerity.

"Luc, please. Please trust me! Trust me. Surrender the *Galant*. It's your only chance. *Our* only chance."

He took a strangled breath, reason warring against the compelling truthfulness in her gaze. Captivity. The pain of it exploding through his brain. The stench of it rose, burning his nose, searing his senses. The endless darkness where he dared not sleep for fear that rats would come to feast on him in his bound helplessness.

"Cap'n, they're coming about!"

He retreated another step, closing his eyes against the sight of his family slaughtered at his feet. He choked, breathing in that vile mix of blood and sludge again, drowning.

"Luc!"

Eliza's voice penetrated the smothering red fog. He blinked his eyes open, seeing not the tragedy of his past but the hope of his future in her uplifted face. He turned to his crew, commanding, "Stand down and prepare to be boarded!"

The *Delight* was quick to come alongside her submissive prey. The crew of the *Galant* waited, tense and unarmed, for hooks, then planks, to join the two vessels. The first man across drew a welcoming shout from Eliza from where she stood next to the proud French privateer.

"Nate!" Then a more wondrous cry. "William?"

Following the somber-faced captain wobbled a very green-tinged William Montgomery.

Jean-Luc stepped forward to offer his outstretched saber in both hands, his manner stiffly formal.

"I surrender myself, my crew, and my ship into your care."

Nate's furious gaze swept over his sister, taking in the signs of her abuse. When his stare met Luc's, it was blazing with hellfire. Nate ignored the extended sword, drawing his own pistol.

"I'll take your ship, sir, and I'll have your black soul."

At close range, the pistol discharged with a roar like cannon fire.

Chapter 29

The sound was tremendous, echoing with huge vibration. As it eased within Luc's head, an engulfing pain swelled up to take its place. It was all he could do to grit his teeth and open his eyes to face a roomful of his antagonists.

Nate's bullet creased a nasty furrow along his brow. An inch over and Eliza would have been scooping up his brains instead of stanching the flow of his blood. She now stood a room away, pale and anxious, her gaze never leaving him even as William Montgomery's arm lent her support. A swooning Philomena draped across the settee beside them.

The Parrish parlor room dripped with affected elegance. Against its calculated wealth, Luc felt soiled and insignificant in his seaman's clothing, with his hastily bound head. He stood even though Eliza bade him sit. One didn't sit in the presence of one's enemies—even when one was close to falling down. He remained straight and unflinching beneath the combined glares of Nate Parrish and Justin Montgomery. The *Galant* bobbed helplessly, moored to Parrish Wharf, its crew anxiously awaiting the outcome of this discussion.

"So," Nate Parrish drawled out. "My sister pleads

a good case for you, Frenchman. What have you to add?" Clearly, he didn't believe the women had come to no harm under the care of Coeur Noir.

"I stand by my honor, m'sieur. I need say no more."

"Stand by it and hang by it, you mean."

Luc's chin notched higher. "*C'est la guerre.*"

Alarmed by his unwillingness to speak in his own defense, Eliza took a step forward only to be pulled back by a possessive William. "Luc—"

Nate held up his hand to hush her. "Coeur Noir. Your name precedes you, Captain. I had always assumed it to be a bold, brave name linked to daring deeds during wartime. I cringe to think that such skill and cunning has turned to abducting helpless women for ransom."

Luc's black stare narrowed slightly, but his voice betrayed none of what he was feeling. "Monsieur Montgomery owes me for services rendered. He paid me in treachery, and I but sought to remind him of his vows. I am no pirate. I sailed under his letters of marque. His lies saw me unjustly imprisoned."

"And for that you sought revenge against his helpless daughter and my sister?" Contempt froze those words.

"*Non.* Not revenge. Payment. I had no plans to take what I had not already earned."

"You did not . . . harm either of these ladies?"

Luc's gaze flickered briefly to Eliza, but his stoic expression didn't change. "*Non.*"

"Why are you listening to this, Nathaniel?" Montgomery blustered. "The man is disreputable. All he says are lies!"

"The only lies are yours," Eliza challenged with a sudden fierceness.

"Your dear sister is obviously overwrought by the experience."

"Do not try to mollify me, sir," Eliza said. "And I believe in your last address, you called me whore and threatened to see me hanged."

Nate's severing gaze quieted further protest from the seething merchant. He turned back to Jean-Luc. "And what exactly does Mr. Montgomery owe you?"

"He knows the amount. The fifty percent for my crew and me for our part in the capture of the *Britannia Rule*. He was to settle with my first mate, and they decided on betrayal instead."

"Nathaniel," Montgomery began in a condescending tone. "You know me—"

"Yes," Nate cut in. "I do, Justin. I know that in my absence, you snatched up all my family's properties, broke your betrothal oath to my sister, and cast her into despicable bondage. Now you expect me to believe that a man who would commit such nefarious acts against a peer and partner would not also betray a man known for his noble reputation upon the seas."

Montgomery clenched his jaw. "You will not cast the blame upon me, sir."

"But it is your fault; don't you see?" All were surprised by Philomena's thready accusation. "Your greed, your ambition drove you to any means necessary. You trod upon your neighbors, your friends, your son's fiancée, your own daughter, and would do so again without remorse. What manner of man are you, Father? I am ashamed of ever having bowed to your will. You are more pirate than this man, for you would sell off your own kin to better your social standing."

Her condemnation tore through the arrogant facade of Justin Montgomery. His mouth quivered briefly as he sought some way to vindicate himself. He could not, and so he bowed beneath his beloved daughter's scorn, seeking to ensnare her sympathy. "I thought I had lost you, Mena," he moaned.

"You did, Father. When you sent me away in disregard of my wishes. When you refused to recognize my Jonathon for his own merit, you forced me into a life of intolerable hardship, a life I loathe but will not leave because I love my husband. And now you risk losing William by discarding Eliza's worth, as I did. And I do beg your pardon, Eliza!"

Eliza came down upon the sofa next to her weeping friend, enveloping her in a forgiving embrace.

Faced with the loss of his family and the greater threat of losing his reputation, Montgomery sucked in a deep breath and squared up to a proud bearing. "I will make amends. I will take Jonathon in as partner and honor Eliza's claim upon my son."

Philomena regarded him coolly. "You shall have to discuss that with my husband. He makes the decisions for our family."

Because he did not know the woman his daughter had become, he was sure he could win her over in time. Then Montgomery turned to the more difficult attack. "I have acted shamefully toward your family, Nathaniel, and for this, too, I apologize."

Nate regarded him narrowly, not as easy to convince as his children. "Deeds speak louder than empty words, Justin. I suggest you extend a show of faith by paying your debt to Captain Gautier and by admitting to the falseness of the charges against him."

Montgomery balked, knowing the minute he did so, his credibility would be forever compromised within Salem society. But realizing as well that Nate Parrish had the power to totally disgrace him made the choice a bit easier.

"I will have payment brought to your ship, Captain, along with a letter from the magistrate exonerating you of all crimes."

Nate turned to Jean-Luc. "Will that satisfy you, sir?"

But Luc wasn't thinking of the money or the clemency. He was tortured by the picture of Eliza Parrish surrounded by the comforts of her home and the closeness of the Montgomery family. She held Philomena in a consoling embrace, while William's pale hands massaged her shoulders with damning intimacy. She had her dream returned: the enviable social standing, the devoted fiancé, the security of a prestigious heritage. She could not wish to be reminded of past horrors, of the degradation and suffering she had endured. What was he but that reminder? How could he compete with this cherished dream come true?

Suddenly, Eliza's gaze lifted, meeting his from across the room. A surge of longing passed between them, as unwise as it was now impossible. Before he could fall again into those tempting green seas, he looked to Nate and claimed tersely, "It is enough."

A lie. It was all he could take with him, but it would never be enough.

Nate nodded toward the foyer. "A moment of your time, Captain Gautier, if you please."

Luc followed him out of the sight of the others. Though he'd never met Nate Parrish, he, too, was aware of the other's reputation. He was leaving Eliza in good hands. A small consolation.

Nate faced him squarely. "My sister says you did her no harm, and I must believe her. Since you've returned her safely, I feel I owe you my thanks as well as my apology." He nodded toward the bandaged gash made by his bullet.

Luc shrugged. "None are needed. Your conclusion

was a reasonable one under the circumstances."

"Still, I would feel better if you would accept a token from us, a reward—"

Luc cut him cold with a look and a terse, "I ask for no reward. I must return to my ship and my crew. Am I free to go?"

"I will walk you to the door, Captain," Nate was quick to offer. As he followed the rigid Frenchman, he was troubled by a glimpse he'd caught of his sister's expression as Gautier left the room, one so woeful it could twist tears from stone. He gave a start in recognizing its meaning.

She was in love with the Frenchman.

And she was letting him go.

At the door, Nate halted Luc with the weight of his palm upon his shoulder. Luc stood stiffly beneath it, a fierce pride starching his stance while weakness from his head wound threatened his senses.

"Again, I apologize for my earlier misinterpretation."

Luc said nothing, not trusting himself with words while his heart was breaking and his head pounded with misery.

"If ever you should choose to earn a more responsible wage with that hellcat of a ship, come see me. I could use her in my coastal ventures when steered by such a valiant crew."

"I am flattered, m'sieur, but I have retired from the sea. I have my own home to return to. You might discuss the matter with her new captain, Mr. Sterns. He will be back this way. I will not." He said that with a grim finality.

Damn! The man was in love with Eliza as well!

"Smooth sailing in your journey home, Jean-Luc, if I may call you that."

Luc nodded his acceptance of the familiarity. Under

other circumstances, he could have formed a liking for Nate Parrish. With a sketchy bow, he took his leave of the Parrish home. And all his dreams.

Never had Eliza felt so completely fatigued than after the carousel ride her emotions had taken over the past hour. She was aware of William chafing her hands, but the warm friction annoyed rather than consoled her. She pulled her hand away.

William smiled at her and produced a fancy gold signet ring bearing the Montgomery crest. She stared at it in dismay as he scooped up her hand once more.

"Let me put this in its proper place, my love."

She was aware of her brother watching enigmatically from the doorway, of Philomena's happy smile and Justin Montgomery's cautious relief. With the ring, William gave back everything she'd longed for: acceptance, security, position. Everything except the one thing Luc taught her never to surrender—her own sense of self-worth.

And she was worth more than a passionless marriage, socially merging two families together.

She deserved to be loved for who she was.

She pushed the ring back into William's soft palm. "I believe this belongs to Miss Wiggins."

Looking aghast, William glanced at his father, then scrambled to explain. "I'm sure she will understand that yours was the prior claim to my affection."

"But I don't, William. I don't understand. I do not wish to belong to a man who must seek the approval of others in order to claim me as his bride. Good-bye, William."

Before he could protest, Nate had him by the forearm and was steering him toward the door. "This has been a trying homecoming for all concerned. My sister is very weary."

Philomena surprised her new friend with a snug embrace. "How very proud I am of you," she whispered fiercely. "William will soon recover, but will you, I wonder, if you let your captain sail away?"

She straightened, smiling at Eliza's look of astonishment, before she allowed her father to lead her to the door. A forlorn William trailed behind.

Justin Montgomery lingered, hoping to salvage something from the disastrous turn of the day. "Shall I call upon you tomorrow, Nathaniel, to discuss the terms of the loan I made to your father?"

Nate's stare cleaved his ambitions in two. "Sir, how do you dare ask such a thing? Our good faith agreement was voided the moment you allowed my sister to fall into penury. I think your share could best be used in payment for her suffering, don't you?"

Montgomery's mouth thinned, but he dared say nothing more.

Nate wasn't finished. "We will have our discussion, sir. But it will be witnessed by a board of your peers, ones who have the power to rule over your treacherous dealings. I would not be surprised if you found no welcome remaining for you in Salem. Good day, sir."

Dismissed and facing disgrace, Justin Montgomery exited with pride dragging.

Once alone in her family's familiar rooms with her doting brother in attendance, Eliza sank back against the couch cushions with a plaintive sigh. Nate came to sit on the rolled arm, stroking her hair as he'd done to soothe her as a child.

"My poor darling, what a time you've had of everything."

Her attention sharpened. Her gaze flew toward the hall. "Where's Luc?"

"He left."

"You let him go?"

"He said he had ship's business to attend to. Relax, my girl. I don't think he'll go far."

Uncertain of that, she rested her head upon his lap, her eyes closing against the welling sorrow.

"At least you're home now, and you'll never want for anything again. How happy that must make you."

Her shoulders began to tremble, sobs following too quickly for her to stem. "Oh, Nate, I'm so desperately unhappy. Nothing here matters at all."

"Thank you, miss," he chided, but when she lifted her head, she discovered he was smiling.

"Oh, Nate, you know I adore you, but—" She broke off wretchedly, convinced he wouldn't understand.

"But you love him."

She blinked, amazed at his unbiased insight. "Yes. Yes, I do."

"Where is his home?"

"New Orleans."

"That's not so very far to go for a visit to one's relatives when you have a fast ship at your command." He grinned wide and endured her squeezing embrace. "I expect him to make an honest woman of you."

She leaned back, wiping at her eyes. Her expression was solemn. "But first he must learn to be honest with himself."

Luc stood at the expanse of glass within his cabin overlooking the harbor. In his hand, he held the Montgomery crest, a token from Eliza to earn her meal. He smiled ruefully, remembering her tenacity, then purposefully gave the medallion a toss out the open window. He couldn't hear it hit the waters far below but felt the impact in his belly. She was gone. A cold sinking that went on forever.

From out of his jacket, he drew the papers of indenture that Montgomery had signed. They were meaningless now. Eliza had her freedom. He was the one who would be eternally imprisoned by her memory. The parchment crumpled in his tightening fist.

"Cap'n, the crew awaits your orders."

He found he couldn't give the command to leave Eliza behind. He wished to linger, pulled back to her by his unrelenting need to claim her as his own.

But she already belonged to another, bound there by past ties he hadn't been able to sever. If she wanted him, she wouldn't have let him leave—a hard fact he must nonetheless face.

Perhaps if he had one last chance to speak from the heart, she would listen from hers.

"You give them, Mr. Sterns," he called back without turning. "The *Galant* is yours to command. I've come to pack my belongings."

Attuned to his melancholy, Shamus advanced to place a hand upon the Frenchman's shoulder. "And where is it you go, lad?"

"Home. To France. To say a proper good-bye to my family. They deserve that from me, don't you think?"

"Yes." His fingers pressed briefly. "And what is it you deserve, Luc?"

His shoulders rose and fell in a weighty sigh. "I do not know, my friend. I have never made a journey for myself before. I suppose I will return to Coeur Desir to see it finished. That was my plan."

"A good plan, lad."

Luc said nothing about his other hopes.

"I shall miss you." The Irishman's gruff voice caught in a fragile snag. Slowly, Luc looked around, his eyes shining like wet slate. He started to speak. No words came. Soundlessly, Shamus tugged him into a rough embrace, letting him sag there as his emotions buckled. But the moment passed quickly, and Shamus let him go.

Luc surprised him by not stepping away. Instead, he curled an arm about the big Irishman's neck for a tight hug of his own as he said, "You are family, *mon ami*. Do not forget that. And do not forget me." That stated, Luc shoved away, averting his head until his sleeve made a pass across his eyes.

Guilt fell from Shamus like the parting of heavy shackles.

"Cap'n Luc," Remy called from the doorway. "You got a visitor."

Luc straightened, his features impassive once more. "That will be Montgomery's man with our just rewards." He smiled a bit bitterly. "Take care of him, Shamus. Divide the moneys and distribute your fair share. The crew has earned it."

"And if this reward does not wish to be shared with the crew?"

Both men turned at the sound of a tart female voice. Luc swallowed down the ache of emotions bobbing up into his throat. It was like forcing down one of his boots.

"M'am'selle Parrish. Have you come to wish us bon voyage?"

She didn't look away from the intensity of Luc's stare. "Shamus, would you please excuse us?"

"Yes, ma'am," he said, grinning like a fool.

Luc hadn't moved so much as a muscle when the door closed, leaving them alone together.

Her gaze touched upon the rolled parchment crushed in his hand. "What is that?"

He extended it, allowing her to take it from him. Her brows knit together as the significance struck her. "Did you plan to hold me to the terms yourself, Jean-

Luc?" How displeased she sounded. It made him nervous.

"*Non.* They were to be a gift to you, so you could choose what you would give to whom."

The paper crackled as her hands clenched tight about it. "Thank you."

Silence swelled between them. She made no move to go.

"Have you forgotten something, *ma petite*?" Oh, how carefully he couched that question.

"Just this."

Her mouth smashed up against his, open, wet, and hotly searching.

The aggressiveness of her kiss rocked him. Then his arms were about her, too, and he answered with his own demanding passions. She tasted of paradise lost then found again, delicious, rewarding, so soul-deep satisfying he groaned aloud. Her fingertips trembled against his lean cheeks, then slowly sank back to weave through his hair, anchoring his head for more of her voracious kisses. Finally, he twisted away, breathless, light-headed.

"Captain, wasn't there something you wished to ask me again?"

He blinked in surprise; then a sudden urgency overcame his features.

"I love you, Eliza. I was coming to tell you but . . . I was not sure it would make a difference."

With a glad cry, she hugged him fiercely about the neck. "Oh, Luc! It makes all the difference!"

The discipline of a lifetime abandoned him as he held her close, murmuring, "You will come with me?"

"I belong with you."

"Your family—"

"My brother insists that we marry here so he can see it's properly done."

"I would be happy to oblige him. Be my wife. I am asking you, Eliza Parrish. What do you say? *Oui* or *non*?" He held her back, his hands kneading her shoulders anxiously, his gaze drowning in warm blue-green seas.

"Yes. I will be your wife, the mistress of your house, and—" She drew a lingering trail down his chest with one fingertip. "On those hot nights when we're alone in that big bed, we can work on your reading."

Laughing, he caught her errant hand, bringing it up to his smile to press a possessing kiss upon it. And then he grew completely serious.

"I look forward to the lessons, *mon coeur desir*."

Avon Romances—
the best in exceptional authors
and unforgettable novels!

WICKED AT HEART
by Danelle Harmon
78004-6/ $5.50 US/ $7.50 Can

SOMEONE LIKE YOU
by Susan Sawyer
78478-5/ $5.50 US/ $7.50 Can

MINX
by Julia Quinn
78562-5/ $5.50 US/ $7.50 Can

SCANDALOUS SUZANNE
by Glenda Sanders
77589-1/ $5.50 US/ $7.50 Can

A MAN'S TOUCH
by Rosalyn West
78511-0/ $5.50 US/ $7.50 Can

WINTERBURN'S ROSE
by Kate Moore
78457-2/ $5.50 US/ $7.50 Can

INDIGO
by Beverly Jenkins
78658-3/ $5.50 US/ $7.50 Can

SPRING RAIN
by Susan Weldon
78068-2/ $5.50 US/ $7.50 Can

THE MACKENZIES: FLINT
by Ana Leigh
78096-8/ $5.50 US/ $7.50 Can

LOVE ME NOT
by Eve Byron
77625-1/ $5.50 US/ $7.50 Can

Discover Contemporary Romances
at Their Sizzling Hot Best
from Avon Books

Avon Romantic Treasures

*Unforgettable, enthralling love stories,
sparkling with passion and adventure
from Romance's bestselling authors*

DREAM CATCHER *by Kathleen Harrington*
77835-1/$5.99 US/$7.99 Can

THE MACKINNON'S BRIDE *by Tanya Anne Crosby*
77682-0/$5.99 US/$7.99 Can

PHANTOM IN TIME *by Eugenia Riley*
77158-6/$5.99 US/$7.99 Can

RUNAWAY MAGIC *by Deborah Gordon*
78452-1/$5.99 US/$7.99 Can

YOU AND NO OTHER *by Cathy Maxwell*
78716-4/$5.99 US/$7.99 Can

WILD ROSES *by Miriam Minger*
78302-9/$5.99 US/$7.99 Can

LADY OF WINTER *by Emma Merritt*
77985-4/$5.99 US/$7.99 Can

SILVER MOON SONG *by Genell Dellin*
78602-8/$5.99 US/$7.99 Can